Andrea Leoncaballo

About the Author

JULIAN SMITH is an award-winning travel writer whose work has appeared in *Outside*, *National Geographic Adventure*, *National Geographic Traveler*, *Smithsonian*, *Wired*, the *Washington Post*, and the *Los Angeles Times*, among other publications. He is the author of guidebooks to El Salvador, Ecuador, Virginia, and the southwestern United States, and he has been honored by the Society of American Travel Writers for writing the best guidebook of the year. He lives with his wife and daughter in Portland, Oregon.

HARPER ● PERENNIAL

NEW YORK ● LONDON ● TORONTO ● SYDNEY ● NEW DELHI ● AUCKLAND

CROSSING
the HEART of

An Odyssey of Love
and Adventure

JULIAN SMITH

HARPER ● PERENNIAL

HarperCollins books may be purchased for educational, business,
or sales promotional use. For information please write: Special
Markets Department, HarperCollins Publishers, 10 East 53rd
Street, New York, NY 10022.

FIRST EDITION

Designed by Betty Lew

Library of Congress Cataloging-in-Publication Data

ISBN 978-0-06-187347-8

10 11 12 13 14   DT/RRD   10 9 8 7 6 5 4 3 2 1

For Laura,

of course

There is no journey upon this earth that a man may not make if he sets his heart to it. There is nothing, Umbopa, that he cannot do, there are no mountains he may not climb, there are no deserts he cannot cross, save a mountain and a desert of which you are spared the knowledge, if love leads him.

—H. RIDER HAGGARD,
King Solomon's Mines

PROLOGUE

The Nile slides thick and silent beyond a grid of barbed wire. I slump in a plastic chair that's soft from the heat and watch a cloud of tiny silver fish leap from the water with a hiss like rain.

In the next chair, a young Sudanese woman holds a baby in her lap. She croons to it to the tune of "Frère Jacques."

"Bay-bee Jesus, Bay-bee Jesus, I love you. I love you. Yoo-hoo are my savior, yoo-hoo are my savior, every day, every day."

Clumps of vegetation the size of refrigerators drift downstream toward Cairo, seventeen hundred miles north. The air is like a wet wool blanket. My focus blurs, and I envision a boat that floated past this same spot, 108 years ago. At the helm is a twenty-five-year-old Cambridge University dropout named Ewart Grogan, a man whose story has taken over my life.

In the past two months, I have followed Grogan's trail over four thousand miles through eight countries in Africa. My fixation has led me here, the city of Juba in the pseudo-state of Southern Sudan, one of the most desolate and impoverished places on the planet.

I had no idea this would happen when I first heard about him. It was an amazing story, for sure: after almost two years of unimaginable hardship, Grogan was close to becoming the first person to travel the length of Africa, south to north. Even more astonishing was that he had been virtually forgotten.

What really grabbed me, though, was that his true goal was even loftier. The five-thousand-mile trek was merely the means to an end. Grogan was in love. Her name was Gertrude, and she was waiting for him in London. She had long dark hair, a radiant smile, and a suspicious stepfather who wouldn't let her marry until her beloved had proved himself worthy.

Like Grogan, I'm here because of a woman. Her name is Laura; she's my fiancée and the love of my life. She's also waiting for me on the other side of the world: Portland, Oregon, to be exact.

I am retracing Grogan's journey to see how much this cross section of Africa has changed—and how little—in the past century. I'm also doing it because Laura and I are planning to marry less than a month after I get home, and as much as I'm thrilled at the thought, it also scares the hell out of me. Her father has no problem with it; any hurdles are purely my own. I left home hoping to find some answers in Grogan's footsteps, some kind of equanimity in the tangle of self-doubt and hesitation I've woven in my head.

But I've never felt this far away from home, or from Laura. And I don't know how much farther it makes sense to go.

Two hours in Juba and already it's starting to look like the end of the line. To the north, native groups are fighting with machine guns left over from the country's fifty-year civil war, and heavy flooding has closed the roads. Too dangerous, not enough time. It kills me to think of turning back so close to the finish.

Grogan kept going north, through trials that made his struggles up to this point—charging elephants, hungry cannibals—seem like parlor games.

Should I? How far is it worth it to push?

The sun sags toward the forest on the far side of the river. Frogs start to chirp among the plastic bottles on the riverbank as the light turns amber.

Coarse electric melodies split the silence. The woman is holding a cell phone to her baby's ear, pressing buttons to cycle through the different rings. The child's eyes are open wide.

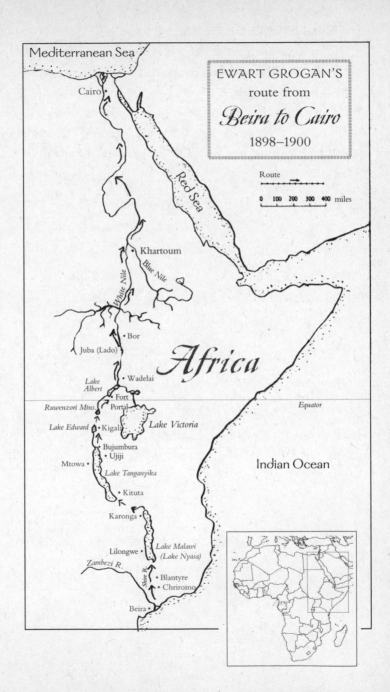

Mediterranean Sea

EWART GROGAN'S
route from
Beira to Cairo
1898–1900

Route ▸▸▸▸▸▸▸

0 100 200 300 400 miles

Cairo

Red Sea

Khartoum

White Nile

Blue Nile

Africa

• Bor

Juba (Lado) •

• Wadelai

Lake
Albert

Fort
Portal

Ruwenzori Mtns.

Equator

Lake Edward • Kigali

Lake Victoria

Bujumbura
• Ujiji

Mtowa •

Lake Tanganyika

Indian Ocean

• Kituta

Karonga •

*Lake Malawi
(Lake Nyasa)*

Lilongwe •

Zambezi R.

Shire R.

• Blantyre
• Chriromo

Beira •

PART I

Africa is mystic; it is wild; it is a sweltering
inferno; it is a photographer's paradise, a hunter's
Valhalla, an escapist's Utopia. It is what you
will, and it withstands all interpretations. It is
the last vestige of a dead world or the cradle of a
shiny new one. . . . It is all these things but one
thing—it is never dull.

—*Beryl Markham*

CHAPTER ONE

When Ewart Grogan pushed off into the White Nile five days before Christmas, 1899, the sun over southern Sudan fell on his back like a hot sheet of metal, and his diseased liver hurt so badly he couldn't stand up straight.

His open boat groaned with supplies and sweating bodies: a dozen native soldiers, a small boy, a tall man from the Dinka tribe, an elderly Egyptian prisoner with a broken leg, and a mad criminal in chains.

At full height, Grogan was six feet tall and strikingly handsome. He had a strong jaw, a narrow nose, and startling yellow-green eyes, which seemed to spark with intelligence and humor. It was because of that piercing gaze, and his almost superhuman determination and endurance, that Africans had nicknamed him *Bwana Chui:* the Leopard.

On that day, however, he was nearly unrecognizable: haggard, hunched, half starved, and baked brown by the sun. He had been traveling through Africa for almost two years. His route wound from the salty breezes of the Indian Ocean to the indigo lakes and smoking volcanoes of the Great Rift Valley, where the steep jungles teemed with pygmies and gigantic apes.

Naked cannibals had pursued him for days near the lava

beds of Mushari, and just a few weeks ago he had celebrated his twenty-fifth birthday by fleeing a bull hippo for half a mile. Abscesses on his liver burst in blooms of agony, and a recurring malarial fever threatened to bake his brain.

His only European companion had left for home nine months earlier. For most of the journey his only company had been a handful of African soldiers and porters who tended to desert at every opportunity, when they weren't busy plotting mutiny.

And the worst was still ahead. Between him and his goal, a remote British outpost hundreds of miles downstream to the north, lay the most godforsaken swamp on earth. The Sudd was tens of thousands of square miles of clotted vegetation and miasmatic air, home to the fierce giants of the Dinka tribe and cloud banks of insatiable mosquitoes. Hippos lurked in the black water, ready to snap canoes in half, and six-foot Marabou storks stalked across floating islands of green like reanimated corpses.

If he made it to the outpost, and then descended the Nile to Cairo, Grogan would join the ranks of legendary explorers like Sir Richard Burton, David Livingstone, and Henry Stanley. If he didn't, well, no one would ever know what happened. The swamp would swallow him without a trace.

As the prow sliced the blood-warm water and high grasses hissed against the sides, Grogan was filled with uncertainty.

He had no idea how far he still had to go, or whether Dinka warriors would ignore his tiny party or slaughter them. He didn't know if his band of reluctant volunteers would remain by his side, shoot him in the back, or abandon him to shrivel and starve in the sun.

He was sure of one thing, though. He had to make it. Because Gertrude was waiting.

At age twenty-two, three years before he pushed off into the Nile, Ewart Grogan was already a war veteran and world traveler who thought he understood his way around women. He knew the barmaids of Melbourne were the most beautiful in the world. He'd seen how difficult it was to tell the men from the women in Sri Lanka, and he had once killed a man barehanded in a bar fight over a Portuguese beauty.

Grogan had just returned to England after serving as a soldier in Rhodesia, where he had fought in a bloody native uprising and fallen so sick he had almost been buried alive. His doctors advised a long rest to convalesce—an extended sea voyage would be perfect—so when his friend Eddie Watt from Cambridge invited him to stay with his family in Napier on New Zealand's North Island, Grogan accepted.

There, on the Watt family estate, Grogan met Gertrude, the oldest of Eddie's three sisters. A year younger than Grogan, she was almost as tall as he was, with luminous skin and kind blue eyes. She was shy, but her calm elegance erupted frequently into a booming, infectious laugh. More than anything, it was her laugh, and Gertrude's tender heart, that made her irresistible to Grogan. He was instantly infatuated.

Gertrude saw how people were drawn to the eloquent Englishman's overflowing confidence and wit. He could talk for hours on just about any subject, with a well of jokes and stories that never ran dry. Grogan had it all, or so it seemed—looks, brains, ambition, passion—and she found herself falling for him as well.

Within days of their meeting, Grogan brought up the idea of marriage, and Gertrude agreed. But there was a problem: she was rich and he was not.

In the late nineteenth century, the concept of marriage was shifting from purely practical to one that was more romantic. But among the upper classes of Victorian England (and her colonies, such as New Zealand), marriage was still more akin to a business merger than a starry-eyed union of hearts.

Gertrude was a direct descendant of James Watt, the Scottish inventor of the steam engine. She lived in a forty-room Mediterranean-style villa overlooking the Pacific Ocean, with double tennis courts and a retinue of servants.

Grogan came from a respectable family, but after being kicked out of Cambridge and serving in the army, he was painfully aware of how little he had to offer a wife except "a skinful of amoeba, malaria germs and similar parasitic mementoes . . . [and] . . . a head full of vagrant ideas." He couldn't offer Gertrude a fraction of what she already possessed.

It didn't matter to her, but it did to her stepfather, James Coleman, a stern, arrogant man with a thick waist and a white walrus mustache. At the death of her father, Gertrude and her fat inheritance had become his responsibility. When he looked at Grogan, Coleman saw not a charming suitor but a cocksure young man with questionable prospects, one more overconfident cad after Gertrude's fortune.

One afternoon the two men were alone in one of the estate's many drawing rooms. A squall spit across the ocean, and the popping fireplace made the room stuffy and close. Grogan took a deep breath and told Coleman he was in love with his stepdaughter and wanted to make her his wife—with his blessing, of course.

"My dear sir, do you consider yourself in a position to marry?" Coleman scoffed. "Sent down from Cambridge! No job! Forgive me, sir, if I say that I do not consider you worthy of my stepdaughter. You appear to be drifting down the river of life without a rudder. A girl in the position of my ward can expect to marry an outstanding man."

He huffed and stood up, ready to stride from the room.

Grogan swallowed and asked him to wait. His guts were churning, but his voice was steady.

"You say I am unworthy?" he said. "Very well. Now suppose I were to make the first crossing of Africa from south to north, from the Cape [of Good Hope] to Cairo. Would you consider that worthwhile?"

Only a madman would consider such a thing. "The Dark Continent," as it was known in the popular press, defeated the toughest and smartest men in the world, chewed them up and spit them out, broken for life, or else swallowed them forever.

Vicious animals, biblical weather, ferocious native tribes, in-curable diseases unknown to science. There were more ways to die in Africa than there were crocodiles in her rivers or lions on her savannahs. Grogan might as well have proposed some-thing as impossible as climbing Mount Everest or trekking to the North Pole.

"I can only presume that you are trying to be funny," Cole-man replied. "If so, I do not appreciate it."

"I am quite serious," Grogan said. "Never more so."

"You mean to say that you really contemplate crossing the entire continent? My good man, do you realize what that would mean?"

"Perfectly."

During his army career, Grogan had served under the leg-endary British imperialist Cecil Rhodes, founder of Rhodesia and the De Beers diamong mining company. As Coleman lis-tened in disbelief, Grogan explained the man's grand plan to link British colonies from one end of the continent to the other by train and telegraph. One potential route followed the western branch of the Great Rift Valley, which curved through central Africa in a progression of great lakes and volcanoes.

Grogan would survey the route and in the process would become the first person in history to transect the continent from end to end.

He'd survived Africa before, he said. (Barely, he didn't say.) In fact, as far as he was concerned, he had already done the first leg of the trip, from the Cape to the coast of Portuguese East Africa, while he was a soldier.

Coleman asked how he would cross the impenetrable jungles of central Africa, the ones that Henry Stanley had needed a small army to bludgeon through during his descent of the Congo River two decades ago.

Grogan said he would travel light and fast, with a minimum of native soldiers and porters. A large expedition would only attract attention. He could sense Coleman's scorn and disbelief. But arguing logistics was a good sign.

"Anyhow, I mean to try." Grogan's confidence was back. "After all, if I fail, nothing is lost. On the other hand, if I succeed— well, I shall hope to have proved worthy of your stepdaughter."

Coleman was a successful entrepreneur himself, having made his own fortune in sheep and cattle ranching. He could respect a bold plan. Perhaps he saw a bit of his younger self in the ambitious young man. Maybe, in his own pompous way, he could even appreciate the romance of the gesture.

Regardless, Grogan probably wouldn't even make it back alive. Coleman accepted the challenge.

Later, Gertrude found Grogan, still trembling with adrenaline. She looked confused.

"What's this about crossing Africa?"

He explained to Gertrude his plan and the agreement with Coleman. The thought of Grogan alone in Africa terrified her, to say nothing of how long it would keep them apart. But she knew that only a feat like this could convince her stepfather to give his blessing.

And even though she had only known Grogan a matter of weeks, she knew it was something he had to do—for her, for them, for himself. She assured him there would be no other suitors before he came back.

Inevitably Grogan had to return home. When he and Gertrude said goodbye, he said, "I won't hold you to your promise, of course. And I give my word you won't hear from me until I'm successful. I'll send you a cable as soon as I reach Cairo. Then, if you are still able to return my love, I shall make you my wife."

"You will succeed," Gertrude said softly. "I know you will. And I will wait for you, no matter how long."

Damn, I'm going to miss you. I know everything's going to be fine, but I'm going to miss you so much."

Laura's slim frame trembles as she speaks into my shoulder. The fine mist of a gray Pacific Northwest dawn hides the sun. The drop-off lane at the Portland airport smells like car exhaust and wet asphalt.

I wasn't expecting this. She'd been so cool on the drive to the airport. I was quiet, still groggy from late-night packing and anxiety dreams of disasters in strange places. "Dancing with Myself" came on the radio. I turned it off—too prophetic.

I looked at her perfect profile in the driver's seat. What was going on in there? I always found Laura's rare silences unsettling, but this was unusual.

Here she was, sending her fiancé off on a solo journey through places that were more catastrophes than countries: Burundi, the Congo, Rwanda, Sudan. I'm leaving her in a city we just moved to, where she knows nobody, to follow an obsession that has peaked at the least convenient moment possible. Less than a month after I return—if everything goes according to plan; if I'm not stricken with a strange disease, or crumpled in a bus accident or plane crash; if nothing changes between us while I'm gone—we're getting married.

This will be the longest time we've spent apart since we became a couple seven years ago.

So where are the emotional fireworks? For weeks I've been a knot of nervous energy, trying to plan and pack for thousands of miles of public transportation through backcountry Africa: ancient buses, decrepit minivans, homemade bicycles, and boats dating to World War I.

Laura kept her composure all the way to the airport. But that's her way: happy face forward, smile through the sadness.

In our time together we have already survived two cross-country moves, a simultaneous leap into full-time freelancing, reappearing exes, and one dead pet. We know each other's stories, answer each other's cell phones, finish each other's sentences. I love her like no one else I've ever met, and I know I'd have to be a drooling idiot to let her get away.

I don't plan to. But the thought of making an eternal commitment is terrifying. As an introverted only child, independence is a pillar of my identity. No matter how compatible Laura and I are—and we are, wondrously—every argument we have leaves behind tiny splinters of uncertainty. Sometimes we seem *too* alike to ever coexist peacefully, both of us too headstrong, too self-reliant.

And of course, I'm a guy. The concept of being married appeals, but the reality keeps me up at night. I've always found ways to justify my hesitations. Am I ready to consign myself to one person, completely, forever? Do I even deserve Laura?

The months before the wedding seemed like a window inching closed. I could see the domino line of Major Life Changes start to tumble: house, kids, PTA, retirement. It was clear that something drastic still needed to happen before I could make this lifetime promise with all my heart. I needed inspiration. I needed a kick in the ass.

One day I was reading a book about the evolution of language. In among the graphs of primate mating success versus testicle diameter and descriptions of how far males will go to impress females, I read this:

> The young Captain Ewart Grogan walked the 4,500-mile length of Africa from the Cape of Good Hope to Cairo in 1899 to gain the hand of the woman he loved. Her family had dismissed him as a ne'er-do-well who would be unable to keep their daughter in the manner to which they thought she should be accustomed. Grogan banked on the fame (if not the fortune) that a dramatic adventure would bring him to persuade them to reconsider.

That was it: three sentences, nothing more. But I had to know more. I tracked down the few biographies of Grogan and his firsthand account of the journey, *From the Cape to Cairo.* The more I read, the more the adventure and romance of his story captivated me.

The proud tradition of men doing crazy things for love goes back at least to the Trojan War, triggered when Paris eloped with Helen, the most beautiful woman in the world (and someone else's wife). A seventeenth-century Mughal emperor built the Taj Mahal as a memorial to his favorite wife, who had died in childbirth. In 1936, King Edward VIII did the unthinkable and gave up the British throne to marry an American divorcée.

Grogan's story was just as astonishing, but nobody seemed to have heard of him. I became convinced I could sense a lesson in there: some insight into the wisdom, courage, and conviction it took to go to such extremes just to be with someone else, to make a life-changing leap and follow through to the end, no matter what.

Even though our personalities, our lives and times were vastly different, Grogan and I were really after the same thing: lifelong happiness with an incredible woman. There was the challenge and, yes, the buzz of danger; he certainly felt that, too. One final taste of true autonomy. But in the end it was about love.

No one had ever retraced his route. Perhaps crossing Africa as he had would help me find peace with this radical new direction my life was about to take. Maybe some of Grogan's mojo would rub off on me.

I ordered every book and article about him I could find. I plotted his route in guidebooks and maps, tracked down and cold-called his living descendants around the world. The wedding countdown kept clicking: six months, five. If I didn't go now, I never would.

I was flabbergasted when Laura gave her blessing. She was a gut-level decision maker, with instincts that had yet to steer her wrong. She was also the last person to want to tie her partner down against his will. If this is what it took for me to settle down, she said, hell, she'd buy my plane ticket and drive me to the airport.

Now her eyes are inches from mine, swimming above a wrinkled grin. A hazel ring surrounds each pupil like a reef around a tropical island. She runs her hand across my newly shaved scalp. "You look like someone else," she said.

Behind us a sleepy-looking skycap in a baggy black jacket pushes a cart full of suitcases. A 737 howls overhead and the months apart hit me like a heavy door. We're both crying now. All the gates are down.

The things we don't say outnumber the ones we do.

"Be safe."

"Don't worry."

"Stay in touch."

Don't be sad.

Don't get hurt.

Don't meet someone else.

Don't have second thoughts.

She presses a packet of red envelopes into my hand. "Open one a week."

Then I'm lifting my bag and all I can see is a blur of blond hair in the car getting smaller and disappearing in the drizzle.

Chapter Two

William Grogan had so many children that he sometimes mixed up their names. But Ewart Scott Grogan, born December 12, 1874—number 14 of 21—was the one no one ever forgot.

A rebellious streak seemed to run through the male side of the Grogan family tree. Ewart's great-grandfather Cornelius Grogan participated in the unsuccessful Irish rebellion against British rule in 1798, and ended up with his head on a pike. His father, William, enjoyed the prominent position of surveyor general to Queen Victoria, until he did the unthinkable. When the queen requested that he return from a vacation in Scotland to attend to her at the Isle of Wight, he sent back a reply that perhaps a later appointment would fit both their schedules better.

One did not offer the queen a rain check. He lost the appointment.

William's first wife, Mary, had died at age forty-two after bearing thirteen children, one of whom died in infancy. Five years later, in 1873, he spotted an elegant young woman with a black wave of hair and lovely ankles walking past his office window. When she passed again the next day, William leaped up, chased her down, and introduced himself. He and Jane Sams were married a month later. He was twenty-two years older than she.

Ewart was Jane's first child and by far her favorite. Named after his godfather, Prime Minister William Ewart Gladstone, he was unusual from the start. Gregarious and bright, self-confident and independent, he had the ability to excel at almost everything he tried—music, sports, schoolwork—and poured his excess energy into stunts and pranks.

He spent a large part of his childhood terrorizing his siblings, locking his brothers on the balconies of their forty-two-room house in Kensington and tying his sisters to tree branches by their hair. At preparatory school, he had to have his stomach pumped after he swallowed a sausage whole to win a bet. He could usually charm his way out of any punishment, whereas his siblings suffered his mother's discipline.

His father was delighted he had spawned such a "thruster," who would surely blaze his own path through life.

At night, Ewart dreamed of Africa. When he wasn't fattening his vocabulary by reading the *Oxford English Dictionary,* he pored over the latest accounts of men like the missionary-explorer David Livingstone and the great white hunter Frederick Courteney Selous.

He loved the pulpy adventures of H. Rider Haggard, whose *King Solomon's Mines* was his favorite. Published in 1885, the tale of intrepid adventurer Allan Quartermain, the evil King Twala, and the doomed beauty Foulata was the first adventure novel set in Africa, and its vivid, melodramatic vision of the continent made it a bestseller.

Africa represented many things to upper-class Britons in the nineteenth century. It was an escape from the stifling crowds and conventions of Victorian society; an enigmatic id to countless repressed egos; a place to prove one's manhood by hunting, pioneering, or simply surviving. Regardless of her millions of inhabitants and ancient cultures, Africa was seen as a blank canvas where a man of bold action could make his name and fortune while bringing "civilization"—the British version—to "savage" races (often, ironically, by re-creating the same social structure the settlers had fled, albeit with them on top).

Ewart read and reread tales of vast animal herds, fierce native armies, and treasure maps sketched on yellowed linen. He swore he would do four things in life: hunt an elephant, a rhino, and a lion, and see Lake Tanganyika.

When Ewart was sixteen, his father died and left him the head of the household. To distract his mother from her grief, he packed the family off on a vacation to Zermatt, Switzerland. There he met the famous mountaineer Edward Whymper, the leader and only surviving member of the first team to summit the Matterhorn, the most majestic summit in the European Alps, in 1865.

Inspired by Whymper, Grogan took to mountaineering with his typical intensity. He decided he wanted to become a member of the selective London-based Alpine Club, the world's oldest mountaineering association. This required climbing "a reasonable number of respectable peaks," so with Whymper as his tutor, Grogan began to scale every noteworthy and difficult peak in the region during his family's repeated summers in Zermatt. He climbed the twin knife-edged peaks of the Aiguille du Dru, made one of the first ascents of the Aiguille du Grepón on Mont Blanc, and summited the Matterhorn twice.

His mother was horrified. She had just lost her husband,

and now her darling was hanging off cliffs all over the Alps. Grogan, now six feet tall and fearless, patted her hand and kept climbing.

One day he and two local guides were crossing a glacier on the Weisshorn, a difficult peak taller than the Matterhorn. Without warning, Grogan vanished into a crevasse. The men were roped together, and he dragged one of the guides in after him and knocked himself unconscious. The other guide managed to sink his ice axe into the snow and keep them all from falling to their death. He held on desperately until two other groups of climbers could help drag them to safety.

After four seasons of climbing, Grogan was elected both to the Alpine Club (as its youngest member) and to the Swiss Alpine Club. Satisfied with his accomplishment, he hung up his crampons and never climbed again. He had achieved his goal, and now he turned his energies elsewhere.

In 1893, Grogan had entered Jesus College at Cambridge, where he studied law and convinced his crew coach to let him smoke a pipe while rowing. Everything still came easy for him, from writing to playing the banjo, and he was often bored.

He refused to run with either the intellectual "smugs" or the sporty "pugs." When the socialist Fabian Society invited him to join, he told them he wanted nothing to do with such a "very unwholesome gang of chinless men and bosomless women."

To him, the world was a place where you did what you wanted and had fun doing it. It was also full of fools who needed to be put in their place. One day he screwed shut the door of an undergraduate he disliked, trapping the boy so securely that he had to be fed through the mail slot until a carpenter could arrive to let him out.

Grogan almost set a don's house on fire with fireworks. Another evening he was leading a drunken procession through the streets of Cambridge when two constables ordered them to stop. The boys collared the men, tied them up, and proceeded, in Grogan's words, "to stuff the contents of a fish and chips shop down their throats."

Grogan didn't seem to grieve his father very much, but when his mother died unexpectedly at age forty-nine from heart disease, he was devastated. They had always adored one another. She was one of the few people to whom Grogan, otherwise almost completely self-reliant, felt a strong emotional attachment.

Her death left him responsible, at age nineteen, for six siblings, the youngest only seven years old. (William's children by his first wife had already left home.) Grogan's stepbrother Walter, twenty years older, was chosen as legal guardian for the children so Grogan could continue his studies.

He was still grieving his mother when his life shifted again. A school tutor he disliked left town, and as a prank Grogan locked a goat in his study. But the man stayed away longer than expected, and he returned to find that the starving animal had eaten his books, ripped the stuffing from the furniture, and chewed the wallpaper.

Grogan was expelled.

The Grogan family was financially comfortable as a result of Jane's wise handling of the trust fund her husband had left. But Grogan had no interest in taking his father's place at Grogan & Boyd, the family real estate business. He wanted to make his own way in life, but his dreams of African exploration and big-game hunting would require more than the regular income he received from the trust.

Grogan had to get a job.

His first stop was a brief stint at art school. The teachers praised his work, but he still didn't fit in with the "long-haired lizards with Machiavellian beards and Bohemian mannerisms" who were his classmates. One day in April 1896, a teacher told him that he could become a great artist if he was willing to "work for many years, living, dreaming, thinking nothing but art, art, art."

Grogan said he wasn't sure he was cut out to be an artist. Maybe being a policeman would be more exciting. It was a strange choice for someone so allergic to authority.

"A policeman!" the man sputtered. If a man of Grogan's education and talents wasn't ready to dedicate himself, he said, he should leave and stop wasting everyone's time.

"I tell you what," Grogan said, pulling out a shilling. "I'll toss for it. Heads, I become an artist; tails, a policeman."

He flipped the coin and slapped it on his wrist. He lifted his hand: tails.

Grogan thanked the teacher for his time, put on his hat, and left the studio for good.

But he didn't head for the police academy. That spring, the newspapers had started carrying reports of a native uprising in the British colony of Rhodesia (the part that is now Zimbabwe). Cecil Rhodes, then prime minister of the Cape Colony at Africa's southern tip, was advertising for volunteers to join the fight in the colony that bore his name.

Grogan was tempted. Here, finally, was a chance for income and excitement—in Africa, no less.

Less than a week after turning in his paint brushes, the twenty-two-year-old two-time dropout was on board a ship to Cape Town to become a soldier.

At last—Africa! The sun-reddened landscapes, the endless herds of animals, all the people and places he had dreamed about since childhood, ready to serve as backdrop for men of bold action and the spread of British glory. Grogan's excitement grew every day of the two-and-a-half week journey. He arrived in Cape Town at the foot of wide, flat-topped Table Mountain, full of patriotic pride and ready for adventure.

Instead, his army career was sheer misery from start to finish. The Matabele, a branch of the ferocious Zulu tribe, were in revolt against the European settlers who were slowly spreading across their territory. Native warriors armed with clubs and axes were raiding white camps, killing men, women, and children indiscriminately. Rhodes's troops responded just as savagely, mowing down ranks of Matabeles with the newly invented Maxim guns.

Grogan's first assignment was to lead a convoy of mules loaded with food and ammunition to Bulawayo, the main white settlement. The route crawled more than six hundred miles through dense, sweltering bush. Half the mule drivers deserted the first night. When he finally arrived at his destination, there was no place to sleep. He collapsed under a thorn tree, filthy and exhausted. The next morning he awoke to an awful stench. He looked up and saw two rotting bodies hanging in the branches.

As the fighting continued into the summer, Grogan saw men pinned to the earth by their hands and feet and left to die in the sun. He saw women who had been raped, tortured, and killed and their children dismembered, tiny skulls crushed.

Meeting Rhodes was the one bright spot in the whole experience. The man was already a living legend. Tall and thick-chested, with curly hair and a surprisingly high-pitched voice, Rhodes was a one-man engine of Empire, virtually the czar of southern Africa.

As part of Rhodes's personal escort, Grogan sat around the fire at night and listened to the man's vision of telegraph lines and trains connecting Her Majesty's colonies from Cape Horn to Cairo, spreading the civilizing influence of British culture from one end of the continent to the other. But large parts of the route were still a mystery, and it wasn't clear if other countries had already laid claim to crucial stretches.

When the fighting ended in August 1896, Grogan found himself in the port city of Beira, recently established in the Portuguese colony on Africa's southeastern coast. Looking for some excitement that didn't involve people shooting at him, Grogan went on a buffalo hunting trip with three men from Holland.

The excursion quickly devolved into a fight for survival. The Dutchmen fell sick and one died. Grogan suffered a burst liver abscess, caught amoebic dysentery and malaria, then developed blackwater fever, a complication of severe malaria that turned his urine the color of port wine.

Grogan made it back to a small settlement on the railway, but he was so sick he was given up for dead. His pale and seemingly lifeless body was tossed on the train back to Beira. When the train arrived, a railway engineer named Alfred Lawley lifted the blanket and saw the motionless form. He took a sniff. If Grogan really had been dead, he thought he'd have smelled a lot worse. Lawley had Grogan taken to his home and nursed him back to health "like a mother," earning a lifelong friend.

One night after his recovery, Grogan and a few fellow troopers went to a local Portuguese dance hall. At the time, Portuguese authorities were worried that Britain had plans to take over their coastal colony, but the men didn't care that things were tense between the two countries. The soldiers were waiting for a ship home, and the seedy place looked as good as any to blow off steam. Plus, there were women.

A string band plucked out lively tunes and the drinks kept coming. Grogan spun around the dance floor with any girl who would let him. Enjoying a drink at the bar, he spotted the most attractive girl in the place and flashed his best smile.

His eye caught a movement in a mirror on the wall. An enraged man was raising a knife to plunge into his back.

Grogan whirled and punched his attacker in the face. The Portuguese struck his head on a table and fell to the floor. He lay too still even for an unconscious man. A quick check showed he was dead.

All hell broke loose. An angry local mob surrounded Grogan and his companions, demanding blood. The British consul arrived to smooth things over, but the crowd threw him in the gutter.

Only the quick arrival of more British troops saved Grogan and the soldiers from being beaten to death. The army took them into custody for their own safety, and the bruised consul telegraphed the Royal Navy for help.

The next morning Grogan was safely on board a ship headed to Zanzibar. (A friend asked him later if the girl might have been the man's girlfriend, his sister, or even his wife. "How could I know?" Grogan said. "I didn't speak Portuguese.")

When he finally caught a ship to England, Grogan shook his fist at the receding shore of Africa and swore he would never return to the "accursed sands" of "Satan's summer palace."

Yet a little over a year later, he was back. The months that followed his trip to New Zealand and Coleman's acceptance of the challenge had been a tornado of packing and planning. On his way back to England, Grogan stopped in San Francisco, where he saw the "indescribable scene of human degradation" of the opium dens in Chinatown, a notoriously dangerous part of the city. He was eating alone at a restaurant called the Puppy Dog when he noticed that the only other customer was a menacing thug who happened to be sitting between him and the only exit.

The incident in the dance hall in Beira had left him acutely aware of dangerous situations. Grogan walked over and gave the man a quick one-two punch and a kick "where it hurts," then fled as two knives embedded themselves in the door frame.

Back in England, Gertrude and Eddie's wealthy aunt Caroline Eyres agreed to help finance Grogan's expedition on one condition: that he take along her brother, Arthur "Harry" Sharp. Grogan had spent time with Eyres and Sharp after leaving Cambridge. In fact, it was she who had urged Eddie to invite him to New Zealand expressly (but secretly) so he could meet Gertrude.

Sharp was more than two decades older than Grogan, a stout man with a beard and mustache to balance his thinning hair. He was in good shape and an avid hunter. He was also single, wealthy, and bored, with a law degree he had never used. His sister thought a little travel would do him good.

Together, the men took a crash course in surveying and cartography from John Coles, the mapping curator of the Royal Geographical Society, the world's most elite society of explorers. Livingstone, Burton, and Charles Darwin, among others, had benefited from the society's support on their expeditions. They packed carefully and said their goodbyes, then set sail for Africa.

On February 28, 1898, Grogan and Sharp, along with "sundry German officers and beer enthusiasts," arrived in Portuguese East Africa in memorable style when their passenger liner "violently charg[ed] a sandbank in the bay of Beira on a flood-tide, to the ear-smashing accompaniment of the German National Anthem."

Grogan stepped ashore in a tweed jacket and a wide-brimmed bush hat. His pants were tucked into tall leather boots. Sharp's mustache and beard were freshly combed and his hat tilted stylishly over one eyebrow. Grogan could see the port city was still a miserable place, consisting mainly of "galvanized iron, sunbaked sand, drinks, and Portuguese ruffians."

But their spirits were high, and there was plenty to do: gather porters and supplies, set their chronometers (used to calculate longitude), and organize their equipment.

Compared to most nineteenth-century African expeditions, Grogan and Sharp traveled light. Their main weapons for hunting and defense were two magazine-fed .303-caliber rifles, which could bring down anything from ducks to large antelopes. Grogan brought a giant black-powder "elephant gun" for bigger game, and both men had backup rifles and cases of ammunition.

Wooden boxes held tents and folding cots, shoes and clothing, fishing rods and mosquito nets. They took surveying tools and a camera, three Union Jacks, a phonograph, and books of poetry and classic literature, including the complete works of Shakespeare. For trading with Africans, they packed beads and multicolored rolls of "Americani," a type of cloth made in the United States.

There were sixty-four cases of food and drink in all, including whisky, brandy, and champagne, and plenty of Worcestershire sauce, Grogan's favorite, "without which life . . . is intolerable."

The medicine chest held quinine for malaria; Elliman's Universal Embrocation, a cream made of turpentine, eggs, and vinegar, for aches and pains; and plenty of permanganate of potash (potassium permanganate), dark purple crystals that made a disinfectant and antiseptic when mixed with water.

Just being in Africa required a huge adjustment, both mental and physical. Everything about the place was alien: the scenery and climate, the people, plants and animals, the tastes and sounds and smells. Grogan was as excited as he had been when he first saw Cape Town as a raw recruit. Now he was here on his own terms, with a concrete goal to guide his energies.

His army experiences had quashed most of his romantic notions about the place. But he could still appreciate its raw beauty, writing of sunlit clouds that formed "a sinuous mesh of molten red, a ghostly sea from which the peaks reared their purple silhouettes, until they faded into the uncertainty of lilac mists."

Amid months of packing and preparations, Grogan admired hippos strolling past at night, their wet backs glistening in the moonlight. The first time he heard a lion roar at full volume, the sound seemed "to permeate the whole universe, thundering, rumbling, majestic." It rose and echoed and trailed off into a sobbing chorus. "The joy of it! Never had I heard such music," he wrote. "Thousands of German devotees, backed by thousands of beers, could never approach the soul-stirring glory of one *Felis leo.*" Then he killed it with five shots, achieving the first of his childhood goals.

Hunting was the quickest way to get used to life in the bush. Grogan and Sharp stalked rhinos and buffalo and gazed across swampy plains filled with tens of thousands of wildebeest. On one trip out of Beira, they walked sixty miles in nineteen hours. On another, Grogan dove into a crocodile-infested stream to avoid a wounded buffalo that finally dropped three yards from Sharp's feet.

The activity helped toughen the explorers to the ordeals ahead, but it also helped conceal the true nature of their mission. As the age of exploration morphed into the era of colonization, the "Scramble for Africa" was in full gear.

Europe had salivated at the thought of controlling Africa's vast expanses, manpower, and natural riches since Roman times. For more than a century before Grogan arrived, foreign powers had been slicing up the continent into colonies and protectorates like a pie at a murderous family gathering. By the turn of the nineteenth century, European governments were still fighting over poorly defined colonial borders and wiping out native groups who stood in their way.

Missionaries and explorers like Livingstone and Burton served as vanguards of colonialism. Their maps and information helped governments establish and hold territories. But much of the interior was still terra incognita, and with so much at stake, explorers guarded their goals like inventors protecting their ideas.

Grogan's planned route would take them from Portuguese East Africa through territory controlled or claimed by three other countries. To the north, German East Africa extended from the coast to the eastern shore of Lake Tanganyika, including most of what is now Tanzania, Rwanda, and Burundi.

British claims sandwiched Germany's to the north and south. The Crown's holdings in southern Africa extended as far north as modern-day Zambia. British East Africa, a territory three times the size of the British Isles, encompassed what would become Kenya and Uganda. King Leopold II of Belgium personally controlled almost a million square miles of the Congo basin to the west.

Before leaving London, Grogan had visited the Foreign Office and the War Office to see how his journey could help the British Empire directly. He left with requests for information on the activities of Portuguese, German, Belgian, and French forces, especially when it related to colonial boundaries. He also promised to bring back the first accurate map of the region around Lake Kivu and Lake Edward.

"From end to end every tribe seemed at war with its neighboring tribes or with the white man," Grogan wrote about their route. Local conflicts merged with international disputes from Lake Tanganyika to Sudan, while native troops in the Congo were rising up against their Belgian masters.

The Sudan was the most worrisome part of the itinerary. Six years before, a Muslim religious leader claiming to be a returned messiah (the Mahdi, or "Chosen One") had led an uprising against the colonial forces of Egypt and Britain. The revolt had bloomed into all-out war.

In January 1885, after a siege of almost a year, the Muslim army had captured the key trading center of Khartoum, where the two main branches of the Nile meet before flowing into the Mediterranean. The Mahdi's forces (whom the British mistakenly called "Dervishes") slaughtered an entire seven-thousand-man British garrison and killed or enslaved most of the city's thirty-four thousand Egyptian, Sudanese, and British inhabitants. A British relief column arrived two days late. As the Crown scrambled to respond to the humiliating defeat, the Sudan had become a religious state governed by sharia, the strict interpretation of Islamic law.

This bloody maelstrom was where Grogan and Sharp were heading. The conflicts "rendered the success of our enterprise extremely problematical," Grogan wrote. "And as failure is unpardonable, we wisely refrained from announcing our intentions."

CHAPTER THREE

The only sound at the tiny crossroads north of Beira is the steady thunk of an empty Coke bottle hitting a block of ice. I lay my pack in the shade under a tree and watch a man make his own ice cubes next to a cooler bristling with bottles of cola and orange soda. It's a little after nine in the morning and already the air is suffocatingly hot. I wonder how long I'm going to be stuck here.

After the twenty-four-hour flight to Johannesburg, it took me three days to cover the six hundred fifty miles to Beira by bus and plane. Since this was where Grogan and Sharp started their journey—and I have a lot less time than they did—I decided it was where I'd start as well.

I'd flown in from Maputo, Mozambique's bombed-out capital, last night. As the taxi pulled up in front of the hotel, the driver had nodded at an orange building across the street, apparently a nightclub, and grinned.

"Many women here at night."

No thanks, I thought. Even if I were ten years younger and single. A country where almost a sixth of the people have HIV is not a place for casual liaisons.

Just after dawn, the fog off the Indian Ocean had erased the tops of buildings around the main plaza, where men in skull-caps and ankle-length robes had strolled under sodium lights the night before. Mozambique's second-largest city smelled like a damp towel.

The crack of breaking glass interrupts the iceman's rhythm. In the row of cinder-block food stalls, a few heads turn in mild curiosity. He blinks in the sudden silence and examines his palm. No major gashes. He fishes the largest chunks of broken glass from the slushy pile of ice, grabs another empty bottle, and resumes hammering.

I need to get moving, but no buses have passed for three hours. I try to will myself to patience. I have far to go and only so much time: two months to retrace Grogan's entire route—or at least as much of it as I can. I had originally planned three, but Laura was adamant that I needed to be back at least a month before the wedding. She would handle most of the planning while I was away, but she insisted that we make up a guest list and mail save-the-date cards before I left. An extension is out of the question.

It's July 24, 2007, almost exactly 109 years after Grogan left Beira himself.

"I would like to ask what is your name?"

A tall man in a green T-shirt, a black leather cowboy hat, and a wide grin has appeared out of nowhere. "I am Mandinho," he says, pronouncing it *man-deen-yo*. He offers a limp handshake and asks where I'm from.

"Ah, America!" His face lights up. I have yet to meet someone here with a neutral opinion of the United States. "And you are going where?"

"Vila de Sena, I hope." The city near the Malawi border looks so close on the map: just a few red, white, and yellow roads, some solid, some dashed, and across the thin blue stripe of the Zambezi River.

"Really? Today?" The smile sags. "Would you like to come wait at my bar?" He points to a stall where two more men sit at a table covered with glasses, bottles, and flowery plastic placemats.

For the past half hour I've been fighting the urge to walk north into the dusty glare, hoping for some sort of passing vehicle to hop aboard. I don't want to chance missing the next ride, if there is one.

"I will tell them to look for a car for you," he says, sensing my hesitation.

I've been to Africa twice before, both times for short trips in Kenya and Uganda. The last one was six years ago. I'm slowly readjusting to African public transportation, which mostly consists of learning to wait. Peace of mind is proportional to giving up control; things happen when they happen, or don't, often for no discernible reason. The best strategy is usually to trust that things will work out. Sometimes they do.

Under a corrugated metal awning, he pulls up another chair and introduces his friends. They work at the military base nearby, where Mandinho teaches English. All three are affable and half drunk, with heavy-lidded, bloodshot eyes.

Rounds of homemade wine circle the table, followed by questions. They don't get many foreigners out here, away from the beaches and national parks that draw Mozambique's trickle of tourists.

I draw the basic outline of my trip in the air: six and a half thousand miles through seven more countries, a crooked line heading north and west up the scar of the western branch of the Great Rift Valley (technically the East African Rift System), a massive fracture in the earth's crust where the continent is tearing itself in two. My goal, like Grogan's 109 years ago, is to go as far as I can down the Nile into southern Sudan, a place as foreign to these men as Tibet or the United States.

They understand maybe a quarter of this but keep nodding and pouring. Every time the conversation falters, Mandinho gives me a wide grin and a palm-slapping handshake. Bottles of Cream Head Stout replace the wine. The tipsy joviality is infectious, but I'm itching to get going, peeking at my map and watch when I think no one's looking.

I don't want to look ungrateful. But I'm off-balance, alone and anxious. How will I make it to Sudan if I can't even get to Sena? Life has just become radically simplified. Everything I need for the next two months—I hope—fills the dark green backpack at my feet. The three essentials: Swiss Army knife, Pepto-Bismol tablets, and earplugs. Flashlight, toothpaste, dental floss: check. Notebooks, digital camera, carefully marked and folded map. No wallet, no keys, no cell phone.

There are four twenties under the insole of each of my shoes and another five hidden inside my bulging medical kit. I don't think I've ever taken so many pills on a trip: vitamins, malaria pills, little Chinese kill-anything tablets that look like yellow lentils and taste horrendous. The cash is tucked inside a box of SpongeBob Band-Aids. It was part of a going-away goodie bag Laura gave me the night before I left, along with a pack of Gummi Worms, a tube of sunscreen, and a tiny silver locket with her picture inside.

I started packing three days before I left, but I still feel half-cocked. Between moving to Portland five months ago and all the wedding planning that had to happen before I left, I haven't had much time to look into the current state of the route. The Democratic Republic of the Congo (formerly Zaire), northern

Uganda, and southern Sudan are all in turmoil. I don't know if I'll be able to get into any of them, or if I'll even want to try. Grogan was willing to risk his life; I'm not.

A woman brings over clean glasses from behind the bar.

"This is my wife!" Mandinho says. "My friend Justin!" We shake hands and she bends over for a two-cheek kiss, Portuguese style.

"Again! Again!" one of his friends says, laughing. Mandinho snakes an arm around her hips. She rolls her eyes and hip-checks free, then goes back behind the bar.

A man trots up and says there's a truck heading to Sena. I try to hide my excitement as Mandinho and I perform the ritual of exchanging contact information. I know already that I'll go home with a notebook full of street numbers and email addresses. No matter how friendly people are, it's hard not to be a little cynical, since more often than not each address comes with a hint or outright request to become someone's sponsor, a key step in getting a U.S. visa.

"I will call you! When will you come back here?"

I don't know how to answer that. I mumble something about "soon."

"You just ask for me, the teacher, Mandinho Comboio. It means 'train.'" In my notebook he writes in big letters: *Mandinho Comboio = TRAIN. English-teacher.*

Goodbye is a round of backslaps and high-fives. The truck is a shiny red pickup—not only brand-new but with an empty passenger seat. In fact, it's just me and the driver in the spotless cab, not the usual four people and a baby. There's even air-conditioning. It's the Presidential Suite of African hitchhiking.

More people are climbing into the back and handing up bags and boxes. Soon the bed is overflowing. Coins and crumpled bills make their way to the driver. I assume I'm paying more than anyone else for the front seat, or for just being a white foreigner. Fine with me.

"I am glad we met! I am crying lots!" Mandinho is smiling, but his eyes are brimming as he clasps my hand through the open window. I think of Laura at the airport. There's no sad sense of tearing here, just the urge to move and a sense of ridiculousness. For a second I have to concentrate not to giggle. Then—maybe it's just the alcohol or the exhaust fumes—I do feel a hitch in my chest, tiny compared to four days ago, but there nonetheless. For whatever reason, my new friend is just so sincere.

"Never forget me!" he cries as we roll off in a cinnamon-colored cloud.

Grogan's journey up the Zambezi River by steamer was a "dreary, hot, monotonous" affair. As he and Sharp left Beira and headed inland, islands and sandbanks broke the wide flow, and coconut and sugarcane plantations stood on the grass-covered banks. Huge flocks of geese, flamingos, and pelicans spotted the sky.

The expedition bought eggs, chickens, and tomatoes at villages along the way, but there was no bread, butter, or milk. Worse, they had run out of Worcestershire sauce. They found Sena home to "a few miserable huts, and a few yet more miserable Portuguese." Then came Chiromo, a small but important gateway town to Nyasaland, the protectorate of British Central Africa (today the country of Malawi). The local coffee industry was booming, and European-run companies were busy turning out bricks, cordage, and soon, Scotch whisky.

Grogan and Sharp enjoyed the hospitality of the British vice consul, who caught dinner by shooting his rifle into the river and collecting the stunned fish. The day before they arrived, a lion had sauntered into town in the middle of the day and carried off a local. Almost everyone in town had taken a shot at it, but the man-eater escaped unharmed, "the least excited individual in the place."

By now it was autumn back in England. The nights were turning crisp, and fiery colors were spreading through the trees in Kew Gardens. At Chiromo the thermometer read 120 degrees Fahrenheit in the shade. "Periodical waves of fever prostrate the population when the wind blows from the Elephant Marsh," Grogan noted, referring to a huge nearby wetland, "and the death-rate assumes alarming proportions." People everywhere were alarmingly thin and weak, he noticed, with the classic symptoms of beriberi, a debilitating sickness caused by a lack of thiamine (vitamin B_1).

One evening Grogan decided to take a bath outdoors. He had just eased into the water when a swarm of bees filled the air and attacked every inch of exposed skin. He leaped from the water and sprinted through a nearby native village, naked. He crashed into a hut and collapsed in front of a terrified old woman. When she saw the welts that covered the pale stranger from eyebrows to ankles, she took pity and helped nurse him through the raging fever that followed.

Amid their boxes of gear, Grogan and Sharp almost certainly carried a copy of *Hints to Travellers*, a handbook for gentlemen explorers published by the Royal Geographical Society. Heavy-weights like Richard Burton, Robert Falcon Scott, and Ernest Shackleton all looked to *Hints* for detailed advice on every-thing from weather forecasting to field surgery. In the front and back were ads for adventurous essentials like Jaeger's Pure Wool

Underwear, the Tuckett Insect-Puzzler, and something called Bovril, which could be made into a drink or spread on toast.

While the book's instructions on packing and surveying were generally helpful, its medical advice was par for the period. For the recurrent malarial fevers that would plague Grogan throughout the journey, it prescribed quinine, which was correct, but also large doses of opium or tablets of arsenious acid, a liquid form of arsenic. (Granted, it said the latter "should never be taken on an empty stomach.")

The book also urged him to try a "full purge" (evacuation of the bowels) using calomel, a tasteless white powder made from mercury. Calomel was widely used as a cathartic in the nineteenth century, even though it tended to inflame the linings of the mouth and digestive system and occasionally kill patients.

Grogan had caught malaria during his first trip to Africa. It was far more widespread then than it is today, common as far north as London. Doctors no longer thought the disease was caused by "bad air" (hence the name, from the Italian), but the vector of infection—the bite of an *Anopheles* mosquito infected with the *Plasmodium* parasite—had been pinpointed barely a year before Grogan's departure by a British army officer in India named Ronald Ross. (The discovery earned Ross the 1902 Nobel Prize in Medicine.)

Of the four kinds of *Plasmodium* that infect humans, the deadliest can kill in less than a day. Grogan had the classic symptoms of chronic *Plasmodium malariae* infection: exhausting cycles of chills, fever, and bed-soaking sweats repeated every four to six hours for two or three days. The parasite could lay dormant for years, like a spy in deep cover, before erupting again.

Quinine, the only known treatment, originally came from the reddish bark of the cinchona tree, which grew in the foothills of the Andes Mountains. The bitter alkaloid was priceless; an eighteenth-century Italian doctor called it the medical equivalent of gunpower. The isolation of quinine for commercial production in the 1820s essentially made African exploration possible. Pre-quinine death rates from malaria were astronomical, sometimes on the order of 95 percent or more. From the 1850s onward, expeditions that packed powdered quinine sulfate often didn't lose a single person to the disease.

As bad as it was, chronic malaria was just one of Africa's awful diseases. Yellow fever, spread by a different mosquito, could make the victim's mouth, eyes, and intestines bleed until his vomit turned black. Dengue fever caused such agonizing pain in the joints and muscles it was nicknamed breakbone fever or the bonecrusher's disease. Tiny nematode worms that clogged the body's lymphatic system could make the scrotum swell to the size of a rugby ball, a condition called elephantiasis.

An African ran up during lunch one day, shouting that he had been bitten on the finger by a poisonous night adder. *Hints to Travellers* recommended a dose of carbolic acid (used by the Nazis to kill prisoners by injection during World War II), followed by searing the bite with a hot iron or live coal. Grogan went one better. He threw a tourniquet on the man's arm, sliced open his finger with a pocket knife, dumped gunpowder in the gash, and lit it.

The man's chest, arm, and entire left side swelled enormously. They gave him repeated injections of a solution of potassium permanganate, and someone poured most of a bottle of whisky down the victim's throat. Then Grogan had three other men run the African around camp until he collapsed.

He couldn't have been more misguided. The bite wound should have been left alone, the limb bandaged and splinted, and the patient immobilized. (Even *Hints* got this last bit right: "Let the patient be quiet. Do not fatigue him by exertion.") Extreme swelling calls for antivenin, which, alas, French scientists were just starting to develop at the time.

When the swelling hadn't gone down by the next morning, Grogan decided it was time for stronger measures. He boiled up a pot of permanganate of potash solution and had six people grab the man, who by now was probably wishing he had just crept off into the bush and died. The explorer took a firm grip on his wrist and thrust the swollen hand into the boiling liquid again and again.

"His yells were fearful," Grogan wrote, "but the cure was complete." The swelling went down, and the next morning the bite victim seemed to be doing reasonably well, "with the exception of the loss of the skin of his hand."

I could use some painkillers myself by the time I arrive in Sena, stiff and sore on the third bus of the day. It's after dark, and the only places with lights on are the bars and brothels. Half-dressed women circulate boldly among glassy-eyed men to the distorted thump of dance music. It takes three tries to find a room available for the entire night. I lock the door with a sigh of relief that's becoming a nightly ritual: *This is now my space.*

I sweep the bright blue sheets for stains and stray hairs and open the first of Laura's cards: *I can't wait to spend the rest of my life with you. Let the adventure begin!* A picture of us smiling on the rim of the Grand Canyon falls from the envelope.

This ache wasn't supposed to start so soon. Seven more cards to go. The night before I left, I'd hidden a dozen pink paper hearts around the house: in her sock drawer, inside the dishwasher, under her laptop. Now that last-minute gesture feels weak.

The next morning I'm eating breakfast in bed, a peanut butter PowerBar, when a hoarse warble outside tells me Sena's goats are up, too. A spotted puppy chases chicks across the motel's dirt courtyard. The sun is blinding as I look for someone to pay.

I've run out of Mozambican cash, and when I offer the owner crisp new dollar bills, he shakes his head. The new bill design and my kindergarten Portuguese don't help ("Big heads! Yes! Good!"). But when I turn out my pockets to show it's all I have, he grabs the notes with a scowl and waves me off.

A group of men with bicycles are lounging under a tree. The bikes are Heros, single-geared black metal monsters with plastic seats and metal shafts instead of brake cables. The India-based company is the largest bicycle manufacturer in the world, cranking out 18,500 machines every day. They're one of the main modes of transportation in sub-Saharan Africa.

I hire one to cross the Zambezi River—Malawi is just a few miles on the other side—and climb aboard a rack made of rebar that's been welded over the back wheel. The pilot stands on the pedals and we wobble off.

Bare metal bites into tender flesh as we roll onto a bridge across the fourth-largest river in Africa. The Zambezi drains six countries and roars over Victoria Falls, three times as high as Niagara, before sliding into the Indian Ocean north of Beira.

The Hero sounds like a swing set disintegrating in a hurricane. The owners of these two-wheeled tanks make up for a lack of replacement parts with ingenuity. Already I've seen broken plastic seats replaced with hand-carved wooden ones and a repairman hammering out a bent rim with a rock.

Below us, the early morning sunlight eats through the mist

over the garden patches spread across the floodplain. We cast a strange shadow: two men, two wheels, and a backpack. Workmen in yellow hard hats laugh and call out and point. Riders ferrying crates of empty beer bottles swerve around us, and women with babies tied to their backs simply stare, heads swiveling as we pass.

Then we're out over the water, swallows swooping and fishing boats carving whorls in the wide brown flow. I try to keep my heels out of the spokes as my ass goes numb.

The driver leaves me on the far side of the bridge near a pickup parked by a shack in the shade of a broad, thorny tree.

"This is going to the border?" I ask a man sitting against the shack. He has a scrubby mustache and wears clean jeans and bright white tennis shoes. He nods. "Do you know when?"

"Oh, not until it is full. There are not many people today."

He finds a milk crate for me to sit on and tells me about living as a refugee in Malawi during Mozambique's civil war, which began in 1977, the year he was born, and ended in 1992. Now he lives with his family just over the hill. His name is Tomé.

"Mozambique is very poor," he says. I'm starting to get used to fiscal non sequiturs like this in casual conversation. I'm never quite sure how to respond without sounding guilty or condescending. Sometimes they seem like simple statements of fact— the average *moçambicano* earns less than one percent what the average American does—and sometimes like a veiled plea. Either way, it's discomfiting to have the interaction framed in monetary terms right off the bat.

"Mmm." I nod in agreement, or sympathy.

"All these people sitting around, waiting for something to do." He looks at the crowd gathering slowly around the truck. Three men are buried to the waist under the open hood. The bed is still empty. Not going anywhere anytime soon.

A voice comes through the window of the hut behind us, where a group of men are drinking in the dimness. "My brother-in-law," Tomé says.

All I catch is *mzungu*, so I know he's talking about me. The word (plural *wazungu*) is used to mean "white person" throughout East Africa. It may have its roots in the Swahili for "someone who moves around," from the early days of European traders. Today it's directed—often loudly, by children, with fingers pointing—toward any Caucasian. It isn't overtly derogatory, but it's not completely innocent, either; like a semi-affectionate "honky."

"He says there are too many." Tomé shrugs. I haven't seen another *mzungu* in a day and a half; I wonder how long it's been since the last one passed through, this far off the tourist trail. Weeks? Months?

Almost as an apology, Tomé says, "I would like you to come to my house for breakfast. We have tea and cassava."

His home is three brick huts with thatched roofs. Chickens scratch in the packed dirt courtyard. He pulls up two chairs in front of the largest building and introduces a young woman with cornrow braids as his wife.

She seems annoyed at my unexpected arrival. Now she has to make tea and boil enough starchy roots for both of us. I can see Laura feeling the same way if the roles are reversed—but she would expect me to help, unlike Tomé, who clearly doesn't intend to raise a finger. Our efforts to divide up domestic responsibilities usually end up, if anything, gender-reversed: she does the finances; I do the laundry.

"Her teeth are hurting," Tomé says. I dig a tube of oral pain reliever from my medicine kit and give it to her as a peace offering. Three toddlers emerge from the building, a boy and three girls. Any shyness evaporates in a minute, and soon they're giggling at my attempts to repeat Portuguese words.

"My firstborn died," Tomé says. "He was a boy."

His wife reemerges with mugs of steaming clear liquid, a cup of brown sugar, and a bowl filled with bone-colored chunks of hot cassava. I give a silent prayer that the water was boiled and take a polite sip, then a nibble of one of the fibrous, tasteless morsels.

Tomé tells me he built the buildings himself. I cluck appreciatively; paint and lightbulbs are the limits of my contractor skill set.

The children wrestle in a pile at our feet. The boy is a happy hellion who tackles his siblings like a linebacker. He pins his youngest sister to the ground and blows raspberries on her belly.

Then he tackles one of the other girls, and her dress flies up and a tiny wiener waves at the sky—another boy. His older brother pounces and grabs it, setting off an anguished wail, but he hangs on like a rodeo cowboy. The boy in the dress finally thrashes free and runs crying to his father. Tomé pats his back and brushes off the dirt.

"Michael Jackson is in America?" he says. Yes, he is.

"How much does a bicycle like that cost?" I point to his Hero. At least sixteen hundred meticais, about fifty dollars.

"Are there people like me in America?" he asks, touching his dark forearm.

"Ah, yes, many." I wonder if he's waiting for something, a gift or cash, and then I feel guilty for suspecting his hospitality. Sometimes there's no need to bring up money at all. When your shoes cost more than someone makes in two months, the gulf is obvious.

The kindness of strangers offsets much of the aggravation of traveling in the developing world. It's amazing how admitting your own helplessness and ignorance can bring out the best in people. But I still can never predict when someone will ask for money. Sometimes an awkward request follows the most trivial gesture. Other times people won't take a cent for going hours out of their way, no matter how much you insist.

Grogan encountered something similar—many of the people he met had never seen a white man before, let alone the things he carried—but I doubt he lost any sleep over it. His encounters with locals were almost purely commercial; as long as they weren't robbed or attacked, he and Sharp couldn't care less if the natives liked them.

Tomé's wife retrieves the cups and bowls and the children squirm at our feet. The sour smell of wood smoke drifts from inside the hut.

"Are you married?"

"Not yet. Three months."

"So soon! She is waiting? You have been together a long time?"

Laura and I had met seven years before, in fact, in a dark pub in downtown Washington, D.C. I hate to admit it, but my initial thought when I saw my future wife for the first time wasn't about the surge of electricity that coursed through me when our eyes met, as I imagine happened to Grogan when he met Gertrude. It was how much I hated Irish music.

The wood-paneled walls of the Dubliner vibrated with the overamplified sound of an acoustic guitar and a deep voice singing about star-crossed lovers. Two women about my age were sitting at a table near the stage. One was blond and petite, with a smile that almost stopped me cold. Laura's nose was dusted with freckles and her mannerisms were quick and delicate, almost deerlike. The brunette to her left was Kerry, her best friend, on security detail.

Fresh out of grad school and unemployed, I had found Laura's name in the alumni directory of the University of Virginia. She had graduated two years after me. Her listing said she worked for the *Washington Post*'s website, which was just the kind of job I had in mind. But when I emailed, she apologized and said she'd switched jobs to *National Geographic*'s TV channel and hadn't updated her profile.

Even better, I thought. After a few months of sporadic emails, I suggested meeting in person the next time I came to Washington.

We had to shout over the music. It turned out we had both majored in biology, overlapping by two years.

"Did you ever take genetics?" I said. "Kicked my ass."

"I can't believe I never saw you around Gilmer Hall," she said.

We had both also joined the Greek system, almost certainly hitting some of the same parties, and then bailed our sophomore year when the beer-soaked mind-set grew stale.

"I can't believe I even lasted a year," she said.

I wanted to make a good impression. Careers were all about personal connections, I was learning quickly. At the same time, there was an undercurrent to the conversation that wasn't strictly professional. Laura seemed bright, fun, interesting. Definitely attractive. A mountain-biking world traveler who made nature and science documentaries: quite a combination. I wasn't looking for someone to date—this meeting was part of my job hunt, Bass Ale pints and all—but she definitely seemed like someone I'd like to get to know better.

I know now it was all there at the beginning, all the warmth and wariness, the similarities and sticking points. Laura's unalloyed confidence and cheeriness, tinged at odd moments with a strange shy deference. My curiosity about this woman who seemed so straightforward and complete, so simply *there* in a way I hadn't ever encountered.

The singer finally took a break and the women went up to talk to him. Laura had said she loved this kind of music—the only strike against her I can remember from the entire night. I took a deep breath. Having to be "on" was tiring. It felt like playing doubles tennis with no partner, part job interview, part chaperoned date.

At least there hadn't been any eyebrow-raising silences. Laura had agreed to introduce me to friends at work. And as far as I could tell, she was single.

They came back, and after a few more songs I excused myself.

"See you later," I said.

"Definitely."

A full moon hung over the dome of the Capitol when I left the bar. A taxi blared its horn down half the block.

That seemed to go pretty well, I thought. Even if it didn't lead to a job, maybe it could go somewhere else.

CHAPTER FOUR

The angry rhino was fifteen yards away when Grogan reached back for his four-bore rifle and grabbed nothing but air.

With a barrel an inch across, the elephant gun was essentially a shoulder-mounted cannon. Each four-inch shell held a bullet as big as a man's thumb and enough black powder to send it through a rhino's inch-thick hide or even the skull of an elephant, if you hit the right spot—and if you could fire it in time.

But Grogan's gun bearers, who were supposed to caddy his rifles and hand them over loaded and ready at a moment's notice, had dropped the weapons and bolted up a thorn tree in terror. The bull rhino snorted and stamped, ready to charge at any second. Grogan normally thought these "choleric, dyspeptic, unsociable old fellows" were overrated as game animals, and their blundering, unprovoked charges almost comical.

No one was laughing now. The rhino pawed the ground and snorted, blinking myopically. Grogan fell to his knees and scrabbled through the undergrowth in the dust and the heat, searching for the rifle. It had to be somewhere.

A few days before, Sharp had gone north to hire porters for the crossing between Lake Nyasa (called Lake Malawi today) and Lake Tanganyika. Grogan had gotten tired of waiting for their misdirected baggage to be shipped to Chiromo. When he heard there were rhinos and elephants in the hilly country to the east, he leaped at the chance to check off two more of his life goals.

First he needed to get permission from the Portuguese to enter their territory. He knew nothing impressed petty officials in remote postings like a gaudy uniform. He donned a set of spurs and a red-and-white medal ribbon he made from a pin-cushion and rowed across the Shire River to Portuguese East Africa, a riding whip under one arm, amid waving flags and blaring trumpets. The official on duty was appropriately dazzled and gave him a "viesky-soda" and permission to shoot.

A few days later, the chief of a native village asked Grogan what he was going to shoot the next day. Like Babe Ruth point-ing to the bleachers at Wrigley Field, he casually predicted he'd bring home a rhino. After five hours of tracking, he surprised one sleeping behind an anthill but then found himself unexpect-edly unarmed.

Now he was groping frantically in the dirt, with his porters hanging from a branch "like a cluster of bees" and a ton of angry pachyderm gauging the shortest distance between the tip of its horn and his spleen.

His hand closed on the barrel. He jerked the gun up and fired. The recoil was like a horse kick to the shoulder. The bul-let slammed into the rhino's shoulder and the animal crashed off into the bushes, squealing. A thick cloud of gunsmoke hung in the sudden silence.

He scolded his men out of the tree, and they tracked the bull across steep hills and gullies. It was November, the start of the rainy season. New grass pushed through the dark soil and young leaves filled the trees. Grogan led the small party across icy streams lined with bamboo, ferns, and orchids. From the shoulder of Mount Chiperoni, forty miles east of Chiromo, they could see an endless plain covered with flowering trees in all the colors of a British autumn, shading a carpet of purple and green flowers.

When they found it three hours later, the rhino took four more shots to kill. Exhausted and famished, they cut out the liver and grilled it over a quick fire. Fourteen hours after setting out, they were back in the village, where the chief was impressed by Grogan's skill. Hundreds of people left to go cut up the carcass.

Few things made Grogan feel as alive as tracking an animal that could kill him. The only thing that compared was mountain climbing. Both offered "the same glorious feeling of space, the same communing with Nature in her wild grandeur, the same gulp of excitement, the same fierce joy of life only to be had in grappling with death."

A successful hunt gave a feeling of "solid satisfaction . . . that one does not find on the top of a peak, and then one has not got to come down." While climbing was all about camaraderie, big-game hunting was generally done alone or with, at most, one or two companions.

African natives were legendary for their skill at hunting and tracking. But Grogan was starting to think that most of them were just "an abominable nuisance" in the bush. The men and boys he hired as gun bearers or porters would lag behind or whistle loudly when they saw an animal. Some would flee whenever animals charged.

A self-described "lover of nature," Grogan would only hunt on foot in the bush, eye-to-eye with elephants, lions, or hippos. It was only sporting. The animals had at least some chance of turning the tables; they could turn around and attack directly, hide and tackle him from behind, and play dead and spring up when he came close. He considered letting a wounded animal suffer to be inexcusable, and using bait and waiting on a platform or in a blind "an unpardonable form of murder."

The lost luggage finally arrived in Chiromo, six weeks late. Grogan was so impatient he left the next day, November 28, 1899, on a boat up the Shire River. He and Sharp had been in Africa for nine months. They'd spent a third of the time waiting for misdirected supplies. "Such is African travel," Grogan wrote. "Even after this wait some of our things never turned up at all."

A peloton of Heros-for-hire is waiting at the Malawi border. I pick one with a padded passenger seat that's nowhere near as comfortable as it looks, and we weave down the dirt track toward the immigration post.

Moving through Mozambique felt like a constant struggle, but Malawi makes a good first impression. The countryside becomes greener almost immediately. The immigration officer welcomes me in English like an old friend and says the health officer will be back in a moment to look at my yellow-fever card.

I unfold my map and calculate it's only another hundred miles to Blantyre, and a hot shower, and an Internet connection. In three days I've covered what took Grogan nine months. I've started measuring my progress by map folds. Beira was fold one. I've made it to fold two. Sudan is eight. I do the numbers in my head one more time: two weeks to get to Burundi, maybe another week to Uganda . . . Beyond that, I have no idea. But covering Grogan's entire route looks at least possible.

A group of men are bent over a board in the shadow of the building. They're playing *bao*, a deceptively simple-looking strategy game that's a national obsession in Malawi and Tanzania. They shout in triumph or frustration as two players move seeds between rows of round divots. There are no draws, only victory or defeat.

Malawi has a reputation as one of the friendliest places in Africa. It's also one of the poorest countries on the planet. Two out of every five people here live on less than a dollar a day. The only reason many people even know the country exists is that Madonna recently showed up to adopt a local orphan.

The health officer gives me a thumbs-up and it's bicycle time again. The first ride lasts twenty minutes before the driver pulls over, gasping.

"So tired, so tired," he says. Sweat is streaming from under his knit hat. He unties my pack from the handlebars and drops it on the ground. "No more."

It's strange to be ferried on the back of some sweating stranger's bicycle. But I'm sure not walking this far, and they're eager for the business. The next bicycle breaks a spoke after ten minutes. But number three is the charm, and two hours later I'm sitting in a minibus idling near the Chiromo post office. The seats look as if they've been mauled by a wolverine.

A man in the front seat introduces himself as Zola Emanuel. He's good-looking in the gaunt way of a long-distance runner.

"In Africa there is no happiness," he says.

"Sorry?"

"There is nothing here." This keeps happening, these conversational bombs out of nowhere. It's like a first date bringing up her colon issues before the appetizers arrive. He looks out the cracked windshield at the town square, where people stumble in and out of the Why Not Booze Garden. "Nothing."

He has a point. For whatever reason—politics, geography, misguided attempts by outsiders to help—two-thirds of the least-developed countries in the world are right here, between South Africa and the Sahara. The average Malawian barely earns enough in a year to buy an iPod. According to some estimates, the country has a million AIDS orphans out of 13 million people.

I'm mystified why misery is so often a conversation opener. Everything that's said and written about Africa, all the hand-wringing and blanket generalizations and dismal statistics—I wonder how much of that sinks into your consciousness, living here, like acid rain into limestone. How could you not absorb the pessimism, like a child who's always told he's not good enough?

"Africa is crying, always," Zola says. Am I wrong to wonder if he read that somewhere?

The idling motor fills the bus with carbon monoxide until we leave a half hour later. Then the engine coughs and dies after just a few miles. I find myself standing on a corner in a one-street town too small for the map. Hissing propane lanterns light a few tiny market stalls, and the western sky is bloody with sunset.

I'm starving, but I don't have enough local currency to buy a hard-boiled egg. I haven't seen a bank in days. After a thirteen-hour day of bikes, buses, and equatorial sun, it almost seems like too much effort to ask someone if this place has a hotel or a place to eat. The chances of either are slim to none. There's not even a bicycle in sight.

I can't imagine Grogan having a what-now moment like this. Even at twenty-three he was incredibly self-confident, all decisive action and no regrets. What would he do? Probably stride up to the nearest man over fifty and demand—politely but firmly, using sign language if necessary—to be shown the nearest place of lodging, and how about a nice plate of rice and fish while you're at it.

I just don't have it in me. What seemed doable this morning looks futile now. Grogan had a clear goal. What am I trying to prove, sitting on the curb in a mystery town in Malawi—and to whom?

I barely notice the portly man in glasses as he approaches. He's a teacher, he says, and when he learns I'm a writer, his face lights up.

"I plan one day to write four books. Would you like to hear their titles?" What I'd really like is somewhere to curl up in a ball and rock myself to sleep. I nod.

"The first will be called *A World Denied Me*. The next, *No Teacher in Eden*. And the third . . ."

He frowns. It's on the tip of his tongue.

"Anyway, are you looking for a hotel?"

Grogan was just one of the characters aboard the steamer chugging up the Shire River toward Lake Nyasa. The liveliest passenger was a "Bible-flaunting, prayer-moaning, evangelical madman in a state of charity-seeking destitution." Grogan thought missionaries upset Africa's traditional cultures more than they helped. "Such men should be caged, or at least prevented from running loose amongst the natives."

He had little patience for organized religion, especially when it meant meddling in other's affairs. He had no problem when people kept their beliefs to themselves, and he even went out of his way to accommodate those of his men who were Muslims, who would only eat an animal that had had its throat cut before dying. "Although this is a great nuisance (as cutting the throat spoils the head skin), it is right to respect such customs, . . . they should not suffer for their belief," he wrote.

Alfred Sharpe, commissioner of British Central Africa, was also on board. He was a living legend from his years as a professional hunter and soldier in southern Africa. Sharpe gave Grogan plenty of welcome advice, including what to do when an elephant charged: "Remain quite still till the brute [is] within four yards, and then . . . blaze in his face. This almost invariably turns the brute or makes him swerve." Grogan couldn't wait to give it a try.

He was disappointed that men like Sharpe didn't write up their experiences more often, so that "much of the misleading balderdash that now passes current as representing the Dark Continent would be happily crushed out of existence." As it was, the reading public was left with "the imaginative literary efforts of missionaries and week-end tourists," in addition to the accounts of explorers like himself.

Grogan was as guilty of overgeneralizing as anyone. That said, it can be hard for outsiders to write about a place as alien as Africa. A cloud of caricature and distortion has surrounded the continent since at least 1733, when Jonathan Swift penned:

Geographers in Afric-maps
With Savage-Pictures fill their gaps;
And o'er unhabitable downs
Place Elephants for want of towns.

Joseph Conrad's *Heart of Darkness* helped cement many of the clichés that persist, starting with its title.

Africa has always been a concept as much as a place: an exotic backdrop for outsiders to have ennobling experiences, a land of theatric extremes of violence and beauty. In modern accounts, the native stereotypes have simply shifted, from barba-

rous and bloodthirsty to impoverished or corrupt. Simply saying
Africa "is" anything implies a single amorphous entity, instead
of fifty-three countries with a billion inhabitants. Not to mention that "Africa" often refers to just the most destitute part of
the continent: the region south of the Sahara, not including
South Africa.

The steamer's captain was so sick with fever that the passengers
took control of the ship. They steered it past the Elephant Marsh,
where uncontrolled hunting in past decades had decimated huge
herds of elephant, buffalo, and other animals. The area had since
been set aside as a game reserve and the animals were slowly
recovering.

Grogan rode as far north as he could and then set out on the
road that climbed into the highlands toward Blantyre, the ad-
ministrative post for British Central Africa.

He passed coffee plantations with tidy homesteads and rows
of bushes laden with blooms. This was the industry that would
solidify Britain's claims in East Africa, he wrote, keeping the
"wily Teuton" (Germany) at bay. The parts of the continent
that lacked mineral wealth tended to be overlooked in the grand
scheme of colonization, but that was a mistake. The problem as
Grogan saw it was that Britain kept sending over idiots to run
things. "No country requires a more delicately-adjusted combination of dash, tact, and perseverance than Africa."

The view at sunset was superb: forested hills, new grass, and
a carpet of purple flowers that looked like crocuses.

Blantyre, the first vaguely urban center in this part of Africa, had a passable hotel and streets lined with eucalyptus trees.
Grogan enjoyed the hospitality of British officials, days of tea

and tennis amid tropical gardens. He felt as if he had been transported back to England.

All in all, Africa didn't seem nearly as awful this time around. Aside from the delays, the trip was going smoothly. Gertrude might even have enjoyed it so far, snakes and bees notwithstanding.

How are you doing! I was just thinking about you! Where are you now!?

Laura's instant messages, like her emails, bristled with exclamation points.

I'm okay I guess. Blantyre, Malawi now. Ass is throbbing from riding on bike racks for half of yesterday.

Aww. Take care of it for me!

Blantyre has as many people as Austin, Texas, but it's small enough to walk across in fifteen minutes. My first goal, after luxuriating in a real cup of coffee at the poshest hotel in town, was to find an Internet café. I'd promised to stay in touch as much as possible, whenever I could get email access. A satellite phone was too expensive, and I'd assumed that crossing so many borders would make a regular cell phone impractical.

I'll do my best to preserve my tush. You too!

A trio of high school students, obviously American, chitter like birds at the next table. I add a few more exclamation points, but they seem forced. The ache I'd felt in Sena has faded. Now I'm back to my default on-the-road mind-set: happy and content to be moving, absorbing new things, alone.

This lack of longing has always seemed wrong somehow. Since we both work from home, we see a lot of each other. When Laura asks me after a trip if I missed her, I usually feign nonchalance and say no, airily enough to call it a joke if she takes it seriously. More often than not she acts just offended enough: *I know you love me, but I know you're not really kidding, either.*

I'm never sure if missing someone has to mean I wish we were together right now, or whether it's enough just to feel the separation as an ache, an unwelcome but bearable pain.

Miss you! Be safe! Laura adds a smiley for good measure.

Miss you too!

It wasn't until three months after we met that I saw Laura again. It was November, and I was visiting Washington again from my temporary home base in Utah to hustle up more job contacts. On the spur of the moment, I invited her to a movie on my last night in town.

We met in line outside an ornate old theater near the National Zoo.

"Hey, welcome back," she said. Her smile was as radiant as I remembered.

There was a fleeting moment of awkwardness: handshake? Quick peck on the cheek? I went with brief hug, barely a shoulder toucher.

"This is Jeff." I introduced my college roommate and best friend, who worked for the Treasury Department. If she was surprised it wasn't just us two, she hid it well. She looked at the line for tickets, which wound around the block and out of sight down a side street.

"What was this movie again?"

"*Lord of the Rings.* It's getting great reviews. Total epic." People were dressed like wizards and elves.

To her credit, Laura kept smiling, at least until the lights went down. Cheers went up at the opening credits and about every fifteen minutes thereafter, especially during the big battles.

It was three hours and eighteen minutes of hobbits, orcs, and huge, burning eyeballs.

I was too absorbed in the spectacle to wonder what she was thinking. At twenty-nine, I could count on two hands the number of bona fide, mutually acknowledged dates I'd been on in my life. Not one of my smattering of relationships had lasted much more than a year without serious (and always, ultimately, deal-breaking) turbulence, usually instigated in one way or another by me after the initial exhilaration cooled down. I had fallen hard a few times, but it never seemed to last. I'd never even come close to living with anyone. Apparently it wasn't enough, on our first explicitly non-work-related encounter, to invite her to this übergeekfest. (What sophisticated professional woman doesn't love Tolkien?) I had to seal the deal by bringing my own chaperone. At least Jeff didn't sit between us.

My social instincts must have atrophied after three years in the teetotaling cultural vacuum of Utah.

Outside afterward, cigarette smoke and conversation steam eddied above the giddy crowd. Laura actually seemed to have enjoyed the movie, although I doubt she'd have let on if she hadn't. We said good night and promised to stay in touch. Then she left to catch the Metro home. Jeff and I went to a bar nearby.

"I'm thinking of asking Deb to marry me," he said over the second pint.

"Seriously? Wow."

I wasn't really surprised. He and his girlfriend had known each other since grade school. It was inevitable they would take the plunge, and she was getting impatient.

Jeff had a steady government job that was the opposite of my peripatetic freelancer's lifestyle. He made getting married seem so easy, so obvious.

We clinked glasses and I wished him well with hardly a trace of disappointment.

"Laura seems cool," he said. "So are you guys dating or what?"

CHAPTER FIVE

M yfrend, myfrend, you need taxi!"
The teenager in the black stocking cap won't stop tugging my sleeve. I hate giving in to touts—the more insistent they are, the more the overcharge you, in my experience—but it's already dark, and Nkhata Bay, halfway up Lake Malawi's western shore, is still half an hour away. It took a day longer to get here by bus from Blantyre than I thought it would. I need to get to the bay tonight to catch the weekly ferry up the lake first thing tomorrow morning.

"Taxi!" The kid is persistent. We settle on nine kwacha, about five dollars, for a one-way ride to Nkhata Bay. He herds me outside and into the front seat of a battered black Ford sedan. His climbs into the backseat and says his name is Noel. The guy behind the wheel is Harold.

Another taxi driver leans through my open window. "They are drunk," he says, bouncing an eyebrow at the pair. I buckle my seat belt.

"Okay okay, let's go, let's go," Noel says, shaking the back of Harold's seat.

They ask for money up front for gas as we pull out. I refuse, as I do five minutes later when a policeman flags us down and practically demands we let him and his friend climb in. Usually I'm happy to share a vehicle—you never know when it's going to be you begging for a spot—but tonight I'm tired and feeling selfish and unreasonable. I don't want to open the floodgates and end up packed in with ten other people, stopping every three minutes for the next hour and a half. I just want a meal and a bed.

Noel keeps mumbling "noprublem, noprublem" until I'm ready to hit him. "I like Jeanclaudevandamme," he says, and promptly falls asleep.

There's a gate across the road. Harold tells Noel to open it.

No response. Harold reaches back and starts punching his friend in the leg, harder and harder. *Whap! Whap!* "Get up!" Nothing.

"Stupid guy," he says. I get out and open it.

We vibrate downhill through the dark. Snores rise from the backseat. Then we can see a semicircle of lights sparkling on the black surface of Lake Malawi. Harold drops me in front of an inexpensive hotel on a steep hill above the water.

Music from dueling sound systems echoes around the bay. It's Saturday night, and I find the hotel is swinging into party mode. Tourists and well-dressed locals crowd the place, clinking bottles of Carlsberg beer at a bar under a flat-screen TV.

I squeeze in and a stout woman behind the counter orders me dinner from the kitchen. Mary wears a red bandanna and has a Letterman-sized gap in her front teeth. Her husband died and left her with three children, she says. She looks barely out of her teens.

Neon green snakes writhe on the TV. A familiar yellow rectangle appears in the corner of the screen. It clicks that it's the National Geographic Channel and I feel the sudden shock of Laura's absence.

"My fiancée works for them. My girlfriend." I point to the TV.

"Why is she not here with you?" Mary says, sliding a plate of pasta across the bar.

"She's . . . waiting at home."

"You should be with her." She smiles. "Next time you should come here together."

When Grogan reached the southern end of Lake Nyasa, he hadn't seen Sharp for weeks. On the final stretch upriver, the steamer had churned up the shallow muddy bottom, releasing so much marsh gas that the water looked like it was boiling. Other passengers told him that "men had been blown out of their cabins, after igniting the gas with a stray match."

The settlement of Fort Johnson, barely a few months old, was full of rats. "[They] amused themselves all night by tobogganing down my face, rushing along my body, and taking flying leaps from my feet into outer darkness," Grogan wrote.

But he had made it to Lake Nyasa, the first of the Great Rift Valley lakes. It stretched almost due north for three hundred sixty miles, no more than fifty miles across at its widest.

Livingstone had been the first European to see the lake a little before noon on September 16, 1859, during his expedition to explore the Zambezi River. The southern end of the lake was the most crowded place he had come across in two decades in Africa. "On the beach of wellnigh every little sandy bay, dark crowds were standing, gazing at the novel sight of a boat under sail," he wrote in his popular account of the expedition.

Whenever his group landed, hundreds of men, women, and children surrounded them in seconds "to have a stare at the 'chirombo' (wild animals)." To the locals, "blue eyes appear savage, and a red beard hideous." He decided to cut their stay short when the natives, assuming the white men were slavers, offered to sell them children.

By the time Grogan arrived, Great Britain, Germany, and Portugal all claimed parts of the lake's shoreline. He was given a tour of the HMS *Guendolen*, a 136-foot British gunboat that had just been launched to patrol the lake against rival powers. It was odd but reassuring to see a Royal Navy ship this far from England.

Fifteen years later, the *Guendolen* took part in the first naval engagement of World War I. In 1914, four days after Britain declared war on Germany, Commander E. F. Rhodes received orders to destroy the *Hermann Von Wissmann*, a smaller German warship piloted by one Kapitan Berndt, who happened to be Rhodes's drinking buddy. The British gunboat tracked the *Von Wissmann* around Lake Nyasa for five days before disabling her with a lucky shot from two thousand yards away. Berndt hadn't even known war had been declared. When he rowed over to the *Guendolen* to find out what was going on, Rhodes politely took him prisoner.

On December 15, 1898, three days after his twenty-fourth birthday, Grogan started up Lake Nyasa aboard the SS *Domira*. Monkey Bay, the first stop, reminded him of the South Sea islands he had visited on his way home from New Zealand. "Bold rocky headlands plunge into the lake and enclose a white strip of sand with straggling villages at the back. The water is clear as crystal, and broken by the heads of hundreds of natives diving, swimming, and splashing about. Ringing peals of laughter echo in the rocks and startle the troops of baboons that sit watching with curious eyes."

As the boat continued north, it steamed through dark clouds that turned out to be made of tiny flies natives called *kungu*. They rose from the surface "in such stupendous clouds that they blot out the whole horizon," Grogan wrote. "Seen in the distance, they have exactly the appearance of a rainstorm coming across the lake."

Livingstone had encountered these hordes during his Zambezi expedition. "They filled the air to an immense height, and swarmed upon the water, too light to sink in it. Eyes and mouth had to be kept closed while passing through this living cloud: they struck upon the face like fine drifting snow."

The flies (technically phantom midges) are essential to the lake's ecology. They spend most of their short lives as aquatic larvae, food for the lake's fish. As adults, they gather in mating clouds that were once so dense, it was said, that they could suffocate fishermen caught inside.

Sometime they blew ashore and died en masse, Grogan heard, filling rooms a foot deep and leaving a horrendous stench. Pressed into patties and cooked with tomatoes or onions, the flies make a nutritious meal, full of protein, calcium, and three times as much iron as ox liver. Locals eat them with rice or *nsima,* the ubiquitous cornmeal porridge. According to one European visitor, they taste like "dry chocolate and badly kept anchovy paste." Grogan tried one and found it "by no means bad."

Local culinary conventions seemed to change with every new district the expedition entered. Once, the natives were amazed the explorers wouldn't eat snakes. In another district, Sharp and Grogan tried to buy eggs from a tribe that had an abundance of chickens. The natives were appalled: they ate the birds but never touched the eggs.

Grogan persisted, and eventually an old man brought over a

basketful of eggs. The Englishman cracked one open and found a chicken embryo inside. All the eggs were fertilized. He told the man to take them back. "I knew you people didn't really eat eggs," the man said crossly.

At one stop, a missionary settlement that was once an Arab slave hub, Grogan made the mistake of joining in a game of soccer. The exertion brought on a sharp attack of fever that lasted for days. He spent the time writing postcards to his siblings and a few friends (not Gertrude—not until Cairo). He knew he would soon be entering the true unknown. Every chance to connect with home might be the last.

Each card took more than a year to arrive and consisted of two words: *Cheerio. Ewart.*

The next night Laura and I connected started innocently enough. It was February and I was visiting Washington again for a job interview.

We met at a sushi bar near Dupont Circle. It looked like a set from *2001*, all curving white plastic and DJs playing electronica. The other patrons seemed sleek and self-contained, like show dogs. A glowing panel above our table slowly changed from pink to blue.

After a decade living out west, ultra-hip places like this intimidated me. It was light-years from the fleece-and-beer aesthetic I was used to, though Laura seemed perfectly comfortable. Even "meeting for drinks" sounded glamorous, never mind with someone who had such an enviable job.

So I overcompensated. At the next place we went to, another Irish pub (I detected a theme), I described in glowing detail my life to date: writing travel guidebooks straight out of college, working as a park ranger in southeast Utah, studying grizzly bear ecotourism in grad school, and climbing mountains in South America.

She told about growing up in the suburbs of Philadelphia and escaping to Australia after college, where she lived on a boat and taught tourists to dive on the Great Barrier Reef. After another scuba stint in the Caribbean, she had moved to the capital to work for the *Washington Post*, then found her dream job at "NG."

We let our guard down a little more with every round of drinks.

"So many of the guys here are so boring," she said, confirming my impression that Washington had a plurality of dull, J.Crew-wearing workaholics who talked a lot but had little to say. Nobody chose to live here for any reason besides work, so that was all most people, men and women, had to talk about.

I countered with the outdoorsy but ambitionless women who bounced from city to city in the West, from Durango to Missoula to Moab. Fun at first but quickly disenchanting, with priorities limited to rock-climbing routes or new bands passing through town.

I was dying to meet someone with an interesting job that inspired her—one that wasn't the main focus of her life but was more than some temporary gig to pay the bills. Someone who was passionate. Adventurous.

Now we were into the intricacies of relationships.

"Do you think there's just one person out there for each of us?" she said with a flirtatious directness. The classic soulmate problem: Do you get a single chance at love in life, or more? In other words, how romantic are you?

"No, I'd say more like hundreds." (Answer: semi-romantic.)

"Or thousands. It's just a question of meeting one at the right time—when you're both available and interested." I didn't mention that my closest friends have always been female, but I had a bad habit of falling for them and ruining a good thing.

"So, have you met any?" Was this a test?

"One or two, I think. I don't know—it never worked out, anyway." I told how I'd been head over heels at least twice, maybe three times. The most recent had been one leg of an interstate love triangle I'd just emerged from, a tangle of secrecy, guilt, and infatuation entirely my own creation. It ended in the stone-coldest dumping I'd ever experienced, one I thoroughly deserved, and left me deeply suspicious of my own judgment when it came to relationships. Nothing serious for me for a while, thanks.

Laura's most recent relationship, her most serious yet, had seesawed well past its expiration date before ending. He was still around, in a new social circle that occasionally crossed hers. But they were "just friends" now, she said.

We stepped into the night buzzing with potential. Ten minutes later we were elbowing through a sweaty mass of bodies in a Latin dance club that filled three floors of a converted row house.

I dance salsa like I play pool: poorly, but well enough to fake it with exactly the right amount of alcohol in my system. That's where I was now. We were both at that magical inebriation balance point, enough to loosen stiff gringo hips but not enough to get sloppy.

"You have to let me lead," I said into her ear as we gyrated. "Salsa is the macho dance." She laughed back. My hand was on the small of her back, and the crowd kept pushing us closer together.

After a few songs we took a break in a dark corner. Maybe I should come up and see her apartment, she said.

An overstuffed green couch and an etching of a canal in Venice. Photos of sea fans and coral.

On her bed, kissing. Then she was pushing me away and sitting up.

"You should go."

"What?"

"You should. I'm kind of seeing someone. We're breaking up, but it's not official yet. I'd feel bad."

"You'd feel—" I played it as cool as I could. Stay civil, chin up, casual goodbye.

I left Laura's building. It was 2 A.M. and a tide of bodies was streaming in and out of the bars that lined the street. College students shouted drunkenly across the traffic.

Had I missed something? Nobody had ever kicked me out like that. Was I supposed to protest? I didn't buy the sudden-guilt-attack story. (That shows the kind of person I was used to dating—I didn't know yet that she really was that decent.)

I headed back to my hotel irritated and confused but with a new respect for Laura. From start to finish, the night had done nothing but make her more appealing.

Along Nyasa's coastline, Grogan wrote, "the hills are heavily wooded, and their bases are broken by the waves into fantastic caves and rocky promontories against which plays the white line of surf. Small rocky islands stand out here and there, and form the resting-place of myriads of cormorants."

When the ship stopped at Nkhata Bay, he went ashore to bring medicine to a British telegraph official who was also suffering from fever. Farther north, he climbed the steep hills that rose west of the lake to visit a Christian mission named Livingstonia.

It had been named after the man who, when he wasn't crossing the Congo or searching for the source of the Nile, was busy drumming up support in England to help spread commerce and the Gospel across Africa.

In four years, Livingstonia had had to be moved twice because of malaria. But this spot, high above the lake on the Khondowe Plateau, seemed like it might work.

Dr. Robert Laws, a missionary-explorer in the Livingstone mold, had bought three hundred acres from Cecil Rhodes in 1895. The Glasgow Presbyterian welcomed Grogan and proudly showed him how much they had accomplished in just three years. There was a school and a church, a farm and a quarry. A printing machine churned out books and magazines. At the carpentry workshop, Laws presented Grogan with a folding camp chair he would carry for thousands of miles.

Grogan returned to the ship laden with butter and giant watermelons and a little less opposed to missionary efforts in Africa. "If ability, whole-hearted earnestness, and hard work can accomplish any good in missionary endeavour, Dr. Laws ought to succeed."

The ship reached Karonga at the north end of Lake Nyasa the next day. Grogan disembarked and asked around for Sharp, who was supposed to wait for him there. He was disappointed to find his partner had gotten impatient and left two days before for Lake Tanganyika, to arrange transportation up that much longer lake.

The southern end of Lake Tanganyika was two hundred miles due west across a scrubby plateau. The most direct route would be weeks of rough going across bogs and countless streams.

Grogan's most recent crop of porters had fulfilled their contracts and left for home. He needed to find more locals to carry the expedition's food and equipment and to provide defense. But in Karonga, good men were hard to find. The explorers had arrived during the local planting season, and workers were needed in the fields. A Belgian telegraph-laying expedition had recently camped nearby on its way to the Congo and hired most of the remaining hands.

Grogan stayed busy by reorganizing the expedition's boxes of supplies to lighten the loads as much as possible. When he opened them, he was shocked. The supply firm they had contracted with in London had done a terrible job of packing the food. Much of it had spoiled, and worms were everywhere. Chocolate bars had been packed in hay in a leaky wooden box and were furry with mold. "As a practical joke it was weak, but as a venture in fungi-culture a complete success."

Tins of sausages had gone bad and swelled to the size of rugby balls. "I was careful to throw them down wind," Grogan wrote, "when they exploded on contact with the ground in a manner most satisfactory, to the utter consternation of six Kaffir [wild] dogs and a hyaena."

He spent Christmas Day of 1898 in bed with fever, nursing a cup of tea. In ten months, he and Sharp had traveled more than seventeen hundred miles from Beira. Their journey had barely begun.

CHAPTER SIX

As soon as Grogan recovered from his latest attack of fever, he started looking around Karonga for men to go north.

He strode into a meetinghouse full of men from the Watonga tribe and called out, "Now, which of you would like to come with me on a journey?"

Staring faces surrounded him.

It would be a long walk, Grogan said. But the men who followed him would be more than porters. They would be his right-hand men, responsible for organizing camp, handling weapons, and ensuring the expedition ran smoothly. And they would see many wonderful things. There were lakes larger than Nyasa, and "mighty mountains that made fire." Other mountains were "so high that the water became as stones."

He heard snickering. Someone asked how he knew all this. Had he been there to see it?

"No. Not yet."

"Then how do you know what is there?"

"White men know many things," Grogan said, tapping his forehead. And what they didn't know, they read about in books. He waved a copy of *Whitaker's Almanack*, a yearbook full of esoterica on foreign countries, British government offices, and London social clubs.

His approach wasn't quite as patronizing at it sounds. Grogan was asking these men to leave their homes and families and accompany a complete stranger farther than any of them, or anyone they knew, had ever gone. He needed to impress them, but he also had to find men he could trust. Their lives would depend on each other.

"And where does this journey end?" someone else asked.

"Beyond these lakes and mountains, we shall find a great river that will lead us to the far north of Africa. There you will see the homes of the White Man—houses as large as *kopjes* [hills]. Then we shall come to the end of the land, and reach the sea."

Blank looks all around. The what?

"The sea. Water without end." When the journey was over, the brave men who came with him would come home in "steamers as large as villages," and could tell stories about the things they had seen and done for the rest of their lives.

It could have gone worse, Grogan thought. "The people were much impressed and . . . realized that I must be even a finer liar than they had at first taken me to be."

But after an hour of debate, a Watonga chief named Makanjira stood up and said, "I come with you." Three more men—named Chacachabo, Kamau, and Kapachi—also volunteered.

The next day a boy named Pinka came into camp, naked and covered in dirt, and said he'd like to go, too. Grogan had him washed and clothed and welcomed him aboard. The five Watonga became Grogan's loyal companions and close friends, in effect his noncommissioned officers, and would stick with him to the end.

Their first job was to find porters. Different expeditions had different methods. Some explorers had natives captured and pressed into service, chaining them up at night and treating them like beasts of burden. Others, like Grogan and Sharp, hired men voluntarily for a fixed wage and a regular supply of some trade good—usually a yard or two of cloth per week—to buy food. A cash advance let porters buy provisions, pay off any debts, and leave their families something to live on while they were gone.

Only part of the reward was financial. It was dangerous work, but as Grogan had promised, anyone on an expedition was almost guaranteed to see things his peers could only imagine. Those who made it home brought specialized knowledge valuable to future employers, from the most (and least) sociable villages to the location of springs and streams.

Restless as ever, Grogan spent some of the time hunting and exploring. After a long chase, he shot a reedbuck, a kind of antelope with a beautiful bright silver-gray coat, dark brown legs, and white underparts. Certain it was a new species, he skinned it carefully and had the hide wrapped up and sent home through the local British trading post.

He walked through native villages with neatly arranged huts and avenues of banana palms. The people grew pineapples and pumpkins and seemed pleasant and well mannered. British occupation of their lands, he wrote, had saved them from extinction at the hands of warlike neighbors and slave-raiding Arabs.

By modern standards, Grogan's attitudes toward Africans could seem schizophrenic. One moment he would describe them in respectful, even glowing terms like "noble" and "magnificent." (It helped if they were tall, dignified, and had good hygiene.) Most of the time, though, he was a typically Victorian colonialist, impatient and condescending. He was capable of astonishing contempt toward "cringing," "insolent," "grotesque" natives, especially ones who were trying to rob or kill him.

Grogan was a product of his time, hyperaware of race, appearance, and social standing. But he was also an equal-opportunity offender, as likely to insult an Englishman as an African. He had no patience for sluggards, liars, or deserters of any shade.

As one observer said, "he didn't actually think that Britons were any more civilised than Africans, [and] in many cases vice versa." All Grogan expected was that you kept your word and pulled your weight.

A tan young woman with tribal earrings leans against the ferry's railing next to me. She has a tattoo of a cross on the back of her neck.

"We're behind schedule," she says. "We've been on board since Monkey Bay, and almost all the food and drinks and beer are gone."

The *Ilala* chugs up the western shore of Lake Malawi, past steep forested hillsides that plunge into jewel-blue water. Flecks of ash from the ferry's smokestack settle on my forearms and leave black streaks when I brush them off.

Boarding in Nkhata Bay was a rugby scrum of disembarking passengers and shirtless stevedores humping boxes up and down a single gangplank. It took me three tries to make it on board and up to the open top deck, where a bar shares a wall with the pilothouse and wooden recliners line the railings.

"People keep thinking I'm a missionary, white guy traveling alone," I say. It's been days since I've talked to another *mzungu.*

"I guess you could say that's why we're here." A church-based charity in Ontario sent her and two friends to Malawi with three shipping containers filled with used bicycles, parts, and tools.

After teaching the locals how to repair the bikes, they left the containers behind as a prefab bike shop and set off on their own for some sightseeing.

While they waited for the ferry at Monkey Bay, they had gone snorkeling: "Unbelievable."

Long, deep, and ancient, Lake Malawi has more species of fish than any other lake in the world, estimated at one thousand or more. It's famous for its cichlids, perchlike fish that can fetch $150 each in the aquarium markets of the United States and Europe.

The long isolation and intense competition for food have forced the cichlids to evolve to eat just about anything. Some have massive jaws to crush snails, while others mimic weeds or rotting fish to sneak up on their prey. One sucks insect larvae out of rocky crevices by placing its huge lips over holes and inhaling. Another has learned to ram female cichlids in the head, making them spit out the eggs they carry in their mouths and gobbling them up.

Since Grogan's time, pollution and overfishing have started to threaten the ecology of the lake and the species that depend on it, fish and human. Chemical runoff from farms, silt from deforestation, and development and ash from open fires cloud the water. The fishing industry is a major source of animal protein and jobs in Malawi, but fishermen are pulling in fewer fish and smaller species.

An older couple is seated in two recliners by the rail, watching the sun slide behind the hills. Black clouds of *kungu* flies hover where the slate-colored sky fades into the water. The full moon spills orange shards across the water.

I head for the shower room, a sweltering box above the engine. Cockroaches climb the walls, but the hot water—probably sucked straight from the lake and heated in rusting, greasy pipes—comes in a magnificent, endless torrent.

The older couple, Matthew and Christina, invite me to join them for a dinner of fried fish and rice in the dining room. They booked the best cabin on the ship for a vacation up the lake and back.

"We waited on the beach at Nkhotakota for three hours in the middle of the night to get on board," Matthew says. He has knobby knees and an aquiline nose. "Eventually they carried us out through the water on their backs, one at a time." They both chuckle.

When Christina excuses herself and goes to bed, Matthew orders two more beers. He talks about traveling in Thailand in the early 1970s with a previous partner. "When you brought your wife to Bangkok in those days, they charged you a corkage fee."

It's dark on deck, cold and windy. I squirm into my silk sleeping sack fully clothed, wrap myself in my poncho, and stretch out on a foam pad I rented from a crewman for two dollars. I can see Laura and me ending up like Matthew and Christina, traveling the world for decades after the kids are gone, laughing at experiences that would send most people screaming for a concierge or a lawyer. I couldn't imagine anything better.

The subject of marriage came up on our first trip together. A month after she kicked me out, Laura, Kerry, and their friend Bill entered an adventure race in Moab in southeast Utah. I was still living in northern Utah, and on a whim I offered to drive down and help.

We hadn't talked about what had happened that night, and she seemed surprised at the offer. We hugged hello at their hotel and sat down with her teammates to go over the course map and checklists of gear. Nothing seemed strange or sensitive. It felt the way it had from the start: easy, relaxed. Comfortable.

Southeast Utah's canyon country is my favorite place in the world, and the view from Dead Horse Point is enough to inspire enlightenment: hundreds of miles of bone-and-ochre desert, eroded into cliffs and spires and banded mesas by the pea-green Colorado River two thousand feet below.

Maybe that's what brought the idea of lifetime commitments to mind when we all pulled up to the state park overlook at sunset, just as I planned. The sun spilled across the terrain like orange paint, and the spicy-sweet smell of pines drifted in the updraft as the four of us walked to the edge.

"I'd like to get married here some day," I said without thinking. Not that I was anywhere close to starting to consider something like that. To fill the subsequent moment of silence, I pointed out where they had launched stunt dummies and a 1966 Thunderbird convertible into the abyss for the final shot in *Thelma & Louise.*

Laura looked at me for a second. I didn't know it, but my stock had just gone way up.

The evening after the race, as everyone packed up to leave, Laura and I found ourselves in the hotel room all four of us were sharing, alone for the first time the entire weekend.

After two days of subtle but steady flirting, I knew this was my chance to respond to that night in Washington, to show it wasn't just a fluke and that I could handle being rebuffed. This woman had just finished ten hours of running and mountain biking and canoe paddling. I was finding her more interesting, and intimidating, by the day. I didn't even have to say anything, just grab her and kiss her.

But someone could come in at any minute. And wasn't she

still "kind of" seeing someone? Besides, why does the guy always have to make the move? Look what happened the last time I tried.

So I chickened out. I did nothing, and someone came in a few minutes later, and the moment passed.

.

Half the *wazungu* on the ferry get off at the stop closest to Livingstonia, the missionary settlement Grogan visited. It's two hours before dawn, and we stumble down the dock red-eyed and half conscious. The Canadians are heading south, so we part in that ephemeral, arbitrary way of travelers. The odds of our paths crossing again are even smaller than meeting in the first place.

I wait alone in the chilly darkness, sitting on my bag with my head in my hands. The rim of the sky is just starting to brighten when the first minivan pulls up, a dusty white Toyota Hiace. Compact, ubiquitous, and usually white, the Hiace is the linchpin of public transportation in sub-Saharan Africa. They're relatively inexpensive, easy to fix, and reliable in the face of near-constant abuse.

There are nineteen people on board already in four rows of seats, counting the driver and ticket man in front. Not too crowded; I've seen more than two dozen people crammed into one, bags and all.

They're called many things—*matatus* in Uganda, *chapas* in Mozambique, *daladalas* (or just "Hiaces") in Tanzania—but all minivans require the same strategy. If you can't score the front passenger seat, an honor usually reserved for pretty girls and the elderly, the next best is the window seat in the second row. That's near enough to the sliding side door to get out in an emergency (there's also the window), but not so close that you get squashed every time someone gets on or off, usually every few minutes. The first row of seats has no legroom, and the back row is a claustrophobic death trap.

Claim your space and defend it at all costs, against grandmothers and children especially, or you'll find a bag of onions where your feet just were or a schoolboy on your lap. Have cash ready to pay, and bang on the side or the roof when you want to get off.

Fortunately, it only takes half an hour to reach my destination, a sprawling hostel on the shore of the lake. One of the owners, a Dutch woman, leads me past papaya trees and banana palms to a rickety wooden cabin.

"The generator comes on at four." There's no need for electricity during the day.

A black Great Dane follows me across the sand to the water, scrotum swinging like two apples in a sock, and collapses in the sand to gnaw an itch. With his head buried in his groin, he looks like a skinny gymnast in dark tights.

The air is warm, the water is cold, and the sky is wide open as I rinse my dirty shirts in Lake Malawi. A hundred yards down the beach, a group of women are up to their hips in the water doing laundry for real. One waves and a boy runs and somersaults into the miniature waves. A stripe of greenery separates the lake from the brown wooded mountains.

Things looked much the same when Grogan passed through in late 1898: "Bold rocky headlands plunge into the lake and enclose a white strip of sand with straggling villages at the back. The water is clear as crystal, and broken by the heads of hundreds of natives diving, swimming, and splashing about. Ringing peals of laughter echo in the rocks and startle the troops of baboons that sit watching with curious eyes."

It's a serene spot, and I wish I could stay more than one night. I wonder if he did, too.

Before he left Karonga, Grogan hired twelve more men to serve as *askaris*, a combination of guard and soldier.

They were a "very unwholesome lot" from the Asiska tribe, whose name meant "rebellious" or "quarrelsome" in Swahili. Grogan gave each one a blue cotton uniform and matching fez and did his best to drill them into shape.

One day he was walking through the bush in short pants when his gun bearer cried "Njoka!" (Snake!) Grogan leaped sideways, barely missing a sleeping puff adder. "It would have been impossible to have slipped a visiting-card between us," he wrote.

Puff adders were already known to be the most dangerous snakes on the continent. They still cause more deaths than all other snakes in Africa put together. The thickly muscled reptiles have long fangs and the awkward habit of sitting camouflaged along footpaths and striking when disturbed. Their venom is a coagulant that can make blood clot so quickly that a bite victim's limbs become locked in place. Even if you don't die from kidney failure, circulatory collapse, or anaphylactic shock, the poison continues to destroy the flesh around the bite for weeks. Infection and gangrene set in as rotten craters spread across the skin and muscles literally melt from the bone.

Grogan was lucky. The snake didn't wake up, and he mashed it flat with a log.

Later in the trip, he stepped on another adder. That one did strike, so hard it flipped completely in midair. It missed.

It took patience to train the men to his exacting standards. Grogan must have told Pinka a dozen times how to set up his campsite at night. The boy was thrilled at the position, but he took weeks to learn how to arrange the camp bed, table, and packing cases correctly inside the tent.

Once, when Grogan was walking back to camp after a hunt, there was an explosion behind him and something screamed past his ear. He looked back and saw the four-bore rifle stuck in the ground by its muzzle. The boy who had been carrying it was sprawled a yard off the path. He had slipped back the safety bolt and caught the trigger on a twig.

At nine on the next morning I'm walking up the road that slithers up the mountainside to Livingstonia. Small numbered signs label each of its twenty hairpin curves. It's already ninety degrees out, I'm dripping sweat, and I've only reached number four. Some bends don't have signs. It doesn't seem fair. *Shouldn't that be number five?*

There's no way I'll make it ten miles uphill on foot, let alone back. I give it two hours, or half my water bottle, before I turn around.

A man on a red motorcycle drives past and stops. He's wearing a black parka that makes my brain hurt. But there's room for two on the seat, and to my infinite relief he offers me a ride and hands me a '70s-vintage mustard-yellow helmet.

Our helmets knock on the larger ruts. Over his shoulder he says he's the primary education coordinator for the local school district, responsible for twenty-two schools.

"How many children?"

"Oh, too many." Students have to provide their own uniforms and supplies. Sometimes owning a notebook and a set of pencils can make the difference between going to school or not.

He points out different schools and stops to chat with community leaders (all men) and teachers (women).

The air has cooled by the time we reach Livingstonia, 1,300 feet above the lake. There's still a European orderliness to the place. Tall pine trees close over the orange dirt of the main avenue, lined with redbrick Victorian buildings.

He drops me off at a stone building that was once the home of the Laws, the missionaries who hosted Grogan. Now it's half guesthouse, half museum.

As I hand him the helmet, he says, "I hope there will be a consideration for . . ." I'm happy to give him a few bills. He asks to write his contact information in my notebook. I realize I didn't even ask his name.

As he putters away, I silently promise Yotam Chiakaka Nyivenda I will put a large box of pencils and notebooks in the mail the moment I get home.

A haphazard collection of dusty relics lines the shelves of the museum: spears and clubs, the Book of Matthew translated into Chechwa, an ancient and ominous-looking anesthesia kit, its rubber tubes cracked with age.

Drawer after drawer brims with glass slides for the magic lantern Robert Laws used to introduce locals to the wonders of the outside world. He stayed here for half a century after Grogan's visit and eventually established Livingstonia as one of the best schools in central Africa, which it still is.

An old woman is selling sodas and snacks in the next room. I'm dying for a Coke.

"No, Sprite," she says, like a Jedi mind trick. "You want Sprite."

At least it's cold. She doesn't have any change, so I throw in a pack of Hav-Sum-More biscuits to munch on the way to the church.

The huge green-roofed building is empty. The stained-glass windows show Livingstone facing a suspicious-looking native family, with Lake Malawi in the background. He has one hand on his hip and the other out in a gesture that's supposed to look nonthreatening but instead seems mildly annoyed. ("Just look at this mess!")

Behind him stand Chuma and Susi, his loyal servants and companions through his years of grueling travels. It was they who found him kneeling in prayer on May 1, 1873, near Lake Bangweulu in what is now Zambia, dead from malaria and dysentery. He had been searching for the source of the Nile in entirely the wrong part of Africa. They buried his organs under a tree and carried his body, dried and wrapped in bark, over a thousand miles to the coast.

Livingstone eventually was buried in Westminster Abbey, his dream of bringing his famous "three C's"—civilization, commerce, and Christianity—to Africa only just begun. His epitaph comes from his final journal:

> All I can add in my solitude, is,
> May Heaven's rich blessing come down on
> Every one, American, English, or Turk,
> Who will help to heal
> This open sore of the world.

CHAPTER SEVEN

Nobody can bitch about a place like an expat. Students, retirees, teachers, fugitives—no matter what the reason Westerners decide to set up shop in other countries, they always seem to spend most of the time complaining.

I'm eating dinner with the Dutch couple who own the lakeside hotel. We're joined by Sam, a burly British man who runs another lakeside hotel nearby. The carping starts almost immediately.

"It's the little things that add up," Sam says. "Like having to give your employees the same instructions over and over: Do we have any eggs today? Did you check the water levels? Well, why not?" The couple nod in agreement.

He waves toward the entrance gate I walked through yesterday. "That nice new road you came on is for the uranium mine they're opening near Karonga next year." Karonga, where Grogan stepped off the boat and hired the Watonga, is my next stop, fifty miles north. "The South African company that built it ended up paying twice as much as they bid because everything kept getting stolen. They'd take the truck tires at night, the headlights. Even the petrol. They dyed it green to keep track of it. Pretty soon the whole country was running on green diesel. I had it in my truck!"

Grogan would have empathized. Theft would soon become a major problem for the expedition.

Complaining is a bonding ritual. From the outside, though, it just sounds like whining. *Why exactly are you here, then?*

Sam is on a roll, his forehead bright with sweat. "You get Europeans coming here and giving ten thousand dollars to the village headman to buy a piece of land." Malawi is cheap and gorgeous, and foreigners are starting to notice. "But he doesn't even own it; the government does. He just goes off and gets shit-faced, and everyone in the village spends years fighting over the money. I bought my place five years ago and they're still fighting. Someone stabbed the chief last week!"

Next up was foreign aid and NGOs. "You have these organizations come here, stay for two years, hand out money, and leave. The people earn huge tax-free salaries, their résumés are padded, but they haven't really done anything for the country. Malawians are happy to take the money. But what are they left with?" I thought about Grogan's disdain for missionaries.

"How about the Peace Corps?"

"That's just a seventeen-year-old plunked down in the middle of Africa, told to start a sewing cooperative. They don't know what the hell they're doing. Twenty years later, sure, it means something to them."

Other situations would have mystified Grogan. Last year Madonna arrived in Malawi to launch a foundation to help the country's orphans and poorest children. While she was here, she adopted a thirteen-month-old boy whose father had left him in an orphanage after his mother died in childbirth.

Critics accused the singer of using her wealth and fame—she's worth about a tenth of Malawi's GDP—to bypass the country's adoption laws. For starters, prospective parents have to live in the country for eighteen months. Even Angelina Jolie, who knows her way around international adoptions, called it illegal. The boy's father initially fought to keep him in the country, and a humanitarian case turned into a tabloid spectacle.

But the law wasn't the real issue, Sam says. "She did it legally, just quietly. She was in and out before anyone knew it was her. She embarrassed the system. People found out she was here, and they were pissed they didn't make anything off of it."

Back in my bungalow, dazed from this onslaught of opinion, I lie awake worrying about catching the next ferry up Lake Tanganyika. I haven't been able to confirm the schedule or whether it's even running. As far as I can tell, it heads north every other week, passing the village of Kasonga, Tanzania (not to be confused with Karonga, Malawi—this is already starting to get confusing), at the lake's southern end every Sunday. That's where I'll catch it or miss it.

First I have to get there. But how hard can that be?

The rain fell in biblical torrents, day and night, as the expedition started west toward Lake Tanganyika. The giant drops soaked through Grogan's oilskin coat and the wide tail of his sou'wester hat, hitting the ground so hard they bounced up and drenched him from below.

Even in the dry season, the route to Tanganyika was just a beaten path through the bush. The route followed the border between Rhodesia to the south and German East Africa to the north; today these are Zambia and Tanzania, respectively. Now the hills were devoid of wildlife, and the swamps in between were swollen with the downpour.

Grogan had left Lake Nyasa on January 24, 1899, eleven months after he and Sharp had arrived in Africa. He and his

Watonga assistants led a column of 150 men. Makanjira, the Watonga chief, became Grogan's second-in-command, carrying his guns and helping organize the group.

By day they plodded along half blind and soaked to the bone, barely making ten miles before they had to set up camp. At night they struggled to light fires and tried to sleep in sodden blankets and tents.

Grogan kept the group under tight discipline, especially the dozen sullen Asiskas. When one of them asked for cord to lead a calf with, he took it as insolence—locals could make their own string easily from tree bark—and decided to teach him a lesson.

"Right. Here you are." He held out a coil of climbing rope that weighed twenty pounds.

"I'll make my own," the man said, handing it back.

"Oh, no," Grogan said. "I never refuse a reasonable request. Don't you dare cut it, either."

The man never asked for rope again.

The halfway point to Tanganyika came at a station run by the African Lakes Corporation. The British company operated trading posts and steamboats throughout Nyasaland, the territory that would become Malawi. (The ALC is still in operation today, having acquired everything from automotive companies to Internet service providers.) The rains had stopped, and the man in charge piled the dining table with peas, cabbage, potatoes, and other fresh vegetables from the station's gardens.

As Grogan gazed over the misty scenery from the veranda, he thought what fine country the Tanganyika Plateau would be for European settlers. The nights were cool, and familiar vegetables thrived.

It took the expedition two more weeks to make it another thirty miles to a settlement called Mambwe. There Grogan met an Englishman named Palmer who worked for Cecil Rhodes's British South Africa Company, set up to promote trading and colonization. After Grogan sent the rest of the caravan on to Lake Tanganyika, Palmer led him on a hunting detour to the south, the territory of the powerful Awemba tribe.

The Awemba lived in stockaded homesteads called kraal, surrounded by deep trenches and palisades banked with clay and pierced with loopholes. Almost every man owned a gun. They herded the women and cattle into dense thickets whenever strangers showed up.

Grogan and Palmer were approaching the kraal of the chief of the Awemba when they heard music approaching. A group of dancers, singers, and musicians surrounded them. Men sang and pounded lizard-skin drums and boys shook pods filled with dry seeds. "Like most African music," Grogan observed, "the strain plays about three notes with untiring repetition, and, though rather pleasing at first, palls after the fourth or fifth hour."

He noticed many of the performers were missing eyes or limbs. Palmer explained that the disfigurement was an honor. Every chief maintained a band that he sent out to meet important guests, and he would blind or cripple the most talented performers to keep them from deserting.

The chief himself rode out on the shoulders of one of his men to meet them, leading a retinue of hundreds. He was a large man, with a face "expressive of determination and character."

The men were tall and well built, with bronze skin, straight thin noses, and hair worn in tufts down the middle of the head. "Many of the young women, with their regular features, beautiful colour, and small, delicate hands and feet, are quite pleasing," Grogan wrote.

They drank *pombe*, a beer made from millet, and made a rust-colored cloth from fig tree bark. When an important chief died, they would dry the body in wood smoke for a year and then bury it in a bark-cloth cocoon.

"Mutilation in various forms appears to be the chief recreation of these autocrats," he wrote. People everywhere were missing lips, ears, hands, sometimes all of the above. Men were castrated and women had their breasts cut off for little or no reason.

The tribe had a grim sense of humor. Grogan heard of one practice in which a victim would have his throat cut with a blunt knife. Then a mask attached to a large sable horn would be placed over his head.

"The blood spurting forth into the horn rang a bell, a performance that gave general satisfaction, with, I suppose, one exception."

The corrugated dirt track across Tanzania's southern border is baked iron-hard by the heat. Mud brick homes, many roofless and abandoned, dot the hills. Every door is shut against the airborne earth that coats everything within fifty feet of the road. Even the donkeys look made out of dust.

Compared to the relatively straight route Grogan took, the modern road from Lake Malawi to Lake Tanganyika zigzags across the plateau. It's August, and the weather is the exact opposite of the monsoon Grogan toiled through in January and February 1899.

I'm stuffed in the last row of a long bus. Big mistake. I feel like a test pilot in a disintegrating plane. The deeper potholes launch me completely off the seat. My head has hit the ceiling twice already.

At first, whenever we passed a village, I looked it up on my map. But our progress is heartbreakingly slow, and I stopped an hour ago.

Tanzania had seemed more lush and better tended than Malawi, at least at first. Just across the border, farms quilted the hillsides and green chandeliers of bananas dangled from forty-foot trees. Workers with baskets on their backs walked down the rows of tea plantations, past hip-high bushes frosted with the electric green of new leaves. Flocks of children in neat school uniforms walked along the road. The matching colors of their sweaters and pants and skirts changed at every town, from navy to maroon to forest green.

Now I'm playing vertical crack-the-whip in a sweltering metal box, clattering through the background of a spaghetti western. My shoulders ache from clutching the seat in front of me, my kidneys feel bruised, and an ominous gurgle is blooming in my intestines.

Carrying on a conversation is out of the question. I need a break from Grogan and Africa. I pull out a ratty paperback from the hotel in Nkhata Bay, about the Uruguayan rugby team whose plane crashed in the Andes in 1972.

It's impossible to hold it steady; I can only read half a sentence at a time. Every so often I close my eyes and picture the snowy mountains and open, silent spaces. The frozen descriptions are delicious, even when they start eating each other.

You will have a long life and come into money soon." The fortune-teller dragged a fingernail across my palm. *But of course,* I thought.

The street outside my apartment building in Washington

thronged with vendors and jugglers and activists at folding tables piled with brochures and photocopies. Summer had enveloped the city like a tropical fever, but the annual neighborhood festival was in full swing.

"Your heart is wounded." *Whose isn't?*

"Now is not the time for romance." *We'll see about that.*

On Laura's recommendation, I rented an apartment in her neighborhood, Mount Pleasant, a mix of expensive brownstones, quaint cafés, and discount grocery stores with signs in Spanish and the faint odor of fish. I settled into my new job and new city, reveling in the sudden abundance of things to do and people to meet. I was still bitter and leery of anything serious. But I hadn't been single in years, and never in a place like this.

As casual dating went, Washington was a bonanza. Congressional staffers, law students, nonprofit grant writers, journalism interns: the city seemed like a lab where they bred idealistic young women and released them into the wild.

There was the Salvadoran aerobics instructor, and the intellectual hipster who collected salt and pepper shakers. One uneventful coffee with my high school Russian teacher, whom I'd always had a crush on.

I went out to dinner with a blond Valkyrie who seemed to live in a surprisingly flashy apartment for someone who worked at a health-care nonprofit. At some point in the evening I gave her my standard line about pro sports, about finding it impossible to care which randomly assembled group of overpaid mutants defeated another.

The next day, the friend who'd introduced us called for a report.

"I think it went pretty well. She seems cool." He seemed to be waiting for something.

"Didn't she tell you who her father was?"

"No, why?"

He named one of the most famous coaches in the NBA. Even I had heard of him.

She never called back.

None of these connections went anywhere, though, in part because no one could measure up to Laura. We did things together once every few weeks at first, then every week, then every few days.

Museums and monuments, Ethiopian restaurants and art openings, jazz clubs and house parties—anything was fun with her. On weekends we'd go rock climbing at Great Falls above the raging Potomac River or bike through Rock Creek Park.

We started competing in local adventure races, usually with Jeff as a teammate. The three of us would train by jogging around the National Mall, past the pools and estuaries and up and down the marble stairs of presidential memorials. Laura kept right up with us, another check mark on the growing list.

She loved her work, but it wasn't the center of her existence. She loved to travel and try new things, from tango lessons to history lectures. And she invariably brightened a room.

In some strange way, her openness and perpetual optimism made my inner cynic suspicious. It was too easy. Without friction, it felt like something was missing. Sometimes I would unconsciously create some, things like making vague plans and backing out at the last moment. She hid her annoyance well.

I wondered how long this best-of-both-worlds arrangement would last: the benefits without the commitment. But we seemed to be on the same page, enjoying each other's company but not looking to dive into anything too deep at the moment, even though by fall we were regularly spending the night at one another's apartments.

We'd cook dinner and watch movies, and sometimes, if someone was feeling particularly open, talk would edge into the subject of relationships. Never ours, though.

"You know, that night you had to leave, it was Bill I was kind of seeing," she said one night, after a barely tolerable chick flick.

"Seriously? You're shitting me." I knew them both better now and found it hard to imagine. He was definitely not her type.

"Nope. Really." I could see she enjoyed surprising me.

"I think four of my exes went on to marry the next guy they dated after me," I said, snorting. "No—five. I should charge for it. Marriage prep. 'Break up with me and you're ready to take the plunge!'"

Laura didn't laugh back.

Chapter Eight

Palmer and Grogan followed game trails along the Chambesi River, the source of the Congo, searching for signs of game. The river wound through a plain of rippling spear grass punctuated by anthills as tall as three-story buildings.

One day Grogan was stalking an antelope when he came across a fresh set of lion prints. He tracked the pad marks for hours, finding and losing them again and again. Then he heard a low growl and glimpsed four tawny shapes disappearing behind a brush-covered anthill.

He sprinted around the other side of the mound and almost ran into the animals. He shot and wounded two before they scattered. He followed them into the bush, determined to put the injured cats out of their misery. He stumbled on the first, an eight-foot lioness, so unexpectedly that he stepped on its tail just as it died. That left one huge wounded predator to track down.

Over the past year, Grogan had developed a respect for lions that bordered on reverence. It wasn't unusual to hear an old lion's roar from six miles away. He looked back with nostalgia on the first time he had heard the sound, near Beira at the beginning of the trip: "Five years of my life would I gladly give to live that morning again, but . . . no amount of lions will ever again bring back that lump, it is gone where the taste for peppermint and mud pies goes, to the irrevocable land of first experiences and boyhood's joys."

Hunting four-hundred-pound cats took focus and constant vigilance. Even then it wasn't always clear who was stalking whom. If you didn't kill it with your first shot, a lion could seem almost indestructible. Back in Portuguese East Africa, one made it to within a yard of Grogan's feet despite having seven bullets in it. Even a lifeless lion couldn't be trusted: "When he appears to be dead, heave half a brick at him, and if he does not move heave the other half."

A lion often lost its teeth and claws as it aged, and the handicap could steer it toward humans, by far the easiest prey to catch. During the first year of Grogan's journey, two of the most famous man-eating lions in history were terrorizing Indian railway workers in the British colony of Kenya to the north.

The Tsavo man-eaters, two maneless males nicknamed "the Ghost" and "the Darkness," dragged their victims from tents and buildings by day and night for ten months, leaving empty beds and bloody trails of body parts. By the time a British officer shot them in December 1898, when Grogan was hiring porters to march to Tanganyika, the lions were thought to have killed more than one hundred people. Recent analyses of the lions' bodies, now on display at the Field Museum of Natural History in Chicago, has put the number at a more believable but still chilling thirty-five.

Grogan searched for the other wounded lion for three futile hours, and returned to camp disgusted. Letting a wounded animal escape was bad enough. Wanton slaughter, though, was even worse. He and Palmer soon reached a pool that had once churned with hippos. All that was left was a giant pile of tusked skulls; a French missionary had killed almost all of them—"for the satisfaction, I suppose, of seeing them float down-stream," Grogan wrote.

The killer was one of the Pères Blancs, a Roman Catholic order called the "White Fathers" for their distinctive robes. The same priests, Palmer said, had built huge fences out on the plains that drew together into narrow openings. They forced herds of red antelope, called puku, into the funnels and butchered them by the hundreds.

Grogan and Palmer came into an unexplored tract of country that had been flooded by recent rains. They waded through waist-deep water and camped on isolated anthills. As they returned to Mambwe, Grogan collapsed with fever.

Once again his body was a war zone. The malarial parasites lurking in his liver had burst forth like a hidden army and attacked his red blood cells for the iron they carried, which the parasites need to reproduce. Infected blood cells swelled and burst, releasing even more parasites. Grogan's circulatory system became littered with ruined cells and proteins. His spleen, overwhelmed by the invaders and detritus, grew large and dark.

The bout would last, on and off, for the next two months. It left Grogan so weak he had to be carried in a *machila*, a hammock on a pole, the remaining hundred miles to Lake Tanganyika. On the way, he "eked out a precarious existence on Worcester sauce and limes" in between bouts of delirium. Every night he pulled out a picture of Gertrude; some nights, when the fever peaked, the men could hear him talking to her.

In all it took Grogan a month to cross from lake to lake, an average of less than seven miles a day. Kituta, the African Lakes Corporation station at the southern end of Lake Tanganyika, had once hosted Arab slave caravans, but with the decline of the trade it had faded into insignificance. Now it was "a beautiful but pestilential spot, chiefly remarkable for its abominable smells."

That didn't bother him, though. It didn't even matter that Sharp had given up waiting once again and headed north without him to arrange more porters. The great inland sea he had dreamed of as a boy, late at night under the covers in Kensington, spread out before him. Just over a year after starting across Africa, Grogan had achieved another of his childhood goals by reaching Lake Tanganyika.

After six hours on the bone-cracking bus to the lake, I'm full of uncharitable thoughts. Can it be that hard to grade a road every so often, even out here? Is there some specific reason the music is always blaring to distortion? How can anyone stand it?

To everyone else on the bus this is all perfectly normal, certainly much better than walking across this wasteland. And I'm covering ground an order of magnitude faster than Grogan did. It makes me feel so . . . soft. A milquetoast *mzungu*, delicate down to his digestive tract, which by now is on the verge of meltdown. Nausea has a way of crowding out all other thoughts.

I'm in a throbbing daze by the time we reach the city of Sumbawanga, about fifty miles from Lake Tanganyika. There's no hot water in the hotel shower. In the restaurant, the ever-present TV is tuned to a South African soap opera and gives off an insect whine that drills into my skull. Prickly chills crawl up my arms, followed by sweaty goose bumps, then more chills. Is this malaria?

What's the blandest thing on the menu? Spaghetti Bolognese, I hope. I can only eat a few bites before dragging myself upstairs and collapsing into bed, where I stay for the next eleven hours except for several trips back and forth to the bathroom. Nothing is staying down or in. My dreams pulse with dark colors and scenes of strange violence. I've come two thousand miles since Johannesburg. Portland is 9,440 miles away.

First stop next morning is the closest pharmacy. "Oh yes, we have Ciprofloxacin," says the woman behind the counter. "You have typhoid?"

"Not yet. There's always hope."

The final leg to Lake Tanganyika is a quarter the distance of yesterday's hellish ride. But the road is so awful it takes just as long. The entire way my gastrointestinal tract is threatening to go full-on China Syndrome at any second.

At one point, disturbing noises erupt from the undercarriage (the bus's, not mine) and everyone piles off. The driver crawls beneath the engine and starts hammering, popping up every few minutes to grab a spare part from the glove compartment.

Sunflowers sway in fields of stubble. I have a terrible thought: What if this isn't even the right bus? All these town names start to sound the same after a while—Kasunga, Kasanga, Kasesya, Kigoma. Half of them are spelled two or three different ways. I've had to start writing them on my hand every morning to keep track. Grogan complained about the same thing: "A name, as we regard a name, has no existence in Central Africa. . . . All native names are really descriptive, and what is Pimbalonga to-day may be Bongowongo to-morrow; as an instance, I obtained thirty-six different names for one mountain."

Could I be going the wrong way? It's a ridiculous idea, but between the language gap and my sickness-scrambled brain, it seems just possible.

At least we're pointing in the right direction, west, because the setting sun is glaring through the windshield. Fires smolder on both sides of the road, farmers clearing fields the easy way. Night falls and we drive past smoke columns bottom-lit by flames. The bus stops in village after village, and in each one the driver blares the horn.

An old couple climbs aboard and starts playing tease-the-*mzungu*. They point and ask me questions and laugh when I don't understand. Every culture has assholes. I'm too drained to care. Cyclic pressure clenches my guts, even though I haven't eaten anything since lunch.

It's not much comfort to think that no matter how rough things get, they'll never equal what Grogan endured. Bumping along in a bus with a bad case of Montezuma's revenge is nowhere near as bad as tramping through a monsoon with a potentially fatal fever.

Need to stop comparing. That and looking at my watch.

"To travel" originally meant to "suffer." A thousand years ago, life was dangerous, but leaving home was worse. The word itself comes from the Old French *travailler*, meaning to toil, as in "travail." It's rooted in the Latin *tripalium*, a torture device made of three poles tied together, to which victims would be attached and lit on fire.

We halt for the hundredth time, and a little boy and a woman stand up behind me to get off. The boy, maybe five years old, stumbles over the luggage and limbs that clog the aisle. As he reaches my seat, he turns and dumps something warm and wet in my lap.

I glimpse a horrified expression and two small hands full of vomit before his mother yanks him off the bus and into the night.

Then I'm standing in the glare of headlights, wiping chunks of a child's lunch off my pants, trying to keep from throwing up myself. The lowest I've felt in a long, long time. The driver and his fare-collecting helpers are sympathetic. One gives me a plastic water bottle to rinse with.

It's another hour of damp pants and bottomed-out spirits before I see a handful of electric lights reflecting off black water. It's Kasonga, a small village and ferry dock near the southern end of Lake Tanganyika. I've never been so relieved to leave a vehicle in my life.

A fellow passenger leads me down dark, sandy streets to the only guesthouse in town. It's attached to the Kibwawa Bottle Store, a bar-cum-liquor-shop where the motto, painted in bright blue letters above the doorway, is "TII KIU YAKO: OBEY YOUR THIRST." Inside, a raucous group crowds around a TV blasting screams and evil laughter.

One of the owners tears himself away from the program long enough to show me the shower—a bucket—and the toilet, a shit-smeared hole in the floor. The filthy white walls of my room end raggedly two feet below the roof, as if they've been gnawed by a giant rodent. There are bars on the window, and on the inside of one green shutter someone has scrawled, "PLEASE USE CONDOMS CORRECTLY."

The *Liemba* has to dock here tomorrow. If I miss it, or if her schedule has changed, she won't pass again heading north for another two weeks. I have no plan B for getting to Burundi, the next country north, besides another five hundred unimaginable miles on a bus, which, with my limited schedule, I don't have time for anyway.

I need some cheering up, so I open Laura's next card. *I'm missing my cute cowboy. You make me feel special even when you're not right by my side.*

It works, and I crawl into bed with a little more optimism.

By the time the leaves started changing our first year in Washington, Laura and I were spending more nights together than apart. The more time we spent together, though, the touchier the topic of our relationship status became.

Laura started to ask, understandably, if we were an exclusive couple or, at least, heading in that direction. I did my best to dodge the question. I liked her, a lot. But I still hadn't processed the last time I'd fallen for someone, part of the love triangle that had ended so badly. I don't know if I'd ever really gotten over a breakup, in fact. I'm terrible at letting go, strangely compelled to keep connections going long past their expiration dates.

For the first time, I was having fun going out and meeting new people, actually dating instead of relationship-hopping. Commitment would end all that. And deep down, the thought of someone who really wanted to be with me always carried a kind of performance anxiety I'd never really been able to understand.

As we became closer, Laura got to see parts of me I didn't show many people, the scars and insecurities, the melancholy and selfish tendencies I did my best to hide, even from myself. Pursuing, flirting, having fun—that was all fine. But living up to someone else's expectations? Much harder.

One night near Halloween she tried to pin me down for an answer for the fourth or fifth time. "Are we a couple?" she said, sitting up in bed. "I need to know."

"I'm just not ready to get deeply involved with someone right now. I just can't."

"I don't understand the difference between not being able and not being interested." She was clearly frustrated. "When am

I going to meet a guy who *is* ready? I haven't met anyone like you here yet."

To my surprise, she was crying. It was the first time her deeper feelings had broken through. I don't know if I was more flattered or frightened.

The first signs of jealousy started to crop up. Did "out with a friend" mean a date with someone else? Why didn't I answer the phone that time? What about her ex?

In November, while Laura was traveling alone through Vietnam for two weeks, I did make a lifetime commitment to a female. She even slept with me the first night. Her name was Truvie, and she was a thirteen-year-old cat who had lost her tail to a dog. She was sweet, needy, and constantly underfoot.

At least she liked Laura, and vice versa. As far as she and I went, by the end of the year it was obvious we couldn't drift through this gray area much longer.

Anxiety over missing the ferry keeps me half awake half the night in Kasonga. In the morning, scratching bug bites in bed, I hear what sounds like a ship's horn. I pack in a flurry and jog half a mile to the dock, over a bridge, through a field, down a dirt road along the lakeshore.

My first sight of Tanganyika hardly even registers, just a wall of reeds and cobalt horizon, and a ship that's not the ferry. It's a cargo ship carrying cement to the Democratic Republic of the Congo, which forms most of the west shore of the lake. Nobody knows when the ferry will arrive.

With serious misgivings, I retreat to the guesthouse and spend the day lying in bed, sweating and reading other explorers' accounts of the lake.

The first Europeans to see Tanganyika were the explorers Richard Burton and John Hanning Speke, who arrived in February 1858 on an expedition to find the source of the Nile. Speke was the first to reach Ujiji, three hundred miles north up the east shore, but seven months of sickness and grueling travel from the coast had left him temporarily blind. "The zenith of my ambition, the Great Lake [was] nothing but mist and glare before my eyes," he wrote bitterly, "seen in all its glory by everybody but myself."

His eyes eventually healed and Speke could see the lake. "In no part of Africa hitherto visited by us had we seen such splendid vegetation as covers its basin, from the mountain-tops to its shores," he wrote.

The lake's crocodiles were notorious man-eaters, and he had to remind his Indian cook-boy repeatedly not to wash the dirty pots in the water, since "the ravenous hosts of crocodiles seldom spare any one bold enough to excite their appetites with such dregs as usually drop from those utensils; moreover, they will follow and even board the boats, after a single taste."

By late afternoon I have to get out and stretch my legs. At the lakeshore a group of boatbuilders are working on a small beach. The light is thick and saturated. One ropy, shirtless man is painting a hull in vivid orange and blue. I can't resist sneaking a picture when I think no one's looking.

I forgot that my camera's shutter sounds like a shotgun being cocked and is almost as loud. One of the other men looks up and grins and says something to the painter. I don't need a translator to understand. *Hey, he took a picture of you!*

The man turns and glares, then stalks over and starts yelling at me. Playing dumb is futile, so I show him the digital image on the camera screen to assuage him. In some places, here included, it might be the only time someone will ever see an image of him- or herself that's not in a mirror. Kids love it.

Not this guy. He seems particularly pissed I caught him without a shirt—probably because he thinks it makes him look poor.

I can sympathize, or at least I could, in the first few minutes of the tirade. Out of politeness, I try not to take pictures of people without their consent. But I don't always have the time or the inclination to ask, and I figure if they don't know, there's no harm done.

Pretending I deleted the photo by flipping through other shots doesn't work, either. It just seems to make him more upset. Then he makes the universal give-me-money sign, rubbing thumbs and fingertips. I don't believe in paying to take pictures of people, except in rare instances that are clearly arranged ahead of time.

I've had enough. Time to retreat after one last apology.

Behind me I can hear the men laughing and whistling. *Come back* mzungu, *we were just yanking your chain!* Maybe I could go back and laugh things off, but I just don't have it in me.

Kasanga slowly comes alive at dusk. Radios start to play and children dart under palm trees as the air cools. Two Germans arrive at the guesthouse, sweating after an all-day hike. They rode the ferry all the way down the lake last week. "It was a real adventure!" one says.

"I'm catching it north. Whenever it gets here."

"Really?" he says. "It is here, at the dock. They are about to leave. You should be on board already."

Exactly the words I've been dreading for days without even knowing it.

Shit, shit, shit.

The Milky Way is the only light outside of town as I sprint for the dock. Across the bridge, through a plowed field, stumbling over invisible stones and furrows. Then onto the road, where I pass the man who led me to the guesthouse last night, going in the other direction.

"Hurry, man," is all he says.

Spotlights on concrete, pyramids of crates, and a ship that looks straight out of *Heart of Darkness*. The *Liemba*.

I vault on board, panting and drenched with sweat. I made it. Next stop: Kigoma, three hundred ten miles north. The air horn sounds a long blast as the ship pulls away from the dock and slowly starts picking up speed.

Just one problem: we're heading south.

L ooking back on that turbulent winter in Washington, I see I must have needed to push things to the edge with Laura for some murky, subconscious reason: to end our gray period without actually having to make a decision; to avoid the risk of opening up to someone again; to test her limits in some perverse way and see how much she really cared, as if it weren't obvious already. I'm sure there was some self-sabotage mixed in there, too. I wasn't even sure I deserved someone like her.

None of this was clear at the time, just the urge to *do* something, to shake things up and end our constant, hovering circles.

In January, an old girlfriend came to Washington for the weekend. I told Laura she was going to stay with me—magnanimously, I wanted to be up front about it—and I must have taken her shocked silence as consent. The visit did provide some long-overdue closure to that particular relationship, but as I predicted, it wasn't a platonic one.

I didn't see much of Laura over the next month, but when I did, I didn't get the impression anything was seriously wrong.

Then I went rock climbing in Nevada with a "friend," neglecting to mention that she was single and that we'd been flirting by email since we met over Thanksgiving.

Just thinking about those months now makes me wince. Laura and I weren't exclusive yet, technically, but it wasn't as if we had just gone out a few times. I just felt less committed to her than she did to me, and acted accordingly.

In any case, it did set things into motion. When I arrived home on a Sunday night from Nevada and turned on my computer, a short email from Laura was waiting:

Fuck off. Don't ever talk to me again.

PART II

I thought life in Africa was so different from
this.

—*John Shaw, Henry Morton Stanley's companion
on his expedition to find David Livingstone,
shortly before dying of sleeping sickness*

CHAPTER NINE

They called her the *Good News*, but the steamer that carried Grogan up Lake Tanganyika promised nothing but trouble. She had a hole in her bottom plugged with cement, and her machinery was "tied together with string and strips of sardine-tins." Mosquito nets over the bunks sagged with cockroaches the size of mice.

The captain spent more time in his bunk than piloting the ship, Grogan wrote. "His only anxiety was lest he should oversleep himself and miss a meal."

They had left Kituta on April 2, 1899, six days after the Italian inventor Guglielmo Marconi sent the first wireless message across the English Channel. One of the official goals of the journey, scouting a route for a Cape-to-Cairo telegraph line, was on the verge of becoming obsolete. Grogan seemed to be going back in time, but the outside world was surging forward.

The *Good News* shoelaced from shore to shore as it steamed north up the lake. At a French mission station on the eastern side, the passengers were paddled ashore in forty-foot dugout canoes, and the Catholic fathers filled the canoes to bursting with fresh fruit, beef stew, and Algerian wine.

Grogan toured a church that could hold hundreds of people

and saw busy workshops and gardens full of fat coffee bushes. The mission's few nuns were the first European women he had seen in months, but "it was very sad to see how ill they looked," he wrote. He thought wistfully of Gertrude. Could she thrive in a place like this?

On the next leg of the journey, winds funneled down narrow gullies between the mountains on the shore and lashed the water into a mad froth. Grogan's men were violently sick, and all the passengers waited white-knuckled to see if the boat would flip before it reached M'towa, a station of the Congo Free State on the western shore.

Despite its name, the Congo Free State was a living hell. A vast unmapped region of central Africa, home to an estimated 30 million people, it was essentially a private rubber plantation ruled by a single ruthless man who had never been anywhere near it.

In 1885, through shrewd political maneuvering, King Leopold II of Belgium had taken personal control of an area larger than France, England, Germany, Italy, and Spain combined. (Governments usually administered colonies.) The Congo's jungles crawled with vines that produced natural rubber latex, which was suddenly in huge demand for everything from car tires to telegraph cables.

Leopold turned the Congo into a corporate state, organized to make money as quickly as possible. The military Force Publique could do almost anything to ensure the native labor force kept the rubber sap flowing. Rape, beheadings, and crucifixions were common. Officers were required to account for every bullet they fired with a severed human hand.

Without any accurate population records, no one is sure how many natives died from starvation, disease, overwork, and abuse during Leopold's rule, but it was unquestionably in the millions. Some historians estimate the population was cut in half.

Word of the atrocities had begun to trickle out by the time Grogan boarded the *Good News*. Joseph Conrad based *Heart of Darkness*, first serialized in 1899, on the terrible things he had seen as a riverboat captain on the Congo River a decade earlier. The international outcry that followed drew in celebrities such as Mark Twain and Sir Arthur Conan Doyle, and eventually forced Leopold to hand over control to the Belgian government in 1908. The worst of the cruelties were stopped, and forced labor was outlawed, at least on paper.

When at last the ship arrived in M'towa, a native rebellion against the Belgians had been smoldering for five years. Grogan found local officials huddled behind barbed wire and other elaborate defenses. They were starving after cutting down all the banana trees to keep them out of the natives' hands. One sentry asked Grogan if he had any poison to spare, in case he was captured by the rebels.

Amid the chaos came one happy reunion. After three months apart, Grogan finally caught up with Sharp. Between them, they had an average fever of 104 degrees, but they were delighted to see each other safe. They caught up on recent events as the steamer carried them toward Ujiji, the most famous town on this legendary lake.

W hy are you calling me? I told you not to." Laura hung up. Again.

For exactly three days I had followed her instructions. Then I started calling. The first few times she let it ring. By the fifth or sixth, she picked up only to tell me to get lost again.

I kept trying, hoping for a thaw. After a week, a hesitant conversation sprouted. Then she surprised me by agreeing to meet the following Sunday. I got a chilly greeting when we sat down to coffee and beignets at a New Orleans–style café.

While I was in Las Vegas, Laura said, she was in my apartment one night and needed to write something down. She grabbed a piece of scrap paper from my computer printer tray. On the back was an incriminating email from the woman I had met that, for some brilliant reason, I had printed out but then decided to recycle.

We were both hurt and angry. To Laura it seemed that I had betrayed an unspoken agreement that we were only seeing each other. I felt unfairly accused of breaking a contract I had never signed. Amazingly, I also was upset at her for violating my privacy. Her explanation felt too close to snooping, I said, grasping at straws for any sort of defense.

In response, she delivered a coup de grâce: "The only reason I was there was to feed your cat!"

It took weeks for the resentment and defensiveness to start to fade. We had crossed some sort of line—actually, I had shoved us over—but Laura had become a big part of my life, and I had hurt her.

A week later, she agreed to meet again at a coffee shop. It felt delicate, almost as if we were starting over. Trying to keep things light, I told her a story about the first and only time I modeled clothes, for a domestic violence fund-raiser at an old movie palace in Albuquerque.

"The pants were so tight I could hardly move. No belt. So there I was up at the end of the catwalk in front of all those people and my zipper just pops open. Bing!" She grinned, grudgingly.

She hadn't cut me off, but she still kept me at arm's length, literally and otherwise. Then one afternoon she consented to come up to my apartment for lunch.

"I can't do this halfway," she said after I cleared the table. "If we're not going to make this real, I don't think I can just be friends."

"I don't know. I don't know what I want."

"I'm willing to give it a try. Are you?"

Now I was starting to tear up. The idea of a capital-R relationship made my stomach clench. But I could tell that with Laura it could be different, that there was more at stake here than one more lukewarm six-month dalliance.

I was guilty of enjoying most of the benefits of companionship without much, if any, of the hard work. We both were. I had an irrational hope that things would quietly go back to the way they were before, like the end of a sitcom. Everything forgiven and forgotten.

"We need to figure this out," she said firmly.

The phone rang like a recess bell and I jumped up to grab it. It was Jeff calling to go mountain biking. I said sure and hung up.

"Do you want to come?" I asked Laura automatically, as I had dozens of times before.

She glared at me. I sat down on the couch next to her.

"Okay. Let's give it a try."

A flicker of surprise crossed both our faces. Then smiles.

Two shirtless men dump sack after sack of dried silver fish into the triangular platform at the bow of the *Liemba*. They spread the glittering drifts with their hands until the room-sized space is ankle-deep. The smell is breathtaking.

"You think they'll leave themselves a path out, or will they paint themselves into a corner with fish?" Chris, a Scottish medical student, lounges on a thick coil of rope next to his friends Andy and Steve. They're all in their mid-twenties, fresh off a month of volunteering at the hospital in Sumbawanga.

The nose of the ship is as far as we can get from the chaos that descends every time the *Liemba* stops. To my immeasurable relief, the ferry had made a U-turn after I boarded last night; she just needed to go south to leave the dock. Now we're hopscotching north up the eastern shore of the lake, from one Tanzanian port to another.

She takes three days to go the length of the lake in either direction, as opposed to the week it took Grogan and Sharp on the *Good News*. But the commotion at these isolated towns, where the ship is one of the few (if not the only) means of contact with the outside world, is still much the same.

We're averaging a stop every few hours by day and night. Most don't involve a dock, just dropping the anchor and sounding the horn, as the captain did five minutes ago. Dozens of small boats are racing from a wide beach covered in smooth boulders as big as houses. Some have motors; others are big dugout canoes powered by a dozen sharp, long-bladed paddles.

Every vessel wallows with cargo and bodies, passengers bailing with decapitated plastic jugs. People climb the sides of the *Liemba* on rope ladders and disappear into portholes. The deck crane lifts rope nets bulging with crates, pallets, appliances, even a Land Rover.

"The hospital was crazy," Chris says. "Doctors here have more authority than experience. The doctor-patient relationship is like it was in the fifties back home. He sits behind the desk, says, 'Do this, do that, next!'"

"There's one guy who knows how to administer an IV, that's it," says Steve. "They don't really know how to monitor patients, keep airways clear or anything."

"Are things sterile at least?"

Andy shrugs. "Sterile-ish. Locals usually can't pay for what little care there is. First they try to ignore an injury, then they go to a traditional healer. Someone comes in with a distended abdomen and they have these wee cuts in lines across their chest." He points to his rib cage. "You can tell how long it's been by how much they've healed. If that doesn't work, then they go to the hospital, weeks later."

Steve tells about how a small fishbone cut on a fisherman's leg became infected and cost the man most of his calf. "Just like people use machines here until they stop working, it's the same with the body. They only come to the hospital when they can't work or can't walk. You almost have to admire it. Back home we overmedicate, look for treatment for every little thing."

"Lots of unnecessary surgery," Steve says. "At home, we take out the appendix at any excuse."

"You have to give the doctors here credit," Chris says. "Most of them do their best with hardly any supplies. It's like you're in a war zone. They're incredibly dedicated."

Soon they're trying to outdo one anther with hospital horror stories.

"There were these two women in the maternity ward," Chris says. "Just lying there naked facing each other, no privacy, no attendants. I looked in—is that a head? And the baby just pops out! A nurse came in and started yelling at her. I think she wanted to show us the birth. She was mad because the mother couldn't wait."

Steve wins. "Once I scrubbed in to assist a surgery. I was

holding open this woman's abdomen when this hand appears out of nowhere. She was waking up! I thought, what do I do with this hand?"

My stifling cabin slowly fills with light on the second morning on board. Someone shouts into a cell phone outside the window and I can hear cargo pallets slamming into the hold. Last night the hum of the ship's engine was strangely soothing, like being in the backseat of a car as a child. But the *Liemba* wakes early and loud.

I'm glad I decided to spring for a private cabin instead of sleeping on deck like some passengers. My temporary haven is the size of a modest walk-in closet or a small jail cell, with a thick, rubber-sealed porthole window. I keep finding dead insects on the floor, and the closet doors won't latch and bang open when the ship rocks. For two more days, though, it's mine.

The face in the mirror over the tiny sink looks tan and leaner than when I left home. Has it only been two weeks? A cold-water shave with soap and a cheap plastic razor leaves my cheeks pink and raw.

It's ten degrees cooler out on deck. A dhow slips across the cobalt water, its patchwork sail at the same rakish angle as the mountains behind it. A bright thread of beach is stippled with people and boats.

The water seems to go on forever. We might as well be tracing the coast of a continent. The largest lake in Africa, Tanganyika is almost a mile deep and holds one-sixth of the freshwater on earth. It's long enough to stretch from New York to Charlotte, North Carolina, but barely forty-five miles across at its widest point. Only Lake Baikal in Siberia is larger and deeper.

I buy two green apples from a vendor on the lower deck, my first fresh fruit in a week. I savor each carefully peeled bite and wander the ship. The *Liemba* is just as crowded as the *Ilala*, but with a rougher edge. Tanzanians are New Yorkers to Malawi's Hawaiians: more hustle, less patience. People bump into each other on the steep narrow stairs and glare.

Countless coats of cream yellow paint, spotted with bursts of rust like lichen, blur every edge and corner. The brass handrails between decks are polished bright from use. After denting my head on two doorways and a steam pipe, I've learned to walk with a Groucho stoop.

The *Liemba* has quite a history. She started life in 1913 as the *Graf von Götzen*, built in Germany and brought to Tanganyika in pieces by ship and train. She served as a cargo ship and troop transport when World War I began and became the key to Germany's control of the lake.

In 1915, the British Royal Navy decided to import a few boats of its own. The navy's top brass chose two forty-foot motorboats, HMS *Mimi* and HMS *Toutou* ("meow" and "woof" in French slang), and shipped them to South Africa. The disassembled pieces were then packed onto a train to Elizabethville, deep in the Belgian Congo, the closest rail link to the lake.

Getting the boats to Tanganyika was a three-month horror show involving two steam tractors, dozens of oxen, and hundreds of Africans dragging huge chunks of wood and metal through almost impassable jungles. The effort was led by Commander Geoffrey Spicer-Simson, a grating bully who wore a knee-length khaki skirt sewn by his wife and showed off his torsoful of snake tattoos at every opportunity.

When they reached the lake, Spicer-Simson's crew assembled and launched the boats and went gunning for the *Graf*. First, they captured a forty-five-foot gunboat and renamed it the HMS *Fifi*. The *Graf* eluded them until July 1916, when it turned out she was unarmed; her guns had been fake. As the British closed in, her captain ordered the three engineers who had brought her all the way from Germany to sink the ship to keep her out of enemy hands.

The poor bastards filled the *Graf* with sand and sent her to the bottom near the settlement of Kigoma, near Ujiji. Less than ten years later, the British refloated the ship, replaced her steam engines with twin diesels, and recommissioned her the MV *Liemba*. Her strange story inspired C. S. Forester's 1935 novel *The African Queen*. Today she is the oldest passenger ship in the world.

You made it halfway! All downhill from here—I'm thinking of you every day. I opened Laura's next card on the *Liemba*'s rear deck, sitting on a pile of orange life jackets. The day is almost over and the sky and water are different shades of silver.

The envelope holds a picture I took of her on a ski lift in Colorado in pink helmet and goggles, gloved fists raised. She looks like a Hello Kitty riot cop.

Think snow, ice, and abomidable snowmen! The misspelling makes me smile. At home I have to bite my tongue at these linguistic hiccups, like her habit of saying an issue is "mute," or adding *l* sounds to the end of words like *draw*. Here, they're just endearing, and it makes me miss her more.

I think of Bogart and Hepburn at the end of *The African Queen*, getting married by the captain of the *Luisa*, the fictional version of the *Graf van Götzen*. They're about to be hung as spies by the Germans, but they're beaming. What matters is that they're being joined forever, even if their lives are about to end. Romeo and Juliet, Heathcliff and Catherine, Roxanne and Cyrano—death always seems to shadow true love in fiction, as if the only way to earn the perfect partner is by paying the ultimate price.

Neither death nor marriage was on either of our minds the first summer Laura and I spent as an official couple in Washington. We slipped back into our groove, cooking dinner, watching movies, going to yoga classes, and complaining about the swampy weather.

My first clue that I'd made the right decision came when we both signed up for a mountain bike race in the Blue Ridge Mountains. The course was steep and wicked, with roots and exposed rocks. On my last lap, I reached for a PowerBar and lost my balance, slamming my hip on a pointed rock. The pain left me breathless. After five minutes of whimpering, I managed to climb back on, teeter across the finish line, and collapse.

Laura arrived five minutes later, in the middle of the women's pack. She was pushing her bike. Blood was streaming from one eyebrow, and her cheeks were streaked with muddy tears. I forgot the throb in my pelvis and led her gently to a picnic table.

"What happened?"

"Shit!" She threw her bike down.

"Wait a minute." I limped to the first-aid tent and grabbed an ice pack. She pressed it to her forehead and explained what happened. She was pushing her bike under a fallen tree across the trail when her front tire hit a rock and the handlebars jumped and gashed her face.

"Then this guy is riding past and he yells at me to get out of the way. I'm sitting there bleeding." Her expression somehow combined anger, distress, and an apologetic smile, embarrassed at her own outburst.

"Who was it?" I was furious. She glanced around but didn't see him.

"It doesn't matter." But it did to me. I wanted to fix her, to make her pain go away—and to smack the asshole who hadn't stopped to help.

In August we went to Philadelphia for a wedding. The bride, one of Laura's cousins, was glowing, and not just because the church was an inferno. (She had to stop the priest mid-blessing to ask for a glass of water.) The guests were giddy, the dress blinding white, and the cake an iceberg of sugar in a sea of flowers. It was an archetypal American wedding, straight out of a magazine.

As we danced after dinner, I could almost feel her relatives' eyes on us. It was easy to imagine the murmured conversations. So this is Laura's new man—what's he like? How serious are they? Will the next one be for them?

Driving back to the hotel, I cranked the air conditioner on high, as if I were trying to drown something out.

"Some ceremony, huh?" Laura said over the roar.

"What?"

She turned the AC down. "Some ceremony."

"Yeah. I don't know. Nice. Not really my style, though. Too frilly."

"That's right. You want to get married on the edge of a cliff."

I was amazed she remembered—I'd forgotten saying it myself. But she was right. I could picture the precipice, clear as day.

Chapter Ten

Grogan and Sharp couldn't wait to get off the *Good News* at Ujiji, one of the oldest and most famous towns in central Africa. For more than a century, it had been the western end of the lucrative Arab trading route to the island city of Zanzibar, almost due east on the coast. Caravans laden with ivory arrived from the Congo trailing long lines of manacled slaves. Those who survived the journey were auctioned in the markets of Zanzibar and Dar-Es-Salaam, its coastal counterpart.

Ujiji's glory days faded as the slave trade was gradually abolished in the nineteenth century. In late October 1871, the explorer Henry Morton Stanley approached the town with a racing pulse and dry mouth. "My heart beats fast, but I must not let my face betray my emotions," he wrote in his journal. He had received word that another white man, a rare find in these parts, was waiting on the lakeshore. It had to be David Livingstone.

Stanley was born in Wales, named John Rowlands. Illegitimate and poor, he grew up in a workhouse before fleeing to America and changing his name. During the Civil War, he started with the Confederates but was captured by the U.S. Navy and decided to defect. He worked as a journalist in the Ottoman Empire, northern Africa, and Europe before being hired by James Gordon Bennett Jr., the playboy publisher of the *New York Herald*.

Bennett commissioned Stanley in 1869 to find the famous British missionary and explorer David Livingstone, who had vanished in central Africa. No one had seen or heard from Livingstone for six years, and many thought he was dead. Stanley knew it was the chance of a lifetime.

Stanley's first expedition was a hellish eight-month, eight-hundred-mile journey inland from the coast. He drove his sick, exhausted men so hard they nicknamed him *Bula Matari*, "the Rock Breaker," for his habits of whipping deserters and using dynamite to clear the way. As Ujiji came into sight, he was giddy with exhaustion and anticipation of success. "What would I not have given for a bit of friendly wilderness, where, unseen, I might vent my joy in some mad freak, such as idiotically biting my hand, turning a somersault, or slashing at trees, in order to allay those exciting feelings that were well-nigh uncontrollable."

At the lakeshore Stanley pushed through crowds of people and saw a pale, gray-bearded man sitting under a mango tree. He briefly considered running over and embracing him but then decided to walk over deliberately. He took off his hat and uttered one of the most famous lines in journalism: "Dr. Livingstone, I presume?"

Except he probably didn't. As Tim Jeal, Stanley's biographer, writes, the explorer probably thought up his immortal phrase months later. Livingstone didn't record it in his account of the meeting, and Stanley tore the relevant pages out of his own journal. Either way, the words stuck and helped make Stanley a household name once he returned home.

Stanley and Livingstone hit it off like a long-lost father and son and explored the northern end of the lake together. Stanley urged his new mentor to come back to civilization, for his health if nothing else (he suffered from malaria and dysentery, among other things). But Livingstone, then fifty-eight, was determined to keep searching for the source of the Nile. He wandered off from Ujiji to the west, weak and addled from decades of hardship in the African bush, and died less than two years later.

Stanley returned to England to a fifty-thousand-pound book advance and a new career as an explorer. He went on to complete the first descent of the Congo River, an even more ambitious and brutal expedition, and spearheaded King Leopold II's plan to control the region. He also helped convince other European rulers of the king's absurd claim that his goal was really to end Arab slavery.

When the dugouts carrying Grogan and Sharp slid up on the beach at Ujiji, the skulls of slaves still lay half buried in the sand. The town itself was little more than a few white buildings and mango trees scattered above a gentle green slope leading down to the water.

A handful of elderly Arabs still lived in Ujiji, some being tended to by freed slaves who had decided to stay. When the Arabs came by to pay their respects to the explorers, as tradition dictated, Grogan shed a few crocodile tears for the once-proud dealers of men. "It was sad to see these venerable old gentlemen in their then condition, and to think of how, in the good old days gone by, they had held undisputed sway over many, many thousand square miles."

Grogan and Sharp were both still sick, but they went to the German station to have lunch and pick up the latest news.

Hauptmann Bethe, the officer in charge, had a mustache to make the Kaiser proud and a bottomless liquor cabinet.

Industrial quantities of alcohol were crucial to avoiding fever, he said, uncorking bottle after bottle of port, champagne, brandy, beer, Vermouth, and claret. The thermometer read 110 degrees in the shade.

Bethe told them how British and Egyptian forces had beaten the Mahdi's rebel army at the Battle of Omdurman, on the Nile River near Khartoum in central Sudan, a few months after they had started out. It was a complete slaughter: more than twenty-seven thousand Muslim casualties versus less than four hundred on the Anglo-Egyptian side. The Muslims were on the run, but the Sudan was still far from safe—especially the southern part, where the remnants of the rebel army had fled.

When Grogan gave him a vague outline of their plans, Bethe dropped his fork in astonishment. Not only were they heading straight for Sudan, but traversing the lakes and volcanoes of central Africa to reach the Upper Nile was suicide. That was Ruanda territory, and even Arab slavers knew to avoid that exceptionally strong and unified tribe. Assuming they made it through, there were still living volcanoes to cross, cannibals to dodge, and who knew what other terrors to face.

"You would need at least a hundred men for protection," Bethe said. It would be much better to follow the safer, established route to the east around the far side of Lake Victoria.

Grogan checked with the Arabs over the next few days, and they confirmed what Bethe had said. There was no food or game in the volcanic mountains, they said, so any expedition would have to carry months' worth of provisions.

The more warnings Grogan heard, the more he was determined to prove them all wrong. He was here to win Gertrude's hand. At the same time, completing the traverse of Africa had taken on its own trophy glow. And not just finishing it, but on his own terms. Grogan simply hated being told he couldn't do something.

First, though, he had to get healthy again. After almost a month straight of fever, Grogan was starting to lose control of his hands.

The *Liemba* docks in the busy lake port of Kigoma, and from here it's a ten-minute bus ride to Ujiji. The turnoff to the monument that marks the famous meeting spot is unmarked, but all I have to say is "Livingstone?" and the driver knows where to stop.

I follow a dusty lane between flat-roofed houses for fifteen minutes, long enough to wonder if this really is the right place. Then I see a stone bulk that looks like a World War II machine-gun bunker. There's a map of Africa carved on the front of the monument, with a cross cut into it that stretches from Cairo to the Cape. A plaque reads UNDER THE MANGO TREE WHICH THEN STOOD HERE HENRY M. STANLEY MET DAVID LIVINGSTONE 10 NOVEMBER 1871.

I can't see the lake, but its presence floats in the stifling air, some subliminal odor or sound that says there's water near.

A wizened head pops from the doorway of a building. "Please come, please come!"

A birdlike old man waves me inside a small museum. A pair of life-size papier-mâché figures stand inside the doorway, both with wide mustaches, cartoonish grins, and hats raised in greeting. Amateur paintings of the historic event cover the walls. The most recent date in the guestbook is ten days ago.

The man swings into a practiced monologue on the lake and

its history, but I can hardly understand his singsong accent. I gather that the lake has retreated half a mile since Stanley was here. (In fact, global warming and decreasing rain levels have caused Lake Tanganyika to drop five feet since the late 1990s.)

I mention that some people think the meeting spot is in Burundi, to the north. He waves this off as absurd. The large boulder overlooking Tanganyika, just south of the capital Bujumbura, is clearly carved with the date "25 November 1871," which was weeks after the men met here.

When he's finished, I put a thousand-shilling note in the donation box, thank him, and walk downhill to the lake. Dozens of weathered wooden fishing boats painted in primary colors are lined up on the beach. Children run up and demand I take their picture, then scatter laughing when I lift the camera. "Hello-*mzungu!*" "What-is-your-name!" "Give-me-money-*mzungu!*"

When Stanley came through Ujiji again five years after meeting Livingstone, he found that the house where they had briefly lived together had burned down. The man who had made him famous was gone, dead and buried in Westminster Abbey, but "the lake expands with the same grand beauty . . . the surf is still as restless, and the sun as bright; the sky retains its glorious azure, and the palms all their beauty."

That's what Grogan saw, too, and what I can see now if I turn my back to the fishing boats, the corrugated metal shacks, and kites made of plastic and wire dancing in the wind. The signs of civilization may change—are there still skulls buried in the sand?—but the background stays the same.

The long boat rides are over. From here I'll follow Grogan overland, north through Burundi, Rwanda, and into western Uganda. To this point his motivation showed no signs of flagging, although I doubt he would have recorded (or admitted) if it was. I'm starting to wonder about my own; moving has felt as important as experiencing lately, and I don't like that.

On the packed minibus back to Kigoma, an old man climbs aboard with a small boy in his arms. He sets the toddler in my lap without a word and crams in, half standing beside us. The boy starts to suck on his fingers. A minute later, his father scoops him up and squeezes out the door, giving me the slightest nod as his feet touch the ground.

The sounds of a Manchester United match drift across the roof-tops of Kigoma in the orange evening. Every radio in town carries the announcers' tinny voices and the staticky roar of the crowd.

I'm wringing out laundry on the roof of the hotel, barefoot and shirtless in the cooling air. It's a moment I know will stick in memory, one of peace and privacy and hygiene, so different from most of the trip so far. Up here, I can relax in a way I can only when I'm alone.

This bone-deep need for space and solitude has always been a fundamental difference between Laura and me. Socializing seems to energize her, while being around other people always eventually wears me out. Sometimes I find the people I like the best to be the most exhausting. The only way to recharge is to be alone.

Traveling can be the ultimate alone time, which is probably why I ended up doing it for a living. Away from home and sur-rounded by strangers, you can be anyone or no one, anonymous or camouflaged.

When Laura and I were living in separate apartments, it wasn't much of an issue if I didn't call for days or if I took off alone for a weekend or a week. Laura had her own life and I was just one part of it. But it can be hard not to take your partner's need for space personally when you live together and you're the only other person around.

I know it's one reason I'm here in Africa: one last deep breath before we bind ourselves closer than ever, forever.

All the same, I want to share the moment with Laura. Yesterday the subject of her email was "34 more days!" I wasn't even keeping track. She admitted she was starting to worry after not hearing from me for a few days. *I feel so disconnected from you. A little kid puked on you and I didn't even know it!*

I was in a coffee shop yesterday and they started playing that song some brides walk down the aisle to these days. Is it Pachelbel's Canon? *Whatever, it gave me the jitters. Ten weeks from now I'll be your wife! Crazy, huh?*

I pull out a cheap cell phone I borrowed from one of the doctors and dial our home number for the first time on the trip. I'm not sure why I haven't called before. My initial excuse was that crossing through so many countries, each with its own network, a prepaid cell phone wouldn't work.

It's also part habit. I'm too used to being out of touch on the road, even though cell phones and email have made that an anachronism. Not like Grogan, of course, with his once-a-year postcards and no word at all from home. But being out of touch, feeling remote and at least somewhat cut off, will always be an essential part of what it means to me to travel. At least until the entire planet is bathed in free wireless Internet.

Listening to our phone ring on the other side of the planet is bizarre, as always. I can see the cherry-wood nightstand and the rubber plant by the phone. Is there a cat curled next to it? Is Laura even home?

"Hello?" Her voice is scrubbed by distance.

"Hey. It's me."

"Hey. Hey!" Her excitement makes me smile. "I was just getting ready to go to yoga. How are you? Where are you?"

"Kigoma. Tanzania. On Lake Tanganyika. Half naked on the roof of a building."

"Ooh, sexy."

"I'm rinsing out my underwear."

"Ah. Nice."

She updates me on her work and the latest wedding plans, and I tell her about the *Liemba* and Ujiji and the kid in my lap on the bus. The time delay leaves small holes of silence. The phone has never been our best means of conversation; our rhythms are just different enough to make us step on one another's sentences.

As early as Washington, whenever I bugged Laura to just *get to the point*, or she asked me to stop mumbling and repeat myself, it was hard not to read too much into it, to see it as symbolic of a larger disconnect.

If we literally couldn't understand each other, whispered my inner pessimist, how would we ever really *understand* each other? As we became more and more attached, I tended to attach greater significance to glitches like these, each tiny thorn of irritation a chance to keep a bit of distance. To stay safe. In a way, I was jealous of Grogan and Gertrude, who never had time to disagree before they made their commitment.

Laura extracts a promise to call her again as soon as I can, or at least to email more often. When we hang up, the moon is out and the game is over.

On April 12, 1899, Grogan and Sharp left Ujiji at the head of a caravan of a hundred fifty porters. The new recruits were from the Manyema tribe, a famous and ferocious group from southeast Congo whose name translated as "eaters of flesh."

The Manyema had brutalized other tribes in the lake region of central Africa for decades. Ten years earlier, the British explorer and soldier Frederick Lugard described how they had ravaged the region near Lake Edward: "From time to time they invent a grievance and a quarrel, and fall upon some helpless tribe, and massacre large numbers of them and carry off the slaves they require."

David Livingstone found them attractive, at least. "I would back a company of Manyuema men to be far superior in shape of head and generally in physical form too against the whole Anthropological Society," he wrote during his final expedition. "Many of the women are very light-coloured and very pretty."

The Manyema were also known for their strength and endurance—the men could carry loads of eighty or ninety pounds without much difficulty—so Grogan and Sharp decided they were worth the risk and hired a company's worth.

Wet grasses overhung the narrow track as the column marched up the eastern shore of Lake Tanganyika. The trail grew rougher, leading across streams and over steep hills. Native huts and gardens appeared wherever the ground wasn't too steep, between deep valleys covered with dense bush. People in the villages wore wooden tweezers on their noses. They were happy to demonstrate how they filled their nostrils with snuff mixed with water and clamped them shut to keep the concoction in.

The chill afternoon mists forced the explorers into their tents early. After reaching seven thousand feet, the trail led to the lakeshore down a slope so steep they had to glissade, using spears for balance. There the path ended, so Grogan and Sharp had to improvise a route along a narrow, rocky strip of land that bordered the water. Over and over, thorny bushes forced them to wade out from the shore into water swarming with crocodiles.

The sun glared off the lake, burning them from above and below. There was no wind or shade. Between the drenching and the scorching, both men's fevers grew worse. Grogan's hands had recovered, but now mosquitoes bit Sharp's hands so badly they gave him blood poisoning. Finally, they hired two large canoes, rigged up deck chairs and awnings, and continued by water while the rest of the party slogged up the shore.

Every new campsite meant a visit from the local chief, trailed by an entourage and bearing presents ranging from millet beer and bananas to goats and sheep. They wore white clothing adapted from the Arabs, including turbans and long shirts called *kanzu*. The explorers reciprocated every present with something of equal value, handing out beads and cloth from their stores.

At one campsite they found that the cook and ten of the *askaris* had gone AWOL, leaving a pile of rifles and bayonets on the ground. Grogan offered the nearest chief a hefty reward for any deserters he captured, but they never saw any sign of them again. This left the five Watonga and the two remaining *askaris* the party's only defense.

By the time they reached the northern end of the lake, the explorers were burning up inside. Grogan had a temperature of 106.9 degrees and was too weak to move, completely dependent on Sharp—suffering from a fever and sunstroke himself—to cook and care for him.

In rare lucid moments Grogan wondered if this was how it would end. Africa had already reduced them to "a couple of wrecks," and they hadn't seen the worst of it yet. Sharp just kept dosing them both from their last bottle of quinine.

A few more days of misery brought them to the German

military post of Usambara, at the northeast corner of Tanganyika. The surrounding Kingdom of Burundi, along with the Kingdom of Ruanda to the north, were both part of German East Africa. The colony stretched seven hundred miles from the Indian Ocean to Lake Tanganyika, encompassing most of what would become modern Burundi, Rwanda, and Tanzania.

The post was laid out with "characteristic German thoroughness," Grogan saw. A wide lane of bananas and pawpaw trees led from the government headquarters to the lakeshore, and gardens thrived between the buildings. The marketplace overflowed with grains, rice, chickens, beans, bananas, and fish.

But Grogan was too sick to appreciate it. He lay in bed for days, too weak to walk, thinking about what lay ahead up the broad valley of the Ruzizi River: the mysterious waters of Lake Kivu, the powerful Ruanda tribe, the huge volcanoes vomiting smoke and cinders.

The region between Lake Tanganyika and Lake Albert Edward, two hundred miles north, was almost completely unknown to Europeans. Grogan and Sharp would be among the first to explore it and, they hoped, the first to map it accurately. If they could get there, that is. Nobody even knew if it was possible to reach Lake Kivu from the south, the way they were going.

And Grogan had never felt worse in his life. "It seemed as though I had struggled thus far only to die at the very gate."

Chapter Eleven

"They are so very quiet today." Shaibu, the park ranger, sounds like the embarrassed parent of misbehaving children. He has been calling the chimpanzee trackers on the radio for hours, but no one in Gombe Stream National Park has seen a chimp all morning. Not even a shaking treetop.

At least the view is outstanding from Jane's Peak, named for the primatologist Jane Goodall, whose research in the 1960s made this place world-famous. From here we can see most of the park; it covers just thirty square miles, barely twice the size of the National Mall in Washington. Steep forested valleys plunge toward the lake, and fishing boats move slowly across the bright water.

Two British women make up the other half of our group. Both have charming Cockney accents; I keep hoping one will call me "guv'nah." Neither has heard of Grogan. I have yet to meet anyone, British or not, who has. I found his story compelling enough to follow it here, but sometimes I wonder if I've lost all perspective.

"In the dry season, the groups disperse farther looking for food," Shaibu says, sheepishly. "Maybe we will see some below." He leads us down a steep path into the trees. His shiny leather hiking boots crunch over dry leaves. The steep descent is as tough as the hour-long climb up.

It's hard to imagine Grogan and Sharp's horizontal grind over these same ridges and valleys and streams, both of them exhausted and smoldering with fever. Maybe that's why they didn't record seeing any chimpanzees, since the hills would have been full of them. Or else the animals just heard the group coming from miles away and hid far out of rifle range.

The path leads past stands of bamboo and trees with buttress roots like serpentine rocket fins. Some are enveloped by strangler figs, parasitic climbing vines that eventually squeeze their hosts to death and take their place in the canopy.

We reach a clearing where two paths meet near a rusted metal structure overgrown with grass. "This was Jane's feeding station," Shaibu says. "She would hang bananas above a scale so she could weigh the chimps as they ate."

I've wanted to visit Gombe since high school, when I read *In the Shadow of Man*, Goodall's 1971 book about her research on the Kasakela chimpanzee community. In her first year at Gombe, the twenty-six-year-old former secretary documented a chimp named David Greybeard fishing termites out of the nest with a grass stem. (Goodall broke research tradition by giving her subjects names instead of numbers.)

That simple act set off seismic ripples, since tool use, along with language, was considered part of the definition of human culture. All of a sudden, one of the things that separated us from the rest of the animals wasn't just ours anymore. Since then, creatures from crows to dolphins have been shown to use tools.

At a small waterfall, Shaibu sits on a log and tells how the Batongwe tribe, who had lived in this area for centuries, were forcibly relocated when the park was created in 1968. Some of the stragglers had to be evicted at gunpoint.

"We need to show locals that that they weren't just kicked out for no reason, that the animals are bringing them money," he says. Poaching and illegal wood-cutting are both down in recent years, encouragingly. The park's evergreen vegetation has been growing denser, in contrast to the surrounding forests, most of which have been clear-cut and converted to farms.

Shaibu is only in his mid-twenties, and already he has one of the more dependable and well-paying positions in a country where just having a job is a kind of victory. His dream growing up was to attend wildlife management college, but it was too expensive.

Five years ago, he was hired to lead an elderly American couple on a hike up Mount Meru, near Kilimanjaro. "When we came down, they asked me, 'Shaibu, would you like to go to school?'"

They agreed to sponsor him, buying him a laptop and paying his tuition of $3,500 per year. (Many students at the school are sponsored by foreigners.) They didn't know it, but the American couple were following a tradition started in the nineteenth century, when Germany set up elementary, secondary, and vocational schools for locals living in its east African colony. It was the only colonizing country that did.

Shaibu stands and brushes off his pants.

"It changed my life."

Blue-and-black butterflies quiver from bright light to shadow. There's movement overhead. A group of monkeys leap from limb to limb like skinny kids on rope swings, chirping like birds. They have red crowns and long silver fur, dark at the roots.

Goodall's next major discovery was documenting that the supposedly vegetarian chimpanzees methodically stalk and devour smaller primates like these red colobus monkeys. They even use weapons—chimps in Senegal have been seen to sharpen sticks with their teeth and stab them into tree hollows where doe-eyed primates called bush babies sleep.

A dark shape clings to a tree trunk up ahead. "Just a baboon," Shaibu says dismissively. With a huff, a scruffy form climbs down and lopes into the forest. Baboons are the redheaded stepchildren of the primate world: barely cute as infants and downright frightening as adults, with close-set eyes, canine snouts, and pit bull teeth. Though barely half our size, baboons have little if any fear of people. "They will follow you into your house, close behind," says Shaibu. "You don't leave the key in the lock—they know how to open it."

We're all starting to get impatient and hungry—there's no food allowed in the park—when what looks like a hairy, barrel-chested child appears on the trail ahead and stops.

It's a twenty-six-year-old female chimp named Fanni, and her backside is about all we see as she turns around and ambles back the way she came. We scramble behind like inept private eyes, trying not to get too close in our excitement. Her butt-swinging knuckle walk is adorable, but her body bulges with muscle. Her arms look twice as large as her parenthetical little legs.

Chimps are unbelievably strong, at least twice as powerful as humans pound for pound. Researchers have seen them crush truck tires with their hands. They can be unpredictable, even when they're habituated to humans. Chimp attacks are notoriously vicious—they tend to go for the groin, fingers, and head. A chimpanzee can literally rip your face off, as a male named Travis did to a woman in Connecticut in 2009.

One of Goodall's original subjects, an aggressive male named Frodo, almost broke her neck. She never came near him again without bodyguards. In 2002, Frodo killed and partially ate a park employee's fourteen-month-old daughter. He's still out there.

Every few minutes Fanni sits in the trail and scans the tree-tops, hooting softly. It's next to impossible not to anthropo-morphize an animal that shares 98 percent of your genes. I can almost hear her saying, "Where is everyone?"

She flows up a tree, showering us with leaves and bark as she reaches for fruit in the highest branches. She extends her arms and swings gracefully from limb to limb, perfectly at ease in her three-dimensional world.

Fanni leaps into the crown of a palm tree, then another, until she's out of sight.

Did Grogan see something like this through a throbbing haze of sickness and fatigue, even if he didn't record it? I hope he did.

Grogan and Sharp started up the Rusizi Valley, "the path that led to the yet unknown," on May 7, 1899. Both were still feeble with sickness, but they hoped the highland climate ahead would improve their health.

The watery vein of the Rusizi River flowed seventy-five miles from Lake Kivu to Lake Tanganyika. Streams slipped from the mountains on either side, attracting clouds of butterflies. Antelope roamed the grassy flats among palms and cacti that looked like giant cabbages from a distance.

One night a cry of agony rang out from Grogan's tent. Sharp and the Watonga rushed in to find him clutching his foot and howling. Everyone's first thought was snakebite. But when Grogan took off his boot, he found a parasitic flea the size of a pea embedded in his pinkie toe. The female "jigger" was feeding on his blood and getting ready to lay a batch of eggs.

Using a pocketknife, Kamau, one of the Watonga, sliced Grogan's toe to the bone to excavate the insect and its egg sac.

The field surgery left him covered in cold sweat, with a toe that looked like a lollipop. He was worried he would lose it, but between Kamau's care and liberal applications of permanganate of potash, "that panacea for all African ills," the toe eventually healed.

The problems with the hired help started midway up the valley. One morning the explorers found that the cook and three porters had deserted, taking a month's pay and two months' worth of rations. The baggage carriers began straggling into camp hours behind the main party, hoping to avoid their evening duties. This put the whole group at risk. They were entering dangerous territory, and a scattered party was harder to defend.

To round things off, they discovered that the men who cared for the cows were keeping the fresh milk for themselves and buying sour milk from local chiefs to give to Grogan and Sharp.

Grogan announced that anyone who was more than half an hour late would have to stand in the middle of camp with his load on his head until he was told he could go. The punishment worked not only because it was exhausting and uncomfortable. "The native enjoys his afternoon nap [and] likes to stroll into the neighbouring villages, show his best clothes off before the local beauties, and pass the time of day with the village cronies. It jars on him to have to stand doing nothing while he sees his friends chatting."

The caravan crossed tributary rivers and deep ravines and passed scattered settlements. The Germans had built three forts in the Rusizi Valley to strengthen their claim to the area, under the pretext of guarding the border of the Congo Free State against native rebels. Near the first fort Grogan saw his first herd of elephants. He grabbed his four-bore and set off after them, ordering his men to keep the litter close behind in case he collapsed.

The herd was gathered in the open, but to his astonishment they ignored him completely as he drew closer. There were twenty-nine in all, some twelve feet high at the shoulder, with tusks longer than he was tall. He approached slowly from down-wind until he could have touched them with his rifle. Their eyes looked impossibly old.

He picked out a black-tusked male and fired the four-bore, both barrels. He was still so feeble that the recoil knocked him flat on his back. The elephant fell, too, but two others used their tusks to help it back to its feet.

Grogan watched from the dirt in disbelief as the animals supported their wounded comrade until they were out of sight. Then he fainted.

A gap-toothed man turns to me on the minibus to Burundi and says, "My name is Michael. I preach the Gospel of Jesus."

Christ! It's too early for this. Evangelical Christianity is every-where in sub-Saharan Africa, from impromptu bus-aisle ser-mons to weeklong tent rallies on the outskirts of cities. But the sun is barely over the eastern hills, and I'm still too groggy for proselytizing.

"Really."

"We have a problem here."

"What's that?"

"Many Muslims. They all believe their Prophet is the only one."

"Must be tough, all that close-mindedness." He nods.

"How do you talk to God?"

I tap my temple, meaning *I think for myself.* But he must take it to mean I'm thinking about his question, and waits patiently. Finally he seems to realize we don't exactly bat for the same team.

"I am sorry I made your mind disturbed. It is an important question. We will all die soon. It will be hot." Hell, I assume.

"More than this?" The air is already thick with dust and heat.

"When will you come back?" Another question I get a lot. I shrug. "Well, when you do, you are welcome at our church." He stands up for his stop. Now I feel bad for being such a grouch.

"Nice to meet you, Michael." He waves and smiles as he disembarks.

The bus climbs and climbs out of the Tanganyika basin and Tanzania. We pass herds of goats and flame trees like frozen fireworks. Men push bicycles loaded with mountains of pineapples and green bananas that seem secured by faith alone.

A Tanzanian woman in an orange fleece jacket takes Michael's place. Anastasia is going to visit her husband, who works at the Tanzanian embassy in Bujumbura, as Usumbara was renamed when Burundi became independent in 1962.

She is in her fifties, sweet but tough, with fine crow's feet around her eyes. When a soldier in the front seat doesn't want to take a stranger's child in his lap, she says, "Do it for the mother," and he does.

Every time we stop she haggles relentlessly with the food vendors that surround the bus, using an aggrieved eye roll to drive the prices down.

Four of her five children live in the United States, three in Las Vegas and one in Washington, D.C. One of her daughters is married to a Swedish man. She shows me a picture of a Nordic-looking girl with bright blond hair. "I hate it when people here treat her like a doll. They touch her hair, her skin."

We share cashews and bananas for lunch, and I show her a photo of Laura and tell her about the wedding in October. It still sounds strange to say things like "my fiancée" and "we're getting married."

"In a church?" I don't have the heart to tell her the ceremony will be in the mountains of Utah, led by a gay friend ordained on the Internet.

Anastasia still feels the need to advise me against sleeping with anyone in Burundi.

"People here lie. The women will do anything, follow you to your hotel, come to your room. There is so much AIDS. They do not care you have someone back home." She touches her temples. "I have a headache. I think I have malaria."

At the border, we each hire a bicycle taxi and roll sidesaddle through a eucalyptus forest into Burundi. The next bus to Bujumbura, the country's capital and main port on Lake Tanganyika, skirts the green northern edge of the lake. It's so shallow in places that Grogan saw hippos raise their heads above water two miles from shore.

We're stopped half a dozen times at police checkpoints. Every other truck bears the logo of the UN High Commission on Refugees, and guns and uniforms are everywhere. Men are hanging sheets of corrugated metal on wood frames along the border of a field. "For returning refugees," Anastasia says.

Burundi's recent history is just as tragic as Rwanda's, although here the bloodshed stretched over a decade instead of erupting in a hundred days. The setup was similar: a Tutsi ethnic minority, about 15 percent of the population, dominated a Hutu majority in a system encouraged by Belgian colonial rulers. Between Burundi's independence in 1962 and 2006, ethnic conflict and civil war left more than three hundred thousand people dead.

The country's economy is in ruins, with four out of five people living in poverty. In a 2006 study asking people around the world how happy they were with their lives, Burundi ranked last. Earlier this year, rival factions of the last remaining rebel group started fighting again in the streets of the capital. People have started fleeing the city, and everyone is worried about another wave of violence.

The tidy Teutonic settlement that Grogan found is long gone. So is the sophisticated city of two decades ago, its optimism and colonial-era art deco buildings both hammered by violence.

Today downtown Bujumbura is dun and dusty chaos. Cranes and huge piles of dirt are everywhere, but I can't see a single traffic signal or streetlight. People on the street give me hard looks as I leave the bus station. In a bank, cashing travelers' checks, I can see liquor bottles sitting on half a dozen desks.

There's a one-handed beggar sitting outside my hotel. Both take only cash.

In the early evening, the Havana nightclub across the street is still mostly empty.

"You have to laugh or you'll go crazy." Sarah lights a thin French cigarette and pushes a slice of pizza across her plate. She is a writer, a friend of a friend. Four months ago she left a doctor boyfriend in New York and a position at Oprah's magazine to come work for a private radio station in Burundi.

"I'm thrilled to be here and I'm totally overwhelmed," she says. "I've never seen anything like it."

The bedlam of "Buj" and the amused fatalism of its upper crust remind her of her Louisiana roots. "Burundians like a good story, just like in New Orleans. And they lie all the time." A few weeks after she arrived, she heard a noise in her house in the middle of the night. It was her security guard, robbing the place. "When I told my local friends, they just laughed. 'Fire him? No, that's not the Burundian way!'"

Later she threw a big party and someone stole her Black-Berry. "It was a friend, someone I had to look in the eye later!" She shakes her head. "I was so pissed off. But then you realize even people who are successful here can still be hungry."

She says a friend of hers, one of four qualified doctors in the country, earns the equivalent of one hundred dollars a month, twice the average salary of a government employee. Two of the four doctors only speak Chinese.

As the place starts to fill, Sarah talks about how strange it is to be black in Africa. She is tall and light-skinned, so people assume she's a Tutsi. "At home I'm one of the darkest, but here I'm one of the lighter ones. It's like New Orleans—lighter is better."

Before the war, Burundi was more developed than Rwanda. Now the roles have switched. The government is ineffective to the point of comedy, or tragedy. "Here's one of the president's great ideas," she says. "Every Saturday morning everything will stop, the roads will be closed for three hours, and people are supposed to clean their houses. Do they? Of course not. They're home screwing."

Burundians laugh at everything, as a survival mechanism, but there's a terrible sadness beneath the surface. "People will suddenly get serious, talk about how everyone—*everyone*—knows someone who was killed. I know someone with a Tutsi father and Hutu mother. During the war he was like, 'Who do I kill?'"

Music has started blaring now, bass beats pulsing like a giant racing heart. We pay the bill with Burundian francs so soft and dark from use they're almost illegible.

A dozen young women have trickled in, slim and mocha-skinned, their hair straightened and colored. Most are wearing skimpy ensembles that draw the gazes of a handful of schlumpy old *wazungu*, each sitting alone with a bottle of Primus beer.

Our change arrives and we head for the door.

A few give me predatory glances and the rest glare at Sarah. She smiles back. "This place is usually crawling with prostitutes. They're thinking, 'Look at her, she snagged one of ours!'"

Sarah climbs into a car, promising to call tomorrow to show me something "uniquely Burundian." I cross the street and climb the stairs to my room. Even though it was utterly platonic, I know Laura won't be thrilled to hear about me meeting an un-attached woman for drinks halfway around the world.

I briefly consider not telling her, but that would just make it worse. That first winter's stupidity had shaken her faith in me, and trust never heals scar-free. I hate feeling guilty for no reason. I can't say I didn't earn it, though.

Chapter Twelve

Grogan drank in the view of Lake Kivu and its chaotic shore-line "dotted with a hundred isles and hemmed in by a thousand imposing hills." The walls of the Great Rift Valley rose to the east and west, and the warming early morning air sucked trails of mist toward the sky.

He was the first Englishman to lay eyes on the thousand-square-mile basin, and Sharp, the first New Zealander. If only Gertrude could be here to share his triumph! He had climbed another rung on the explorers' ladder, from simply organizing and enduring to actual trailblazing.

The southern tip of the lake was almost cut off by a narrow neck of land. Grogan named the appendage "Gertrude's Bight." Then he named four peaks at the southeast corner of the lake after his sisters, Hilda, Margaret, Dorothy, and Mrs. Eyres's daughter Sybil.

From here forward, the explorers would need all of the surveying skills they learned at the Royal Geographical Society. The existing maps of the region were completely inaccurate. This was their chance to add to the almost-finished map of central Africa.

Surveying was laborious and time-consuming. It was also the

only way Sharp and Grogan could even guess where they were. They used a tool set standardized from centuries of exploration to calculate their location in three dimensions: latitude, longitude, and altitude.

A mercury barometer and boiling-point thermometer gave them altitude, since air pressure, and therefore the temperature at which water boils, decreases with height. (The barometer also helped predict the weather, of course.) By measuring the height of the sun at noon with a sextant, they could determine their latitude to within about one hundred yards. Like ship captains in the open ocean, they used highly accurate chronometers to calculate the time difference from Greenwich, England, giving them their longitude.

The exhaustive daily drill started with barometer and thermometer readings at camp in the morning. As they marched, Grogan and Sharp took repeated compass and sextant bearings on distinctive landmarks along the way. By estimating how far they had walked in a given time, they created a series of vertical and horizontal triangles whose corners, after a little trigonometry, they could pinpoint as fixed locations.

The barometer and thermometer readings continued all day. With the camera gone, they sketched nonstop, especially Grogan. Every night they spent hours making mathematical calculations, filling in the map and writing everything up carefully in journals.

Kivu's eastern side was gorgeous, fertile, and packed with people. Long rugged promontories, the roots of taller mountains, fractured the steep shoreline into countless bays and inlets. Beds of papyrus showed where streams flowed into the lake.

This was "the terrible Ruanda country" that the Germans and Arabs had warned them about. The kingdom appeared prosperous and densely populated. (Modern estimates put the number then at about 1.5 million.) Acre after acre of banana plantations covered the lower hills. Higher up, butterflies danced across purple, red, and yellow pastures and vast green fields of beans and peas.

Rice, maize, millet, and pumpkins grew in terraced fields drained by complex irrigation systems and lined with hedges of euphorbia and thorn. Huge herds of cattle, goats, and sheep provided excellent milk and an endless supply of butter.

Beneath this picture of success, though, they found a society split in two. The ruling Watusi minority were tall and slim, with delicate features and a manner Grogan found graceful and nonchalant. "I noticed many faces that, bleached and set in a white collar, would have been conspicuous for character in a London drawing-room. . . . The legal type was especially pronounced."

The Watusi had run things for centuries. They refused to do any other work besides tend their beloved cattle, and seemed proud and contemptuous of other peoples, even Europeans. The Watusi king, whose royal symbol was a drum adorned with the genitals of conquered enemies, ruled with the help of a powerful army.

Then there were the agricultural Wahutu, the opposite of the Watusi in almost every way. "Hewers of wood and drawers of water, they do all the hard work, and unquestioning, in abject servility, give up the proceeds on demand," Grogan wrote. "Any pristine originality or character has been effectually stamped out of them."

Overall, he thought, Ruanda seemed like a successful example of what native races could accomplish when left to their own devices. But that wasn't the case. Like the Belgians in the Congo, the Germans had actively favored the Watusi (today's

Tutsis) and encouraged their domination over the Wahutu (Hu-tus) in both Ruanda and Urundi. Divided kingdoms were easier to control, and it was easier to keep tabs on two castes instead of dozens of tribes.

With their slender height, longer noses, and air of superiority, the Watusi looked and acted more European than the Wahutu. It was only "natural" they ran things, colonial thinking went, even though they were outnumbered a hundred to one, and even though it was generally accepted (and later proved by anthro-pologists) that the Wahutu had lived here for centuries before the Watusi arrived from the north.

Colonial census takers categorized natives based on qualities like height, nose size, and how many cows they owned. Every native had to carry an ethnic identity card, and over time the distinction between the groups widened and took on a life of its own.

In the long term it was a recipe for disaster. But in 1899 Gro-gan wrote, "In spite of the obvious hatred in which [the Wahutu] hold their overlords, there seems to be no friction."

Birds warble in the flowered vines of the hotel patio beside pho-tos of Louis Armstrong and Ella Fitzgerald. I'm enjoying the finest breakfast in weeks: fresh fruit, a croissant, and real coffee from an actual coffeemaker.

It's easy to understand how much Grogan and Sharp looked forward to every mission station and army outpost, temporary islands of civilization in a sea of wilderness. At this point, a news-paper and a cup of non-instant java are enough to make my day.

The *Burundi Post* has more bad news for Bujumbura. The president has announced that the government is planning to move its capital to Gitega, the country's second-largest city, so it will be closer to Uganda, Burundi's main trading partner. I almost feel bad for this decrepit city. It's like they've given up on it and just want to start over.

The next article is worse: local witch doctors are hunting local albinos for their body parts. The condition is unusually common in East Africa, affecting one in every three thousand people, compared to about one in twenty thousand worldwide. In Tanzania and Burundi, albino heads, tongues, and genitals are used in "blood money" rituals that promise wealth or social advancement. It's getting so bad that Burundi's few hundred remaining albinos now need police protection.

Grogan saw native albinos early in his trip, which he chalked up to inbreeding. In fact, about one in seventy people carries the recessive gene that, in combination, disrupts the production of the pigment melanin.

As if the situation wasn't bad enough, it also clicks neatly into the "savage Africa" stereotype that so many of us in the West still carry, consciously or not. I hate to say, but I'm sure it accounts for some of my own horrified fascination. Witch doctors, bloody rituals, female genital mutilation, genocide—none of these is limited to Africa, but they've become attached to the continent nonetheless, shouting from headlines and drowning out good news, such as how Tanzania's president nominated a female albino as MP in 2008.

When I leave the hotel, Bujumbura's streets are strangely deserted for a Saturday morning. (Is everyone home scrubbing the floor?) Flames dance in the center of a huge stump near the empty marketplace. The smell of smoke hangs in the air.

It takes ten minutes on a motorcycle taxi to reach Saga Beach, the most developed part of the lakeshore. We pass a long yellow wall with PRIMUS painted over and over in six-foot red letters. The Brarudi brewery, source of Primus beer, almost single-handedly kept the Burundian economy afloat during the worst of the conflict. In 1995, the government's largest single source of revenue was beer taxes. Soldiers guarded the building from rebels and enjoyed three free bottles of Primus each per day.

Next are United Nations compounds ringed with coils of barbed wire big enough for a child to crawl through. The UN recently shut down its three-year peacekeeping mission in Burundi to focus on reconstruction—just before the fighting started again.

Open beach bars line the soft white sand. I head for the upper deck of the nearest and order my own Primus. A hundred yards up the beach, a plump *mzungu* in a skimpy black Speedo wades cautiously into the water. His bright pink body looks flayed next to the local children splashing close by.

Pouring the first glass at exactly noon, I wonder how many tourists who swim here have heard of Gustave. Not coldblooded former president Pierre "Gustave" Buyoya, but the giant man-eating crocodile that (not coincidentally) shares his nickname.

Africa's most famous reptile is said to have killed and eaten hundreds of people here and up the Ruzizi River toward Lake Kivu. He is estimated to be twenty feet long and weigh two thousand pounds, which would make him one of the largest Nile crocodiles in the world. Wild crocodiles typically live to around forty-five, but from his size Gustave could be sixty, older than the country of Burundi.

Bullet-scarred and fearless, he has dragged victims away in front of horrified crowds. He is rumored to leave bodies uneaten, content simply to hunt and kill. Scientists are itching to examine his apparently indestructible genome, and Burundian soldiers have orders to shoot on sight. So far, Gustave has avoided everything from a hail of Kalashnikov rifle fire to a custom cage that took forty men to move.

Bujumbura is barely visible through the haze that blankets everything but the lake. The valley of the Ruzizi vanishes to the north, bookended by green-furred mountains.

If I hold up my hands to block out the cars and buildings, I can see the same thing Grogan did as he lay ill, watching hippos and wondering if he'd live to continue his trek. I doubt Bujumbura is any more alien to me than it was to him. At least I can check my email, rent a hotel room, buy drugs in a pharmacy and a drink in a bar. Even call home, if I want.

Like Grogan, I know almost nobody within hundreds of miles. It's liberating and lonely but starting to skew more toward the latter every day.

How isolated did Grogan feel, this far out in the bush with only Sharp to talk to? By this point they'd been on the road for fifteen months. I've been going for just over three weeks. That's about one day of travel for every three weeks of his.

They did have many of the comforts of home, and an army of porters to carry them: beds, chairs, books. But it was still incredibly tough and dangerous going.

Could I have even survived three weeks here in 1899? Maybe, if I could have brought sunglasses, antibiotics, and some powerful bug juice. Iodine for the water. And ibuprofen—lots of ibuprofen. Maybe.

Young locals have started to gather on the ground floor of the bar. With their Oakley sunglasses and tight jeans, they could pass for rich, bored teens just about anywhere. They're lighter-skinned than the moto-taxi driver and the barman, with narrow jaws and prominent foreheads.

A baby-faced girl with sleepy eyes dances on a table. The party is starting early today.

On my last night in Bujumbura I meet Sarah at an outdoor dance club. We sit at a plastic table and watch people of every shade shimmy across the floor, which is open to the night air on all sides. There's a disco ball and tilted mirrors, but the music is pure Afropop, with fast, complex beats.

Expats are making a solid showing, dressed and dancing as if they just got out of an IT convention. "Most of them are here with Catholic charities," Sarah says. She promised something interesting tonight. This is it?

Then the polyrhythms shift to a familiar shuffling pulse and the words change to English. *Goodness, gracious, great balls of fire!* One couple spin like freshmen at a sock hop. In moments, everyone is swinging to "La Bamba," "Louie Louie," "Tutti Frutti." Faces shine with sweat and delight as Elvis sings about dancing in prison. The sight is joyfully surreal, *Happy Days* goes to Africa. Beyond the spinning bodies and swirling lights is darkness.

After the Latin nightclub that first aborted evening, Laura's and my favorite place to dance in Washington was Ghana Café, a second-story sweat box a few blocks away. We'd shove our way in at midnight and bounce to Afrobeat and highlife until the crowd threatened to burst through the windows onto the sidewalk.

Now that we had clarified our relationship, it felt like a weight had been lifted, or at least shifted. We seemed to get along better every week. I liked this new side of her, up-front and direct. Sweet and easygoing were wonderful, in moderation. But it was reassuring to find she could dig in when necessary.

I loved to listen to her steamroll stubborn customer support drones on the phone, from cell phone carriers to overbilling doctor's offices. Strangers always convinced me to take no for an answer, but Laura would pit-bull them until she got her way. It was beautiful to hear, if not receive.

She was adventurous and, even better, a remarkably good sport when things didn't go according to plan. She would grin through experiences that would have most people whining or quitting in disgust: mountain biking in the rain, painted head to toe in mud, or paddling a kayak through a mosquito-infested marsh. I loved her drive to push through and even enjoy temporary discomfort in pursuit of a larger goal, a quality that was deserting me here in Africa.

In the late spring we took a weeklong trip to the Southwest. We planned to hike to the bottom of the Grand Canyon down a short, steep, and little-used path. We left at 11 A.M., and not even halfway down, the black lava rocks along the trail were already too hot to touch.

"I'm so tired. My head hurts," Laura said, then dropped her backpack and sat on the ground. Her face was flushed.

"Are you okay?"

"No, I'm . . . okay. What?"

Something wasn't right. I drenched her head with water from our shrinking supply. It didn't seem to help, and I recognized the early signs of heat exhaustion.

Abruptly I knew we were balanced on the edge of something serious. Heatstroke was next. People died in the Grand Canyon every year. They sell books of the stories in the gift shops.

The trailhead at the rim was a thousand feet almost straight uphill. The Colorado River looked so close, a latte-colored ribbon that reappeared over every small rise but was still miles down the trail. Even though the canyon was hottest at the bottom, I decided we had to get there before Laura became sicker or we ran out of water.

I hid her pack behind a boulder—by now she was too weak to carry it anyway—and for the next two hours led her down the crumbling trail as fast as we could go.

I kept reassuring her, and myself, that everything would be all right. We slid down a final ski slope of gravel and gasped as we hit the water. Laura came back to life as she cooled down, her smile blossoming under a dripping hat.

I second-guessed myself through dinner and into the chilly night. It had been my call to sleep late and start hiking close to noon. Was going down the right choice? I was the only one who had hiked in here before, and I knew that it took twice as much water and effort to hike out as to hike in.

Lying awake in the darkness, burritoed with Laura in our single sleeping bag, I calculated gallons and mileage and elevation. (The night before we'd discovered that our bags serendipitously zipped together, but hers was still in her backpack.) I was more worried about this woman sleeping against my chest than about myself. I was used to risking my own hide; now I was responsible for hers.

Compared to the descent, the hike out in the cool early morning was almost effortless. We had barely cleared the canyon rim before Laura was asking what park we were heading to next. Within days we were looking back on the experience and laughing, potential tragedy turned to comedy. ("Remember filtering that nasty river water through your hat?")

But I never forgot that moment on the trail when everything seemed to warp in the heat and I felt a concern for this suddenly fragile person that startled me in its depth. That was when I first realized it wasn't just the flicker-taste of fear I felt at the bottom of the gorge. It was love. I would do my best to remember it later in moments of friction or doubt, when it seemed like we spoke different languages or saw the world in diametrically opposed ways.

Whether I deserved it or not, I was a lucky guy.

Chapter Thirteen

Grogan and Sharp learned more about the Ruanda tribe as they marched up Lake Kivu's eastern shore. Most of them carried some form of *dawa*, small sacred items to guard against sickness and misfortune. Large red beans were said to prevent leopard attacks; the tip of a cow's horn inlaid with ivory was good for abdominal pain; and anyone who wore two small leather bottles around his neck could never die.

"Such a thing as a natural death they cannot understand," Grogan said, "and always attribute the event to some form of violence, which, if not obvious, they describe as the effect of the 'evil eye.'"

Lying seemed to be some kind of national sport. "I have pointed to a mountain 13,000 ft. high, at a distance of three miles, and asked my native guide whether there was a mountain there: he would say 'No!' On the march, if I asked whether there was water near, and he told me 'yes,' I knew that it would take at least six hours to find the next stream."

A powerful district chief named Ngenzi came to welcome the explorers with a retinue of a hundred, including a cupbearer with a royal gourd of *pombe*. When he learned their intended route, Ngenzi offered to accompany them up the lake and provide protection. "From his pleasant manner," wrote Grogan, "we little guessed what a source of trouble he was to prove in the near future."

Then the thefts started. One night someone entered Grogan's tent, avoiding a sentry, and stole a pair of pants from under his pillow. The explorers couldn't risk losing any of their irreplaceable gear, so Grogan ordered that their most important goods be put in a single tent with men sleeping at both ends all night.

The next morning they found that someone had snuck into Grogan's tent again and made off with a tin box weighing sixty pounds. It contained their sextant, artificial horizon, boiling-point thermometers; a bag of a hundred gold sovereigns; all of Grogan's trousers, stockings, and socks; and perhaps worst of all, many of their written notes, books, and photographs.

They immediately suspected Ngenzi, who had been tagging along for the last forty miles, growing smarmier by the day. The Germans had spoiled the chief with extravagant presents, Grogan had learned, and as a result "he imagined that he could bleed any one who came into his country."

Grogan always made it a policy not to pay *hongo*, the tax-cum-bribe that local chiefs often charged for permission to pass through their territory. He also made it a policy never to give presents unless he was offered one first. In that case, if the gift was generous, he would give a more valuable one in return; if it was stingy, he would offer one of the same value (in his judgment), unless the stinginess was due to poverty.

He had to keep the upper hand. If word spread that the expedition had been robbed so handily, the Wa Ruanda would see them as easy prey. Grogan summoned the wily chief, who arrived with "a supercilious smile and a host of attendants."

Ngenzi played dumb. "There are many bad men in my country of whom I know nothing," he said, shaking his head sadly. It was a ludicrous response. Chiefs had the power of life and death over their subjects, and very little happened in their districts without their knowledge. If he didn't have them stolen himself, Ngenzi could have had the items found and returned in an instant.

Grogan knew this, and he also knew he had to take action. Stolen coins and clothes were one thing, but it couldn't have been a worse time to lose their notes and most of the surveying equipment. All they had left was the compass. This was his first real test as expedition leader, and how he handled it would set the tone for the rest of the journey.

He had Ngenzi seized and confined in a tent guarded by bayonet-wielding *askaris*. Grogan told the chief's attendants that if their things weren't returned by noon, they would be forced to take further steps.

It was an audacious move. If Ngenzi called their bluff, their endgame options were roughly zero. This deep in Ruanda territory, the expedition was outnumbered a thousand to one.

A few of the items of clothing appeared the next day, proving their suspicions. Grogan knew his hunch had been right. Now he had to push harder. At noon, he climbed a hill to the largest local village to demand the return of the rest of their stolen goods. He took his revolver and an old French cutlass he had bought in a London junk shop. Two of the Watonga followed, each carrying a rifle. Alarm drums began to pound in nearby villages as Sharp passed out cartridges to the *askaris* and prepared the camp for defense.

An enormous woman in a pink bathing cap topples slowly into the shallow end of the sky-blue pool. Waiters in bow ties thread their way between guests sprawled on lounge chairs. Half of Kigali, Rwanda's capital, spreads out below the manicured lawn of the Hôtel des Mille Collines, but the sounds of the city are far away.

I'm halfway through the trip: one month to go. I had to detour to Kigali, in the center of the country, to buy a permit to visit the gorillas in the volcanoes on the country's northern border. I also wanted to see two places that commemorate the 1994 genocide in very different ways.

The first, this posh place in the center of the city, is probably the most famous hotel in Africa, but not for reasons any publicist would want. A room is too expensive, so I head for the pool, grabbing a thick towel from a pile near the bar and claiming a chair with the confidence of a guest. My nylon shorts can double as swim trunks.

I order a mango cocktail from a roving waiter and watch children in inflatable water wings dog-paddle past. Aside from a few interracial couples, most of the guests are white. Within five minutes I've heard French, Russian, German, Spanish, and English. The clink of silverware and Lionel Richie's buttery voice drift from the café.

In 1994, this was an entirely different kind of oasis. As the gears of genocide started to grind across Rwanda, more than one thousand people took refuge in the hotel. Manager Paul Rusesabagina managed to bribe, cajole, and plead with government soldiers and local militias to spare their lives.

Today, the "Hotel Rwanda" has been cleaned up and restored, and is back on the list of the country's most luxurious lodgings. It's also completely generic and boring as hell. Not that I was hoping for bloodstains and bullet holes. It's just impossible to reconcile this tour-brochure scene with what happened here thirteen years ago, those weeks of hysterical anxiety as supplies of food and water dwindled and bloodthirsty mobs clamored outside the gates. It's become a place of denial, of forgetting.

I finish my drink and leave. A moto-taxi is waiting outside the gate. The driver hands me a red helmet, still warm inside from the last passenger. I swing my leg over the seat.

"Gisozi."

He nods as if to say, of course.

Hundreds of angry Wa Ruanda met Grogan at the village, shaking spears and shouting threats. Thousands more looked down from nearby hilltops and waited to see what the interlopers would do. Grogan surveyed the sea of hostile faces. He knew every explorer has his own ways of dealing with upset natives. Some, like Stanley, tended to shoot first. Others, such as Livingstone, did everything they could to avoid bloodshed.

Before leaving England, Grogan had read Francis Galton's bestseller *The Art of Travel*, a comprehensive instruction manual for would-be explorers. Its advice for dealing with the locals suited his personality perfectly: "A frank, joking, but determined manner, joined with an air of showing more confidence in the good faith of the natives than you really feel, is the best . . . they thoroughly appreciate common sense, truth, and uprightness; and are not half such fools as strangers usually account them."

Grogan waved the cutlass to make sure he had everyone's attention. Then he spoke in his most authoritative voice. "I explained what had happened, and told them that my quarrel was with Ngenzi, and with Ngenzi only; that he had allowed thieves to come and steal the goods of strangers in his country, strangers who had come to see their country, to pass through it on a long journey to far lands, and who had come in peace paying for what they [the natives] brought."

Now, he said, they were going to confiscate all of Ngenzi's cattle and take them to a nearby German post. The soldiers there could decide what to do. Anyone who threatened the camp would be shot, but people selling food were welcome as always.

Some of the Wa Ruanda made tentative rushes as Grogan and the Watonga rounded up Ngenzi's herd of about two hundred cattle, but a few swings of the cutlass kept them back. The explorers gathered the animals in their camp and helped guard them through a tense but uneventful night. The next day they drove the animals to the German post without firing a single shot.

No more of the stolen items turned up. Thinking only the clothes had any value, the thieves had tossed everything else over a cliff. Eventually Grogan had to release Ngenzi with a warning. If nothing else, the experience had humbled the chief. "The smaller fry were delighted at the humiliation of the mighty Mtusi," Grogan wrote, neglecting to mention whether Ngenzi ever got his cattle back.

The experience bolstered Grogan's belief that it was best to treat Africans as he treated everyone else: bluntly and firmly, showing no more fear, or hostility, than was necessary.

He sounded almost disappointed the situation hadn't escalated. "Such were the terrible Ruanda people, whose reputation has spread far and wide, and whose country has been left alone for fear of their military organization. At least five thousand men sat on the hill-tops and watched three men with a revolver, cutlass and two rifles drive off one hundred and ninety head of cattle."

All the same, for days none of the porters would leave camp without "two spears, a sword-knife, and, if possible, a gun with fixed bayonet."

As word of the Englishman's boldness spread, entire villages started to empty at their approach. Part of the reason was the fierce reputation of the Manyema porters, who took full advantage of their notoriety.

The porters, who earned an average of three shillings a month (about eighteen dollars today), would subcontract locals to carry their loads for pennies. Sometimes the stand-ins would hire even poorer replacements until three or four people were walking beside every load.

The Manyema weren't above blatant extortion or theft. One trick was to hide a load of cloth at night and blame the theft on the locals—the plan being to collect and sell the cloth on the way home.

To solve the problem, Grogan made each porter personally responsible for his own load, with any loss or damage deducted from his pay. He also required that all transactions between camp members and natives be performed in front of him, and encouraged the locals to bring any complaints directly to him.

For the moment, their celebrity kept them safe. Nevertheless, Grogan wrote, "masses of natives in a silvery sea of glinting spearheads watched us from every hill-top." If he couldn't keep control of the situation, that sea would come crashing down on top of them.

Two porters caught stealing were punished in front of a group of locals, but eventually all the Manyema had to be confined to camp. Grogan explained that they were being punished for the actions of a few bad apples. They seemed satisfied, but as he and Sharp were sitting down to lunch, Grogan noticed a stirring among the men.

It was the Manyema packing up to leave. Thirty of them had already started back down the trail.

This deep in hostile territory, the deserters wouldn't last a day on their own. The problem was, neither would the rest of them. "If the camp broke up," Grogan wrote, "the entire expedition would be inevitably massacred."

Every town I've been to in Rwanda has had a memorial to victims of the genocide. But the Gisozi Genocide Memorial Center, on the outskirts of Kigali, is the Smithsonian of them all, a professional multimedia experience that traces the events before, during, and after those unimaginable months in 1994.

It's cool inside, and dim after the glare of the ride here. The displays start right inside the door. Captions in English, French, and Kinyarwanda tell how long-simmering tensions between the Hutu majority and the Tutsi elite led to a three-year civil war that ended in 1993. A peace agreement was foundering along when, on April 6, 1994, a jet carrying Rwanda's Hutu president and the president of Burundi was shot down as it approached the Kigali airport.

The machinery of genocide was already in place, planned at the highest levels of the Hutu government. Weapons had been gathered and homicidal militias, called *interahamwe* ("those who work together"), were ready throughout Rwanda. The president's assassination—responsibility for which is still a mystery—provided the spark, fanned by rumors of a Tutsi uprising. The massacres of Tutsis and moderate Hutus started within hours.

The farther I walk into the museum, the more the images and details start to blur. Roadblocks and house-to-house searches. Whispers on transistor radios: "Kill the cockroaches." Ethnic identity cards become death warrants. Rape, torture, burning, disemboweling, drowning in latrines. Churches, schools, homes, streets. Guns, machetes, hoes, axes, stones, hands.

An army of Tutsi rebels called the Rwandan Patriotic Front took the capital in early July, ending the worst of the killing. But by then, as one panel says, "Rwanda was dead."

Next come hundreds of portraits and snapshots of victims clipped to wires, some smiling, many beautiful. One section is nothing but children and babies.

The only sound is the murmur of film clips, where survivors describe hiding in terror or making hairsbreadth escapes through luck and the kindness of strangers. I'm riveted by one looping montage in particular. It begins by showing children with horrible head wounds, then four bodies on a road, one leg twitching. Last is a grainy, distant shot of men in an alley chopping something on the ground with machetes. Over and over, it repeats, silently.

Back outside in the sun, a family is standing near a wide patch of salmon-colored ground. It's a mass grave holding more than a quarter of a million bodies. I want to talk to them, to find out if they were here when it happened and what they think of this place, but in the past hour I've gone from curiosity to incredulity, revulsion, then numbness. I'm dumbstruck.

This was supposed to give some insight into the ethnic inferno whose roots Grogan noticed almost exactly a century earlier. But the events are so incomprehensible they become abstract, facts and photos and faces dissolving into a fog of data. Almost one in five Rwandans, dead. That's the equivalent of 60 million Americans or 12 million in the United Kingdom.

"The death of one man is a tragedy—the death of millions is a statistic," wrote Erich Maria Remarque, who based his book *All Quiet on the Western Front* on his experiences in the trenches of World War I. The Battle of the Somme, the bloodiest of that war and almost all others, claimed an average of ten thousand casualties every day for four and a half months. By most estimates, the Rwandan genocide had the same body count: between eight hundred thousand and a million people dead in one hundred days. Six every minute.

In some ways, Rwanda has recovered admirably. The "Land of a Thousand Hills" is as beautiful as it was when Grogan passed through, but now the roads are paved and free of trash. Crime and corruption are down, and the government is angling to promote Rwanda as East Africa's high-tech hub, wiring the entire country with fiber-optic cable and sending students by the hundreds to tech schools in India.

Foreign aid has poured in, much of it a kind of monetary mea culpa from countries that didn't intervene before it was too late. All talk of ethnicity has supposedly been banned. "There are no more Tutsis and Hutus; we are all Rwandans now," says president Paul Kagame, former head of the Rwandan Patriotic Front, whose Tutsi government tolerates no dissent.

Yet one study a year after the genocide found that more than half the children and teenagers who survived had symptoms of post-traumatic stress disorder. Out of every twenty who were interviewed, three reported having to hide under corpses.

The family walks off to their car, which is just as well. Visiting the museum feels like being at a stranger's funeral, except for an entire country. How do you strike up a conversation about something like that?

I've been finding it harder to interact with people lately. The constant low-level stress of traveling alone is wearing me out. Everyone is a stranger and every action a conscious decision: where to eat, where to sleep, what to do, how to get there. No comfortable defaults. I feel like I'm going into touch withdrawal, and my mood has plunged.

Not good, considering I haven't even reached the Congo, northern Uganda and Sudan, the most problematic parts of the route. Instead of hitting my stride and unmixing my feelings about the imminent wedding ceremony, I'm standing on a mass grave feeling sorry for myself.

Ewart Grogan

Gertrude Watt, the inspiration for Grogan's
legendary transcontinental trek

Grogan's sketch of Arthur "Harry" Sharp, his companion for part of the journey

Grogan fumbling for his 4-bore rifle in the sights of a rhino (*Illustration by A. D. McCormick*)

Arthur A. Sharp.

One Mozambican, one *mzungu*, a bike, and a backpack (*Julian Smith*)

Catching a ride near the Mozambique-Malawi border (*J.S.*)

Lake Malawi shoreline, Chiluma, Malawi (*J.S.*)

Food vendors at a minibus stop, Blantyre, Malawi (*J.S.*)

Bananas for sale in southern Tanzania (*J.S.*)

Loading the *Liemba* en route to Kigoma, Lake Tanganyika (*J.S.*)

The beach at Ujiji (*J.S.*)

Barbershop in Kigoma, Tanzania (*J.S.*)

Genocide memorial to the 11,400 victims of Kibuye, Rwanda (*J.S.*)

A wedding in Fort Portal, Uganda (*J.S.*)

Silverback mountain gorilla on Mount Sabinyo,
Virunga Mountains, Volcanoes National Park, Rwanda (*J.S.*)

A mountain gorilla baby enjoys the ultimate jungle gym (*J.S.*)

Soccer under the Virunga Volcanoes, Ruhengeri, Rwanda (*J.S.*)

Grogan's sketch
of camp near
Mount Götzen

Grogan's sketches of a
Manyema pipe, antelope
skull, and elephant that
appeared in *From the Cape
to Cairo*

Docent at the Stanley-Livingstone Museum, Ujiji, Tanzania (*J.S.*)

Children near Queen Elizabeth National Park, Uganda (*J.S.*)

Semuliki National Park ranger, Uganda (*J.S.*)

Grogan's expedition fighting off hippos
on their descent of the Upper Nile
(*A. D. McCormick*)

The White Nile at Wadelai (*J.S.*)

Male hippos jousting for dominance, near Queen Elizabeth National Park, Uganda (*J.S.*)

A face only a mother, or another warthog, could love (*J.S.*)

A portrait of contemporary Africa: Main minibus station in Kampala, Uganda (*J.S.*)

Dinkas attack Grogan's party in the Sudd (*A. D. McCormick*)

Grogan meets Captain Dunn's party at the end of his trek (*A. D. McCormick*)

Photograph of an exhausted Grogan taken by Captain Dunn just ten minutes after his arrival in camp

AFRICAN TRAVELER HERE

Ewart W. Grogan Tells of His Journey from South to North.

WALKED THE ENTIRE DISTANCE

Unfriendly Natives Were Encountered, but Explorer "Bluffed" Them— On His Way to New Zealand.

Across Africa from south to north, traversing 400 miles of Nile swamp—a feat hitherto thought by many explorers to be impossible—is the record of Ewart W. Grogan, a young Cambridge student, who is now staying at the Holland House in this city, and who is going from here to New Zealand. For the first time in the history of the Dark Continent, an explorer has succeeded in crossing it along its length.

New York Times article noting Grogan's accomplishment, dated November 18, 1900

Grogan's portrait taken after his return; frontispiece of his memoir, *From the Cape to Cairo*

Grogan and Gertrude

A wedding in the snow
(*Garret Vreeland*)

CHAPTER FOURTEEN

Grogan grabbed his rifle and ran after the disappearing porters. He topped a rise and saw the ringleader, "one of our
worst villains," two hundred yards ahead. He called at him to
stop, but the man shouted back an insult and kept going.

Grogan aimed and fired. The man's fez leaped from his head.
He dropped to the ground in terror, followed by the entire
group. Grogan shot his rifle a few more times in the air for good
measure. Then he sent another porter to tell the deserters the
affair was over. As long as they returned to camp, no one would
be punished.

As he had hoped, at the evening roll call everyone was present and accounted for. Grogan impressed on everyone how crucial it was to keep peace with the natives. Not only were they
surrounded and hugely outnumbered by the Wa Ruanda—but
who else could sell them goats, tobacco, and "all the things that
rejoiced the stomachs of men"?

"Today I have been very lenient. I shot off your leader's fez,
but I could just as easily have shot off his head." In fact, he had
been aiming to kill, but the lucky shot turned out to be even
more effective. The anxiety lifted. The men cheered and returned to the campfires to talk and laugh into the night.

Relations with the Wa Ruanda took longer to repair. At one point, when no natives responded to his request to buy provisions, Grogan had to send men out to gather bananas from a nearby field. They tried for two days to convince the local chief to show up for payment, with no luck. It was the only time on the trip Grogan had to commandeer anything from the natives. Many explorers did this as a matter of course, but Grogan thought it would be wiser to stay on peaceful terms whenever possible instead of leaving a trail of tension.

Eventually the Wa Ruanda began to venture back into camp. "The hordes of warriors whom we had seen sitting on the tops of the hills in the distance came and mingled freely with our men, and a brisk trade started in the numerous products of the country."

Lake Kivu's shoreline was a complexity of bays and inlets backed by hills so numerous they looked like they had been "sprinkled out of a pepper-pot." Cranes and ibis flocked on small islands and large otters frolicked in the bays.

"There was an air of *dolce far niente*"—the "carefree idleness" of the Italians—"heavy with the lush glamour of the tropics that carried me back to the South Seas," Grogan wrote, thinking of his voyage back to England after meeting Gertrude. Sharp said the scenery reminded him of Japan.

When the explorers reached a hilltop at the easternmost point of the lake, they could finally see its full expanse, "deep set in its basin of innumerable hills, dotted with a thousand islets, stretching far away till it was lost in the shimmering haze of the northern shore, where, crisp and clear, towered the mighty mass of Mount Götzen"—an active volcano named after a German explorer—"whose jet of smoke alone broke the steel-blue dome of sky."

Determined thieves still snuck into camp almost every night.

One evening an exasperated sentry shook Grogan awake and told him it was becoming impossible to stop the infiltrations. Grogan dressed and crouched under a small bush just outside the camp, waiting.

Soon a figure crept past. Grogan leaped up to grab him and found the man was completely coated with grease. He tightened his grip and brought the surprised burglar down with a rugby tackle. The next day he turned him over to the local chief. The standard punishment for thievery was swift and final: the man's head was cut off and set on the path as a warning. The stealing stopped.

Another night Grogan was turning in for bed when hordes of ants appeared and swarmed over everything, him included. He yelled for help, then snatched the blanket with the least insects on it and ran to the spare tent.

He was busy setting up a bed with each leg in a basin of water when Sharp poked his head in.

"What the hell's all this?" He saw the water basins and burst out laughing.

"Bloody funny!" said Grogan. Painful welts were already rising all over his body.

When Sharp left, Grogan stripped naked, brushed off as many ants as he could, and passed the night "without more than three or four hundred" aboard.

A few hours later he awoke to howls coming from the direction of Sharp's tent. Grogan smiled in the darkness, rolled over, and fell back to sleep.

A man sweeps the flagstone patio of the guesthouse on Lake Kivu with a straw hand broom, his back bent almost double. All the other guests in the open-air restaurant are speaking French.

On the TV above the bar, James Brown howls in what sounds like another language.

Cloudy skies cast a subaqueous light over the water and the city of Kibuye, near where Grogan first saw the lake in its entirety. Vacation homes and hotels line the shore, and terraced fields make ziggurat steps up the hills. Tongues of land trail off into ellipses of green in the water.

Three fishermen paddle between islands in a trimaran of dugout canoes. Their voices carry across the water, a call-and-response rhythm halfway between a chant and a song.

The genocide reached an awful climax in Kibuye, at the time one of the poorest places in Rwanda. Between hills and water, with no paved roads to escape to other provinces, Kibuye turned into a death trap. Four out of five Tutsis were killed, close to sixty thousand people. Hundreds of bodies were dumped into the water.

On the road into town, tall cacti droop under the weight of small red fruit. There's a church on the first hilltop. A sign in three languages says it's a memorial to 11,400 victims. What look like rows of pale, hollow-eyed faces in the front windows resolve into skulls. Leg bones lean against the glass.

I'm pulling out my camera when a teenage boy walks over. He's carrying a notebook, probably on his way home from school for lunch.

"What are you doing?" he says curtly.

I lower the camera without pressing the shutter. "Taking a picture."

"Why?" he says. The Rwandans I've met have an edge, a flat-gaze brusqueness that can border on mild hostility. It's understandable, but it still catches me by surprise. "This is a memorial. People are sensitive. It is not for pictures."

I want to be considerate. But they are on public display.

"It's just to show people at home." Isn't part of the point to spread the word about what happened, to prevent it from ever repeating?

"Oh. All right. *Pas de probleme*." He seems to relax, and steps aside for me to take the shot.

His name is Marcus, and he's studying agriculture. Like half the country, he's under eighteen, too young to remember the genocide. I wonder if he's among the 20 percent that are orphans.

We part amicably. Before he leaves he asks me for *un peu d'argent*, a little money.

"Sorry." Personal policy. It's not always easy to say no, but traveling so much I've had to make a blanket decision, erring in the same Republican direction Grogan did. Otherwise I'll drive myself crazy having to decide every time if someone "deserves" a handout, whatever that even means.

A few minutes down the road I pass a billboard with a mother and baby sleeping peacefully. Above them looms a mosquito the size of a cow, stamped with a red circle and slash. The sign is in Kinyarwanda, but I know it's urging people to use mosquito nets to protect their family from malaria.

The disease that dogged Grogan is still a major public health issue. According to the World Health Organization, malaria kills almost a million people every year, and 85 percent of them are African children under five. The parasites have developed resistance to drug after drug, so governments and organizations like the Bill and Melinda Gates Foundation are putting hundreds of millions of dollars into multi-pronged campaigns that include vaccine development and mosquito control.

Sleeping under a net treated with long-lasting insecticide is one of the simplest and cheapest ways to avoid the disease. In one week, in September 2006, the government and donor groups distributed 1.3 million of these to every child in the country between six months and five years old.

Through efforts like this, Rwanda has cut its number of malaria cases in half since 2000. Being a small country helps.

It's mid-afternoon on a Tuesday, but every roadside shop is closed: all the barbershops, the eateries, even the public phone offices. I reach the city stadium and see one end is full of people, but they're not watching a game. Half a dozen men and women are sitting behind desks, facing the crowd at that end of the field. I ask a soldier standing along the road what's going on.

"*Gacaca,*" he says.

When the killing was over, more than 120,000 accused *genocidaires* filled Rwanda's jails. It would take a century for the judicial system to handle all the cases, so in 2005 the traditional custom of public tribunals (*gacaca* means "justice on the grass") was revived to handle the bulk of the trials. Now accused criminals stand eye-to-eye with survivors and the families of victims. Volunteer judges hand down sentences of prison or community service; the country abolished the death penalty last month.

The system isn't perfect. No lawyers are involved, the judges have no legal training, and eyewitness testimony is often years old. But there's little other choice.

Gacacas are usually held outdoors to accommodate crowds. Kibuye's stadium is an especially fitting place, though. When the killing started, government officials across the country urged people to gather in churches, schools, and stadiums for safety. Many of the refuges became slaughterhouses. In Kibuye, a panicked crowd was told to take shelter in the stadium. The gates were locked. Days passed. Some people were so hungry they ate the grass. Then government soldiers, policemen, *interahamwe* militia, and armed civilians entered and surrounded the crowd. A gunshot cracked and a massacre began. The killers came back the next day to finish off survivors.

Today people are streaming quietly out of the stadium. Judgment day is over. Snack vendors are doing a brisk business by the gate, and shopkeepers are lifting their awnings up the street. Three women walk past with babies tied on their backs, tiny feet at each hip like gunslingers' pistols. Talking and laughing, they leave behind the stadium and the carefully tended field next to it, a cemetery with ten thousand unmarked graves.

There, you see—I promised to show you mountains that spit fire!"

Grogan and the five Watonga stood on a hilltop overlooking the great plain north of Lake Kivu. A thousand huts speckled the landscape. Men drove herds of goats and long-horned cattle down to the lakeshore. Hundreds of women worked in fields of peas, bananas, and millet, topless in the afternoon heat. It was the most fertile, prosperous, and crowded place on the continent that Grogan had seen yet.

Above everything rose the Virunga volcanoes, six black and olive cones that average 12,500 feet high. Grogan took the liberty of naming one Mount Eyres, after Gertrude's generous aunt. Another, formed just two years before by a violent eruption, he dubbed Mount Sharp. A third became Mount Watt. (The names didn't stick—a 1908 British survey map lists only the native names they are known by today: Mikeno, Kazene, and Visoke, respectively.)

Mount Götzen, the closest, was a monster spewing black

smoke into the sky. Fog swirled around its base, mixing with the smoke and the clouds and filtering the sunlight into patterns of white and gray.

The Watonga stared, speechless. They had never seen mountains this big, much less ones that lived and breathed.

Then Makanjira, Grogan's personal gun bearer, smiled. "You put them there!" The rest agreed, and Grogan couldn't persuade them otherwise.

In any case, it was the finest view he had ever seen. He stayed out, lost in thought, until the sun disappeared behind the hills and the moon rose to paint the lake silver.

It was going to be a long, waterless march over the seven-thousand-foot pass between Mount Götzen and Mount Eyres. Natives came to the camp by the hundreds to sell animals and produce, and the expedition bought all the supplies they could carry. Grogan insisted that everyone in the group have a gourd to carry water.

The trek seemed cursed from the start. The pitiless sun baked their throats and blistered their skin, white and black alike, and the men drained their gourds with alarming speed. The track grew rougher with every mile until it disappeared completely. Every step from then on had to be hacked through dense jungle with axes.

Just when they had dragged themselves to the top of the pass, an *askari* rushed up and said a group of locals had speared one of the expedition's herders and stolen thirty of their goats and sheep, one of their main sources of food. There was nothing Grogan could do.

They set up camp in an open glade on the flank of Mount Eyres. Grogan led ten men on a recon mission into the forest. Climbing along slippery tree trunks and hacking through fishnets of vines, they felt like rats crawling through an endless hedge. For hundreds of yards at a time their feet didn't touch the ground.

There were thornbushes waiting below if you slipped, and something even worse: ten-foot nettles covered with poisonous spines, which Grogan called "the most appalling creation that I have ever dreamed of." These vicious plants bristled with long, almost invisible needles that passed through skin, khaki, flannel—anything, in fact, but leather. The slightest touch caused a fiery pain that lingered for ten minutes.

His men gave up one by one, and eventually it was up to Grogan alone to cut trail through "mile upon mile of reeking forest, where the pungent sweat of hypertortured life drifts in a maze of liana-strangled trees." Every man was painted with mud and sweat and blood.

"Careful!" Grogan stopped short and threw out his arms. The men looked up and saw a taut cord leading up into the branches. A careful check showed that it ended at a spear attached to a heavy block of wood. It was an elephant trap set by pygmies. Another step and Grogan would have broken the cord and dropped the weighted point on their heads.

They began to see toppled trees and postholes in the forest floor. Crunching sticks and shifting shadows showed something immense through the jungle up ahead. Eighteen feet up, a wrinkled gray trunk wrapped around a tree as thick as a man's torso and snapped it like a celery stalk. A slow munching sound followed.

Then Grogan's third and final childhood goal, a bull elephant, was standing in front of him. Without a thought, he fired twice. The animal fell but was up again in an instant and crashing away through the forest.

How did an animal the size of a small cottage slip through

that merciless tangle so quickly? The jungle seemed to reknit behind it within seconds. Armed with an axe and rifle, Grogan followed the trail of blood.

Breezes stirred the leaves in every direction, making it impossible to stay downwind. In the stillness a breaking twig sounded like a gunshot. In this snarled vegetation the elephant could be yards away and still invisible.

Every few steps Grogan paused and held his breath to listen, fighting a growing desire to shoot, scream, do anything to break the unbearable silence. Every hour felt as if it aged him a year.

A shriek rang through the trees—just a monkey, but it left Grogan covered in cold sweat and gasping.

He heard a series of grunts, then an uproar rose somewhere through the trees. He hurried forward, certain it was the elephant rushing away again. But the noise became louder, and he realized the bull wasn't fleeing. It was coming straight for him.

He didn't dare move—he couldn't have run if he wanted—so he stopped and slowly cocked the double .500 Magnum.

The clamor grew and the forest shook. Then the branches overhead opened with a roar and he fired both barrels straight into the charging elephant's face.

Chapter Fifteen

Grogan awoke in a thornbush ten feet above the ground, covered with blood. His gun lay on the ground ten yards away.

He felt as if he'd been thrown from a speeding carriage. He could hear an uproar fading into the distance and frantic voices nearby. Dead? Someone was dead?

A head appeared in the leaves beside him. It was Zowanji, one of the bravest of his men. His face lit up when he saw that Grogan was still breathing. He helped him climb down.

To everyone's amazement, Grogan had suffered only a tweaked knee and a backside full of thorns. His gun was also covered with blood, even the inside of the barrels. But it was the elephant's, which was long gone. "I do not believe that I ever knew what real excitement was till I had crept quietly into the dim, dense, mysterious forest on the trail of a wounded elephant," Grogan wrote.

The group spent the night huddled naked in the rain around a fire at nine thousand feet. No clothes were apparently better than sopping wet ones. No one had had anything to eat or drink since dawn. The next day they staggered back to camp, half dead with fatigue. Grogan slept for fifteen hours straight.

Before they marched north to Lake Edward, Grogan wanted to investigate the area west of the volcanoes, up and over the western edge of the Great Rift Valley. The region was called Mushari, and people had been warning him against it for months.

To get there they would have to cross a sea of lava that an eruption two years before had spread across the west side of the valley. The surface was like broken glass, far too rough for cattle, so Sharp would have to stay behind with the animals and most of the party.

There was no water for dozens of miles in that direction. The best they could hope for was a purple liquid the locals made from banana palms, but even this was in short supply and expensive.

"You will all die of thirst," a village headman warned. "You will never get through. Turn back before it is too late."

Their first attempt, by skirting the lava beds to the north, ended in less than a day when their local guide disappeared with Grogan's axe. The next day they tried a more southerly route around Mount Götzen. Before they even left, the next guide they had hired tried to bolt as well.

When the fugitive was caught and brought back, he fell to his knees, begging Grogan not to make him go. The stones were like knives and would slice their feet to pieces, he said. There was no trail, and no food or water for two days. Even if they made it to Mushari, they would wish they hadn't. "They will eat us!" he wailed. "They eat everybody!"

Grogan wasn't convinced. He ordered his men to tie a rope around the man's neck. He couldn't risk getting lost in the lava field without a guide, he explained. To make up for the humiliation, he promised the man an extra payment when they were through.

The guide reluctantly led them into the dense forests of Mount Götzen. The men carrying the food and camp supplies became separated from the main party. Grogan and the rest of the party spent another miserable night in the rain, hungry and tentless.

The next day they were sitting down to eat when Grogan felt eyes on his back. "Turning round, I saw the hideous, distorted features of a pigmy leering at me in open-mouthed astonishment through the bush against which I was resting." When he realized he had been spotted, the pygmy dashed away, easily outrunning some of Grogan's men who tried to catch him.

The Twa (or Batwa) pygmies were the original inhabitants of the Great Lakes region of Burundi and Rwanda, pushed aside and subjugated by the Hutu and Tutsi cultures that arrived later. Other European travelers had reported that pygmies were hostile to strangers, but Grogan never had a problem with them. They had no farms or villages, the natives said, but lived free in the forests, where they gathered honey and hunted elephants. They traded meat and honey for grain from other tribes.

Grogan was impressed with how tough and quick they were. To him they seemed a perfect example of Darwin's theory of natural selection, published forty years earlier. "It is curious to notice how perfectly adapted they are to the surroundings in which they live; the combination of immense strength necessary for the precarious hunting-life they lead, and of compactness, indispensable to rapid movement in dense forest, where the pig-runs are the only means of passage, is a wonderful example of nature's adaptability."

The food and water soon ran out, and Grogan had to turn the group back again. On their return, he set fire to the empty hut of the first guide who had deserted them, "a punishment that he richly deserved."

Guides were abruptly in short supply. Sharp wondered aloud whether they should just keep going north.

In his notes, Grogan recorded his frustrations with the natives and his men, who seemed to be having a contest to come up with the scariest rumors of lava and cannibals.

Finally he had had enough. "If we'd listened to a fraction of the twaddle we've been told we'd have abandoned our trip long ago," he barked. "Lies, lies, lies, I was sick to death of them," he wrote, "and resolved to go to Mushari by the direct route, cost what it might."

That meant straight across the blackened moonscape. Grogan picked twelve men and ordered them to make sandals and gather two days' worth of food and water. On the morning they were to leave, the unlucky dozen limped up, leaning on sticks and insisting they were too sick to go. None had sandals or supplies.

Unmoved, Grogan led them to the lava's edge. Sunlight shattered across volcanic boulders with edges like razors. The air was gluey with heat. The men wept, certain they were being led to a slow and certain death.

Grogan took a step onto the lava, and suddenly "the whole scene changed. Beads were produced, natives with sandals for sale brought forth, guides sprang up in bewildering plenty, and, as I had half suspected, I found there was a well-used track across."

Troops in camouflage uniforms march single file along the road to Gisenyi, each one carrying either a machine gun or a mortar. The bus is still an hour from the northern tip of Lake Kivu, where Grogan's men had marveled at the mountains that breathed fire.

"I was in the army." The man next to me looks out the window. The line of men seems like it will never end. "For five years." He has a sparse mustache and a V-shaped frown that reminds me of Ice Cube. His name is Innocent, and his voice is so quiet I have to lean in to hear him talk.

In 1993, he joined the Rwandan Patriotic Front, the rebel force of Tutsi exiles that eventually toppled the Hutu government and ended the genocide. During the civil war that preceded the genocide, his unit fought in the north around the Virunga volcanoes.

"Did you ever see a gorilla?" I suppose it's not the most inane thing I could ask. Straddling the intersection of Rwanda, Uganda, and the Democratic Republic of the Congo, the Virungas are home to half the world's seven hundred or so remaining mountain gorillas.

"Oh, yes, when I was in army in the forest. We were protecting them."

No one knows exactly how many mountain gorillas were killed in the crossfire when Hutu and Tutsi troops clashed on the bamboo-covered slopes. The headquarters of Rwanda's Volcanoes National Park was left in ruins.

Innocent left the army in 1998. Now he works as an accountant for a secondary school in Ruhengeri, the park's gateway town. He sounds more proud of this than his time as a soldier. He's going to visit his sister to give her money for college.

Here in northern Rwanda, the countryside has gone from fertile to downright fecund. A checkerboard of fields covers every available surface, down to the narrow strips between houses. Women hoe the dark earth and goats make spastic leaps near walls of pitted volcanic stone. A bicycle rolls downhill laden with a bundle of sugarcane the size of an outhouse, and the medicinal smell of eucalyptus floats through the windows.

We pass a small city of white plastic tents, where a crowd waits outside prefab buildings marked TOILETS. White Land Rovers bear the side-door labels of the UNHCR, the UN's agency for refugees. It's a refugee camp for people from the Congo, Innocent says, the smallest of five around here.

Gisenyi sits on the border of the Democratic Republic of the Congo, the latest incarnation of the region once known as the Belgian Congo, then Zaire. When we arrive, Innocent offers to show me the lakeshore. I follow him through town, past the Hotel Dian Fossey and the Che Guevara Beauty Parlor, to a wide beach under an overcast sky. The white sand is empty except for two women sweeping up leaves and a guard lounging in front of a luxury hotel with a rifle over his shoulder. On weekends, tourists, expats, and rich Rwandans fill the city's vacation villas and private clubs.

"Nyiragongo is there." Innocent points into the clouds to the northwest, where the volcano, Grogan's Mount Götzen, looms ten miles away like an angry parent. Across the border two miles down the shore is the Congolese city of Goma.

It would be hard to find a more miserable place. Originally developed as a posh resort for Belgian colonialists, Goma has been torn by fighting and crammed with refugees continually since the 1990s.

In 2002, the volcano erupted and sent rivers of molten rock through the city. The main stream of lava followed the border almost exactly—on the Congolese side. Gisenyi was spared, but over half of Goma was destroyed, including two of its four hospitals and a third of the airport runway.

"You could walk faster than the lava," Innocent says. "Not many people were killed."

War and lava aren't the only things people have to fear here. Geologic activity has saturated Lake Kivu's deep, cold waters with dissolved methane and carbon dioxide like a huge can of soda. A large enough disturbance (say, a volcanic eruption) could release huge clouds of deadly gases that would gather invisibly on the surface.

In 1986, a similar lake in Cameroon released enough carbon dioxide to smother seventeen hundred people in their sleep. Kivu is almost two thousand times larger, with 2 million people living near its shores.

We walk back up into the city and stop at a restaurant near the bus station for lunch. The buffet is heavy on the starches, rice, and cassava and potatoes, along with small dried fish and chunks of meat in some kind of red sauce.

"I want to start my own accounting business," Innocent says, popping the top on a can of Coke. "But it is difficult—you have to pay so much just to live. I say I have a job, but I only earn a little." Over half of his monthly wage of $160 goes toward rent.

"Do you think it would be safe for me to go to Goma?" I ask, changing the subject from money.

Grogan's route around the volcanoes entered this corner of the Democratic Republic of the Congo, now the province of North Kivu, and right now that's one of the most dangerous places in Africa.

After King Leopold II's disastrous rule, the Congo was administered by the Belgian government for the next sixty-three years. Then came two and a half decades as the country of Zaire, personal kleptocracy of the dictator Mobutu Sese Seko, who amassed a personal fortune estimated at $5 billion while his subjects foundered in poverty.

Rwanda's ethnic conflict crossed the border during and after the genocide. In 1997, Zaire renamed itself the Democratic Republic of the Congo just in time to be invaded by troops from

Rwanda and Uganda with an eye on its vast mineral wealth. The turmoil eventually drew in almost every neighboring country.

Despite allegedly free elections in the DRC last year, "Africa's Civil War" still grinds along with a body count of over 5 million, more than any conflict since World War II.

This summer, most of the conflict has been in North Kivu province, where fighting between government troops and rebel forces has displaced hundreds of thousands of refugees. It's hard to tell the players even with a scorecard: the DRC army, UN peacekeepers, and Hutu and Tutsi groups from Rwanda are all involved. Violence against civilians is epidemic, including rape, torture, murder, and the kidnapping of child soldiers.

This will probably be my only chance to enter the actual Congo. But is it worth it? On top of the fighting, I'm almost a week behind schedule.

Innocent advises against it. "It is not safe. All the people will see you and think you have money."

He offers to pay for lunch, but I insist on covering my half. He wishes me luck and leaves to find his sister. I need to get online, to check in with Laura and see if there's anything in the news to help me figure out what to do.

I have a problem trusting my instincts. I tend to think decisions to death, even when I'm not procrastinating. Especially with big life changes, my usual method involves picking the least unappealing option—nothing binding, just keep it in mind—and then, six or nine or twelve months later, if no better alternative has appeared, go for it.

It works well enough when the choices only involve yourself and things like buying a mountain bike, moving cross-country, or going to grad school. Not so much in a relationship.

As Laura and I grew closer, my instincts started to yank me in opposite directions. She would make a great lifelong partner—that was increasingly obvious—probably more so than anyone I'd ever met. Yet my tension increased in direct proportion to her appeal.

At first I chalked it up to the different ways in which we weren't perfectly compatible: the everyday burrs and annoyances, the sore spots and sensitive topics. But I gradually came to see it wasn't just that I was afraid of being unhappy—I was, but in a more profound way I was worried about being happy.

Every one of my previous relationships had been a roller coaster, or else I'd turned it into one—painful, sometimes, yes, but at least not boring. I conflated contentment with stagnation, discontent with progress. I was scared of being satisfied.

The realization didn't make the problem any easier to solve, but it was a start. Being aware of the emotional moat I instinctively kept in place was the first step to breaching it.

One evening we were walking home to my apartment after dinner in Adams Morgan. Recent rain had left the streets shining darkly and the air warm and moist. We reached my block, where my well-worn Volvo was parked.

"Son of a *bitch*." The passenger-side window had been smashed in, the second time this year. I'd already had two bikes stolen. All I needed was a mugging to complete the D.C. crime trifecta.

I slumped on the couch in the apartment. "God, I hate this place." It was my mantra lately. Work was getting boring, fast. Washington was starting to feel like an angry city, with only moderate rewards that didn't outweigh its high hassle factor.

"Aw." Laura patted my knee. "No, I know, it sucks."

"I need to get out of here." The urge to go west, again, had been building since the day I arrived. A few years ago it would have been simple: quit my job, pack up, and drive toward the sunset. Find freelance work, volunteer somewhere, go back to school. Reboot my life as I'd done half a dozen times before. Now it wasn't just my life, though.

"Tell me about it," she said. I knew she loved her job, but after three years there she felt like she'd hit a ceiling. Quitting and doing the same work as a contractor might be the best way to advance her career at this point.

"No, seriously. I need—*we* need to get out of here."

"But we've never even lived together." She was right. Neither of us had ever lived with a partner, let alone each other. I changed the subject.

A few days later we were instant messaging at work. Laura had just learned that her landlords weren't going to renew her lease. She would have to find a new place by next month.

I had another half a year on my lease. If this relationship was going anywhere, literally or figuratively, it would never happen without a dry run.

Why don't you move in with me?

The pause before her reply was longer than usual.

Really?

Yeah. It makes sense. No use paying two rents. Then, realizing that might sound too businesslike, I added, *We should do it for the right reasons. Not just to save money.*

Let me think about it.

The biggest Internet café in Gisenyi has four computers and a baby-blue clock shaped like a cat with a bow tie on the wall. Waiting for Hotmail to load, I open Laura's next red envelope. *I never tell you how special you are, how I love watching you sleeping in bed in the mornings.* A photo of me holding a friend's baby is captioned, *Now this is hot!*

A young man in a baseball hat is at the next computer. Valentin is originally from the Congo. He came to Rwanda in 1994, at age nine—what a year to immigrate—and his mother was killed in the genocide. He works at a hotel in Ruhengeri and speaks five languages: English, French, German, Swahili, and Kinyarwanda.

"German is the hardest."

I notice he's emailing someone at the University of Virginia. His girlfriend, he says.

"How do you say 'I would like to send you my hug'? 'I would like to hug my arms around you'?"

"Not really. How about just 'I miss you'?"

An email from Laura tops my inbox. *Can you send your detailed itinerary (as much as you can) for northern Uganda and Sudan? It'll make me feel a little better. I'm behind you 100% in whatever you decide to do, but the instability just really scares—ok, no, I'm going to be blunt, it terrifies me. I'm saying this out of love and being a team, working together.*

Sideways smiley faces end every paragraph, but today they look nervous somehow.

I can't wait till you're home. You're my best friend—the one I can tell anything, the one that makes me feel better, the one who makes me laugh, who makes my days special.

The website of the UN peacekeeping mission to the DRC is full of bad news about the fighting in North Kivu province. With more than seventeen thousand soldiers and a budget of $1.3 billion a year, it's the largest mission of its kind in the world.

Travel advisories from the U.S. and British governments are even more hysterical. One newspaper headline reads, "Congo

Candidate Calls for Calm, Denies Cannibalism." The BBC's top Africa story is about a photojournalist who was just killed in Goma.

That's it. No to the Congo—it's just not worth it. Years ago I probably would have tried. The longer I follow Grogan's trail, though, the more I can see how different our motivations are. He came to prove himself to Gertrude's stepfather and to make his mark in the world, and was willing to risk his life to do it.

I'm here to prove something, too, but not to Laura's father. To myself. Maybe to Laura, too. What it is, I'm not exactly sure. I do know that nothing else matters if I don't get home safe.

North it is, then, to Uganda and Sudan, as far as I can go in the time I have left. But no stupid risks.

As he picked his way through the topography of lava, Grogan thought of glaciers. Specifically, the shattered one on the northwest side of the Aiguille du Dru, near Chamonix, that he traversed as a teenager on his way to climb the peak. Those summers in Switzerland seemed impossibly remote, like a story someone had once told him.

This hellscape was the inverse of the Alps, broiling black instead of frigid white. A misstep meant an ugly gash on serrated stone instead of a thousand-foot plunge or an icy death at the bottom of a crevasse. The going was slow, barely half a mile an hour. Charred tree trunks and the bones of elephants jutted from the surface. The violent eruption had left huge holes in the surrounding forests, which were already starting to fill back in with ferns.

Grogan took another swig from his canteen and wondered how Sharp was doing. His partner was leading the main body of the expedition on a circuitous route around the lava to meet him in Mushari. Whatever he encountered, it couldn't possibly be this awful.

To everyone's relief, the party made it across the lava in four hours without incident. In camp that night, Grogan poked fun at his men, asking how many had perished as they had predicted. "My inquiry as to the death-rate caused much merriment, and the evening passed with howls of joy and those unearthly noises which in Africa pass current for song."

The laughter stopped when stooping figures began to shuffle out of the darkness into the firelight. They were refugees from Mushari. Cannibals from the Baleka tribe had raided their country, they said, destroying their crops and livestock and hunting them down like animals. Those who weren't killed and eaten were starving by the hundreds every day.

The true horrors began the next day. Dead bodies lined the fourteen-mile path around the base of the new volcano. In the afternoon they came across a group of Africans huddled in misery among the boulders along a river. They had been there for six months, they said, too terrified even to make a fire. When they couldn't stand the hunger any longer, they would sprint into the fields for whatever half-ripe grain they could grab. Every time, the Baleka would capture a few and drag them away. Grogan gave the natives beans to eat and lay awake that night wondering what he was getting into.

Few things have done more to bolster the image of "savage" Africa as cannibalism. Even though it occurred from the Americas to the Pacific, eating other people had become one of the continent's most enduring—and destructive—stereotypes long before Grogan arrived.

"Nothing can exceed the terror in which cannibal nations are held by other African tribes," David Livingstone wrote thirty years before Grogan's journey. The specifics are still under debate, but many tribes in the Congo undeniably did consume human flesh at least through the end of the nineteenth century. They did it for a variety of reasons: to absorb the power of strong leaders or enemies, to keep evil spirits from haunting the living, to mark important occasions, or simply to utilize a readily available source of protein.

European explorers, missionaries, and travelers reported lurid details. Human meat was said to be the most delicious of all, and men supposedly tasted better than women. "All [cannibal tribes] agree in saying that human flesh is saltish, and needs but little condiment," Livingstone wrote (although, as one African told him, "it makes one dream of the dead man"). The meat was always boiled or roasted, sometimes with bananas, and occasionally buried for a few days to ripen first.

The Congo was notorious for its cannibal markets, where potential buyers eyed lines of slaves and captives, each one marked with clay to advertise the choicest cuts. Victims were often fattened up before being butchered, their legs broken to keep them from fleeing.

Europeans certainly weren't the most objective eyewitnesses. Many writers made it sound as if human flesh were the equivalent of fish on Friday for everyone south of the Sahara. Others went further: on one of Stanley's expeditions, James Jameson, heir to an Irish whiskey fortune, bought an eleven-year-old girl so he could sketch her being dismembered and eaten. Cannibalism sold books, but it also reinforced the prevailing view that Africa's native cultures were brutal and primitive and needed to be "civilized," which translated as converted and exploited. In places like King Leopold's Congo, cannibalism was used to justify almost any atrocity in the process.

In the morning, Grogan led the men into the uplands of Mushari, every sense on high alert. It was beautiful country, with fields of banana trees and rust-colored grain melting into rolling purple hills and a dark band of jungle.

Along the trail they saw torn sacks spilling drifts of grain. Then the dark stains of dried blood, then skulls and skeletons. A slow cyclone of vultures spun overhead.

Back among the volcanoes, Grogan had assumed that the tales of cannibals in Mushari were overblown, like so many of the warnings he had heard. The Baleka were probably exaggerated bogeymen, and the fighting some routine intertribal squabble.

Now he realized the locals had been telling the truth.

They topped a ridge and heard shrieks coming from a nearby hill. A line of figures was streaming toward them, spear points dancing.

"What do they want?" he asked his guide.

The man looked at him. Wasn't it obvious?

"They are coming to eat us."

PART III

A journey is like marriage. The certain way to be wrong is to think you control it.

—*John Steinbeck*

Chapter Sixteen

I step over an earthworm as fat as my middle finger, coiled like a loop of intestine on the yellow bamboo leaves. We've been climbing the plant-choked slope of Mount Sabinyo, the volcano Grogan tried to name after Gertrude, for half an hour. In places we have to scramble on all fours through soggy tunnels of green. The odors of flowers mingle with the musk of decay.

I'm about to see one of the rarest animals in the world, something my grandchildren will probably only read about in books. I'm half-expecting to hear distant drumbeats and people chanting *"Kong."*

Elie Musabyimana, a ranger with the Parc National des Volcans, leads the way in a dark green jacket and black military boots. Next is a guard armed with a serious expression and an AK-47, then our group of eight visitors. Another rifle-toting guard brings up the rear.

We had come before dawn from Ruhengeri in northern Rwanda at the base of the volcanoes. Two hours earlier at the guard station, Elie gathered us under a tree and explained the setup. We were going to see the Hirwa group of gorillas, one of seven in Rwanda that have been habituated to visitors.

"Hirwa means 'lucky.'" He smiled. "Lucky gorillas, lucky

tourists." It can take hours to find a family group by following its trail from the previous day's location. Sometimes the trackers can't find them at all. In that case, tough luck. No refunds.

We must stay seven meters away, not because the gorillas are dangerous, but because they're susceptible to many of the same diseases we are, and they have no natural immunity. To illustrate, there's a long wooden ruler on the ground with a pair of boots nailed to one end and a little carved gorilla at the other. If they approach you, that's all right, as long as you cover your mouth when you sneeze or cough.

No smoking or eating, obviously. If you absolutely have to relieve yourself, tell him or one of the trackers and they'll show you where to go.

Don't point or stare at the gorillas; they interpret both as signs of aggression. And if you're charged, don't run. It's almost always a bluff.

During his time on the volcanoes, Grogan came across the skeleton of a gigantic ape, larger than any primate he had ever seen. He never spotted a live gorilla, although the natives assured him they were everywhere, "and were a great source of annoyance to the villages, being in the habit of carrying off stray women."

It's a shame, because just three years later a German officer, Captain Oscar von Beringe, became the first European to see a mountain gorilla, at ninety-three hundred feet on this very peak.

We follow Elie up the muddy track through dense groves of bamboo like green plastic lampposts, and chest-high thickets of thornbushes and ferns. Sabinyo's serrated peak (the word means "old man's teeth") looks like a bite taken out of the sky. Its summit marks the intersection of Uganda, Rwanda, and the DRC, the heart of mountain gorilla country. Or at least what's left of it.

Less than seven hundred mountain gorillas survive today in an area the size of Connecticut. About half live here in the Virungas. The other half are twenty-five miles north in another small national park in Uganda.

I grab a vine to haul myself up a steep section of trail. I'm dripping with sweat and the misty rain that can't decide whether to stay or go. We're each paying five hundred dollars to spend an hour with the gorillas. That's eight dollars a minute. What else costs that much, I wonder, as I scramble for a handhold. A doctor? A lawyer? A high-end hooker?

All three countries are planning to raise the fee a hundred dollars a year until it reaches a thousand dollars. And people will pay it.

By the time I catch up with Elie, I'm panting almost too hard to talk. "Do you do this every day?"

"Yes, seven days a week." He's not even winded. "We have two days off every month. After a tough one they give you an easy hike." He's been a guide for four years, after studying animal husbandry. And he's getting married in December.

"I'll beat you by two months—we're in October."

"Maybe you can invite me to your wedding." He laughs. "Will you bring her here?"

This is the kind of thing Laura and I bonded over: outdoor exertion, often in another country, ideally involving animals. She would love this; she'd practically skip up these slopes, earthworms and all.

"Have you ever been charged by a silverback?"

"Oh yes. Many times."

"Hurt?" He hesitates. It's his job to reassure visitors.

"Once a silverback seized me here." He grabs my left bicep. "He threw me into the trees."

The Baleka warriors sprinted toward Grogan and his six men, howling with fury. He waited behind a clump of grass until the cannibals were almost upon them. Then he stood up and opened fire.

Six Baleka fell and the rest scattered, stunned by the rapid firing. The only guns they had seen were the slow muzzle-loading rifles of the Arab slavers.

Grogan led the group forward. Every village they came to was a smoking ruin humming with flies. It was too much to process all at once. He could only record individual images, like flashbulb photos of a murder scene:

"A bunch of human entrails drying on a stick."

"A skeleton with the skin on lying in the middle of the huts."

"A pot of soup with bright yellow fat."

"A gnawed forearm, raw."

"A head, one cheek eaten, the other charred; hair burnt, and scalp cut off at top of forehead like the peel of an orange; one eye removed, presumably eaten, the other glaring."

"A howling baby."

"A head, with a spoon left sticking in the brains."

In the heat the stench was beyond description. "It was a scene that made one wonder if there be a God."

They fled, and the Baleka followed.

The next days were the worst of Grogan's life. "Rapid movements alone could save us from annihilation, and we traveled from sunrise to sunset, camping in patches of forest, and concealing our route by leaving the paths and forcing our way through the grass." The men were ragged with exhaustion, but fear of a night attack kept everyone awake.

The region's beauty was a dreamlike backdrop to the carnage. They passed "wild stretches of undulating hills, streaked with forest and drained by a hundred streams, each with its cargo of bloated corpses." Vultures spun gracefully through the sky. "Flights of gorgeous butterflies floated here and there, and, settling on the gruesome relics, gave a finishing touch to the horrors."

He later estimated the cannibals had razed three thousand square miles of well-watered country. "Not so much as a sweet potato, which grow almost as weeds, was left." Thousands of people had died in the massacres and the resulting famine. They could smell every defiled settlement long before they reached it.

On the edge of a papyrus swamp, the party captured a Baleka woman with two boys and a girl. They were starving and terrified. "Things are very hard with us," the woman said. "There are fifty people in our party and in the last week, our men have only been able to catch two people." She offered to help Grogan find the rest of her group. She led them through a patch of dense, tall grass. As Grogan turned a corner in the path, his guide bolted past in the other direction, half a dozen Baleka warriors on his heels.

Grogan sprang to one side, dodging a spear, and shot one of the cannibals through the heart. The others ran. He chased them to their encampment in a banana grove, but they disappeared into the grass. The remains of two victims were still simmering in the pots. Baskets of grain lay on the ground, but even though his men were suffering from dysentery and famished, they refused to touch "so much as a yam growing in that accursed ground."

It took them five days to march back to the volcanoes, with nothing but green bananas and a few pumpkins to eat. In a brief encounter the next day, a timid guide surprised everyone by rushing in and spearing a cannibal in the chest. It was the last they saw of the Baleka, aside from their miserable prisoners. The skulls and scorched bones trailed on for miles.

"This was the Congo Free State," Grogan wrote with disgust. He was all for orderly colonization as practiced by England, Germany, and France, where trained men surveyed the land and European settlers arrived in a carefully planned manner, ideally with minimal bloodshed.

But in the Congo, the brutal tactics of Belgian administrators, combined with decades of raids by Arab slavers, had set the stage for abominations like this.

As he hurried down out of the highlands, Grogan's anxieties turned to Sharp. If he couldn't warn his partner soon, the caravan could be ambushed and destroyed by the cannibals. He pushed on with a growing fear he might be too late.

In the forests near the volcano, Grogan met an elderly pygmy with a beard down to his chest, "squat, gnarled, proud, and easy of carriage." He told them a white man with many belongings had passed by two days before en route to the lakeshore, where he was camped. ("These people must have a wonderful code of signs and signals," Grogan marveled, "as, despite their isolated and nomadic existence, they always know exactly what is happening everywhere.")

Thank God—Sharp was safe. Grogan sent two of his men running with an urgent note telling his partner to stay put: CANNIBALS IN MUSHARI. DANGEROUS TO PROCEED. HAVE HAD A HELL OF A TIME.

Rumors filter down the line: the gorillas are fifteen minutes away. Ten minutes. Five.

"We leave our packs here," Elie says. The slope is steeper than ever now, corrugated with roots, but it isn't just the exertion making my heart pound.

The trackers start clearing their throats loudly. "They are saying, 'Here we come, it's okay.'"

We top a slanting ridge and look down into a wide valley filled with thick vegetation. Fifty yards away, a black bundle sits in the crook of a tree, rattling the branches in a tantrum. It looks like an infant in a wooly snowsuit. The baby gorilla hangs by one stubby arm for a moment, then tumbles to the ground and scampers into the undergrowth.

"See the bebbie? He has six months."

A female gorilla lies on a bed of leaves, nursing an infant with bright black eyes. She holds the baby with a graceful strength, somehow cradling and manhandling it at the same time.

The silverback male sits veiled in greenery, a scowling linebacker with maroon eyes and man-boobs. He faces sideways, glancing at us out of the corner of one eye, plucking at leaves with hands like hockey gloves. He yawns to reveal the nastiest set of canines I've ever seen on a vegetarian.

Every time the group moves, the trackers grunt or make a low hooting as a heads-up. Half the time the silverback answers.

The tree climber re-appears and starts tussling with another female. He's wider than he is high, all thighs and forearms. She pushes him away and he rolls down the slope, then clambers back up for more, panting and grinning.

When he saw his first mountain gorillas in 1902, the German officer Beringe did what any naturalist or explorer of his time would have: he shot them. Two fell "with much noise" into a canyon, and it took five hours with ropes to haul one out. Bringing back a specimen was the only way to prove an animal existed. And what difference could killing a few make?

A century later, mountain gorillas are one of the ten most endangered species on earth. Females bear just one infant every four to eight years, and only half make it to their first birthday. They're in what biologists call a population bottleneck: even if the species does survive, it has already lost much of the genetic diversity that is key to surviving in an unpredictable world.

A restaurant in Ruhengeri had a sign painted on one wall: "Given peace, gorillas bring in currency." It's true: each animal is worth thousands of dollars every year, simply by existing. Gorilla tourism is Rwanda's third-largest source of foreign revenue after coffee and tea. Even though 5 percent of the money and three-quarters of the jobs go to local villagers, people keep clearing the forests for farms and firewood, often out of desperation, and apes are maimed or killed by snares set by poachers after other animals.

Visitors had only been trickling back into Rwanda for a few years when, in 1999, Hutu rebels kidnapped fourteen foreign gorilla tourists in Uganda, just across the border. After forcing them to march for days, they killed eight with clubs and machetes.

Tourists are safe in the Virungas for now, at least in Uganda and Rwanda. (Nobody is going to the DRC.) But more than one hundred rangers have been killed in the Virungas in the past decade by poachers, soldiers, and militia. And this year is turning into the worst for the gorillas since Dian Fossey started studying them in the 1960s. Six have been killed already. In the DRC's Virunga National Park, rangers recently found the bodies of two silverbacks who had been dismembered and partially eaten. A female was found shot in the back of the head. Her infant was still clinging to the body.

The execution-style killings were meant to send a message,

though it's not clear from whom. Hutu rebels? Local farmers, jealous of the land set aside for the animals? Hunters desperate for food, or profiteers in the illegal charcoal trade, with their eyes on the protected forests?

At least the Hirwa group is safe, for now. It's the newest in the park, formed just last year by members of three other family groups.

Our hour is almost up. We're all gawking like babies; so much for not staring. By now some of the gorillas are just ten feet away. Every so often Elie or one of the trackers tells someone to move back slowly or get out of a gorilla's way, but most of the time they just smile with a custodial pride.

Time evaporates. As a biologist and travel writer, I've had my share of wildlife close encounters, enchanting and otherwise: nuzzled by sea lions; pooped on by penguins; swarmed by hammerhead sharks; bluff-charged by grizzly bears.

This is something else entirely. It feels like we're not exactly welcome, just grudgingly endured.

Yet it's their entire existence that's tenuous, on these forested islands in a sea of farms and people. A fragile peace among the ferns. It's magic.

Every time the enchantment gets too thick, one lets loose with a fart like an air horn.

"We have two minutes." Elie and the trackers start to herd everyone back toward the trail. The guards stand up stiffly and sling their rifles on their shoulders. Clouds are moving in.

The silverback watches us go with a sidelong look that seems equal parts bored, grumpy, and sad. What is he thinking? Probably relief that we're leaving. Even habituated gorillas tend to cluster around silverbacks and spend more time looking around and moving away when people are around—all signs of stress.

I'm guessing he's aware something isn't right and hasn't been for a long time. The world has changed drastically in his lifetime: less forest, more people, some friendly, most not.

He couldn't possibly know that every one of his kind would barely fill a large theater, that there are probably far too few left for the species to survive—that by now it's just a matter of time.

Could he?

CHAPTER SEVENTEEN

After a relieved reunion on the lakeshore, Grogan and Sharp turned north again on June 26, 1899. They left the volcanoes behind and entered the wide valley of the Rutchuru River, which led fifty miles to Lake Edward. After the vine-choked slopes and the terrors of Mushari, the open space that spread before them was sweet relief.

A herd of elephants sailed through the sea of grass that filled the valley. With their huge flapping ears and swaying gait, both legs on each side moving together, the animals reminded Grogan of an old print of the Spanish Armada.

When he was done marveling at the procession, Grogan shot one. It was his first confirmed elephant kill, and his last childhood goal accomplished.

The porters gathered in a circle around the carcass, chanting a song in the animal's honor. Each threw a handful of grass on its side to show respect. They refused to eat the meat, as did the locals.

As an experiment, Grogan simmered a section of the trunk for half a day. The taste was passable, but the blackened, bristly skin and the two rubbery tubes down the middle killed his appetite. He offered the trunk to the cannibals they had taken pris-

oner. (A few more had joined the woman and three children.)
The Baleka devoured it.

Away from their horde, the Baleka weren't so terrifying. Between them they wore "one string of beads, half a dozen wire
bracelets, and a human tooth as a pendant to a necklace of elephant hair." They did smell like death, though. Grogan produced a large block of soap and ordered them to bathe in every
available stream.

His men resented how much of the party's food the prisoners
ate. When two elderly cannibals went missing one night, Grogan shrugged and ordered the expedition forward.

They walked through the grasslands for three days, past
bone-white salt pans and the occasional candelabra euphorbia, a
poisonous, cactuslike plant. One of Grogan's feet began to hurt,
but he couldn't afford to let the others see him limping. At the
southern end of Lake Edward they bought fish from the natives
who lived in the reeds along the shore along with thousands of
geese, storks, and pelicans.

When Grogan took off his boots, he found the skin on one
heel had been sandpapered off. The lingering fever had wrecked
his immune system, and the foot became badly infected. "When
I pushed my finger into the swelling, it left a cavity which did
not swell out again for some minutes."

Grogan was forced to ride in the hammock again as they continued up the eastern shore of the lake. The foot finally healed,
thanks to—or despite—a nightly regimen of permanganate of
potash soaks and poultices of Elliman's Universal Embrocation.

The explorers took careful measurements of the shoreline,
bays, and adjoining hills. They were the first to map this side
of the lake, and soon realized that it was much smaller than it
appeared on current maps. The shallow water seethed with hun-

dreds of hippos, and the beaches steamed with piles of dung. At night their grunts and bellows made sleeping difficult.

They passed native villages with plots of dwarf-banana plants and canoes of fiber-sewn planks bobbing among the reeds. Dense tracts of jungle showed where rivers flowed toward the lake to meet in vast marshlands. Geysers shot columns of steam into the air. Sometimes they saw log scaffolds that held heavy weights attached to spearheads pointing downward. These were hippo traps, designed to impale by force of gravity when they were triggered.

One chief offered to sell Grogan a large elephant tusk. First, he insisted, they must become blood brothers. The expedition's headman, serving as Grogan's proxy, sat down opposite a man representing the chief's tribe. Both men were given small pieces of raw meat to hold. An elderly native called down evil on anyone who broke the pledge they were about to make: "May hippopotami run against him; may leopards tear him by night; may hunger and thirst gripe him; may his women be barren; may his children wither, even as the grass withers; may crocodiles rend him; may lions howl round his couch by night; may elephants crush him."

The master of ceremonies made a small cut in each man's chest and rubbed the meat in the flowing blood, then gave it to the other to eat. "You taste our blood and we taste yours," the chief explained. "Then we are always friends." Guns roared into the sky and the ritual was over.

Grogan reciprocated by teaching the chief to shake hands. He pointed to the British flag rippling in the breeze. Wherever the tribe saw this cloth, he said, they could count on being received as friends and treated fairly.

They were near the northern end of Lake Edward when

Grogan's malaria flared up again, worse than it had in months. Sharp stayed by his bed round the clock, dosing him with quinine. Racked by chills and drenched with sweat, Grogan twisted and howled, hallucinating that all the animals he had ever killed were coming back for revenge. He was convinced he was dying.

"Nonsense." Sharp said. "You're not dying. You're going to live. But you must fight the fever. Fight, man, fight!"

The thermometer reached a staggering 108.4 degrees. Any higher and brain damage or death was virtually guaranteed. It might already be too late.

At one point Grogan bolted upright in bed. His fingernails were blue and his eyes were on fire.

"Elephants! Elephants! They're charging!" he shrieked, and collapsed.

Look!" Sam points to a dark gray shape in the trees as we flash past. A broad, leathery forehead lifts at the roar of the motorcycle. Bat-wing ears track us like radar dishes.

Yes, elephant, great, I think. *Now please, eyes ahead, two hands on the handlebars.* I'm crammed so close against his backside I feel like I should buy him a drink. The dirt road to Katwe is rocky and furrowed, and at the moment I'm more interested in staying upright and uninjured than watching wildlife.

Lake Edward's southeast shoreline, where Grogan writhed in feverish dementia, is now part of Queen Elizabeth National Park, the most popular game reserve in Uganda. So few people visit the southern part, where we are, that there wasn't even a sign when we drove in early this morning.

We're heading for the park's main entrance, near Katwe at the northern end of the lake. Five days ago I crossed into Uganda, whose southern end is as fertile and folded as Rwanda. Every day involves a different vehicle: motorcycle, bus, pickup truck. The map is a varicose tangle of red and blue back roads. I have to start writing the names of towns on my hand to remember which comes next: Kisoro, Kabale, Kihihi.

I hired Sam at the hotel last night. After picking me up this morning, he stopped by a small office in Kihihi and ran inside. A tall man about my age came out and introduced himself as Gideon Orombi, director of the Stay Safe from AIDS Children's Organization. Sam was the project coordinator.

"We are trying to take care of six hundred AIDS orphans in Kihihi," Gideon said. "Those are just the ones we have registered. There are many more."

The AIDS epidemic has left almost 12 million children in sub-Saharan Africa missing one or both parents. Ten percent of these orphans are in Uganda.

"We are trying to raise money, teach them crafts, and organize a drumming group." Gideon's deep voice was full of pride. He explained how they were trying to slow the spread of the disease in the community.

"Circumcision is very important." (Circumcised men are less likely to have HIV and don't pass it on as often.) "It's cultural. Only two tribes practice it, out of sixty-two. I am from the east—I am circumcised."

I nod, as if hearing a stranger talk about his foreskin before breakfast is the most natural thing in the world.

"I should be infected," he says.

"Why?" Is it my turn to share next?

"I was exposed. I have had many tests, but they all came back negative."

Uganda is a rare example of an African country fighting

AIDS and HIV successfully. In the 1990s, prevention and education campaigns helped cut infection rates of the "slim disease" by two-thirds. Last year they started to rise again. Some blame it on a shift from a proven approach, combining abstinence, monogamy, and condoms, toward abstinence-only programs backed by the U.S. government.

Yesterday I saw a billboard with a photo of a smug, successful-looking older man with the caption, "Would you let this man be with your teenage daughter? So why are you with his? Cross Generations Sex stops with you."

It was part of a nationwide campaign against "sugar daddies," older men who sleep with younger women in exchange for gifts and money, spreading the disease. One story in wide circulation told of a university student whose friend convinced her to meet a sugar daddy in his car behind her dorm one night. Climbing into the Mercedes, she found her father sitting behind the wheel.

Sam emerged from the office and climbed on the bike. Gideon asked where we were going. "Katwe," Sam said.

"On that?" Gideon said. I've been here long enough to learn to pay attention when locals raise their eyebrows about something logistical. It's like a Sherpa saying, "You're going to climb that?"

The hills melted into flat savannah as we neared the lake. Now the way forward is a tan line through thorny brush that seems to stretch on forever. Cape buffalo stand half hidden by bushes. Baboons dart off the road and glare from the bushes.

Clouds rise ahead, mirroring the anvil shape of the acacia trees. We pass a few cargo trucks and fishermen on bicycles bringing their catch from the lake. Mostly it's just us and the motorcycle, hour after hour. The sound and vibration are numbing, hypnotic.

Sam pulls over every hour or two so we can stretch and drink water. Every time we stop, I can't help eyeing the nearest acacia. This part of the park is famous for its tree-climbing lions. No one knows why they do it—all lions can climb trees, but they hardly ever do—but seeing them draped over the branches like cats on a sofa is one of the few reasons visitors venture this far south.

We veer toward a pothole every time Sam looks anywhere but straight ahead. He keeps killing the engine on the downhills to save fuel. The starter doesn't work right, though, and it takes at least a few strong kicks to get the motor going again. Every time I'm thinking, *Come on, man, there are* LIONS IN THE TREES *out here!*

It starts to rain and the road turns slick. Sam slows down but still almost dumps us, then does it again. The forest closes in on both sides, giving off the odor of a damp pet shop. My hands are cramped from clutching the seat. Sam starts gunning the engine on the straightaways until I'm ready to throttle him. I don't want my trip to end in a muddy pileup. But he wants the ride to be over, and so do I.

I hate skating across the surface of a place. But sometimes, like now, it's unavoidable, especially with so much ground to cover and the deadline of a ticket home. The pants-on-fire approach was the one Laura and I usually ended up taking when we traveled together. As much as we said we wanted to take our time, see fewer places and really get to *know* them, we would usually fall into the do-everything trap: vacations are expensive, in time and money, so why not cram in as much as possible?

Besides, she loved to try new things as much as I did, and grew bored just as easily. It was just one of the many ways we clicked. When she moved in, we found we fit together like the hybrid couch that appeared in the living room: my futon, her frame. My apartment received a much-needed makeover, and errands to pick up domestic items like dish racks and end tables started to feel alarmingly comfortable.

Laura had grown up with dogs and was even a little allergic to cats. Within a week she was Truvie's second parent.

It took us six months to save up enough money to quit our jobs and move west. Before Utah I had lived in Albuquerque, and I had been extolling the Southwest since the day I arrived in Washington. Santa Fe, the state capital, topped our short list of potential destinations. I'm sure the city's mystique as a place for escape and reinvention helped, although we'd never have admitted it at the time (much too canny to fall for that). It was arbitrary as much as anything; we had to choose somewhere. We eventually cut every other city for one reason or another: too big, too remote, too dreary. Santa Fe it was.

We made our escape in February. It was becoming our special month; to end the debate over when we actually became a couple, we'd picked Valentine's Day as our anniversary, with no regard to luck or irony. *Two birds with one stone,* I thought, but kept my mouth shut. Now, just when the mid-Atlantic winter was at its gloomiest, we both gave notice and traded sea-level swampland for bright desert at seventy-two hundred feet.

We took our time driving cross country, enjoying the best barbecue joints and backyard art installations of the Deep South. We were nervous and eager to start a new life together, but we also wanted to savor the transition from full-time employment to working for ourselves, and by "savor" I mean "postpone."

At a campsite in Georgia, Laura elbowed me awake in the middle of the night.

"What's that?" Something was rustling in the leaves outside our tent.

"Nothing. Some critter. Go back to sleep." The only thing I hate more than being woken up is being woken up for no reason.

"There! What is that?" She shook my shoulder, sincerely freaked out.

I could tell she wanted me to go out and take a look, even though she wouldn't just come right out and say it. She hated asking for help. It made her feel vulnerable, less than fully self-sufficient. (And why did she have to ask, anyway? Shouldn't I just automatically offer?)

The indirect approach made me feel manipulated, like I had to read her mind to see if she had too much on her plate. I had a tendency to ignore obvious clues, to "encourage" her to be more direct. We had noticed the pattern, unraveled it—different conversational styles; part gender, part upbringing—and still we kept falling into the trap.

These were the kinds of things we were learning by living together: not just how we both operated, alone and together, but why. We were deciphering one another like puzzles, and then trying to fit the pieces together to make one big new picture.

This time I did the right thing. I grabbed the flashlight, grumbling, and crawled out of the tent in my socks.

The air sizzled with insects. I swung the flashlight around and caught a scaly silver football rooting in the underbrush. A step closer and it shuffled off, grunting.

"Armadillo," I said, crawling back in beside her. "Okay?"

"Thank you, sweetie." Laura pinched my side and snuggled close. "My hero."

The explorers breathed a sigh of relief when they reached Katwe, a frontier post of the British protectorate of Uganda, three weeks after leaving Lake Kivu. Grogan's fever had broken, for the time being. The madness receded, and his mind emerged as sharp as ever.

They had reached the equator, twenty degrees of latitude from Beira. Cairo was another thirty degrees north.

At Katwe they resupplied and slept under a roof for the first time in months, "despite the uncomfortable accessories of thousands of mosquitoes and armies of rats." Then they continued northwest across the flank of the Rwenzori Mountains.

In the second century, the geographer Ptolemy included the "Mountains of the Moon," an icy range in central Africa whose snows fed the Nile, in his map of the continent. Geographers debated their existence for the next sixteen hundred years. Then, in 1889, one of the men on Henry Morton Stanley's final expedition in Africa swore he saw a snowcapped mountain north of Lake Edward.

Stanley scoffed. Snow on the equator? A few months later he saw the mountains for himself, after first mistaking them for clouds. Their higher reaches were almost always shrouded by mist and fog rising from the jungles to the west. The tallest of the six main summits was eventually named after him; 16,761-foot Mount Stanley is the third-highest mountain in Africa after Kilimanjaro and Mount Kenya.

A decade later, Grogan's column snaked across the eastern side of the range, crossing ice-clear streams that seemed to spill from the clouds. But not once in the entire march did they even glimpse the jagged peaks.

At the end of July 1899, the expedition climbed the last steep hill to the British settlement of Fort Gerry near the north end of the range. They were overjoyed to find the fort stocked with recent newspapers and books. One piece of news was especially encouraging: soon after they had left Beira a year ago, British forces had recaptured Khartoum from the Muslims. It was the first step in getting the state back under British and Egyptian control—at least the northern part. The remote southern section, which Grogan would have to traverse as he descended the Upper Nile to Khartoum and Cairo, was still lawless and wild.

Grogan caught up with his correspondence. In a letter to Alfred Sharpe, the senior British official in central Africa, he summarized their findings since Tanganyika and added a warning about the Baleka: "none of your ritualistic amateur cannibal, but a real earnest man-hunting gentleman who makes a regular business of the thing."

The explorers met Kasagama, ruler of the native Toro kingdom, in his palace on a hilltop near the government station. His kingdom was larger than Ireland, stretching from Lake Edward to Lake Albert. A few years earlier, British forces had brought Kasagama back from exile and helped him take back his throne from a rival. Now he reigned again through the grace of Her Majesty's government.

There wasn't much for the men to do in Fort Gerry but drink *pombe*, the native beer, and the porters started to grow rowdy. One evening they stole milk from the fort's Sudanese officer and beat up his men. Ten were arrested and put on a chain gang as punishment. Another night a group of drunk porters threatened Grogan with spears, forcing him to shoot his revolver at the ringleader's feet to back them off.

The next day the men approached Grogan peacefully. Instead of asking for forgiveness, they said they wanted to go home to Tanganyika.

Losing the porters now would be a disaster. None of the locals would even consider going north into the Sudan. They knew how desolate and dangerous it was.

Then Sharp dropped his own bombshell. He had just received a telegraph message that told of pressing business affairs back home. After agonizing over the choice, he decided he couldn't afford to be away for another year or two, or however long it took to finish the journey. He had to return to London immediately.

"I feel dreadful deserting you like this," he said.

Grogan was flabbergasted. He tried halfheartedly to convince his partner to stay, but Sharp's mind was made up.

After days of negotiations, the explorers arranged for thirty of the Manyema porters to continue north with Grogan. The rest would accompany Sharp to Kampala, a settlement 160 miles east that was connected by train to the coast. A hundred local porters would help carry everything Grogan didn't need anymore: native artifacts, elephant tusks, animal skins, and most of the weapons.

At Kampala, the Manyema would be free to return to their villages on Lake Tanganyika. Sharp would send supplies ahead to an outpost on the Upper Nile called Wadelai to await Grogan's arrival. Then he would finish the eight-hundred-mile journey to the coast by train and take passage to England through the Red Sea and the Mediterranean.

The sudden changes left Grogan shaken and depressed. For the first time he started to question whether he could succeed alone. He suspected there was more to Sharp's story than he let on. The older man had held up to the rigors of African travel, but he had clearly had his fill of fever and exhaustion and the constant tension of life in the bush.

Now everything was up to Grogan: route finding, discipline, defense. There would be no one to talk to, to trust unconditionally, or to nurse him back to health. On the positive side, the abbreviated caravan would be able to travel even faster. Without the security of a large group, they would have to.

If there was one thing he couldn't comprehend, it was quitting. Tellingly, he refers to the separation in his book with just two terse sentences expressing his great regret that Sharp couldn't "risk the possibility of being buried in the wilds for another two years."

When his mood was at its darkest, Grogan would pull out a photograph of Gertrude he had carried since New Zealand. It was discolored and torn from years of travel, but her lovely face was still clear; and her calm gaze helped clear his mind and focus his scattered thoughts.

The equation was simple. He was determined to make Gertrude his wife. Reaching Cairo was the only way to make that happen. He could never face her as a failure. So he would press on, no matter what it took.

A few days later, Grogan paid the departing porters and thanked each one for his services. He and Sharp faced each other one last time as explorers. They had been through so much in the past eighteen months. They'd had their differences—with Grogan, it was impossible not to—but the shared struggles and triumphs had welded a strong friendship.

"Good luck, and—may God be with you," Sharp said as he shook Grogan's hand firmly. "You'll win through!"

"Yes, but I'm going to miss you, Harry," Grogan said. His eyes held no bitterness, just regret. "Thank you—for everything."

Sharp turned to go. Grogan watched the column wind into the hills to the east until it was out of sight.

CHAPTER EIGHTEEN

Santa Fe was the opposite of Washington in almost every way: small, quiet, artsy, bathed in sun, and dry as a dead leaf. There were mountains and rivers and deserts to play in, bike trails and art galleries and native pueblos to visit. I had almost forgotten how inspiring and energizing New Mexico's scenery and near-constant sunshine could be. The summer monsoon thunderheads trailed rain like lace gowns, leaving behind stream-scoured gullies and the smell of damp earth and sage.

Starting over in a new city is always exciting. And for the first time, we both had someone to share it with. At the same time, by leaving our jobs and moving simultaneously, we had combined two of the most stressful life events into one. I had worked as a freelance writer full-time before, but Laura hadn't. I was so entranced with being free of the desk job and back in the Southwest that it didn't occur to me right away what a huge leap of faith this whole thing was for her.

We worked on laptops and chased down gigs wherever we could: books and magazines for me, TV documentaries for Laura. We alternated between working at home and in coffee shops, carefully planning a schedule to keep us from crossing paths constantly. We still saw a lot of one another.

Our new home had many quirks that we'd missed during our quick reconnaissance visits. In Washington, work was central to the lives and identities of most people we knew and met; the first thing anyone always asked was what you did for a living. Here, half the time you couldn't even get a straight answer to the question. "Fanta Se" was a place to hide out and nurture your inner something-or-other. A job was a necessary evil. People like us, gainfully employed thirty-somethings who loved their work, were in the minority.

Scarce jobs, ridiculously priced real estate, and a glut of retirees created a pronounced demographic dip around our age. Almost everyone seemed older or younger than we were.

That fall, the changing aspen leaves painted the mountainsides gold, and we finally started to feel settled in. Truvie lay in the sun and rolled in the dirt in the small garden in front of our rental house. Christmas meant backcountry skiing and bonfires in the snow among the swank art galleries on Canyon Road.

The new year brought something else: a few days into January, sweet, stump-tailed old Truvie died suddenly of feline leukemia. We brought her back from the vet in a small black box. I dug a hole in the sandy soil behind our rental house.

"Our little monkeybutt," Laura said. Her eyes were red.

"Remember how she used to scoot around, scratching her ass on the floor?" I said, sniffling. "Every time a dog barked she practically had a heart attack."

I told Laura about a book I had as a child. It was about a boy who tries to think of ten good things about his cat who just died. At first he can only come up with nine.

"Your parents got you a book about a kid's *cat* dying?" Laura's expression slid from sadness to disbelief.

"No, it was sweet. Really." In the end, the boy does think of the tenth: now Barney is helping the flowers grow.

We came up with twelve things about Truvie.

The house seemed too empty. Six weeks later, we went to Santa Fe's new $10 million animal shelter and brought home a dark striped kitten with huge ears. We watched her sniff around the corners of the kitchen.

"It feels like we're a family again," I said. *Whoa—where did that come from?*

Laura squeezed my hand.

Three months later we brought home another.

Sam pulls up to the main entrance to Queen Elizabeth National Park in the late afternoon. My face feels skinned from the wind and I'm so stiff I can hardly lift my leg over the seat. He pulls away and I wave goodbye, relieved it's over and a little sad to see him go.

The Mweya Safari Lodge is a plush affair, high on a stubby peninsula at the north end of Lake Edward. The lawn in front of the lodge is crawling with animals. Dozens of striped mongooses snuffle about fearlessly, crawling between my feet and rooting under the manicured bushes. For some reason each one has a different pattern shaved into the hair on its back.

Within fifty feet are two of the ugliest animals in Africa. A marabou stork stands motionless near a hedge. It's a small one, only four feet high (they can reach six, with a ten-foot wing-span), with a spearlike bill and bone-thin legs. Its head and neck are pink and featherless, both spotted like an old man's hands and covered with white fuzz.

A pair of warthogs graze the grass on bent front knees. Africa's ubiquitous wild pig doesn't have the stoned-Creator feel of, say, a giraffe, or the acid-inspired whimsy of a sea anemone. The warthog, in comparison, has an almost vindictive homeliness. Feed a serving tray through a dull wood chipper, stick on two stumpy tusks, and cover in coarse hair. Finish with stubby legs, a wispy tail, and hooves like cloven high heels.

The lodge is way out of my budget, but I can at least afford three dollars for a late-afternoon cocktail on the veranda. Yellow and black weaver birds steal strips from the potted plants to add to their hanging nests. I couldn't weave something that tight with ten fingers, let alone a beak and claws.

Copper light ignites a bend in the channel that connects Lake Edward to Lake Albert. This was where Sharp had to ferry the expedition's loads and cattle across after Grogan had gone ahead in a canoe, ablaze with fever. Two men had to grab each cow by the horns and swim alongside it.

Grogan had no idea he would soon be on his own. I wonder how soon he started to miss Sharp after he left, or if he ever did. I usually prefer traveling alone, but I've been wishing for company more and more lately. If Laura were here, I'm sure we'd find things to argue about, but more important, we would be able to support each other, to share the pleasures and frustrations together.

All right—to cuddle at night, too.

The man at the next table turns out to be the owner of the hostel next door, where I'm sleeping. He ticks off the visitors killed by wildlife this year with macabre relish.

"A hippo got one in May." The channel is home to thousands of hippos, one of the largest concentrations in Africa. We can hear snorts and splashes far below in the darkness. A galaxy of insects swirls around the lights.

"And in March, an elephant killed two people," he says. "It

got one, and the other tried to swim away. It saw his head out there in the water, then it swam out and"—he smacks his hands together—"whomp!"

The next morning I walk down to the channel with a graduate student from the hostel named Matt, who is here to study the park's tourism potential. On the way down he identifies the mysterious mongoose shaver: it's a zoologist from the University of Cambridge, Grogan's almost alma mater, studying the animals' reproductive patterns.

A small crowd and a flotilla of fishing boats are gathered at the foot of the bridge. When we ask about taking a boat tour of the channel, we're steered toward a twenty-foot dugout canoe with an outboard motor. In hippo territory, the bigger the boat, the better. It belongs to the local community, used for rescues and patrolling the park. We wait in the shade as someone rounds up fuel and guides.

"A few weeks ago a guy asked me how much this cost," Matt says, taking out his small digital camera. "I told him and he said, 'That's how much a year of school costs me.'"

We're soon surrounded by children in tattered clothes. They erupt with laughter when we take pictures and show them their faces on the camera screens.

"Give me your sunglasses," one boy says, grinning. "Give me your camera!" Straight-faced demands for your things are another staple of African travel.

I play along. "Okay, but you have to give me your pants. Give me your shoes!"

He calls my bluff and holds out a green flip-flop. Touché.

Luckily the boat is ready. We climb in next to two guides,

Vincent and Brahim. Water trickles through caulked seams at our feet. At least there are a few life jackets on board.

Hippos huff spray into the air like whales near the shore as we motor past. Eyes, ears, and bristly brows glisten pink and gray in the cloudy water.

Almost every famous explorer, from Burton and Speke to Livingston and Stanley, had at least one unpleasant hippo encounter. Three-ton males can outrun a person on land, and in the water they tend to attack without reason or warning. Males' curved canines, used to joust for dominance, can grow three feet long and snap a dugout canoe like a breadstick.

The surest way to provoke a hippo to attack is to get between it and the water, or between a female and her baby. One morning early in his trip, Grogan came across an old cow hippo and a calf. "I accompanied them for some time watching them, but when I caught the youngster by the tail the old lady turned round in answer to its squeals, and opening her mouth to its fullest extent, some 6 ft., gave vent to a terrific roar, which reminded me that it was breakfast-time."

Each family group is led by a single old male, Vincent says. The rest are females and young. If a female has a male baby, she has to go far away or the old male will kill it, removing a potential future competitor.

A trail of bubbles blooms to one side and moves under the boat. A huge male surfaces twenty feet away and eyeballs us.

"He is scared of the motor," Brahim says, "but if we were in a paddle canoe he could bite us, owee!" He does the wrist-snapping finger slap that seems to be the universal sign for "holy crap."

Vincent waves to two men paddling past in a small canoe. "They were scared of us," he says. "They thought we were park patrollers. They're not allowed to land in the park to rest, to make a meal. Just to fish in the channel."

The locals aren't huge fans of the park. "Their land was taken, and populations are rising here. They can make arrangements to do some things in the park, like gather food or firewood." But the needs of rich foreign visitors come first.

The conversation turns, as it so often does, to HIV and AIDS. Vincent and Brahim know Sam and Gideon well. Both are AIDS orphans themselves.

Standing on the escarpment at the northern end of the Ruwenzoris, Grogan felt like he was on the brink of a new world.

He was the sole boss of a lean, road-tested crew, on an expedition that had always been his to begin with. It was still more than two thousand miles to Cairo, and the most difficult part of the journey lay ahead, in the Sudan. From now on, he had only himself to blame if anything went wrong.

But he had come so far already, with no major disasters. His group was fed and rested. And just look at that view: to the north, half a mile below, spread the vast sunlit basin of the Semliki River Valley. Beyond it was Lake Albert, the last of the chain of great lakes, shining like an ocean of mercury under a turquoise sky flecked with pink.

Behind him rose the purple mass of the Ruwenzoris, peak after peak painted black with forest. Evening mists curled up gorges and past gigantic buttresses into storm clouds that fed snowfields and glaciers.

Scenery like this would draw people from around the world one day, he predicted, especially once trains arrived. With the classic travelers' resentment of other tourists, Grogan envisioned a future of "Cook's tours, funicular railways [and] personally-conducted ascents (with a sermon and ginger-beer thrown in)."

For now, though, the view was his. "Well! thank God I have seen her first—seen her as she has stood for countless ages, wrapped in impenetrable mystery, undesecrated by human tread."

It was August 28, 1899. The party had left Fort Gerry three hours earlier, passing through a scattering of small volcanic lakes before reaching the escarpment. Now they scrambled two thousand feet down through dense forests to the valley floor. Black and white colobus monkeys leaped between rubber vines, and okapis—bizarre animals that look like deer with white cheeks and zebra-striped legs—edged along the banks of streams.

Up close, the river valley was less inviting than it had looked from up high. It alternated between stinking, impassible marshes and grasslands decimated by drought. "It might well have been named the Valley of Death."

The men were already in a morbid mind-set. Before they left Fort Gerry, word had come back that the main party of porters had been attacked on their way home to Tanganyika, after they had taken some items from the locals without asking. Twenty were killed in the brawl that followed.

The news reminded Grogan how much they owed their lives to sheer luck. It also made him even more certain that stealing from the natives was a bad idea.

After a nightmare in which a rooster with ten-foot tusks was dancing on his chest, Grogan led the party across the Semliki River in a leaky canoe. The riverbanks writhed with crocodiles. When they landed on the other side, a native told him a woman had been snatched from that very spot earlier that morning.

Elephants moved through the dense forests on the other side

of the valley. Grogan was as impressed as ever with the giant animals as he stalked them through the trees. "A whole regiment of lions cannot produce the same moral effect as one elephant when he cocks his ears, draws himself up to his full height, and looks at you, letting off at the same time a blood-curdling scream, while in all probability others invisible are stampeding on all sides with the din of an earthquake."

Elephants seemed to be able to telegraph alarm over long distances. "The extraordinary ease with which they pass on the danger-signal has often made me wonder whether they have another sense, which we, by disuse, have practically lost," Grogan wrote.

He was right: researchers have discovered that elephants can communicate over miles by sending low-frequency vibrations through the ground. They "hear" the infrasonic signals with the sensitive skin on their trunks and feet, and may even be able to triangulate the source.

Hunting them in the damp press of jungle was terrifying. The bulls were gigantic—Grogan measured one that was fifteen feet from ear tip to ear tip. Their skulls were like armor plating, some sixteen inches thick. Only a perfect shot, or many, many imperfect ones, could bring an elephant down. "When wounded, they have a nasty knack of looking to see who did it."

During a jungle hunt "one seems to shrivel, and the very gun to dwindle into a pea-shooter; try as I will, I can never quite stomach it, and always feel inclined to throw down my rifle and run till I drop."

Throughout his trip Grogan saw huge herds of elephants, buffalo, hippos, and antelopes of every description. But it was already clear that the enthusiasm and deadly weapons of European hunters like himself were taking a toll.

"In the greater part of Africa the elephant is now a thing of the past; and the rate at which they have disappeared is appalling," he wrote. "Ten years ago elephant swarmed in places . . . where now you will not find one." When he spotted a small group of Congo buffalo on Lake Albert, locals told him that the "evil beast [had] once been very numerous, but was now finished." Outbreaks of rinderpest, a lethal viral disease imported with European cattle, had devastated the once-massive herds.

Grogan had no problem shooting an animal—after a fair chase, of course—for the thrill of the hunt and a trophy, or for a specimen of a new species, or for food. Yet it was Africa's animals, as much as her cultures and terrain, that made it unlike any other place on earth. They needed some sort of protection, and soon, "for in a few years' time it will be too late" as more and more European settlers arrived.

Only large-scale, top-down efforts would work. A good example was the two game reserves—Africa's first—that had recently been set aside to control hunting in the Transvaal Republic, part of what would become South Africa. (Virunga National Park, the first national park in Africa, wouldn't be created until 1925.)

When Grogan brought down another elephant one day, a crowd of natives emerged. They had long, greased hair and were "rather short, but well-set-up, innocent of clothing as a babe unborn." They swarmed over the still-warm body like ants:

> Hacking away with knives and spears, yelling, snarling, whooping, wrestling, cursing, and munching, covered with blood and entrails; the new arrivals tearing off lumps of meat and swallowing them raw, the earlier birds defending their worms in the form of great lumps of fat paunch

and other delicacies; while others were crawling in and out of the intestines like so many prairie marmots. Old men, young men, prehistoric hags, babies, one and all gorging or gorged; pools of blood, strips of hide, vast bones, blocks of meat, individuals who had not dined wisely but too well, lay around in bewildering profusion.

Two hours later, all that was left were the ribs, "like the skeleton of a shipwreck."

Grogan's route along the east side of the Ruwenzoris is now smoothly paved, with street signs and white-striped speed bumps. Our taxi driver slows down just enough to keep the car from launching into the air. He says the most people he's ever fit in the small sedan is eleven, not counting himself. Today is slow, only eight passengers.

The green foothills are spotted with trees like pilling sweaters. Metal roofs glint in the sun. The slopes build in larger and larger waves, blue and gray and bruised purple, before disappearing into a cap of thunderheads.

Somewhere up there are glaciers and snowfields, though not likely for much longer. The Ruwenzoris are one of three places in Africa, along with Mount Kenya and Kilimanjaro, with permanent snowfields. But they have shrunk by half in the past fifty years, most likely from global warming, and will probably be gone in another three decades. Climate scientists estimate the snows of Kilimanjaro, which Hemingway called "as wide as all the world," could vanish by 2022.

In twenty minutes we pass three long processions walking along the shoulder. Each one starts with a veiled bride in white, followed by men in dark suits, bridesmaids in bright pink or yellow dresses, and a well-dressed crowd trailing behind, singing and clapping.

I wonder what ideas Laura has come up with for our ceremony. We haven't discussed it in detail yet, just that we both want something simple, secular, and heartfelt. I love that she's not determined to make our wedding all about her, her Special Perfect Day to be achieved at any cost. On the contrary, she hates being the center of attention. The thought of us walking down the side of a road, trailed by our wedding party and all our guests—she would die.

At the ten-foot white concrete circle that marks the equator, the driver pulls over for a "short call" (a "long" one requires toilet paper). The nearby buildings are painted in bright primary colors, each matched to the logo of a local cell phone company: blue for Uganda Telecom, yellow for MTN, and red with yellow doors for Centel.

Just twelve years after the country's first mobile phone company opened, more than two million Ugandans have cell phones. Africa is the fastest-growing market for cell phones in the world. Mobiles have transformed daily life. People who never had a landline, bank account, or even electricity can now keep in touch with distant relatives, transfer money, report violence, exchange health information, and haggle over prices without having to go anywhere.

Everyone crams back in the car and we flee a blue wall of rain racing up from the south. Wind-whipped leaves and plump raindrops speckle the windshield as we climb the last hill to Fort Portal, the city that sprang up around Fort Gerry after Grogan was here.

I drop my bag at a hotel where a sign in the lobby reads:

"Lollers, loafers and gossips are not welcome at all, nothing to do—not here." My first task is to find the fort. But all that's left of the place where Grogan and Sharp gorged themselves on newspapers and books is an outline of stones on a hilltop near the first tee of the Toro Club golf course. Caddies sit on white benches waiting for work. Every few seconds a thwack sends another ball soaring down the slope toward the city.

It takes half an hour to walk across town and up Fort Portal's other prominent hill, where the modern palace of the Toro kingdom has an even better view of tea plantations and rippling blue mountains. The circular building looks more like an avant-garde office than the home base of the world's youngest monarch.

Prince Rukirabasaija Oyo Nyimba Kabamba Iguru Rukidi IV—Rukidi IV to his friends, or just King Oyo—was three years old when he became the ruler of the Toro kingdom, one of Uganda's four remaining traditional kingdoms, after his father died. Now, at fifteen years old, he rules almost a million people. Photos on the walls inside show a handsome teenager sitting in an elaborate crown and robes, looking bored. According to the glossy pamphlets by the door, Rukidi IV likes to play soccer and computer games and wants to study tourism. His favorite movie is the *Chronicles of Narnia*.

The weather looks touch-and-go in the afternoon. I decide to chance it and visit the crater lakes near town that Grogan passed on his way north. They're small and round, like gigantic thumbprints amid the undulating hills, with the steep, almost unnaturally straight wall of the Ruwenzoris as a backdrop. A footpath loops from lake to lake. Halfway around I meet a young man in a red T-shirt named Edward. He's twenty-four, studying public administration at the new Mountains of the Moon University in Fort Portal. We walk together to the next lake.

"Are you married?" he asks without preamble.

I tell him the story and ask if he has a girlfriend.

"Oh, no, they are too expensive." He shakes his head and smiles, showing perfect teeth. "When you get a girlfriend in Uganda, she expects you to buy her everything: clothes, shoes, jewelry. And good things, too, not local things."

He launches into a soliloquy on the traditional Ugandan engagement process.

"First the man goes to the family of the woman. He brings some old men, they have some old men. They sit together. 'Hello, how are you, what do you want?' He asks humbly"—Edward hunches his shoulders beseechingly—" 'We would like to be part of your family.' 'Oh, you want to marry?' they say." He's leaning back and forth, speaking the parts in different voices.

"Everyone sits down, out comes some women from the family. But not the one you are interested in. They are dressed up in suits, they sit down on mats in front. 'Is the one you want here?' 'No.' But then the women say, 'We did not come here to model, you must give us some money.' So you have to pay them each from your pocket, maybe five thousand shillings"—three dollars—"and then some more women come out, but again, the one you want to marry is not among them, and you have to pay them to go away again.

"Then you say, 'Where are the others?' 'Oh, so-and-so, she is in Fort Portal, that other one went away, you will have to pay for transport to bring them.' Maybe fifty thousand shillings now, depending on how much money you have. Then the one you want is finally there in front, and you go up and put the necklace over her head; you put a handkerchief in her pocket."

He's a born actor. I'm not sure who's enjoying the performance more, him or me.

"Then you have to negotiate the dowry. They say 'Ah, this one is the most important woman in our household. She does many, many things. You will have to give us ten cattle to take her.' Or you can pay the money equivalent, say one cattle is worth five hundred thousand shillings. You say"—he clasps his hands again, playing poor man—"'We are sorry, we are not very wealthy, we can only pay two cattle.' " The bargaining continues. Crates of beer and soda are occasionally involved.

"Then, when you have made all the arrangements, then you eat, eat-eat-eat and drink, you have a big party. These same people, the ones who took your money and said the woman you want was not there, come up to you"—he flings his arms open—"'My brother! How are things my brother!'"

CHAPTER NINETEEN

The steep, smoothly rounded slopes of the Ruwenzoris make me think of hips and breasts, a reclining earth goddess in green velvet. You know you've been away from home too long when the scenery starts looking sexy.

The taxi's radio crackles in and out as we contour across folds in the earth, following Grogan's route from Fort Portal around the north end of the range. Next to me, the driver pops in a tape and Bryan Adams starts singing about the summer of '69. A young Israeli couple is snoring lightly in the backseat.

Tiny figures speckle the slopes, tilling fields so steep they can face uphill and chop the ground without bending over. To our right is the broad valley that Grogan gazed across, imagining hordes of tourists. The Semliki River snakes creamy brown across a green plain, marking Uganda's border with the DRC. Enlarged by the Ruwenzoris' melting glaciers, the river changes course frequently, occasionally stranding Congolese communities in Uganda and vice versa.

The jungle grows thicker as the road descends. Now we're on the west side of the range, opposite Fort Portal. Just as the chorus of "Cuts Like a Knife" reaches a crescendo, we reach a small set of hot springs, one of the two main attractions of tiny Semliki National Park. A small man in green fatigues leads us into the forest. The ranger points out four different kinds of primates in three minutes: blue and red-tailed monkeys, black and white colobuses, and gray-cheeked mangabeys. The forest smells old, like cut grass and rot.

A wooden boardwalk leads out of the jungle to the hot springs, bubbling out of a grassy plain. Scalding water spurts over glistening wedding cakes of minerals. The air is thick with steam and the smell of sulfur.

The ranger explains how locals come here to treat skin ailments and cook food. An egg takes five minutes.

"People pray to the springs by sacrificing animals."

"By throwing them in the water?" I ask, picturing a mangabey hog-tied and parboiled.

He looks at me like I'm crazy. "No."

Farther down the road, we pass women and children carrying bundles of sticks on tumplines of woven leaves.

I'm more than a little anxious about our next stop, a village of Batwa pygmies. I was here thirteen years ago, and things did not go well.

I was in Fort Portal with two college friends on my first trip to Africa. We hired a pickup with a few other backpackers and rattled down this same road in the bed of the truck. Everyone was in high spirits.

We arrived to find a filthy village in the trees full of people the size of grade schoolers. All the adults were red-eyed and stumbling, drunk or stoned or both.

About eighty thousand Twa (or Batwa) pygmies, descendants of the ones Grogan met, live around the great lakes in Rwanda, Burundi, Uganda, and the eastern DRC. They have endured centuries of violence, discrimination, and racial prejudice from Africans and Europeans alike. In 1906, one was put on display in the monkey house at the Bronx Zoo. Pygmies have been forced out of the parks and reserves where they once lived as nomads, stuck in miserable permanent settlements like this with little or no economic opportunity.

The villagers were gathered in a clearing surrounded by wooden huts. Eager hands thrust clay pipes and bamboo bongs and fistfuls of marijuana at us.

Someone in our group agreed to a "traditional dance" that turned out to be more *Animal House* than Lévi-Strauss. An argument broke out over compensation.

"We won't pay for that garbage," one abrasive woman in our group kept saying. "You should be ashamed of yourselves."

People started shouting and waving sticks. Our driver began herding us nervously toward the truck. Two villagers held the chief by the arms as he lunged at the woman, apoplectic. Another man leaped from the crowd and shoved a handful of something dark in her hair.

The situation had gone from silly to scary. A mob is a mob, no matter how tall. Everyone finally squeezed back in the truck and we fled in a cloud of dust. The ride back to Fort Portal passed in shaken silence.

I can remember clearly the surge of guilt and disgust I felt—not at the pygmies but at myself for encouraging the farce with my presence.

Today we first have to stop in the village of Bundibugyo (my new favorite place-name) and buy a permit for five dollars, instead of just showing up like the first time. The pygmies were recently relocated to the edge of town, with funding from the European Union. A dozen buildings with mud-and-stick walls and metal roofs have replaced the thatch-roofed huts. A line of T-shirts and underwear slants in the breeze.

It's still a dismal place. The central area of dirt is packed smooth by bare feet and littered with trash exuding the tang of bad fish.

At least everyone seems sober this time. As before, the children are of normal height, but the adults barely reach my sternum. A shirtless old man scowls and a woman with a shaved head nurses a baby.

Nobody is sure why pygmies stop growing in early adolescence. Grogan thought it made it easier for them to move through the dense rain forest. More recent theories point to a lack of ultraviolet light or a lack of calcium in the forest soil. Smaller bodies may have helped keep their ancestors from starving in the nutrient-poor environment, and their cells may carry a natural resistance to a molecule called IGF-I that affects growth.

It is clear that pygmies don't live nearly as long as taller groups of hunter-gatherers. The average adult doesn't survive to see thirty, for reasons ranging from poor nutrition to tropical diseases. They also tend to start having babies at a young age. Some scientists think pygmies' bodies compensate for a shorter life span by focusing energy on early reproduction, leaving less for growth.

Three wooden stools appear out of nowhere, and craft items are spread on the ground: wood and string noisemakers, crude metal knives, a harplike thing that used to be a turtle. The expectation is palpable—why would we come all the way here if we didn't want to buy anything? No one speaks English, understandably.

I'm not afraid for my safety this time, but I'm still squirming inside. There's nothing cultural about it. We're interested in their size; they're interested in our cash.

Grogan sat through countless encounters like this on his trip, buying or bartering goods from locals with hand signals and body language. I doubt he ever felt remorseful about it. His blunt approach, and his confidence in his own cultural superiority, freed him from nagging thoughts of exploitation and voyeurism. I almost envy his insensitivity.

In any case, once again I can't wait to leave.

Grogan led the party out of the Semliki Valley into the marshes at the south end of Lake Albert and promptly got lost.

The group foundered for hours through ten-foot grasses covered with invisible spines that burned their skin like mad. Their matted roots hid thigh-deep holes left by hippos and elephants.

At last they emerged from this "sea of misery" and started up the western shore of the hundred-mile-long lake. Steep mountains met the water for most of the way, making it a much more difficult route than the lake's flat eastern shore. Grogan's task was to map the unknown, though, so that was where he had to go.

The shimmering light turned everything into a mirage. Canoes and their paddlers seemed to glide in the sky. Clusters of huts appeared and vanished on the pearlescent water, and animals transformed abruptly in size. The only sounds were the snorts of hippos and the splash of jumping fish. Flocks of bone-white ibis added to the supernatural aura.

The few natives whom Grogan met lived an amphibious existence amid islands of papyrus and endless bands of reeds.

Swamps gave way to hills, then steep mountains as they marched north. Streams and waterfalls spilled into the lake under enormous silver-trunked trees. Brown-eyed monkeys chattered in the branches among scarlet and yellow blooms.

The more dramatic the scenery became, the tougher it was

to travel. Soon the only path was along a narrow shingled beach between the mountains and the water. Even this kept disappearing whenever the headlands thrust out into the lake, forcing the group to scale cliffs or throw everything into wobbly canoes and paddle around to the next stretch of beach.

The constant soaking and scrambling ate away at Grogan's wardrobe until he found himself down to a single shirt. "Thanks to a classical education and consequent ignorance of the art of washing, [it] had contracted to the modest and insufficient dimensions of a chest-preserver, while assuming the durable but inappropriate consistency of a piece of oil-cloth."

The sun scorched his newly exposed skin. With his tanned face and fish-belly torso, it made him look like a "perambulating three-tiered Neapolitan ice, coffee, vanilla and raspberry." The next day, he wrote, "the alarming desertion of a third of my epidermis so pained me mentally and physically, that after a great effort I produced a double-barrelled garment."

Of all the things Grogan had to teach himself in Africa—"cooking, shoe-mending, washer-womaning, doctoring, butchering, taxiderming, armoury work, carpentering"—he found sewing the most difficult: "The cotton will not go into the eye of the needle, and the needle will go into one's fingers, and then when you think it is all over, you find you have sewn the back of your shirt to the front."

During one midday break, Grogan went looking for some shade. He found a patch of forest where herds of elephants had flattened the undergrowth, leaving "vast shady chambers joined in all directions by galleries." He wandered through the cool green rooms, some an acre in size, as hundreds of black-and-white monkeys bounced from branch to branch and stared at him with fearless curiosity.

I need to stop buying the paper. I'm sitting on the roof of the hotel in Fort Portal with a copy of yesterday's *New Vision*, which has no fewer than three articles about the situation in northern Uganda, where government troops have been battling a cultlike militia called the Lord's Resistance Army since 1987.

What started as an interethnic power struggle metastasized into a guerrilla war between the nominally Christian militants and the Ugandan government. The fighting has left one hundred thousand dead and displaced almost 2 million people.

The LRA's leader, a former faith healer named Joseph Kony, claims to run his army according to the Ten Commandments. But most LRA soldiers are children who have been kidnapped and forced to become porters, soldiers, or prostitutes. Some are made to murder their own parents to prove their loyalty. Peace talks started last year, but civilian vehicles are still being ambushed and people are being shot on the roads that lead to the Sudanese border.

Car horns have started honking, many more than usual, and music is thumping somewhere near the hotel. Over the edge of the roof I see a procession of about a hundred people filling the courtyard of the building next door. There's a large white tent and a bride and groom wearing traditional white and black, like the wedding party behind them.

People keep yelling at each other not to step on the bride's trains, which must be twenty feet long. Six girls climb out of a truck and start singing in crystalline harmony as they join the group, scattering flower petals.

The courtyard gates close and a crowd of onlookers presses up against the wall, everyone craning for a peek. Their color-ful clothing looks like confetti against the monochrome outfits inside. Children perch on the wall, somehow avoiding the broken glass embedded in the concrete. Two policemen in maroon uniforms try to push the gawkers back with truncheons.

A handful of other people have come up to the roof to watch. I ask the nearest man if he knows who's getting married.

"Yes, he works for the government. These people are rich." The groom's family has to pay a dowry to the bride's family, he explains. "For rich people it can be three million shillings"— about two thousand dollars. "You can pay in cows or money."

This is getting ridiculous. First the processions along the road, then Edward's stories, now a full-on ceremony next door.

Laura's latest emails have been filled with updates, questions, and complaints about our own big day. Organizing a wedding is like planning a military campaign, one you're trying to keep tasteful and intimate and within a modest budget.

I feel funny talking about wedding stuff when it seems like that would be the least of your worries right now, she wrote yesterday. I did my best to reassure her that I was more than willing to help in any way I could from the opposite side of the world.

I want to be involved in the process, I wrote back. *There's just only so much I can do.* Frankly, the details aren't as important to me. It's the overall idea I'm grappling with.

And this trip hasn't let me put it aside for very long at all. The universe is trying to tell me something—but what?

My rooftop companion offers a logical explanation for the recent wedding boom. "This is the harvest month. People have harvested their sorghum and they have some money. And the children are home from school."

The photographer finishes up and the procession re-forms and files into the tent. Girls holding blue and green scarves dance to Madonna's "Lucky Star" on the PA.

The show is over and the throng starts to disperse. Three women are talking loudly right below us, obviously critiquing the ceremony.

"I hope to get married next year," he says, "when I finish my studies."

I tell him our plans and get that you're-not-married-yet? look once again. In a world where children and extended family can be crucial to survival, the idea of a financially solvent person my age being single by choice is downright strange.

"No dowry, though," I say. "Guess I'll have to be enough." I don't think he gets the joke.

Getting married is on my mind a lot in Africa, but nothing like it was a year ago. By our second year in Santa Fe, the newness had worn off, and Laura and I were starting to feel like we were trapped on a moon base together.

There weren't many people our age and wavelength in the city, and many of those were oddly insular and cliquish. We kept telling ourselves to give it just a little more time, that things would fall into place. At least social seclusion was good for launching freelance careers.

Board game night became a big deal. We channeled our frustrations into a smoldering Scrabble rivalry that tapped into two deep competitive streaks. We even debated who was more competitive. Laura usually won with strange, high-scoring words, which I was sure she made up on the spot, hoping they'd be in our well-thumbed *Official Scrabble Dictionary*.

"*Neve*. Double letter, triple word, eighteen points," she would say with a face that was all innocence.

"*Neve*? What the hell is that?"

"I know it's a word, I just don't know what it means. I don't have to."

"Is it a verb? Noun? Come on, you have to at least know what *kind* of word it is."

But she didn't, according to the rules, and more often than not, combinations like *neve* ("granular snow"), *wold* ("an elevated tract of open land"), or *lour* ("to lower") would turn out to be in the dictionary. I'd miss my turn and grumble about luck and demand a rematch.

Topics like reproduction and real estate started popping up in conversation. At first they were always in the abstract, like which direction the housing market was headed or the ideal size and sibling spacing for some theoretical family.

Slowly, though, the hypotheticals started to become more tangible, and it became clear we weren't just discussing the latest interesting study in the psychology of parenting or how many rooms in a house you really need for a family of four. We were talking about how *we* would raise *our* children, as partners for life. Hypothetically.

Once marriage became a legitimate topic for discussion, it began to dominate our interactions, and my thoughts.

Laura, to my amazement, said she had known I was The One for a while. There was no one else I could imagine spending my life with. But something held me back.

We could see the echoes of both pairs of parents in our inter-actions, for better and worse. After twenty-five years together, my parents had a deep, loving bond, but it had taken them de-cades to learn to coexist peacefully, leaving an image of mar-riage as something you hammered at like a blacksmith until it worked—and a contract with no escape if things went rocky.

We both have stubbornly self-reliant personalities, thin skins, and sharp tongues. In heated moments it could feel like a tug-of-war as much as a partnership. Sometimes every squabble seemed like the iceberg tip of some deeper, intractable problem. As much as I wasn't ready to get married, I also wasn't ready to stop being unmarried. I couldn't envision what I'd be getting in exchange for my sovereignty. A closer bond? Peace of mind? Inheritance rights? In my imagination, the smallest adjustments were often the most disturbing, like how being married means always having to tell someone where you're going when you leave the house.

That summer Laura radiated love and impatience. In her card for my thirty-fourth birthday, she wrote a quote from *When Harry Met Sally:* "When you realize you want to spend the rest of your life with somebody, you want the rest of your life to start as soon as possible." In less romantic moments, she would actually employ the phrase "shit or get off the pot."

I kept asking for more time. Sometimes demanding. Was Laura the one person I wanted to be with, forever? Was there even such a thing? I needed to be sure.

It's clear now that uncertainty is one reason Grogan's story hooked me so deeply. Compared to how well he and Gertrude knew one another when he left for Africa, Laura and I might as well have grown up together. They made their choice when they were still practically children and could measure their time together in weeks. It was a pure leap of faith.

Laura and I analyzed our decision to death, or at least I did. When it came to love, Grogan's decisiveness intrigued me and spooked me—and I have to admit, it made me a little jealous.

CHAPTER TWENTY

Grogan's makeshift armada reached the northern tip of Lake Albert, where the water narrowed to two miles across, then one, and finally shrank to a thousand-foot-wide channel twisting north.

This was the White Nile, one of the two main tributaries of the world's longest river. In twenty-three hundred miles it flowed from Lake Victoria to Lake Albert, then north through the Sudan to Khartoum, where it joined the Blue Nile, running out of the Ethiopian highlands. The combined stream ran through Egypt and emptied into the Mediterranean at Cairo.

Grogan didn't record his thoughts on seeing the river for the first time, but his heart must have swelled. It had taken him almost two years of sweat and blood to get here. He was tired of Africa, sick of being sick, exhausted with trying to keep his unruly men in line and the locals from killing them.

The muddy flow was Grogan's first direct link to home: a watery, winding, plant-choked road through the desert to Cairo, London, glory—and Gertrude.

Forty miles later, on October 1, they reached the British outpost of Wadelai, consisting of a few "gravitation-defying huts" perched on two small hills above the river. The Union Jack hung on a crooked pole.

Wadelai's sole European inhabitant was a sad-eyed En-glishman named Lieutenant Cape. He was surprised at Grogan's arrival, astonished to hear where he had come from, and flab-bergasted when Grogan told him where he was heading next.

Everyone knew the Nile was impassible through south-ern Sudan. The river and the swamps that surrounded it—the Sudd—were smothered with vegetation too dense to get a boat through but too spongy to march across. The tribes that lived there were as hostile as they were gigantic.

For the moment, Grogan was just happy to have another Englishman to chat with again. ("In six weeks one finds out what a terribly uninteresting fellow one is.") He put on his usual confident face, but in fact, the closer he came to his goal, the more his anxiety grew that something awful was about to hap-pen. If things were going to go to hell, the Sudd was where it would happen.

Cape took him hunting in bleak country that had been scorched by drought down to bark and bare earth. Old rhinos stomped through spiky scrub under a sun "round, red, and glow-ing like a furnace door."

Long-overdue storm clouds bloomed above them. One night the wind snatched away Grogan's tent in the middle of an icy downpour. After that, "life became rather a burden," as the two Englishmen spent the next three nights "in anxious wakeful-ness, desperate hammerings at pegs and holding of poles, to the accompaniment of a running and not too polite commentary on Nature and her ways, sustained in a high falsetto to keep up one another's courage."

When they came across local villages, Grogan found he was an object of great curiosity, "especially to the ladies of these communities, who came in large numbers to inspect me (front seats at bath time being in great request)."

At one village, Grogan noticed what looked like a large pigeon loft. He asked a woman what it was used for.

"We mothers put all our babies together there at night," she said. "Then, if they scream, it does not matter. We do not hear; we sleep."

Grogan thought this was "a very excellent idea, and one that might be introduced at home."

After three weeks at Wadelai, Grogan gave up waiting for the supplies Sharp was supposed to have sent from Kampala. From now on, the expedition party would have to survive on what they carried and anything they could trade for or shoot along the way. He paid off his ten Manyema porters and sent them home.

Now there were nine: Grogan, the five Watonga, two natives he had recruited in Ruanda, and a cook boy from Ujiji. They pushed off into the current, paddling past walls of lilies and hills like brown elephants. The current varied with the width of the river, from quick to barely perceptible. Aquatic plants hid the banks, and black cormorants clustered on small hills in midstream.

When they pulled ashore to eat or camp, they saw game animals such as hartebeest, stout antelopes with narrow black faces and horns like the arms of a lyre. The mosquitoes were typically unbearable after dark, and the men spent the night "in reminiscences of the happy lands flowing with milk and honey now left far behind."

Hippos snorted along the shore and stalked the river bottom. Grogan had heard stories of hippos attacking steel boats on this part of the river. The enraged old bull that chased him the day he turned twenty-five only let off when Grogan shot it with his revolver.

The hills faded away, and soon they saw nothing but "vast

wastes of weed and water" in every direction. They had entered the Sudd.

The blue Toyota sedan bounces east toward the White Nile. Paul, the driver, waves to people as we roll through fields of corn and cotton.

Men in white robes, skullcaps, and sunglasses ride bicycles and swerve out of our way. I realize I'm pressing my foot to the floor, not on an imaginary brake pedal but on an accelerator. It took me more than six weeks to get to Fort Portal. My flight home from Kampala is in a week. Pushing it later isn't an option, Laura has made it clear. Wadelai, or whatever is left of it, will be my last stop in Uganda. Sudan is next.

A sign for the Rhino Camp Refugee Center flashes past. "There are many Sudanese there," Paul says. "And some from the Congo."

"How many?"

"Many."

Tens of thousands, in fact. Rhino Camp is one of the main refugee camps in Uganda for people fleeing the chaos in southern Sudan. It's a city in itself, with schools, hospitals, churches, markets, workshops.

The road descends into a green marshy plain where we splash through stream after stream. Paul stops in front of one that looks especially wide, too deep to see the bottom. He gets out and picks up a fist-size rock and tosses it in the water. It disappears like a depth charge.

He gets back in and rolls up his window.

The Toyota plows forward. Water is up to the hubcaps, then the top of the wheels. Any second it's going to start pouring inside.

Then we're across. "Fearful persons cannot drive here." Paul grins, his eyes turning up at the corners like a cat's.

Nobody can drive up the western side of Lake Albert, the DRC side, even if there were a road, which there isn't. Border tensions between Uganda and the DRC, already high, have been inching toward all-out war since a huge oil field was discovered in the lake basin last year. Earlier this month, soldiers from the DRC entered Uganda and killed three villagers and a British geologist.

It takes two hours to reach Wadelai. Or at least where Paul thinks it is. There are no buildings, nothing but grass and bushes and thorny trees in every shade of tan and olive.

The road dwindles from a dirt lane to twin ruts. Eventually we're down to wide footpaths, two wheels in the dirt and two in the bush. Greenery whips the sides of the car, and a minty smell drifts through the vents.

Paul refuses to ask for directions. I'm impressed he's pushing it this far—he seems to have caught the discovery bug. I just hope he doesn't push the car too far. Hard things smack the bottom of the car, and gravel grates under the floorboards like broken glass.

We drive into a cloud of butterflies and emerge in a dirt clearing ringed by huts. A group of children stands around the base of a tree, arguing. It feels like we've passed through some kind of time portal, except for the T-shirts and the chalkboard on one of the huts that reads THE HUNT FOR/2006.

The children are so startled at our sudden appearance that they don't have time to shout *mzungu* before we disappear into the grass on the other side.

I wonder what they'll think of Sean Connery trying to pass for a Russian submarine commander. Will they give *The Hunt for Red October* two thumbs up?

Where is the river? Paul finally stops to ask a pair of women for directions. One points back the way we came. "This boy will take you." She nods at a shirtless kid carrying a hoe taller than he is. He shakes his head and starts to sidle away.

We're on point five of a six-point turn when the rear axle sinks into dark gumbo mud.

Paul gets out and borrows the boy's hoe and starts digging out the wheels. The only thing I can find to help is a stick.

Three weathered old men roll up on bicycles. One starts hacking next to Paul with his own hoe. Another yells at another boy who's watching to drop the sugarcane stalk he's chewing on and help out. The women stand back and offer suggestions.

"We can push this thing," someone says. Wheels spin, mud sprays. Useless.

I'm sweating, filthy. Nothing here is easy. I miss the cool, clean, efficient world I left behind, the one that eventually bores me to tears after too long. I haven't wanted to go home this much since my first night at sleepaway camp, age ten.

How often did Grogan feel like this—daily? hourly? Did he ever not?

Right now I don't really care. To be honest, I'm getting sick of the guy and his conceit of "walking" the "length" of Africa. He took boats! And started in Beira! I'm not sure I even like this man I've invested so much time and money to follow, putting my life on hold, leaving my fiancée behind.

He's entertaining, sure. Impressive, even intimidating. But he could be a real ass, too.

What was it about him that brought me here, stuck in the mud in God-knows-where, Uganda, trying to find the biggest river in Africa?

The hubcaps emerge. Paul climbs in and guns the engine. We all heave as one, and the car lurches free.

The locals seem as happy as we are, these complete strangers. Nobody asks for anything. They're just glad to help.

Ten minutes later the track ends at the river. A line of dugout canoes in the milky-tea water bobs like huge wooden pea pods.

The Nile at last, I think, trying to invest the moment with some meaning. But it's just a brown river, narrow enough to throw a stone across. Not the least bit impressive.

A group of mothers and children are washing a few yards up the bank. One little boy bursts into tears when he sees me. Everyone else laughs. I don't think I've ever made anyone cry just by showing up before.

The boy sobs himself quiet, and the current flushes clumps of weeds toward Sudan.

Grogan's unease grew with every mile down the Nile. The British had retaken Khartoum, meaning northern Sudan was safe, but for all he knew, southern Sudan was still overrun with Muslim soldiers. Facing down hostile spears was hard enough. What if they found themselves surrounded by Islamic fanatics with rifles?

The farther they could make it downstream before the vegetation closed in and forced them to walk, the faster he could get to Cairo. Anything that floated would do. There was a steamship based at Fort Berkeley, a British outpost a few days downstream, which he hoped could carry them.

At the Belgian outposts on the Nile's west bank, he wrote, "sardine-tins glisten on the banks, and absinthe-bottles drift upon the pools." Native troops in blue uniforms goose-stepped to bugle calls. Many locals had fled to the British-controlled east bank.

At the next British station, Grogan and his men wallowed in

"the unheard-of luxury of glass, china, silver, milk and butter galore" for three days. To avoid a series of rapids, they headed overland across a stony plateau to the east, where Grogan saw his first herd of giraffe. Fortunately for them, the party didn't have the time to detour. He had to be content with a long look through his binoculars, marveling at their size and their awkward but speedy gait.

By the time he reached the station of Fort Berkeley, Grogan was impatient for news, any news—from the Sudan, from Sharp, from Gertrude. He dreamed of being back in England by Christmas, which was more than a month away.

The station commander told him a steam launch called the *Kenia* had set off downstream with a Belgian paddle-steamer three months ago. Their mission was to cut a passage through the Sudd. Nobody had seen them since. He assured Grogan he would probably be stuck at Fort Berkeley through the end of the year, if not longer.

The news was devastating. It would take weeks, if not months, to cover the same distance in a smaller boat, let alone on foot. There was one other option: a Belgian steamer at a post across the river. Instead of waiting for the *Kenia*, which might never appear, Grogan swallowed his growing disgust of all things Belgian and asked for a ride.

The administrator was happy to help, and a few days later Grogan and his party were headed downriver again. It only took a few hours for the steamer to reach a Belgian station located near a number of huge islands in the river, many covered with crops of red millet. Here the hills finally dissolved into an endless expanse of sodden green. This was Lado, a "howling waste in a wilderness of swamps," gateway to the grim heart of the Sudd.

As the Nile flows into southern Sudan, it spreads out across a flat plain and stagnates. Half of the water evaporates. The rest becomes one of the largest freshwater wetlands in the world. In the rainy season, the floating mat of papyrus, grasses, and water hyacinth covers an area the size of England. Living islands, some dense enough to support elephants, regularly break free and block the ever-changing channels. The name comes from the Arabic word for "barrier."

The Sudd inspired horror in everyone who saw it. Thirty years before Grogan, the British explorer Samuel Baker ventured in from the north with his wife, a Hungarian girl he had bought at a slave auction. The Sudd is "a veritable Styx," he wrote. "During the dead calms in these vast marshes the feeling of melancholy produced is beyond description."

"If you can visualize twelve thousand square miles of swamp that seethes and crawls like a prehistoric crucible of half-formed life, you have a conception of the Sudd," wrote the British pilot and adventurer Beryl Markham. It was "one place in this world worthy of the word 'sinister.'"

Another six hours' paddling brought the steamer to Kero, the next Belgian station. Native soldiers paraded daily in the damp heat to the sounds of bugles and drums. The evening amusement consisted of tossing dynamite in the river and collecting the dead fish that floated up. Some weighed two hundred pounds.

He was making relatively good time, but Grogan's fever was back like clockwork and showed no signs of breaking. His congested liver, probably caused by a parasite he had caught during his first visit to Africa, was so swollen and tender he could hardly stand upright.

Grogan was starting to wonder if he would live to reach Cairo. Without rest, proper food, and medical attention, his condition could lead to heart failure. He had to reach civilization as soon as possible.

Luckily the Belgians were about to send a whaleboat, a narrow, oar-powered vessel, downriver to find out what had happened to the two lost steamships. They offered Grogan a ride and even sent word out for volunteers to accompany him.

So it was that, five days before Christmas, 1899, Grogan entered the heart of the largest swamp in Africa in the company of a Belgian officer, a dozen native soldiers, the five faithful Watonga, and a cast of "formidable recruits," including a small boy, a crippled prisoner, and a criminal lunatic.

He was entering a realm of almost quantum uncertainty. To the outside world, until he reappeared in what passed for civilization in southern Sudan, he was in Limbo: neither alive nor dead, just . . . gone.

He set off with an improved opinion of the Belgians and "the sincere hope that never should I set eyes on Kero or any other spot on the Upper Nile again."

After the isolation and emptiness of Wadelai, the crowds and pollution of Kampala are overpowering. The air in Uganda's capital is gray with dust and exhaust fumes.

A day after my own first sighting of the Nile, I'm standing on a downtown street corner, trying to flag down a motorcycle taxi to the embassy of Sudan—assuming there is one, and it's open, and they allow Americans inside—on what is starting to seem like a futile quest for a visa.

I'm freshly scrubbed and shaved, dressed as professionally as possible after two months of hand-washing a weekend's worth of clothes. My nerves are jangling.

With just five days left before my flight home, I'll have to fly to Juba, the capital of southern Sudan. From there I'll go as far north by road as I can, common sense and wedding calendar permitting.

The thought of returning home to Laura and my friends and family without having even made it to Sudan is too much. I've invested so much into this: time, money, myself. If Grogan could swim across crocodile-infested lagoons and eat raw hippo meat, the least I can do is get into the country.

But everyone in Kampala seems to have a different opinion of what I'll need to get into the country. Some say a visa is the only option, but those are expensive and take more than a month to process. "American?" one hotel owner says. "Good luck."

No, wait, says an aid worker at a bar downtown: the Sudanese embassy in Kampala is closed. You'll have to go to Kenya. The U.S. State Department says that I should have gotten a visa back home and that without "appropriate documents," I would risk arrest for espionage, with a penalty up to and including execution. In fact, their advice is to not go at all, especially anywhere outside Khartoum.

Other people have told me a permit from the two-year-old Government of Southern Sudan (GOSS) will work. But nobody knows where the office is or even if there is one in Kampala; this includes two bartenders and three taxi drivers in a row. General consensus: there isn't.

No one answers the phone at the numbers listed for the embassy. That leaves one choice: show up in person and turn on the charm.

I'm armed with my passport, business cards, passport photos, and plenty of cash. If anyone asks why I want to visit one of the most miserable cities on the planet, I have an assignment letter I printed out at an Internet café last night from the editor of an imaginary travel magazine called *New Destinations*. (I found out later there actually is one, for RV drivers.) I'm allegedly writing about the city's "impressive recent strides in transforming from a war-torn ruin to the next adventure-travel mecca."

If this doesn't work, my trip is over.

A motorcycle taxi pulls up, spitting blue smoke.

"You know where the embassy of Sudan is?" I ask as I climb aboard.

"Which one?" the driver says.

"Which—what?"

"The old one or the new one?"

"New one?" No way.

"Yes. The new one. For the south."

I can't believe my luck. There is a GOSS office, and this guy knows where it is. We pull out into the life-or-death game of rock-paper-scissors that is Kampala traffic. Bus flattens minibus, minibus squashes car, car smashes motorcycle. Pedestrians always lose.

Weaving across roads, in and out of incoming traffic, we mount sidewalks and squeeze through tiny spaces between cars and buildings. I'm too excited to be scared.

Ten minutes later we stop outside a brick house on an unpaved residential street. The house is identical to the ones on either side. No guard, no sign or flag. It's starting to rain.

"This is it." The driver seems happily surprised by the fat tip and hearty handshake.

Inside is the unmistakable aura of officialdom, piles of paper and people waiting in uncomfortable chairs, while other sit behind desks doing nothing but looking busy. A woman hands me an application and collects my documents and thirty-five dollars in cash.

"Come back tomorrow. Eleven A.M."

Back outside in the downpour, ankle-deep in the brown torrent raging down the street, I think, *There's no way it can be this easy.*

CHAPTER TWENTY-ONE

Of all the miserable places Grogan had seen in the past two years, the Sudd topped them all. It was "one vast dismal flat, a wilderness of water, weed, and scrub," a "paradise of malaria, misery, and mosquitoes."

The party paddled for hours at a time, seeing nothing but reeds, black water, and the thin violet band that marked the other side of the river. The stench of rotting fish was so thick it was almost visible. They glided past muddy banks where native huts were covered with strips of hippo hide drying in the sun.

As the sun disappeared, the mosquitoes descended "with a long-drawn expectant howl . . . little ones, big ones, black ones, mottled ones, a whirling, wailing fog of miniature vampires, that kept up the mournful dirge till the cold hour before sunrise."

The two men from Ruanda, sick for weeks, were too weak to fight off the insects. One morning Grogan discovered one of them dead, "literally sucked dry" by the mosquitoes. The other died soon after.

Four days later they found an elephant dozing amid scattered skulls in the earth-brick ruins of a Dervish fort at Bohr. They were setting up camp when a group of the tallest men any of them had ever seen materialized out of the bush.

They were Dinka, the gigantic tribe who lived and fished and herded cattle in southern Sudan. Some were easily seven feet tall, and six and a half seemed average. "Strict nudity is the fashion," Grogan wrote, "and a marabout feather in the hair is the essence of *chic.*

"They are all beautifully built," he added, noting their broad shoulders and small waists. They wore their long hair kinked out like a mop or caked in white clay, and coated themselves head to foot in gray wood ash to ward off the mosquitoes. Each one carried a wicked-looking spear and a heavy club of purple wood.

The jet-black giants brought gourds of milk and strings of fish to trade. Then they faded back into the bush, sunlight winking off their spear points until they were out of sight.

Over the next three days, Grogan saw exactly one tree, and that from several miles away. The following morning he spotted what looked like a tall tree trunk swaying in the distance. He looked closer and saw that it bore a tattered Union Jack. It was the *Kenia*, the lost British steamer, heading back upstream full of sick and shattered men.

Her American skipper described the misery they had been through in the past three months, trying to cut a channel through the Sudd. They had labored waist-deep in crocodile-infested marshes by day, sleeping on board or on the floating vegetation itself at night, maddened by mosquitoes, with hardly anything to eat except strange birds and native porridge.

When food ran low, the expedition had decided to abandon the Belgian boat and send most of the men back in the *Kenia* to drop off the sickest and resupply. The rest, including a British captain and doctor, had set off across the Sudd on foot, dragging three lifeboats in case they found open water. The plan was for the *Kenia* to return to look for them, blowing her whistle constantly, once every week for the next three months. After that, they were on their own.

Grogan pictured the men slogging onward, "not knowing where they were, nor, in characteristic British fashion, caring, yet ever keeping their face forward, strong in the knowledge that perseverance must succeed." It stirred his blood and inspired him to keep pushing north.

For the first time in a hundred fifty years, the seasonal rains had failed, and the Nile was lower than it had been in living memory. The low water made the vegetation even denser than usual, the *Kenia*'s skipper said. There was no chance a boat could make it through.

Grogan's only option was to backtrack to Bohr and try his luck cross-country. From Bohr it was about three hundred miles due north to the British station at Sobat, the closest place they could hope to find river transport again.

Fighting despair, Grogan led his party back two days to Bohr, where the natives' opinion of the overland route was "decidedly discouraging."

He ordered the men to dump everything that wasn't absolutely essential: the bed, the collapsible bath, all of it had to go. One night a native who had joined them a week earlier disappeared, taking everything he could carry. Five native soldiers volunteered to take his place.

On December 30, with a group "swelled to the vast total of fourteen," Grogan set out on foot across a wasteland more desolate than anything any of them had ever seen.

He was near his breaking point. "The terror of those stupendous wastes!" he wrote. "With visions of impassable swamps, waterless deserts, and famine in front, I heartily wished myself quit of Africa and all its abominations."

The plane to Juba skims a sea of creamy gray clouds past indigo thunderheads.

I'm still stunned by how painless it was to get the lavender permit that's folded carefully in my passport pouch. I will have to register with the local police, get a separate permit to take any pictures, and find a hotel I can afford—not easy, from what I hear of the city. But I'm finally on the last leg of my journey.

An elegant woman in designer jeans, black calfskin boots, and dangling pearl earrings sits across the aisle. She taps maroon nails on the seat arm and gives me a quick smile. Maybe Sudan won't be all that bad.

On the runway in Kampala I had a momentary fantasy that the plane was taking me home. I've had my fill of the road, of musty beds and fried food and trying to talk to strangers. It's been weeks since I had any sort of exercise beyond the isometrics of clutching a seat in terror.

I'm thinking about Laura more often every day. In her latest email, she told me the British government had just recalled all nonessential personnel from Sudan's capital, Khartoum. *Just thought you'd want to know,* she wrote, which meant she was genuinely worried. I'm back to risking merely my own safety, but it's not just my own peace of mind anymore.

Most of the world's attention has been focused recently on Darfur, in western Sudan. The country has been wracked by civil war for the past half century, pitting the Muslim north half of the country against the Christian and animist south. In 2003, just as the countrywide fighting was winding down, ethnic African rebels began fighting the Arab-dominated government in Darfur. In four years, more than two hundred thousand people have been killed and 2.5 million displaced. The U.S. government is using the word *genocide* to describe the scorched-earth tactics employed by Sudanese troops and Arab "Janjaweed" militias on civilians.

The civil war left southern Sudan in chaos as well. Before the war, Juba was a road and river traffic hub for the brutally poor region. The fighting left it a shell of a city and the capital of a country that existed in name only. Highways to Uganda, Kenya, and the DRC were demolished, mined, or both. A year ago there weren't even ten miles of paved roads in an area almost as large as Texas. Now hundreds of millions of dollars of foreign investment are pouring in, making Juba one of the fastest-growing cities in Africa.

The peace agreement that ended the civil war in 2005 gave the south six years of autonomy from the north. In 2011, a referendum will be held to decide if it should become its own country. The government in Khartoum is especially unenthusiastic about a split because most of the country's five-billion-barrel oil reserves are in the south. At present, oil revenues are shared fifty-fifty between the north and south.

I hope I'm bringing enough cash. Credit cards are useless here, and there's isn't a foreign ATM in the entire country.

Ninety minutes after leaving Kampala, the plane descends under an overcast sky. The city sprawls on both banks of the river, a dun stripe across a moss-colored expanse. This once was Lado, Grogan's "howling waste in a wilderness of swamps." In the middle of the river, the islands he saw covered with red millet are still being cultivated.

Within minutes I'm riding on the back of a talking motorcycle through streets so bad they're three-dimensional. Gerald, the driver, swerves around rusted truck frames and piles of garbage as a tinny voice from the gearbox narrates every turn in French:

Tourne à gauche. Tourne à droite. Turning left, turning right. I have no idea why. Both our shirts are dripping with sweat.

Juba's roads are nothing but thigh-deep ruts and potholes big enough to bathe in. We flash past spindly locals in bright cloth and Western clothes, some with skin so dark it seems to absorb light. One tall man has tribal scars across his forehead, a keloid geometry from eyebrows to hairline.

Gerald hasn't stopped talking since we left the airport. "Oh, the roads get worse than this. But things are better now than they were before."

By "before," he means the first years of the new millennium, when fighting between government troops and militias raged across the region, the latest chapter of Sudan's seemingly endless civil war. Thousands of women and children were kidnapped as slaves, and tens of thousands were killed.

Juba is still filled with the detritus of war, but signs of rebuilding are shooting up everywhere. Foreign aid workers drive white Land Cruisers with plastic engine snorkels for deep-river crossings. Industrious English words flash past: "Procurement," "Logistics," "Shipping Company." Everything else is chaos labeled in Arabic, swooping calligraphy on hand-painted signs.

We pass a high white wall ("Our prison!") and fields full of *tukuls*, round mud-brick huts with thatched roofs, surrounded by charcoal smoke. A group of camo-clad soldiers watch a backhoe rip holes in the ground with the fascination all men have for heavy machinery.

Over the buzz of the engine, I mention I'm hoping to head north, down the Nile River toward Cairo. Gerald almost dumps us in the street.

"No, no, no." He tries to look me in the eye and dodge a goat at the same time. "That would not be wise."

He leaves me at the White Nile Camp, where rows of white prefab structures and olive tents line the east bank of the river. A blast of air-conditioning spills from the door of the trailer that serves as reception area.

"Juba is the most expensive city in the world," the manager, Charles, says proudly as I sign the guestbook. "More than Tokyo, Japan, more than London, England." A tent by the river is available for one hundred forty dollars a night. I haven't paid a quarter that much for a hotel room yet, but I have no choice—demand is high and that's the going rate.

He agrees with Gerald: going anywhere north of Juba is a bad idea. The Government of Southern Sudan has closed the road to Bor, one hundred twenty miles north, because local tribes have been fighting with automatic rifles left over from the war. Skirmishes over cattle have turned into massacres. A dozen women and children were killed two weeks ago.

Besides, recent rains have turned the dirt track into a morass.

"It's not safe!" The cleaning lady holds her broom in midsweep. She seems surprised that anyone is listening. "They're fighting."

"Who?" She shrugs.

"They're always fighting." With a quick shake of her head, she attacks the trail of dirt I tracked across the floor.

An hour of watching the river flow is like meditation. People start to gather in the open-walled dining tent for dinner as darkness falls. A television on one table shows Al Jazeera news. Arabic script crawls across the bottom of the screen from right to left like the readout on an EKG. Images of Donald Rumsfeld and U.S. soldiers are followed by footage of bearded men bleeding on the ground and bandaged in a makeshift hospital. At home they'd be labeled "insurgents." I wonder what the captions say here.

I fill my plate with strips of meat, something spinachlike, and a piece of *injera*, the thin sourdough pancake typical to the Horn of Africa. The dining crowd looks half black, half Arab.

A man with a mustache and a lopsided smile sits down across from me and introduces himself as Assad, an engineer from Khartoum.

"We are here to create infrastructure," he says. His gaze hovers somewhere over my right shoulder as he talks. "With roads, anything is possible." He is part of the huge influx of people—aid workers, UN troops and officials, foreign entrepreneurs, returning Sudanese exiles—who have come to try to build a country essentially from scratch.

He thinks the south will vote to break away in 2011. "Me personally, I think it would be best to stay united." He tears off a piece of *injera* and dips it in meat sauce.

"The north and south look at each other like a cat and mouse. There is fighting with so little cause now, just a word between tribes." He doesn't think the war is really over.

I tell him I'm a writer.

"Write good things," he says.

My tent seems smaller after dark, claustrophobic. So against the advice of everyone at the hotel, including the sad-eyed guard who lets me through the gate, I walk into the dark city.

The streets are unpaved and unlit. Each one seems to have a different odor: spoiled fruit, animals, smoke. I can't remember a day in Africa without the smell of something burning.

On one block men sit smoking water pipes under a string of holiday lights. Someone laughs in the shadows, and silent lightning throbs in the clouds like a slow heart.

I'm abruptly aware of an unfamiliar feeling: the fear of walking alone at night. At home it's not even an issue. I've traveled enough in poor places to know that a decisive stride is the best defense against getting mugged, even—especially—if you have no idea where you're going. I've also been incredibly lucky. But here in Juba I don't have a single foothold: no guidebook, no friends, no plan.

The Bedouin Bar occupies one end of a small compound of prefab offices. All the frontier trappings are new: sand floors, tables on oil drums, the antelope skull under the dartboard. Tough-looking Brits and Australians sit at the bar.

Craig and Mike, the managers, are serving drinks. Both are white Kenyans, grizzled and beefy. The place has been open only a few months. They agree that running a business in Juba is a hell of an opportunity and a nightmare.

"They don't want you here," Craig says. The red tape is ridiculous, and the government seems to make things like regulations and fines up as they go. Sometime "fire inspectors" will show up out of the blue, write a report, and charge business owners a thousand dollars for the pleasure.

"But where else would you pay three thousand dollars a month for a tent?" Mike says. The government has declared a moratorium on building prefab-and-tent camps, but they're still going up. "You just have to pay the right people."

Their opinion on heading north, even just a hundred miles to Bor, is no surprise.

"Forget it," Craig says.

"But how is the road?" I ask.

"What road?"

Grogan and his men fought their way through a world of reeds and water. Over and over they had to wade up to their necks to cross the lagoons and muddy channels that spiderwebbed the vegetation. Some were almost a mile wide. "The prevalence of crocodiles, and a slimy bottom pitted with elephant-holes, did not facilitate matters," he wrote.

Every spongy step was like walking on bedsprings. No matter how careful they were, the men repeatedly plunged into the murky water, the mat of papyrus closing over their heads in an instant.

On one crossing the cook boy stepped in a hole and vanished completely, taking Grogan's revolver, prismatic compass, and coat. An obliging Dinka fished him out, gasping, his hands empty. Game animals were scarce, but there were hippos everywhere, lying in purple banks by the dozens or hundreds.

Herds of elephants stood in the path, and the men often had to shout, throw stones, or fire guns in the air to get them to move. Grogan shook his head to think about what he and Sharp had endured to find elephants earlier in the trip. They were terrible eating and ammunition was running low, but the men were getting so hungry that Grogan shot one and had his men smoke the meat.

The vegetation was full of snakes, including twenty-foot pythons that after a meal could be as big around as a healthy boy. Grogan learned that the monstrous serpents were harmless, even friendly, although they occasionally needed encouragement to straighten out so they could be measured.

"One day, when I saw a particularly pretty specimen, I tried the native trick of stroking his head," he wrote. "Then I scratched him as one would a cat, and found he liked the sensation and that it made him uncoil himself at full length. After that we had no trouble measuring pythons."

The only places to camp were small flat-topped hills covered with palms. They spent the nights praying for morning. Grogan had learned it was essential to stop half an hour before sunset to set up the mosquito defenses: lighting green wood fires at either end of camp, hanging the net, piling everything around the edges to hold it down.

He lay awake smoking the potent local tobacco and listening to the night cries of golden-headed cranes like gunfire in the distance. Each morning he arose "perfectly dazed from the amount of poison that had been injected during the night."

The Dinka strategy to keep the insects away—smearing themselves with a mix of ash and cow's urine, and burning cow dung inside their huts at night—was starting to seem reasonable. Half mad from lack of sleep, Grogan had the men set fire to a twenty-foot-high stretch of reeds. As the flames raced east, he smiled to think of the billions of mosquitoes being roasted.

The exhausted group could barely make ten miles a day. The minerals in the water, concentrated by evaporation, were starting to eat away at their guts. At this rate it would take more than a month to reach Sobat, even though they could only carry a few days' worth of food at a time.

More than once, birds of prey called kites swooped down and stole their dinner out of the frying pan. One morning they discovered that the lunatic criminal had disappeared. Before he left, he had handed out Grogan's blankets, clothes, and mosquito net among the Dinka.

Throughout everything, one part of Grogan's mind was always back home. As they toiled north, their route roughly followed the east bank of a long lagoon the Dinka called the Atem. The previously unknown channel of the great river ran full of clear, delicious water. The men drank their fill for the first time in weeks, and Grogan christened it the Gertrude Nile.

It had been more than two years since he had last seen her, when he and Sharp left London for Cape Town. She had promised to wait for him, no matter how long it took. She couldn't possibly have changed her mind, not after all this.

Thousands of Dinka lived on the barren plains beyond the marshlands, where they surrounded their isolated villages with thorny fences to keep the lions away from herds of goats and sheep.

"From the first moment we struck these people it was evident we were going to have a bad time of it," he wrote. "They were not openly hostile in their demeanor, but it was evident they did not welcome us, and also that they looked down upon us as something quite inferior." They always greeted Grogan in the traditional way, by spitting at him.

He could never get over how tall they were. They reminded him of herons, the way they stood motionless on one leg for hours and took long steps with their giant feet lifted high.

"Height is, of course, a great advantage in the reed-grown country," he wrote, pondering the evolutionary implications. The Dinka seemed the complete opposite of the pygmies, just as "the country in which they live is the complete antithesis of the dense forest that is the home of the dwarfs." Perhaps nature had endowed the Dinka with an extra foot or two to make up for the height they lost to the spongy ground?

If the expedition ever strayed far from the water, natives would materialize to put them back on course. "There was something uncanny about knowing that one was watched by hundreds without ever seeing more than an occasional individual perched on one leg, the other foot resting on his knee, on the top of a far ant-hill, and looking like a long black stork." At night, hundreds would emerge single file from the darkness, to sell fish or just stare.

The Sudd was home to other tribes, like the Woastsch, a "miserable fishing-folk" who would escort Grogan's group for miles, chanting. At one water hole, Grogan wrote how

> a hundred loathsome hags danced a wild fandango around me, uttering the shrillest cries conceivable, and accompanying them with a measured flap-flap of their long pendant dugs; then, as a grand finale, all threw themselves on their faces at my feet, and with one ear-piercing shriek dispersed into the bush, leaving me under the impression that I was in the Drury Lane pantomime [London's oldest theater] outside two bottles of champagne.

One day the party reached a wide lagoon that would take days to detour around. A large crowd of Dinka gathered to watch. Using sign language, the only way he could communicate, Grogan asked them for help finding the best route across. Nobody stepped forward.

He held up strings of beads and rolls of cloth, pantomiming that these would go to anyone who volunteered as a guide. They lived here—someone had to know the way.

Nothing. For two futile hours, Grogan tried to convince anyone to lead them through the water. Finally his patience snapped.

"God, can't you understand anything, you blithering idiots?" he shouted.

Enough with these smirking giants. Grogan strode into the water, livid. His men watched as he inched forward, shuffling his feet in the murk, hoping he wouldn't kick a crocodile or vanish into an elephant hole.

Fifty yards. The water rose to his thighs, his waist. A hundred yards.

He called out for the men to join him. They would swim if they had to.

The Dinka must have realized this strange, angry white man was serious, or else they figured the joke had gone far enough. Either way, several natives stepped forward and showed them the shallowest path.

When they reached the other side, the guides stopped, pointing ahead and making jabbing motions. The meaning was clear: any Dinka who continued to the next village would get a spear in the gut. Grogan gave them some beads and a Queen Victoria Jubilee medal as thanks, for which they were "hugely delighted."

Overall, he thought, the Dinka seemed to consider him "a great joke, and, on the whole, not such a bad sort of fool."

The move to New Mexico may have been ill-considered, but Laura and I did our best to make it work. We hosted cookouts, urged friends to come visit, networked as best we could. No matter what we tried, though, it never really felt like home.

Our growing disappointment with the Land of Enchantment matched the mounting deadlock over the issue of marriage. It was starting to seem like a war of attrition, or a least an endless series of skirmishes.

It felt like Laura had already made her choice, leaving the future of our relationship—or lack thereof—entirely in my hands, and I resented it. For that matter, so did she.

We needed a vacation, so I organized a trip to Ecuador in November. Since I had written a guidebook to the country—and Laura's thirty-third birthday fell during the visit—I had arranged free plane tickets and two weeks of activities.

It was her first time in South America. I couldn't wait to show her around. First came a week of scuba diving in the Galápagos Islands, swimming with marine iguanas and schools of hammerhead sharks. Laura was a certified diving instructor, and I loved watching her do something she knew so well—in tight neoprene, no less, which showed off what I had always called her "nineteen-year-old butt."

We spent most of her birthday on buses in the rain. In the hotel that night, I scribbled out a card while she was in the shower and laid it on her pillow next to a rose I pulled from a vase on the coffee table.

Tomorrow we were heading off on horseback through the foothills of the Andes, then maybe stopping by an indigenous market or craft workshop. Not a bad birthday present, I thought.

She came out wrapped in a towel, sat down on the bed, and opened the card. Her eyes filled with tears, but they didn't seem like the happy kind.

"What is it?" Maybe she was just tired from a long day.

"It's just . . . not what I was expecting." Her shoulders slumped. In so many words, she said: This is it? A last-minute card and a pre-vased flower?

I was stunned. Two days ago we'd been snorkeling with penguins on the equator, for Christ's sake. All of this was paid for. She was *disappointed*?

We exchanged a few terse words of frustration, made up as best we could, and went to bed.

If I hadn't been so indignant, I might have remembered a story from a few months before, when Jeff had taken Deb to Paris for a weeklong vacation before he started a business trip through Europe.

He had been planning to propose for months, but he hadn't gotten his hands on the ring before they left. He figured he'd just pop the question when they were both back home.

Unfortunately, and inevitably, all of Deb's friends had assured her he would propose on the trip. He had to—Paris!

She cried the whole flight home, alone. And it wasn't even her birthday.

(It was right after he got back, though, and Jeff let that opportunity slip by as well. By Christmas she had almost given up, so when he did propose then, he told me later, "she was totally surprised, which worked out well.")

If I had remembered this story, and the abuse we all heaped on Jeff when the news spread, it might have occurred to me that there was only one thing that would have made Laura fully content that night in the hotel room in Ecuador. And it wasn't a fresher flower or a more thoughtful card.

Chapter Twenty-two

Relations with the Dinka started to go downhill just a few days after Grogan entered the swamp on foot. He concluded they were "the most inveterate, pertinacious, and annoying beggars."

They seemed offended he wouldn't hand over anything they wanted. When one hulking warrior demanded his last pair of pants, Grogan, "pleading modesty," said no. The man stomped and howled "like a spoilt child," then stormed into Grogan's tent, brandishing his club.

"I suddenly took him by the scruff of the neck and the seat of where he wished my trousers to be, and, trusting in the superiority of a beef and beer diet over one of fish and thin milk, to his intense amazement, ran him out of camp, and imparted a final impetus with a double-barreled drop-kick, backed by a pair of iron-shod ammunition boots."

The other Dinka roared with laughter.

On January 1, 1900, the first morning of the final year of the century, Grogan found himself surrounded by fifteen hundred "very obstreperous" warriors. A few tried to pilfer items from his tent. Grogan tried to shoot at one who was sprinting away with a bolt of cloth, but his .303 misfired.

He ordered the area around the tent cleared and started shoving the rest of the Dinka away. One pushed back and Grogan knocked him down, slicing his hand on the man's sharpened teeth.

Two of the oldest natives did their best to calm the rest, to no avail. One warrior, without reason or warning, thrust his spear clean through one of the porters "merely as a bit of horseplay." The man dropped dead without a sound.

Grogan drew his revolver and held it an inch from the warrior's forehead. The Dinka, who had never seen a pistol before, closed one eye and peered curiously down the barrel.

To show him what it could do, Grogan aimed at a nearby Marabou stork and fired. The native picked up the dead bird and inspected the bloody hole. He looked more closely at the revolver, which evidently he had thought was some kind of silly-looking little club.

"Then he picked up his goods and chattels and walked away. He had not gone ten steps before he broke into a trot and then into a run, and when last seen, on the horizon the Dinka . . . was galloping."

Grogan spent the rest of the day with one hand on his pistol, expecting to be overrun at any moment. Most of the natives eventually left, but about a hundred of the "most noisy ruffians" lingered.

Two days later, another hundred Dinka warriors appeared and insisted on walking with them.

Something didn't feel right. Grogan noticed two or three natives were crowding around each of his men. Another twenty had gathered behind him.

Then his men did exactly what Grogan had prayed they wouldn't. They panicked, throwing down their loads and running to his side.

"We are all lost!" one cried.

The Dinka attacked.

Juba's immigration office is a mass of slate-blue uniforms. A map of southern Sudan hangs on one moldy wall under a motionless fan.

The lackey who handles foreigners seems flustered. Apparently tourists don't show up alone and unannounced here very often. I can hardly understand what he's saying, but I gather that he'll need my passport and entrance permit and photocopies of both.

He takes the paperwork and then says I need a letter from my hotel confirming I'm staying there. Also, it will cost seventy-five dollars. He'll hold on to my documents in the meantime.

"I'd really rather not—"

He waves off my concerns.

He has a truly impressive set of gums. When he smiles, it looks like he has two sets of lips.

"Will be no problem."

I leave the office with extreme reluctance. I loathe letting my passport out of my sight anywhere outside the United States. But I don't want to pick a fight with a petty official so close to the end, either.

I feel naked walking back to camp without the familiar stiffness of my passport in my money belt. Cash, plane ticket, camera—all those can be replaced. Since there's no embassy in Juba, though, if I lose that little blue book, I'm on my own.

It's a strange floating sensation, as if in some way I don't exist.

A mother duck and eight ducklings waddle across a dirt lane where a boy squats along the road. "Goodmorning," he says, then answers himself. "Imfinehowareyou?"

At the office, Charles is happy to type up the letter. But the power is off, and the computer is dead.

At noon, the recently air-conditioned office is the most comfortable place to wait. I ask him and Franklin if they know anyone with a car or motorcycle I can hire to take me to Bor.

They exchange a look: this again?

"I have a friend, I will ask," Charles says. I borrow Franklin's phone to call two British aid workers here in town, both friends of friends I had emailed earlier for advice. Neither answers.

Franklin says the fighting to the north is nothing new. "In Africa, life is very cheap. Things are expensive, but life, no."

It reminds me of a night near the beginning of my trip, walking down a cracked sidewalk in Maputo, Mozambique, with two young Germans.

"The end of our trip has turned out not so good," one said. His name was Thomas, and he talked quickly, with too many nervous giggles. "We were in a car accident. A bad one. It was a bicyclist. He wrecked our car."

"How? Was he hurt?"

"Oh, he was killed."

"You're kidding."

"Well, he was riding on the wrong side of the road at night. There are no lights. You can't see anything. We were so surprised—the impact, all the glass shattered."

"He killed himself with our car!" his friend interjects, his only contribution to the story.

"We had to go find the police ourselves," Thomas said. "First we call the emergency number and a recording says it is out of service. Then we had to pay someone to go get the police. They don't even have a car. He has to go pick them up!" His friend nods. "We had to stay at the police station the whole weekend, Friday to Monday."

"How inconvenient." They seem more bothered by the logistical hassle than having ended someone's life. "So what happened?"

"Now there is a big dent in the roof of the car. And the cooling system isn't working, where the bike hit. We had to pay a fine to the family, five hundred euros. They were so happy, like, 'Yay, he has brought us some money!'"

I marinate in stress for a few hours in the camp office, waiting for the power to come back on. The only other guest at lunch is a Sudanese lawyer in a pinstriped suit named Michael, with the deep, smooth voice of a jazz radio DJ.

"So you know our boys?" he says. "The Lost Boys?"

Before I left, Laura and I had watched a documentary about tens of thousands of Dinka boys displaced or orphaned by the war who wandered the desert, sometimes for years, dodging wild animals and armed militias. (After the movie, she said, "This is where you want to go?") The lucky ones reached refugee camps and immigrated to the United States.

Until the story of the Lost Boys spread, the most famous Dinka was probably the basketball player Manute Bol, whose insectile frame—seven feet seven inches, 225 pounds—made him an almost unbeatable shot blocker.

I ask Michael if he thinks southern Sudan will vote to break away. He nods.

"It is what we have fought for since 1955. We have all the country's resources: oil, minerals, timber. The Arabs don't want to let us go. The land is so fertile. We will be able to feed all of Africa." As for Darfur, that's northern Sudan's problem.

"Is it getting any better up north toward Bor?" I ask, fishing for any good news.

"At least it is not getting worse."

Franklin and Charles have rigged up a generator in the office. My letter is waiting, stamped and signed. But when I take it to the immigration office, I can't find the official who took my documents. Another official insists I have to pay him part of the fee in British pounds, apparently to stick my file in a drawer. I protest, but he's adamant: twenty-five pounds, no dollars, even the crisp new twenties I flash temptingly.

It's pouring rain and the streets are turning to muck. The foreign exchange offices are closed, but a sympathetic storekeeper takes me to an empty storeroom where we sit on crates and exchange currencies.

I leap puddles back toward immigration, drenched. Trucks splash past and locals stare. Foreigners simply don't walk here, let alone in the rain, by themselves.

"Julian Snell!" says my passport-stealing friend, using the middle name that got me teased to tears in grade school. He's my buddy now that I've jumped through his hoops. He stamps each of my documents with a small black date and hands them over proudly.

"That's it? You're absolutely sure?" There has to be some other form to fill out, another desk to find, a final fee in one more currency. There's no way I'm asking about a photography permit; I'll take my chances with stealth shots.

"Yes, yes, that is all. You are okay. Welcome."

The power is still off at camp. Charles says his friend with the motorcycle refused to drive anywhere near Bor. "Nobody is traveling that road now."

This month alone, the worst floods in recent memory have destroyed seventy thousand homes and killed eighty-nine people in southern Sudan. Close to half a million people have been affected. My desire to continue north abruptly seems as trivial as it does impossible.

I retreat to the tent to brood. Rain on the canvas lulls me to sleep. An hour later I wake to the most profound moment of travel disorientation I've ever experienced. For a full five seconds I have absolutely no idea where I am, or why. My mental GPS is blank.

Then I remember. I've made it to Juba. I finally have full, official permission to move around. Yet all I can think is: *get me the hell out of here.*

Maybe Laura's second-to-last card will help. *My heart's right there in Africa with you, my hand's holding your hand.*

I wish. My suspicion is growing that when I imagined following Grogan, I secretly hoped I'd hate it. That yearning to be home with Laura, instead of here, would prove to my pessimistic self that I've made the right choice.

If so, mission accomplished.

A Dinka spear flew into the heart of the man at Grogan's side. Native clubs swung in skull-splitting arcs. Grogan emptied each barrel of his shotgun into a rushing warrior, then turned to grab his revolver.

The gun bearer had bolted.

Grogan barely dodged another spear. The warrior who threw it closed and swung his club at Grogan's head. He raised an arm to block and thrust the empty shotgun barrel-first into the man's stomach. The warrior turned and fled, but before he made a dozen steps, someone else put a hollow-point bullet in his spine.

The Dinka retreated a few hundred yards away. Grogan climbed an anthill, took careful aim, and shot the tallest warrior in the stomach. Another bullet scattered them in all directions, and the fight was over.

Grogan looked around, panting. His one arm hung useless. At his feet, the speared man was writhing away the final seconds of his life. Three more were sprawled nearby, dark puddles spreading from their cracked heads. Where was everyone else?

"Come on out, you wretches!" Grogan shouted. The rest of the men crept uninjured from the reeds and bog holes where they had hidden.

Together, they tended the wounded. One man had two gaping holes in the top of his head. Another's skull was visible through a deep gash.

They had to get moving, fast. To lighten their load, Grogan had two of the guns and most of the beads and cloth buried. Then the battered group hurried north, terrified the Dinka would return to finish them off. Grogan posted two sentries that night, but the cries of the wounded kept everyone awake.

Grogan lay listening to the agonized moans, filled with "a hopelessness beyond civilized conception." He had fully expected to die when the natives attacked. Another fight would finish them off. At any moment they could hit an impassable obstacle—water too wide to swim, a swamp too dense to push through—and it would all be over.

He made a desperate decision. They would leave the northwest-curving river and head straight north across the vast burnt plain, straight for Sobat. Crossing the waterless wilderness would be a huge gamble, but a direct dash was their only hope.

Ragged and starving, their clothing in tatters, they plodded north into a nightmare. The lush banks of the river quickly faded into tracts of shale and dry lagoon beds cracked by the sun. Load after load tumbled to the ground as the men grew weaker. There was no longer enough vegetation to light fires, and the brackish water caused violent bouts of vomiting.

Grogan's arm was a sleeve of pain from wrist to shoulder. Even if he could have raised a rifle, he found the last box of shells were corroded and worthless. The party was reduced to eating raw hippo meat and sucking mud puddles for moisture. The diet started to turn Grogan's hands black.

The wounded men were half mad from their split heads, and the cook boy was dying of dysentery. One of the native soldiers, hobbled by a wounded foot, lagged a few minutes behind one day and vanished. They couldn't find a trace of him or anyone else.

News of the battle must have spread because every time they passed a village, groups of elders came out waving their arms to show they meant no harm.

One evening at dusk, Grogan heard roars in the distance. Two lions were approaching the camp, growling and snarling as they came. The flaming sky dimmed like a dying filament. The lions fell silent.

Grogan ordered everyone to gather around his tent and light two large fires. Then they waited, trembling with hunger and fatigue and adrenaline. Sleek shapes paced in the darkness, just beyond the firelight.

Two hours passed. Grogan decided the animals must have left. He had just lain down to sleep when a sentry cried out that the lions were in the camp.

Grogan sprang up and grabbed a burning log from one of the fires. He saw the tip of a tail disappear behind a bush. The cats had padded calmly through the camp, almost as if they knew they had nothing to fear.

"They were not in a hurry, and an occasional sniff showed that they were still inspecting, but they would not show in the firelight again." At last, "tired of the game, they strolled away grumbling across the plain, and treated me to a farewell roar."

Every step pushed them closer to death. Some of the men were so weak that Grogan had to force them on at spear point. Still they collapsed, begging for water.

"How much farther?" the men pleaded. "We can't go on!"

"You must!" Grogan said. "If you stay here you will die."

He climbed an anthill and saw a flock of birds far away. Could it be?

Grogan ordered the three men who could still walk to follow him. An hour later he found that his instincts were true. The birds had led them to a flowing stream. The men gulped to bursting, and they brought back gourds full of water for their fallen companions.

Grogan flashed in and out of lucidity. One moment he was staggering across the sunbaked expanse, using his rifle as a crutch. The next he was on his face in the dust, dragging himself forward on his belly.

Then, somehow, he was on the floor of a drawing room in New Zealand, Gertrude watching sadly from the next room. The door between them was slowly swinging shut.

"Yegods, what a land! The old boyhood's desire to shriek and break something that invariably recurred on Sunday morning broke out afresh, and I felt that I was near that indefinable boundary beyond which is madness."

There's an old Welsh wedding custom called *melltith,* where people throw obstacles in the groom's path as he tries to reach his bride on their wedding day. Anything goes, from blocking roads with fallen trees to herding sheep into the church. If the groom perseveres and reaches his bride, the idea goes, he proves his worth as a husband.

Grogan's hurdles came in the form of angry natives, appalling weather, stampeding animals, and deadly microbes, all stand-ins for Gertrude's stepfather's disapproval. Grogan loved nothing more than a challenge, but surely he wouldn't have traveled thousands of miles across Africa if he hadn't been absolutely sure she was the woman he wanted to marry.

I didn't need anyone's help to block my path. I was doing a fine job of it on my own.

By our third year in Santa Fe, my foot-dragging was driving us both crazy. We had passion, fun, great conversations, and nearly identical lists of what we wanted from life. What else was there?

In response, I only had more questions. Didn't the permanence of marriage mean the connection had to be perfect, or else it would mean a lifetime of struggle? Those times it felt like we couldn't communicate clearly, like we experienced two completely divergent realities—would they multiply and condense into disaster down the road?

One more man hesitating to make a commitment—I hated fitting a stereotype so perfectly. Laura's happiness didn't hinge on having a husband, but the longer we waited, the more it was starting to look that way. Her patience ebbed.

Santa Fe wasn't for us: too small, too quiet, too odd. Like half the self-employed people our age in the country, we decided to move to Portland, Oregon. It sounded perfect: a real city, but not too big; progressive but connected; with mountains in one direction and the Pacific in the other.

One night of our last October in New Mexico, we were sitting in the living room after a double-or-nothing Scrabble showdown. Pine logs snapped in the fireplace and filled the room with a faint spice.

"You know," Laura said, "in February we'll have been dating for seven years, unofficially. Six officially."

"Yeah?" I said, thinking, *Here we go.*

"Look. I know I want a family. And kids. With you. You say you do, too. So, I feel like we've been together long enough. I either need to know that's the direction we're going, or I need to move on with my life. By myself."

"So you're saying—"

"I can't move again if I don't know you're really invested in this."

"You mean get engaged."

"Yes."

There it was: the ultimatum I needed, wanted, demanded, dreaded. I don't know if it was from fear or relief, but we were both surprised at my tears.

CHAPTER TWENTY-THREE

Grogan watched the curved pole sway on the horizon for a long time. Anything to distract him from the pain of pushing forward.

It looked like a tree blown by the wind. He pointed it out to his men. One thought it was a palm tree. But no tree could bend that low, Grogan thought. He shuffled faster. The rest struggled to keep up. Then Grogan barked in amazement.

It was the mast of a boat.

They came closer and saw it was the slanting mast of a gyassa, a Nile sailing boat, filled with bustling figures.

Blood pounded in Grogan's ears. There was movement on deck—they had clearly been seen—but by whom?

One of the figures left the craft and began walking toward them. It was a tall black man wearing the cylindrical hat of a Sudanese soldier. He pushed a cartridge into his rifle as he approached.

Grogan straightened his back as the men crumpled to the ground at his feet. He stepped forward and offered the soldier his hand. He hoped his face held a nonthreatening smile, not the grimace of a dying man.

The soldier grinned widely and removed the cartridge from

his rifle. His supervisor was out hunting, he said with a heavy accent, but he would be back soon if Grogan required assistance.

"Who is your master?" Grogan asked.

"Captain Dunn of the Royal Army Medical Corps."

An Englishman.

They had made it.

With what unspeakable content I sat down and waited for Dunn's arrival it would be impossible to describe," Grogan wrote.

Dunn returned and came to meet his visitor. The messenger had to be mistaken, he thought. An Englishman, out here? On foot? Preposterous.

He found an apparition. Grogan wore a ragged jacket, trousers torn off at the knees, and boots held together with twine. His eyes were bloodshot and his unshaven face was blackened by the sun and swollen from mosquito bites. An empty pipe hung from a corner of his mouth.

Grogan removed the pipe, bowed politely, and offered his hand.

For a moment Dunn couldn't speak. He collected himself and shook Grogan's hand and said, "How do you do?"

"Oh, very fit, thanks. How are you? Had any sport?"

"Pretty fair, but there's nothing much here. Have a drink? Scotch?"

Dunn ordered his men to show Grogan the washbasin—and pick up the rest of his party while they were at it.

Over a lunch of chicken and caviar, Dunn said he was the medical officer of an expedition to cut a passage through the Sudd from the north. They were just packing up to leave. If Grogan had arrived a day later, they would have been gone.

Grogan needn't have feared running into Muslim soldiers, he said. The uprising was over. All of Sudan was back under the joint control of Egypt and Britain.

Dunn's curiosity finally overrode his sense of decorum.

"Look here," he said, "would you mind telling me who the devil you are and where you came from?"

His guest smiled. For the first time Dunn noticed the startling color of his eyes.

"My name's Ewart Grogan. I've come from the Cape."

He told his story. Dunn stopped eating and stared in disbelief, then admiration.

"Well, I'll be damned!" he said, and poured himself another whisky.

You're crazy. I never said that." Laura looked almost insulted.

"Oh, yes you did. Why would I make something like that up?" I could still hear the words: that Valentine's Day, our arbitrary anniversary, was as long as she could wait for me to make a decision. That perfect, awful date, a month and a half away.

We went back and forth a few times before she threw up her hands.

"Fine! If that's what you want. Valentine's it is."

The deadline brought us a kind of détente. Six weeks flew past.

We had our last romantic dinner in Santa Fe at one of the poshest restaurants in town. A lovey-dovey couple sat at every candlelit table in the old adobe house.

"Did you know Saint Valentine was a Christian martyr?" I said, slicing a bite of pork loin. "The Romans tortured him and cut off his head."

"Lovely." She sipped her Syrah.

"And Valentine's Day is on February fourteenth because that's when they used to think birds chose their mates for the year."

After dessert, I pulled out a small package. "Something for you."

Laura unwrapped a silver necklace with an angular geometric pendant. She gave me a quizzical look.

"It's a serotonin molecule. The brain chemical that makes you happy and content. Like you do to me."

It caught her off guard. But I could tell she liked it, almost in spite of herself. We weren't going to have another Ecuador episode, at least not here.

At home we curled up on the couch with a bottle of port, chatting about anything and nothing. The fire and the kitchen clock ticked to ten, ten-thirty, eleven.

For whatever reason—to clutch my independence as long as possible, to put off a major life change, sheer stubbornness—I had to push it to the limit. I already knew what I was going to do. I had for a long time, and I think she did, too.

And despite all it had taken to get to this point, we were both all right with it, each of us aware and accepting of the other's needs and limitations, even at one of the most charged moments in our lives. Our life.

"So," I said. I could hear every crackle in the fireplace as if my ear were up against the screen.

"So . . . what?" Laura said, smiling.

"So what do you think?"

"About what?" Playing innocent again.

I had the intense sensation of lameness. Wasn't I supposed to be down on one knee, ring in hand, ideally in some public place—if for no other reason than to give her a good story to tell?

But that was such a cliché, a pressure performance to steam-roll any on-the-spot doubts when you weren't completely sure of the answer. I was sure, or so I thought. This was between us.

I wasn't trying to convince Laura to give me something. She already had. I just had to find the courage to tell her I wanted it, too. Even if I would have to travel across Africa to understand why.

"You want to give it a try? Should we get married?"

She waited a beat. "Do you?"

"Yes."

"Of course!"

And that was it. We kissed as future husband and wife, grin-ning like fools.

An hour later I got up to feed the fire.

"So," she said casually. "A ring?"

I'd always teased her about how bourgeois diamond engage-ment rings were: the "tradition" invented in the 1930s by the De Beers cartel—Cecil Rhodes again—after a glut of South African diamonds threatened to send prices crashing; the ad exec who picked the two months' salary figure out of thin air; the profits from "blood diamonds" mined in war zones that fueled vicious conflicts across Africa, including the DRC.

She didn't deny any of it. But she still wanted one. I owed her that much.

I told her I was going to give her a diamond ring that had belonged to my grandmother. I'd just underestimated how long it would take to have it cleaned and resized and FedExed here.

More procrastination or just poor planning? She knew better than to ask.

A few mornings later I woke up and rolled over and lov-ingly watched my fiancée drool onto the pillow. We had floated through the past few days. Our relationship felt transformed, renewed, scrubbed clean.

The fears and hesitations were still there—I knew that was normal, now, even healthy—but they were overshadowed by the excitement of leaving the holding pattern and lining up for landing. Now we could each look forward knowing someone would be there for the long haul.

Laura was awake, smiling as if she could read my mind.

"Why didn't we do this earlier?" I said.

She punched me in the arm.

It's a toss-up who has the better T-shirt: the man pulling the bottles of beer from the cooler in Juba's crowded market (I AM SPECIAL AND WORTH WAITING FOR) or his swaying customer (ARE YOU READY FOR A 3SOME?).

The transaction would have been different during the civil war, when Khartoum's sharia law made alcohol illegal. It can still earn a Muslim forty lashes and a fine up north. Now it's just one exchange among hundreds. Stalls and shacks overflow with motorcycle helmets and piles of fruit, power tools and knockoff YSL handbags. Two children snicker in a homemade swing in the back of a burned-out truck.

I leave the market, unsure of my direction, brooding. Juba is no summer camp, but it sounds like Disneyland compared to what's waiting up north. I've come so far on Grogan's trail—how far is far enough?

I hear whimpering coming from the ditch by the road. It's a pale dog lying on its side, its mouth and one ear crusted with blood. It pulls itself up on its front paws, but its back legs don't move. It collapses with an anguished yelp.

I stop and squat to look closer. The dog bares its teeth and growls. For once there's no one else around. I feel helpless, but I can't bear to see it suffer.

What can I do? There probably isn't a vet for five hundred miles. I briefly consider trying to put the animal out of its misery somehow, but I'm too squeamish. What if it has rabies?

With all the human misery I've seen in the past two months, I'm almost ashamed to be so affected by an animal.

The dog's eyes are closed, its breathing fast and shallow.

It breaks my heart to leave it there.

It takes an hour to find my tent by the river. At some point, I realize that this is the end of the road. I'm not going on to Bor. I've known it since the day I arrived; as usual, I just couldn't admit it.

I won't say the dog in the ditch was some kind of sunbaked epiphany. It was just a moment of overwhelming loneliness and frustration I instinctively wanted to share with Laura, her presence the one thing that could have made it any less awful. Getting back to her in one piece, as soon as possible, is the most important thing in my life now.

It's not that I can't do this alone anymore. I just don't want to.

I don't have to like Grogan to learn from him, I see now. And after thousands of miles, what is most clear is how different we are. Our ends may have been similar, but our methods—no.

If he were in my shoes, I don't doubt Grogan would keep pushing to Bor and beyond, floods, fighting, and missed flights be damned.

Not me. From here on, every step I take will be toward home.

Grogan lay in Dunn's boat that night, gazing at stars like sand. He was drifting down the Nile again, starting the final leg of his journey back to England. Sleep was out of the question. His thoughts spun like the dust devils that had erased their tracks in the desiccated waste just a day ago.

He just couldn't believe it was over. "The transition from ceaseless anxiety and hungry misery to full-bellied content and tobacco-soothed repose had been so sudden," he wrote. It was like stepping into blinding sunlight after stumbling endlessly in the dark. Now there was nothing to do but sit and be carried along toward "clean shirts, collars, glasses, friends—all that makes life a thing of joy.

"How many people have ever caught the exquisite flavour of bread-and-butter? the restful luxury of clean linen? the hiss of Schweppe's? One must munch hippo-meat alone, save one's sole shirt from contact with water as from a pestilence lest it fall to pieces, and drink brackish mud for days, to realize all this."

He woke in the morning expecting to find himself back in the swamp, Dunn and the boat nothing but a fever-induced fantasy. But there was the ship's mast overhead, that beautiful, slanting spar. They had reached the expedition's base camp during the night. He drank in the sight, half afraid it would fade before his eyes.

Men were busy cutting the floating vegetation, thirty feet thick in some places, into huge blocks to be towed by steamships into open water and released.

The district governor offered to carry Grogan and the Watonga all the way to Khartoum in a gunboat. Grogan paid off the rest of his men, thanked them for their labor and loyalty, and wished them well. How they got home is a mystery.

Within a few hours, the boat steamed past the mouth of the Sobat River, yellow with sediment, and Grogan saw the small outpost that had been his El Dorado for so long.

At the settlement of Fashoda, five hundred miles south of

Khartoum, Grogan handed over "the first trans-continental post-bag" and received his first letter in a year and a half. It said his oldest friend had been killed fighting against the Boers in South Africa. "Curiously enough, the last letter that I had received on leaving civilization had been from him," he wrote. "Verily Africa is an accursed land."

The Nile meandered north through a treeless expanse. One evening Grogan was on deck enjoying the breeze and wondering what was waiting back in England. Had Gertrude's stepfather convinced her Grogan was long dead? Had she given up on him and married someone else?

In the failing light he saw a large animal sitting on the bank up ahead. The boat pulled even and the lanterns lit the eyes of a magnificent leopard. It rose and walked leisurely away from the river, flicking its tail and glancing over its shoulder. The cat settled under a tree, and for a moment their eyes met. Then it faded away in the dusk.

When the boat reached the southern end of the military telegraph line that stretched to Cairo. Grogan could finally let his friends and family know he was alive for the first time in fourteen months.

He couldn't send a telegraph to Gertrude, though, not yet. Part of their agreement was that he wouldn't contact her until he reached Cairo. It was all or nothing.

Grogan learned that the captain and doctor of the steamer *Kenia* had survived after dragging their smaller boats for four months across the Sudd. Like him, they owed their lives to stumbling on a detachment of the Sudd-cutting expedition. Only someone like him, who had experienced the place firsthand, could begin to imagine what they had gone through.

Boats, trains, so many more stops. At Khartoum, Grogan

dined next to the Sirdar, the most powerful man in Egypt, in a fresh-bought shirt and underwear. When the Watonga saw a train for the first time, Makanjira tapped Grogan on the shoulder, pointed at the engine, and solemnly handed him his elephant gun. At Aswan, the colossal dam across the Nile was almost finished.

At last they reached Cairo. There was no one to meet Grogan and the Watonga when they stepped off the train, just six more faces in the throng.

Grogan had completed the first north-south traverse of Africa, as challenging a feat of exploration as any ever attempted on the continent.

But instead of celebrating, he went straight to the nearest telegraph office. He could barely hold the pencil steady as he wrote out a long-overdue message: "Have reached Cairo. My feelings just the same. Anxiously await your answer. Make it yes. Love, Ewart."

It was February 1900, two years and seven thousand miles since Beira.

The Watonga had stayed by his side through things few men could have imagined, much less endured. He took them to see the Mediterranean, the "water without end" he had promised in the meetinghouse on Lake Nyasa. The four men and little Pinka had kept Grogan alive, and vice versa. Now it was time to send them home.

Grogan wrote a letter to the British treasurer of Nyasaland asking him to make sure the men made it home in one piece. He gave them all "indestructible" labels with their names and the location of their village.

After a round of sincere thanks, he put them on a southbound steamship. One of the men died en route, but the rest made it home safely. Grogan would never forget the bond he shared with those "great souls."

He roamed Cairo for days, edgy and impatient. He prowled the bazaars, lingered over meals, and lay in his hotel room until he felt he would burst with anxiety.

One morning a messenger knocked on the door and handed him a telegram. Grogan shoved a coin into the boy's hand and tore open the envelope.

It said, *My feelings also unchanged. Am waiting for you. Gertrude.*

Forty-eight hours after flying back to Kampala from Juba, I'm on another plane home. I open Laura's last card halfway across the Atlantic. *Homeward bound!* it says. *You made it, just like I knew you would! You're coming home! Can't wait to see you!*

As I expected, she was thrilled I turned around. I could hear it in her voice when I called from Kampala. The first few days back would be quiet, she promised. She'd give me time and space to readjust, shake off the jet-lag, and purge any stubborn bugs from my system.

Then she started to list all the wedding decisions we still had to make: DJ, marriage license, wine, seating arrangements. We were only three guests away from our limit. The resort's management was still dragging its feet about having the ceremony outside. Even over the phone it was overwhelming.

"You really aren't in decision-making mode at all, are you?" she said. "I know you trust my judgment, but it means a lot to me to feel like it's our wedding, not just mine. I don't want it to just be MY wedding."

"Don't worry, I'll be there. How's Portland?"

"It's great. I love it. But without you here it's been like being single without being able to date. That sucks."

Grogan had weeks on boats at the end of his journey to soften the transition from Africa to home. I have a little over two days.

After a night at my parents' house in New York, I'm flying to Portland tomorrow.

I've never understood when people say they wish a trip would never end. Coming home is always as exciting as leaving, only sweeter. Everything familiar is new again, sometimes for an entire day or two.

Two months ago I couldn't wait to leave. Now I can't wait to be home. I'm tired of being in transit, itching to get back to the concrete mundanities of real life. And to start this next phase with Laura.

Still, my excitement is tempered with apprehension. I've had too many relationships changed by long trips, some beyond repair, to be able to relax completely. Those first few days together, so intimate and alien at the same time, are disorienting at the least, let alone a month before joining together forever.

As always, half of New York's La Guardia Airport is under construction. Everyone seems so huge and pale, surrounded by an invisible bubble of personal space. The greasy fatigue of a long flight saturates my body. All I want to do is take a shower and go to sleep. I wish I could press a button and be in Portland, curled up with Laura in our big, warm bed.

My father is supposed to pick me up, but I don't see him in the crowd beyond the glass wall of customs. Is he stuck in traffic? I don't even have a cell phone to call him.

"Hey!" I know that voice. That blond hair. That smile.

Laura leaps at me in a running hug.

"Surprise! Welcome back!"

She flew across the country to see me one day earlier. There's a hotel room waiting. I can't put my happiness into words.

It's really her.

It always was.

CHAPTER TWENTY-FOUR

When Grogan arrived at Dover, England, in late March of 1900, almost a month after leaving Cairo, he gave a brief interview to the reporters waiting at the dock, then went straight to 74 Lancaster Gate, Mrs. Eyres's large house overlooking Hyde Park in London.

Gertrude was waiting, shivering with anticipation. Her step-father had continued to oppose the marriage the entire three years Grogan was away. The only reason she was in London at all was to attend finishing school.

The moment Grogan entered the room, they both knew nothing had changed. The bond that had propelled him across a continent, and made it possible for her to wait, was as strong as ever. Even Coleman could see it. He gave his grudging blessing, and soon the couple was officially engaged.

Grogan introduced Gertrude to his friends and family—they loved her—and he charmed the petticoats off Gertrude's two maiden aunts who had come to London expressly to size him up.

Although he was still in delicate shape—his liver hurt constantly and attacks of malaria regularly laid him flat—Grogan spent most of the year reveling in the attention his trek had earned. He was the toast of London. Every time he turned around, it seemed, he was being wined and dined, interviewed, or asked to give a lecture or write an article about his experiences.

On April 30, at age twenty-five, he became the youngest person ever to address the Royal Geographical Society. Even Grogan was nervous speaking in front of such an eminent crowd, which included the king of Sweden and some of the British Empire's smartest and most accomplished men.

"Anything more ridiculous than the possibility of my return to Africa never occurred to me as I wearily munched my ration of everlasting bully beef and rice during the Matabele war of '96," he began, and proceeded to captivate his audience with his eloquence and dry wit.

Harry Sharp sat in the back, happy to let his former partner have the spotlight. They had greeted each other earlier like long-lost brothers. Sharp had been certain he was leaving his friend to die alone in Africa. Grogan didn't hold it against him, especially when he learned Sharp had in fact sent supplies to Wadelai as he had promised, though they had disappeared en route.

Without proper instruments or any prior experience, Grogan and Sharp had filled in a significant portion of the map between Lake Tanganyika and Lake Albert, including the intricate eastern shore of Lake Kivu and the Dinka country of southern Sudan. And they had done it without the financial support explorers usually received from the government or wealthy scientific societies.

For his discoveries in natural history, Grogan was eventually made a Fellow of the RGS. Two new species of butterflies he collected were dubbed *Amauris grogani* and *Gnopbodes grogani*. The silver-gray reedbuck he shot on Lake Nyasa also turned out to be a new species. According to tradition, he was allowed to pick the name. He chose *Cervicapra thomasinae,* "Thomasina's reedbuck," after his pet name for Gertrude.

The explorer's next great honor was a personal audience with Queen Victoria, which amounted to a barrage of royal questions about the places and people he had seen. Grogan presented the queen with one of the three Union Jacks he had carried. She later sent him a thank-you note and a signed photograph of herself. He supposedly sent her a signed photo of himself in return. Queen Victoria died less than a year later, signaling the end of the era of prosperity, global expansion, and relative peace that bore her name.

Gertrude got another flag, and the third went to Cecil Rhodes, who quizzed Grogan intently about his journey. Grogan was happy to comply. He owed his celebrity—and, soon, his wife—to this man's inspiration and motivation. They pored over his maps, discussing potential routes for the train and telegraph.

Meanwhile, Grogan delivered a number of reports to the Foreign Office and Colonial Office, as promised. The civil servants were amazed at the detail in his maps and his information on the relative progress of German and Belgian interests in central Africa. There is no record they did anything with the reports except file them away.

Sir Henry Morton Stanley invited Grogan to come see him. He was fifty-nine, the last of the giants of African exploration. Grogan had seen the fallout of Stanley's efforts in the Congo, and in his speech to the RGS had even made a thinly veiled reference to his policy of "attacking people in case they may attack you," calling it a "superfluous and questionable precaution." Grogan found the Rock Breaker to be "a pathetic-looking little figure like a wizened parrot." Stanley died four years later.

Less than seven months after arriving home, on October 11, 1900, Ewart Grogan and Gertrude Watt were married at Christ Church in West London in front of hundreds of jubilant guests. The master of Jesus College, who apparently had forgiven Grogan for his stunts as an undergrad, conducted the service.

The newlyweds honeymooned in Paris for ten days, then returned to London just in time for the publication of Grogan's account of his trek, *From the Cape to Cairo: The First Traverse of Africa from South to North*. In four months of incredible effort, he had turned his notes into a 377-page volume billed as "The Greatest Book on African Travel and Sport ever published."

It began with a short, bemused introduction by Cecil Rhodes:

I must say I envy you, for you have done that which has been for centuries the ambition of every explorer, namely, to walk through Africa from South to North. The amusement of the whole thing is that a youth from Cambridge during his vacation should have succeeded in doing that which the ponderous explorers of the world have failed to accomplish.

In his preface, Grogan thanked Mrs. Eyres, "without whose hearty assistance the journey could not have been brought to a successful conclusion."

The book included many of Grogan's own drawings and 115 full-page illustrations based on his sketches. In almost all of them, he and Sharp look unusually casual no matter what is going on, slouching and smoking with hats cocked and hands in their pockets.

Its combination of action, humor, vivid descriptions, and stiff-upper-lip attitude made the book a bestseller. In a review, the *Times* of London noted that "[Grogan's] criticisms smack a little of the intolerance of youth, but they are inspired by a robust common sense and by a desire to say the thing that is true whoever may be offended in the process."

Gertrude received the first copy. Grogan made sure to send the next one to Coleman, his new father-in-law, inscribed, "With love."

The new couple made up for their time apart by traveling around the world for the next year. The first stop was New York, where Grogan met John D. Rockefeller, Woodrow Wilson, Mark Twain, and the newspaper tycoon William Randolph Hearst. During their lunch together, Hearst hid a reporter under the table to record Grogan's every word, and within hours the interview was in all the Hearst papers.

Alexander Graham Bell, the inventor of the telephone, presided over Grogan's address to the National Geographic Society. The *National Geographic* magazine ran a brief mention of his claims of elephants and lava fields "without comment" (meaning "take at face value").

The *New York Times* published three articles about his journey with headlines like "Fierce Man-Eating Rage" and "Pygmies and Blood-Drinkers." Grogan and Gertrude made the paper's society column four times in eight days.

They continued to Hawaii, then New Zealand, where they visited Gertrude's family and Grogan met the prime minister. Soon after they returned to London, Gertrude gave birth to a girl they named Dorothy.

In 1902 Cecil Rhodes died unexpectedly at the age of forty-eight. Any possibility of a transcontinental train and telegraph line was buried along with him. Schemes that grand needed an outsize personality to see them through, and the Cape-to-Cairo route had always been Rhodes's personal vision. Marconi's wireless would soon replace the telegraph, and Grogan had shown the geography was too rugged for a rail line.

"Were it not for the big-game shooting, for no earthly consideration would I put my foot one mile south of the Pyramids," Grogan had said to the Royal Geographical Society. But his life was inextricably bound to Africa now. He knew that was where he would make his fortune—the one he would earn himself, not Gertrude's two-hundred-thousand-pound dowry.

So, when he saw the opportunity to help rebuild South Africa after the Second Boer War, Grogan packed up the entire household, including a maid, a nanny, and a valet, and sailed for Durban.

In Johannesburg, doctors drained an abscess on his liver the size of a coconut. He recovered but soon tired of the country's turbulent politics. A friend had mentioned the financial opportunities in the sparsely populated colony of British East Africa, midway up the coast. After two years in South Africa, Grogan and Gertrude sent the servants back to England with the baby temporarily and moved to a bleak little tent city in the East African highlands called Nairobi.

Only about thirty Europeans had settled in Nairobi, out of fewer than five hundred in the whole protectorate. Great Britain hadn't administered the place for a decade yet, and the situation was ripe for "an impetuous young man, self-confident and self-opinionated to the verge of impudence," as Grogan described himself decades later.

Over the following years he embarked on one bold business scheme after another. He founded the colony's timber industry in the densely forested highlands, introduced brown and rainbow trout to its rivers, and developed its only deepwater port in the coastal city of Mombasa.

Grogan built a gabled mansion above the Nairobi River and named it Chiromo, after the sweltering river port in Nyasaland where he and Sharp had waited for their lost luggage. Gertrude filled the grounds with plants and flowers from Africa and Europe.

The protectorate grew slowly but steadily. Grogan eventually came to control hundreds of thousands of acres. His holdings included a large chunk of land near the river that he predicted, accurately, would one day become downtown Nairobi.

The colony's social scene blossomed, and the Grogans were often at the center of things, hosting balls and serving on committees and gathering with friends. "Grogs" was always ready to spin tales about "the walk," as he called it, and his days as a trooper. Gertrude had heard them all before, but she laughed along with everyone else. She had made the transition from a life of privilege to the wild African frontier without skipping a beat. A born entertainer, she could be as funny as her husband. She threw children's parties at Chiromo and even tried her hand at amateur theater.

Those were "the sunshine days," Grogan said later. One of the few dark spots was hearing of Harry Sharp's early death in 1905, four months before the birth of their second daughter, Joyce.

Few things made Grogan happier than butting heads. His entrepreneurial spirit and intolerance of bureaucracy made him a constant thorn in the side of the conservative Colonial Office, which in his opinion administered British East Africa with equal parts incompetence, inefficiency, and idiocy.

People often called Grogan fifty years ahead of his time (sometimes "unfortunately"). He used all his cleverness, stubbornness, and charm to get his way. To illustrate a loophole in the mining laws that allowing speculators to snap up valuable land, Grogan staked out a technically legal claim to most of the city of Nairobi in one evening. The law was changed.

His attitudes toward Africans remained complex. In 1907 he was fined and sentenced to a month of confinement after he flogged two of his own servants in public for allegedly insulting his sister. The "Nairobi Incident" made waves all the way to London, where the Undersecretary of State for the Colonies Winston Churchill condemned it in Parliament, saying, "We must not let these first few ruffians steal our beautiful and promising protectorate away from us, after all we have spent upon it."

Grogan's opinions on race seemed to mellow the longer he lived among Africans. The young man who once wrote how crucial it was to "let the native see that you respect him in his own line, but take your own absolute superiority for granted" became known for his kindness, generosity, and fair treatment of locals and, in most cases, his African employees as he grew older.

As the protectorate grew, the debate over African independence and native self-rule grew heated. Grogan always favored "disciplined co-operation" over "snarling segregation," and advocated strongly for mass education and economic opportunities for people of any color. Yet he never quite believed Africans would ever be able to effectively govern themselves.

His relationship toward wildlife changed more dramatically. Grogan never hunted again after his trek, and he donated most of his trophies to zoos and universities. The archetypal Great

White Hunter became a conservationist, telling anyone who would listen how desperately Africa needed wildlife reserves and regulated hunting seasons. Without them, one day her supposedly numberless animals would be gone.

Grogan and Gertrude bounced back and forth between London and Nairobi in the 1910s and '20s, in part because they wanted their daughters to be educated in England. At one point Grogan was invited to stand for Parliament in the House of Commons. He lost after his opponent accused him of inciting riot during the "Nairobi Incident."

When World War I began, the German and British colonies in East Africa tried to stay out of the fray. This didn't last long, and soon Grogan was made a captain in British East Africa's new Intelligence Service. The reports he sent from his wartime headquarters in Entebbe, Uganda, were signed "Simba."

In Nairobi, Grogan gave a stirring recruiting speech to a crowd of fifteen hundred that would be remembered for years afterward. He made it without notes, as usual, and afterward people started calling him "Kenya's Churchill."

Eventually he found himself back in the Congo near Lake Kivu as liaison to the Belgian army. He became a James Bond of the bush, penetrating a hundred miles behind the German lines and entering cities in disguise to scout out enemy forces. Sometimes he had to fight his way back to friendly territory in hand-to-hand combat. Once he captured a Dutch spy by sneaking up behind him and pressing a pistol to his temple. When the war ended, Grogan received both the Distinguished Service Order and the Belgian Order of Leopold for his efforts.

Even though he was disappointed at never having a son, Grogan doted on his four girls (Cynthia and Jane had joined Dorothy and Joyce). Gertrude later said it was just as well: "God knows what sort of life the poor boy would have had." He drew his daughters pictures, brought them presents from his travels, and was always willing to crack open his billfold for a treat or a toy.

In some ways, he seemed to relate to children better than adults. In the 1930s, he built Torr's Hotel in downtown Nairobi, a four-story redbrick building that was the most fashionable place to stay in Africa south of Cairo. Yet as much as he enjoyed dancing to Sid Zeigler's jazz band and holding forth in the Palm Court lounge, Grogan's favorite part of owning the hotel was hosting the annual children's Christmas party. He would dress like Father Christmas and delight his tiny guests, rich and poor, with magic tricks and presents.

At the same time, Grogan seemed to forget that not everyone had skin as tough as his. His daughters described how his teasing could turn mean without warning, sometimes reducing them to tears. His tawny eyes could inspire fear as easily as laughter. Fellow colonist Elspeth Huxley, the author of *The Flame Trees of Thika*, noted "a certain cruelty in his humour and outlook, a streak (as it were) of the battering-ram." As Grogan's girls grew into young women, their once-playful father began to treat them in the same way he treated other adults: frostily, with little patience.

Grogan grew more distinguished but no less handsome with age. With his ramrod posture, dark, arched eyebrows, and silvering hair, he was often surrounded by a rapt circle of women in the Palm Court at Torr's. "Words poured from his lips like wine at some Bacchic orgy," Huxley wrote, "intoxicating at the time but, when the orgy was over, you wondered what he had actually said."

Those were freewheeling days in colonial Nairobi; as one saying went, "Are you married or do you live in Kenya?" There were rumors of affairs. But he and Gertrude kept their marriage alive, even though they were periodically separated for months at a time when she returned to England.

In his fifties, Grogan developed three huge estates on the border with Tanganyika (now Tanzania) to grow sisal, a fibrous plant used to make cordage. At its height, "Grogan Country" covered eighty-seven thousand acres of scrubland in Taveta, near the base of Kilimanjaro. Well-watered fields surrounded orderly rows of buildings and homes. Grogan invented an intricate irrigation system to direct the water from the mountain's melting snowfields to his citrus groves and other crops.

Thousands of workers lived in houses made of stone and enjoyed a church, a hospital, and a movie theater. Grogan made sure each boy was given a savings account, and he donated money to build a trade school in a nearby town.

In 1932 Imperial Airways invited Grogan to repeat his famous journey in reverse as the first passenger on its new route from London to Cape Town. What had taken him two and a half years to cover by "every then-known form of transport—except camel" took just over eight days by air. "It seems beyond belief that a man could have that double experience in a lifetime," he told the *Daily Express*. "It shows how fast the world is moving."

Grogan wasn't sitting still himself. At sixty, he escaped a charging rhino by jumping into a tree. Five years later, when World War II began, he returned to the Congo, again as liaison officer to the Belgians. Later he was put in charge of three POW camps in Kenya that held Italians.

Then Gertrude suffered a heart attack. Grogan rushed to her bedside and stayed there for two weeks. He promised her they would go away together, just them, as soon as she recovered. But on July 5, 1943, another heart attack took his beloved Thomasina. Several thousand people showed up for the funeral. Even the Italian POWs sent flowers. Grogan was devastated. The woman he had crossed a continent for, the one he called "the mainspring of my life," was gone.

One thing that had always bound them was their love of children. Four years later, Grogan built the first children's hospital in East Africa in memory of his wife. Gertrude's Garden treated children of every race, whether they could pay or not. Grogan visited the little patients daily, spreading ripples of laughter as he went from ward to ward, mugging and joking.

The "Grand Old Man of Kenya" managed his properties in person well into his eighties. With his pith helmet, machete, and white goatee, Grogan was unmistakable as he strode the dirt lanes of his flourishing estates, clearing brush and lighting fires.

In the 1950s, the issue of Kenyan independence from Great Britain erupted in a series of violent clashes. Grogan was far from convinced the black majority could run a country effectively, but he knew the handover was inevitable. "Please do anything you can to adopt a friendly attitude towards the African," he urged his fellow settlers. "Give him every opportunity to participate here, there and everywhere."

On December 12, 1963, Grogan's eighty-ninth birthday, the Republic of Kenya was signed into existence. By then his health had begun to fade. He spent most of his time at his sisal estates with his six beloved Pekinese, cared for by a small, strong-willed woman named Camilla Towers, who had started out as his housekeeper.

By now his family was scattered around the world. He didn't see his daughters, who hated Towers, for years at a time. To his dismay, Joyce had become a nun, as had his sister Mildred. Grogan's skepticism of organized religion never faded. When Towers brought a priest to hear his confession, he sent the man away with "a crisp ticking off." At this point, he grumbled, there was no way he was going to start digging into eighty-five years of "interesting sins."

Grogan didn't seem to fear death. Perhaps he figured he had been through worse. "In the course of a chequered career I have seen many unwholesome spots," he wrote in *From the Cape to Cairo*, "but for a God-forsaken, dry-sucked, fly-blown wilderness, commend me to the Upper Nile; a desolation of desolations, an infernal region, a howling waste of weed, mosquitoes, flies, and fever, backed by a groaning waste of thorn and stones—waterless and waterlogged. I have passed through it, and have now no fear for the hereafter."

Ewart Scott Grogan died quietly on August 16, 1967, in Cape Town, aged ninety-two. His grave faces Table Mountain, the starting point of his great African adventure so many years before.

Grogan's Cape-to-Cairo trek was the last great journey of the Golden Age of Exploration in Africa. Like the death of Queen Victoria on January 22, 1901, it marked the end of both a century and an era.

In his lifetime the continent lurched out of the Age of Exploration and into the modern world. When Grogan was born, only a tenth of Africa was under European control. When he returned from his epic walk, all of it was, except Liberia, Ethiopia, and part of the Western Sahara. Most of sub-Saharan Africa declared its independence during the last decade of Grogan's life.

The world was changing with incredible speed. In his book, Grogan wrote how the trek itself became a memory all too soon: "A few dangers avoided, a few difficulties overcome, many disappointments, many discomforts, and those glorious days of my life are already dim in the haze of the past."

His death went virtually unheeded. The *Times* of London didn't even run an obituary. Only one blood relative, his granddaughter Jean Crawford, made it to his funeral, and then only because she read about it in the local newspaper. Grogan's celebrity flared and faded, and his name never became a household word, unlike those other famous explorers whose exploits he had equaled and, in many cases, surpassed.

Because of politics and topography, the Cape-to-Cairo railway and telegraph, the official premise for his journey, was never really viable anyway. Grogan may as well have been the last man on the moon.

More significantly, he never seriously pursued political power or fame. He could easily have had both, if he could ever muzzle his own bloody-mindedness. Look at Churchill, who was remarkably similar in background, ability, and temperament.

Instead, Grogan appeared content with his own hard-earned financial success and the attention of a small circle, a big fish in the small pond of colonial Kenya. He almost seemed to enjoy making enemies. Someone once described him as the type who "either ended up buried in Westminster Abbey or hanging from a yardarm." Surprisingly, he did neither.

Grogan's sisal plantations are still in operation today, and his home at Chiromo is now a Protected National Heritage Site. Gertrude's Garden, still the leading children's hospital in East

Africa, continues to accept patients whether they can pay or not, and offers free clinics in Nairobi's slums. Their descendants are scattered around the world, but few people who knew Grogan are still alive.

Of everyone who tried to sum up the man's outsize personality, Elspeth Huxley probably did it best: he was "a charmer, a cynic, a swashbuckler, a buccaneer born out of time."

Grogan laid out his philosophy himself at the end of his book: "We all have our allotted portions of black and white paint; how we lay it on is a question of temperament. One mixes the pigments carefully and paints his life an even grey. Another dashes in the light and shade with a palette-knife."

There's no question which applied to him.

CHAPTER TWENTY-FIVE

The reentry into home life is sweet and strange. Laura and I have been apart for two months, longer than entire relationships we've each had. The first weeks are all about reconnecting. Over meals, on the couch, late at night in bed, we share our stories: Laura's favorite things about Portland, her new friends; my pictures and anecdotes from the trip.

Getting used to being around someone else again takes effort. All of a sudden we each have to factor another person into our decisions, even the most trivial. Have you had lunch yet? Do you need the car? Where are you going?

Sleeping in the same bed every night, no more constant movement, a fridge full of food. Things I'd grown accustomed to in Africa—barefoot children, the smell of leaded gas exhaust, the constant curious stares—are memories. Now I'm just one more *mzungu* among millions, no longer the center of attention everywhere I go.

Winter came early this year. October is damp cold and weeping gray clouds, the antithesis of the luminous southwestern dome we left behind or the vast skies of Africa. A lethargy seeps in. Neither of us can seem to get enough sleep.

But there's a wedding to plan. My instinct is to let Laura keep holding the reins, since she's more concerned about the particulars and I'm just lazy. This clearly won't fly, though, so I pitch in as much as possible.

Florist, dinner, cake, photographer, seating, DJ, song list, rehearsal dinner, honeymoon. For the most wonderful day of your life, a wedding is an utter pain in the ass to bring off.

We take a reconnaissance trip to Utah to scope out the resort. While we're there, we apply for our marriage license in Provo, officially the most conservative city in the country. It's as easy as picking up a prescription, and cheaper.

"'Total years of education . . . ethnic group . . .'" Laura scans down the form.

"'Number of this marriage.'" I count on my fingers. "Let's see, one, two, three . . ."

"Ha ha."

"There was that one in Bangkok."

"Shut up. You made sure the . . . whatever, George's church thing is valid here?"

A friend from Washington has graciously agreed to perform the ceremony. Yesterday we had a sudden moment of panic over whether an online ordainment from the Universal Life Church was valid in Utah.

"Yes, dear."

We find an antique silver wedding band to match my grandmother's ring. We also order matching titanium bands, engraved inside with our initials and the big date, now three weeks away.

We're both sensitive and snappish over imagined slights and criticisms. The spats are never about the wedding; on that we're in perfect harmony. They're about routine, minor issues like scooping the litter box and doing the dishes. When we cool down, we remind ourselves it's the stress of two colossal life events almost overlapping: the move to Portland and the wedding (three, if you count the two-month separation).

Yet I still find myself wondering, at the hottest point of an argument, for just a split second: Is this how it's going to be? Forever?

Getting married is absolutely what I want to do. At the same time, it's as daunting as anything I've ever faced. It's not the loss of independence I worry about so much as it is living up to Laura's expectations. Deserving her.

Anxiety isn't always a bad thing. If nothing else, it's proof I care. I want it to be right more than anything. And the thought of it not working bothers me so much—that's a good sign, too.

Like all successful weddings, ours is mostly a blur. It took weeks of effort, but Laura convinced the resort to honor our contract and let us have the ceremony outside. Still, late October in the Wasatch Mountains is a complete gamble, weather-wise. We check the forecast obsessively for two weeks beforehand, and it looks like we're in luck. The day before the wedding is cloudless and almost warm.

With our tiny wedding party—just us, our parents, George, and two friends reading poems—we drive up to an open meadow with a willow-lined stream. The striated pyramid of Mount Timpanogos hangs in the sky. We find a flattish spot and run through the ceremony twice.

The scenery makes it hard to concentrate. Everyone is a little giddy from anticipation and altitude. It may not be a canyon rim, but it's still almost too perfect. The weather just has to hold for one more day.

We wake the next morning to an early-season blizzard. A complete whiteout.

Things start to happen quickly. The reception building is repurposed for the ceremony. Friends and family start to materialize, all of our worlds overlapping: New York, Philadelphia, Washington, Santa Fe, Portland. Jeff is there with Deb, who's due in December.

The cake arrives in one piece, complete with the topper I tracked down at the last minute on eBay: Pepé le Pew embracing his unenthusiastic pussycat *amour*. Laura thinks it's hilarious too.

Then I'm waiting with George by the stone fireplace in front of everyone. Warm light dances on bare-plank walls. Laura appears on her father's arm in a strapless silk gown, both of them beaming. I've never seen her more beautiful.

It's a good thing George has the script. I'm in such a daze I can hardly read my lines.

We've asked both sets of parents to give us the blessings of their combined eighty-four years of marriage. Today is my parents' 16,661st day together.

George leads us in the vows we wrote together. Then the rings, the kiss, and we're walking back down the aisle hand in hand.

Sometime later we step out into the softly snowing night. We need a moment to ourselves. Laura blinks snowflakes off her eyelashes. I drape my jacket over her shoulders. It's cold and quiet.

"Wow. You're my wife." It feels strange in my mouth, a word in a foreign language I've just started to learn.

"My husband!" She giggles.

The white-dusted trees make the moment even more dreamlike. It feels like a pause, a slight flicker between film reels.

"Man, I need a break from these heels." She hoots as I scoop her into my arms and spin us both around in the falling snow.

It's October 20, 2007, exactly 107 years and nine days after another couple pledged their love in a long-awaited ceremony in London.

Not that I'm thinking about Grogan right now. In fact, he's probably the furthest thing from my mind as I dip my wife like a bobby-soxer, trying not to slip and dump us both on the ground.

If I was, I might sense that this is really the end of his trail. In a way—an extremely roundabout one—Grogan led me to this point. Now our paths diverge.

Laura and I are heading into a different kind of mystery. But I know we'll find the answers, as long as we keep pushing forward together, palette–knives dashing black and white and every shade in between.

Because if there's anything I learned from the guy, it's this: compared to making a marriage work, crossing Africa is easy.

Lesson one: lighten the hell up. When someone asked Grogan near the end of his life for the secret of his longevity, he said, "to smoke very heavily, drink and eat very little and not take anything in life too seriously." At least the last part is good advice.

I set Laura back on her feet. Her cheeks are flushed. We're both panting like sprinters. We can hear the first song on our dance mix start to play inside.

"Ready?" she says.

"Of course."

EPILOGUE

"Ba? Ba. Ba! *Ba!*"

Ivy wants her ball back. Right now. She jabs a finger toward the plastic projectile she just launched behind the bookshelf.

"You can get it, sweetie. It's right there."

Laura sits on the floor in a spotlight of sun, folding fuzzy yellow blankets and tiny shirts with pandas and koala bears on them.

Ivy waddles over and leans across a pile of books to reach her ball. After watching her strain for a few seconds, I cave in and move to get it for her. But her attention has already swiveled to the bottom dresser drawer, whose neatly folded contents she is now methodically emptying onto the bedroom floor.

Our daughter has her mother's blue eyes, her father's curly hair, and more moxie than both of us put together. She never seems to stop moving, observing and touching and tasting and laughing, day after day. She's a twenty-one-pound force of nature—a definite thruster, as Grogan's father would have said.

We've been through a few more milestones in the two and a half years since the wedding. We bought a house, watched the economy collapse, got pregnant (well, Laura did), and, fifteen months ago, welcomed this little marvel into the world.

It hasn't been all storm-free sailing. Laura and I are different people than we were when I left for Africa, or when I got back. It's not just us now, and it won't be for a long time. And there are so many more things to argue about.

Our connection is still there, though, as strong as ever, even at two in the morning with a screaming toddler whose damn bottom molars are just about to break through, any day now.

The days of taking off for months alone on the trail of an obsession are gone, too, for the foreseeable future. It makes me a little sad to sense old freedoms fading, as I knew they would.

But then I look at Ivy, now laying her head on the flank of one of our long-suffering cats, and I know that everything is exactly as it should be. Portland is the first place in a long time that feels like home. New opportunities have replaced old ones, and the list is even longer now.

She grabs a purple hippo and a yellow lion from a wooden puzzle and pushes them around the carpet. Her passport just arrived in the mail today. She looks like a stubborn little monk in the photo. The empty pages call out to be filled with stamps and visas.

I pull down a globe from the shelf and put it on the floor.

"Where do you want to go first, Ivy-pie? Huh?" I give it a spin and she gives me the same heart-stopping smile that Laura has behind her.

I know we'll go to Africa someday together. Maybe even Cairo. Probably not right away, though. Baby steps.

"Where should we go, monkey?"

Ivy reaches out, eyes wide, and with a finger stops the spinning world.

SELECT BIBLIOGRAPHY

By far the best of the three published biographies of Ewart Grogan is Edward Paice's meticulous and exhaustive *Lost Lion of Empire*. It's safe to say this book might not exist without it. Written by his nephew while Grogan was still alive, Norman Wymer's *The Man from the Cape* is less objective but full of firsthand detail. Leda Farrant's *The Legendary Grogan* was also useful. Many of the historical sources, including Grogan's own *From the Cape to Cairo*, are available in full online through Google Books and Project Gutenberg.

Akenson, Don. *An Irish History of Civilization*. Montreal: McGill-Queens University Press, 2009.

Baker, Samuel White. *The Albert N'Yanza, Great Basin of the Nile: And Explorations of the Nile Sources*. Santa Barbara, Calif.: Narrative, 2002.

———. *In the Heart of Africa*. New York: Funk & Wagnalls, 1884.

Barrett-Gaines, Kathryn. "Travel Writing, Experiences, and Silences: What Is Left Out of European Travelers' Accounts: The Case of Richard D. Mohun." *History in Africa* 24 (1997): 53–70.

Bright, R. G. T. "Survey and Exploration in the Ruwenzori and Lake Region, Central Africa." *Geographical Journal* 34, no. 2 (1909): 128–53.

Chrétien, Jean-Pierre. *The Great Lakes of Africa: Two Thousand Years of History.* New York: Zone, 2006.

Churchill, Winston. *My African Journey.* London: Hodder & Stoughton, 1908.

————. *The River War: An Account of the Reconquest of the Soudan.* New York: Carroll & Graf, 2000.

Collins, Robert O. *The Nile.* New Haven, Conn.: Yale University Press, 2002.

Constantine, Nathan. *A History of Cannibalism: From Ancient Cultures to Survival Stories and Modern Psychopaths.* Edison, N.J.: Chartwell, 2006.

Dugard, Martin. *Into Africa: The Epic Adventures of Stanley & Livingstone.* New York: Doubleday, 2003.

Dunbar, Robin I. M. *Grooming, Gossip, and the Evolution of Language.* Cambridge, Mass.: Harvard University Press, 1996.

Edgerton, Robert B. *The Troubled Heart of Africa: A History of the Congo.* New York: St. Martin's, 2002.

Farrant, Leda. *The Legendary Grogan: The Only Man to Trek from Cape to Cairo: Kenya's Controversial Pioneer.* London: Hamish Hamilton, 1981.

Fisher, A. B. "Western Uganda." *Geographical Journal* 24, no. 3 (1904): 249–63.

Foden, Giles. *Mimi and Toutou Go Forth: The Bizarre Battle of Lake Tanganyika.* New York: Penguin, 2004.

Galton, Francis. *The Art of Travel: Shifts and Contrivances Available in Wild Countries.* London: Phoenix, 2000.

Gourevitch, Philip. *We Wish to Inform You That Tomorrow We Will Be Killed with Our Families: Stories from Rwanda.* New York: Picador, 1999.

Grogan, Ewart. Letter to Alfred E. Sharp, August 20, 1899. Royal Geographical Society Collection.

————. Letter to Arthur H. Sharp, April 1899. Royal Geographical Society Collection.

————. "The Nile As I Saw It." In *The Empire and the Century.* Edited by Charles S. Goldman. London: John Murray, 1905.

————. "Sixty Years in East and Central Africa." In *Rhodesia and East Africa*. Edited by Ferdinand S. Joelson. London: East Africa and Rhodesia, 1958.

Grogan, Ewart, and Arthur Henry Sharp. *From the Cape to Cairo. The First Traverse of Africa from South to North.* London: Hurst & Blackett, 1900.

Haggard, H. Rider. *King Solomon's Mines; She; Allan Quatermain.* London: Octopus, 1979.

Harbsmeier, Michael, Anders Lindholm, Laurent Gehin, et al. "Cannibalism in Colonial Congo." International Basic Studies in Humanities Thesis, Roskilde University, 2009.

Hinde, S. L. "Three Years' Travel in the Congo Free State." *Geographical Journal* 5, no. 5 (1895): 426–42.

Hochschild, Adam. *King Leopold's Ghost: A Story of Greed, Terror, and Heroism in Colonial Africa.* Boston: Houghton Mifflin, 1998.

Hunter, John A., and Daniel P. Mannix. "Colonel Ewart S. Grogan, Gentleman Adventurer." In *Tales of the African Frontier.* New York: Harper, 1954.

Huxley, Elspeth J. G. *Out in the Midday Sun: My Kenya.* New York: Viking, 1987.

Jeal, Tim. *Stanley: The Impossible Life of Africa's Greatest Explorer.* New Haven, Conn.: Yale University Press, 2007.

Keltie, John S. Letter to Ewart Grogan, dated March 26, 1900. Royal Geographical Society Collection.

"Kenya: Grogs & the Yappers." *Time,* August 13, 1956.

Livingstone, David. *A Popular Account of Dr. Livingstone's Expedition to the Zambesi and Its Tributaries and the Discovery of Lakes Shirwa and Nyassa 1858–1864.* Santa Barbara, Calif.: Narrative, 2001.

Livingstone, David, and Horace Waller. *The Last Journals of David Livingstone in Central Africa, from 1865 to His Death: Of His Last Moments and Sufferings, Obtained from His Faithful Servants, Chuma and Susi.* 2 vols. London: J. Murray, 1874.

Lloyd, A. B. *In Dwarf Land and Cannibal Country: A Record of Travel and Discovery in Central Africa.* London: T. Fischer Unwin, 1900.

Lugard, Frederick D. "Travels from the East Coast to Uganda,

Lake Albert Edward, and Lake Albert." *Proceedings of the Royal Geographical Society and Monthly Record of Geography* 14, no. 12 (1892): 817–41.

———. "The First Expedition from Uganda to Mount Ruwenzori." *Geographical Journal* 76, no. 6 (1930): 525–27.

Miller, Charles. *Battle for the Bundu: The First World War in East Africa.* New York: Macmillan, 1974.

Moorehead, Alan. *The White Nile.* Harmondsworth, England: Penguin, 1973.

O'Brien, Brian. "All for the Love of a Lady." *Field & Stream,* January 1968.

Page, Melvin E. "The Manyema Hordes of Tippu Tip: A Case Study in Social Stratification and the Slave Trade in Eastern Africa." *International Journal of African Historical Studies* 7, no. 1 (1974): 69–84.

Paice, Edward. *Lost Lion of Empire: The Life of Cape-to-Cairo Grogan.* London: HarperCollins, 2001.

Pakenham, Thomas. *The Scramble for Africa, 1876–1912.* New York: Random House, 1991.

"People of Africa's Past: Ewart Grogan." *Travel Africa,* no. 11 (Spring 2000).

Pettitt, Clare. *Dr. Livingstone, I presume?: Missionaries, Journalists, Explorers, and Empire.* London: Profile, 2007.

Roberts, Chalmers. "A Wonderful Feat of Adventure." *World's Work,* January 1901.

Rocco, Fiametta. *The Miraculous Fever-tree: Malaria, Medicine and the Cure That Changed the World.* New York: HarperCollins, 2004.

Royal Geographical Society. "Count Götzen's Journey Across Equatorial Africa." *Geographical Journal* 5, no. 4 (1895): 354–60.

———. *Hints to Travellers: Scientific and General.* Edited by Douglas W. Freshfield and W. J. L. Wharton. London, 1893.

Scroggins, Deborah. *Emma's War: Love, Betrayal and Death in the Sudan.* New York: HarperCollins, 2004.

Sharpe, Albert E. Letter to John Scott Keltie, December 17, 1899. Royal Geographical Society Collection.

————. Letter to John Scott Keltie, March 30, 1900. Royal Geographical Society Collection.

Shillington, Kevin. *Encyclopedia of African History.* New York: Fitzroy Dearborn, 2005.

Speke, John Hanning. *Journal of the Discovery of the Source of the Nile.* New York: Harper, 1864.

————. *What Led to the Discovery of the Source of the Nile.* Cass Library of African Studies, Travels and Narratives, No. 18. London: Cass, 1967.

Stanley, Henry M. *How I Found Livingstone: Travels, Adventures, and Discoveries in Central Africa.* Vercelli: White Star, 2006.

————. *In Darkest Africa, or, the Quest, Rescue, and Retreat of Emin Pasha, Governor of Equatoria (1890).* 2 vols. Kila, Mont.: Kessinger, 2007–2008.

————. *Through the Dark Continent, or, The Sources of the Nile Around the Great Lakes of Equatorial Africa and Down the Livingstone River to the Atlantic Ocean.* 2 vols. New York: Dover, 1988.

Volhard, Ewald. *Kannibalismus.* New York: Johnson Reprint, 1968.

Wainaina, Binyavanga. *How to Write About Africa.* Nairobi: Kwani Trust, 2008.

Weinthal, Leo. *The Story of the Cape to Cairo Railway & River Route from 1887 to 1922: The Iron Spine and Ribs of Africa.* London: Pioneer, 1922.

Wood, James, and Alex Guth. "East Africa's Great Rift Valley: A Complex Rift System." http://geology.com/articles/east-africa-rift.shtml. Viewed 5/20/2010.

Wright, Ed. *Lost Explorers: Adventurers Who Disappeared Off the Face of the Earth.* Millers Point, Australia: Pier 9, 2008.

Wymer, Norman. *The Man from the Cape.* London: Evans, 1959.

Various articles from the *New York Times, Times* (London), *Daily Nation* (Kenya), *National Geographic, National Geographic News, Monitor* (Uganda), *Daily News* (Tanzania), *Juba Post* (Sudan), *Scientific American, Economist, Washington Post, Guardian, Independent, Wired, Science Digest, Daily Telegraph,* BBC News, AllAfrica.com, *Encyclopædia Britannica.*

ACKNOWLEDGMENTS

A book is a little like an expedition; one person takes most or all of the credit, but success would have been impossible without the help and hard work of many more. I'll start by breaking the first two rules of Pitch Club and thank Frederick Reimers, David Wolman, and Rebecca Clarren for reading early drafts and offering priceless comments, criticism, and support. Sana Krasikov, Robert Neild, Carrie Regan, Clifton Wiens, and George Stone also gave essential feedback and suggestions.

A number of librarians helped with the research, including Megan Mummey at U.T. Austin; Kathleen Casey on L-net in Salem, Oregon; Janet Irwin and Kylie Holland at the Multnomah County Library; and Eugene Rae at the Royal Geographic Society.

I'm grateful to Ewart Grogan's descendants, who were kind enough to offer memories, information, and encouragement from Kenya to Australia: David Slater, Charles Szlapak, Samantha Mancuso, and Nicolas Crawford.

For information on (and warnings against) travel in Sudan, I thank Oliver Tunda, James Baldwin, Sergio Rodrigues, Jean Francios Darcq, Ollie Benham, Faith Model, and Melissa Phillips. Sandy Harcourt at U.C. Davis and Maryke Gray of the International Gorilla Conservation Programme provided essential data on mountain gorillas.

Lara Santoro, Edward Paice, Dean King, and Chris Humphrey also helped see this project through to the end in various ways. And thanks to everyone on AskMetafilter who answered my seemingly random but strangely thematic questions about Victorian courtship, nineteenth-century surveying, and the Nile River.

I'd like to express special gratitude to my agent, Byrd Leavell, and my editor, Peter Hubbard, for their hard work, guidance, and patience.

It goes without saying that I owe a large debt to the people who appear in these pages, including everyone I met on the trip and friends back home. Some names have been changed for privacy reasons.

Not many spouses would consent to having the lion's share of their relationship put into print; even fewer would be able to give objective feedback on the process. To do both, as Laura did, well . . . let's just call it more proof of what a lucky guy I am.